Praise for Irene Hannon's Novels

(Daphne du Maurier Awa...   ...e Award)

"A wonderful array of believable characters, action, and suspense that will keep readers glued to each page. Hannon's extraordinary writing, vivid scenes, and surprise ending come together for a not-to-be-missed reading experience."

4½ stars Top Pick, *RT Book Reviews*

"I found someone who writes romantic suspense better than I do."

Dee Henderson, author, the O'Malley Family series

"Hannon delivers big time in this novel. The intercontinental suspense plot combines flawlessly with a fantastic romance that sizzles."

Book of the Month, *The Suspense Zone*

An Eye for an Eye
(RITA Award finalist)

"RITA–Award-winner Hannon's latest superbly written addition to her Heroes of Quantico series neatly delivers all the thrills and chills of Suzanne Brockmann's Team Sixteen series with the subtly incorporated faith elements found in Dee Henderson's books."

Booklist

"Characters that are engrossing, a plot filled with unexpected twists, and a love story that will melt your heart. The only downside to this terrific novel is that you won't want to put it down."

4½ stars Top Pick, *RT Book Reviews*

"An explosive start, followed by brilliant pacing through the rest of the story and the perfect balance of suspense, action, and romance."

Relz Reviewz

In Harm's Way
(RITA Award)

"A fine-tuned suspense tale. RITA–Award-winner Hannon is a master at character development."

Library Journal

"Fast-paced crime drama with an aside of romance . . . and an ever-climactic mystery. Hannon's tale is engagingly sure-footed."

Publishers Weekly

"*In Harm's Way* kept me turning pages as it raced from one twist to another. This book will be a hit with Irene Hannon fans!"

Susan May Warren, RITA Award winner

——————— GUARDIANS OF JUSTICE SERIES ———————

Fatal Judgment

"Hannon's ability to write scenes that cause readers to feel uneasy and to second-guess their safety always makes her stories page-turners."

RT Book Reviews

"Bestselling author Irene Hannon weaves a wonderful story full of suspense and romance. She captures your attention at page one and doesn't let it go until long after you've finished the book!"

Suspense Magazine

"*Fatal Judgment* has all the things I love in a romantic suspense. A strong heroine, and a good man, and a tragedy she might not survive. Irene Hannon is a name I love to find, and *Fatal Judgment* is her storytelling at its best."

Dee Henderson

Deadly Pursuit

"Compelling characters and an emotionally engaging plot powered by a surfeit of nail-biting suspense."

Top 10 Inspirational Fiction 2011, *Booklist*

"Full of action, suspense, and just the right amount of romance."

RT Book Reviews

"The strong character development and suspenseful story line here will win over readers of Lynette Eason, Dee Henderson, and Terri Blackstock."

Library Journal

"An exceptional novel of romantic suspense."

Omnimysterynews.com

LETHAL LEGACY

Books by Irene Hannon

LETHAL LEGACY

A NOVEL

IRENE HANNON

FIC
HANNON
2012

Revell

a division of Baker Publishing Group
Grand Rapids, Michigan

© 2012 by Irene Hannon

Published by Revell
a division of Baker Publishing Group
P.O. Box 6287, Grand Rapids, MI 49516-6287
www.revellbooks.com

Printed in the United States of America

Library of Congress Cataloging-in-Publication Data
Hannon, Irene.
    Lethal legacy : a novel / Irene Hannon.
        p.   cm. — (Guardians of justice ; #3)
    ISBN 978-0-8007-3458-9 (pbk.)
    1. Fathers and daughters—Fiction. 2. Fathers—Crimes against—Fiction.
3. Law enforcement—Fiction. I. Title.
PS3558.A4793L48 2012
813'.54—dc23   2012007246

This book is a work of fiction. Names, characters, places, and incidents are the product of the author's imagination or are used fictitiously. Any resemblance to actual events, locales, or persons, living or dead, is coincidental.

12   13   14   15   16   17   18   7   6   5   4   3   2   1

To Jennifer Leep—
for taking a chance on a newcomer to romantic suspense . . .
and for a letter I will always treasure.

And to Kristin Kornoelje—
for making me a better writer.

Prologue

Vincentio Rossi lifted his glass of ten-year-old Lombardi Brunello di Montalcino, closed his eyes, and sniffed the complex bouquet of the ruby red wine.

Perfect.

Then again, at a hundred bucks a bottle, it should be.

But the cost was of no consequence. After twenty-eight years of forced abstinence, he didn't scrimp on his pleasures. At seventy-four, plagued by high blood pressure and off-the-scale cholesterol, he intended to make every minute count. Who knew how many years—or months—he had left?

Taking a small sip, Vincentio let the peppery flavor linger on his tongue, savoring the hint of wild mushrooms and truffles as he gazed out the window of Romano's onto the familiar Buffalo street scene. The private table he'd occupied every weekday for the past three years suited him, allowing him to observe without being observed.

But he didn't like dining alone. Isabella should be sitting in the empty chair across from him. Romano's had been their place, and during all the years they'd spent apart, he'd looked forward to sharing it with her again. But none of his connections, none of his money, had been able to stop the insidious cancer that had taken her life five years ago.

Worst of all, he hadn't been there at the end, to hold her hand and say good-bye.

Vincentio tipped the glass against his lips and took a long swallow of the earthy wine. Wishing he could rewind the clock. Wishing he could return with her to the hills of Sicily where they'd spent their honeymoon.

Wishing he hadn't made the fatal mistake that had cost him everything.

At the sudden vibration of his cell phone, his hand jerked. The ruby liquid sloshed close to the edge of the glass, and he set the slender-stemmed goblet carefully on the table as he pulled the phone off his belt.

In the old days, he'd had nerves of steel.

One more thing that had changed.

He squinted at the digital display. His vision wasn't great anymore, either. But it didn't matter; caller ID was blocked.

The voice that greeted him, however, was familiar. A spurt of adrenaline set off a tingle in his nerve endings, and he angled away from the other patrons in the restaurant.

"You have news?" Vincentio wasted no time returning the man's greeting.

"Your hunch was correct. He's in town."

Vincentio's fingers tightened on the stem of the wineglass. "You're certain?"

"I've seen him myself. He is older, yes—but there is no question."

A buzz of excitement swept over him, leaving him light-headed for a moment. He'd waited a long, long time for this.

"You know what I need."

"Yes. I'll relay the information as soon as I have it."

"Excellent. You'll be well rewarded, as always."

Hand trembling, Vincentio slid the phone back into its holder and fumbled for a small, folded piece of paper in the inside pocket of his suit jacket. Through the years, the creases had worn thin, and he opened the yellowed sheet carefully. All but one of the names he'd written more than two decades ago had a check mark in front and were crossed out.

He smoothed it out on the tablecloth, retrieved a pen from his jacket, and checked off the final name.

Step one.

He folded up the paper, tucked it and the pen away, and grasped the stem of his wineglass again.

Outside, passersby continued to hurry along in the mid-April chill. Spring wouldn't come to the Lake Erie shore for a while yet, but it suddenly felt like spring to him. He'd almost given up hope of ever finding the traitor who had repaid his kindness with disloyalty. Who had turned his son against him. Who had done his best to undermine all . . .

The delicate stem of the wineglass snapped in his fingers, and Vincentio watched the crimson liquid gush out and seep into the snowy white linen, staining it red.

Like blood.

A smile lifted his lips. He'd always believed in omens.

And this was a good one.

1

Six Months Later

"So what was up with your solo act at Jake and Liz's wedding on Saturday?"

At the question, Detective Cole Taylor stifled a groan. He did *not* want to start his week by rehashing his brother's wedding. Especially with his colleague Mitch Morgan, who had gotten engaged to his sister at said wedding.

"What do you mean?" He didn't look up from his desk. Maybe if he acted busy, Mitch would move on.

"I mean, where was the hot date you usually bring to social events?"

Coming alone had been a tactical mistake. One Cole had recognized five minutes into the reception. He should have brought someone. Anyone. With a woman on his arm, he would have avoided all the kidding from his relatives and the questions about when it was going to be his turn. The grilling had gotten so bad, he'd taken to hiding behind some potted plants—and drinking champagne.

Lots of champagne.

"I wasn't in the mood to bring a date."

"Yeah? How come?" Mitch settled onto the edge of his desk.

So much for getting rid of his future brother-in-law.

Resigned, Cole forced his lips into a cocky grin, swiveled his chair, and folded his hands across his stomach. "The pickings

13

were slim for that night, and I'm particular. I want looks *and* intelligence."

"Since when? That wasn't exactly a rocket scientist you brought to the party at Doug's house two weeks ago."

"That sounds like something Alison would say." Cole's grin morphed into a frown. "Did my sister put you up to this?"

"Nope. But she was surprised you came alone too."

"You know, I appreciate how everyone is taking such an interest in my social life all of a sudden." He laid on a healthy dose of sarcasm. "But trust me, I have it under control."

"I'm glad to hear that. I wouldn't want you to lose out on the chance for wedded bliss."

Cole snorted. "How do you know it's going to be blissful? You only got engaged two days ago."

"Because I know your sister." He grinned at Cole. "And if you need more proof, ask Jake when he and Liz get back from their Bermuda honeymoon." Standing, he stretched. "So you want to go get some lunch?"

"No. Too busy."

"Want me to bring you back a burger?"

"No. I'm not hungry."

Mitch shot him a surprised look. "You're always hungry."

"Big breakfast." He waved his colleague away and swung back to the desk. "I'll hit the vending machines later."

Out of the corner of his eye, he saw Mitch hesitate. Cock his head. Then, with a shrug, his fellow detective walked away. Finally.

Once Mitch exited, Cole leaned back in his chair and stared at the photo on his desk, a family shot taken at his mom's birthday party not long after Jake had returned to St. Louis from a stint in Iraq with the U.S. Marshals Special Operations Group. It had been just the four of them since his dad died six years ago. But now there was a sister-in-law to add. Soon, there'd be a brother-in-law. And not long after that, Cole suspected nieces and nephews would come along. His sister and brother would be busy with their families. His mom lived in

Chicago with her sister now; not that far from St. Louis, but far enough. He'd be the odd man out.

And playing the field was starting to lose its allure.

Annoyed by a sudden empty feeling in the pit of his stomach, Cole straightened up. Must be a case of weddingitis. It was hard not to think about the lack of romance in his life when he was surrounded by cross-eyed lovers and the air was filled with matrimonial vibes. But if it was supposed to happen, it would. No sense fretting about it.

No sense missing meals, either.

Debating what to get for lunch, he stood, snagged his jacket off the back of his chair, and slid his arms into the sleeves. Maybe he'd take Mitch up on the burger offer after all. If he hurried, he should be able to catch him at the elevator or in the lobby.

But he only made it two steps away from his desk before his phone rang.

As he paused, it rang again.

"You gonna get that or what?" Luke Adams looked up from a computer screen at an adjacent desk in the shared office, his expression frazzled. The man was a stellar detective, but he hated computers. And Cole didn't relish being the outlet for his irritation.

"I'm getting it, okay?"

Luke grunted and went back to hunting and pecking while Cole returned to his desk and picked up the phone.

"Taylor."

"Are you in the middle of anything?"

At his unit supervisor's clipped query, Cole sank back into his chair.

He was now.

"Nothing that can't wait."

"Good. I need you to talk with a woman whose father died five months ago. We ruled it a suicide. However, the daughter claims she has new information that could change our minds."

"Who handled the case?"

"Alan. But she doesn't want to wait until he gets back from vacation. And FYI—she wasn't happy with our resolution. Even though she couldn't point us to any suspects or motives, she claims somebody was out to get her father and believes his death was a homicide."

Cole stifled a sigh. Great. A conspiracy theorist. He'd run into them before. And since Alan had just left on a two-week trip to the Caribbean, this woman could be bugging him for fourteen days.

"Okay. I'll meet her out front. What's her name?"

"Kelly Warren. Her father's name was John."

"Got it." Cole replaced the receiver, picked up a notepad, and stood.

So much for lunch.

Perched on the edge of a standard-issue waiting room chair, Kelly clenched the strap of her purse between her fingers, crossed her legs, and jiggled her foot. She didn't want to be here. The whole law enforcement aura brought back all the trauma of her father's death. But calling in the new information wouldn't have the same impact. She wanted the police to know she took this seriously—and that she intended to make sure they did too.

The door to the inner offices opened, and a mid-thirtyish dark-haired man in beige slacks, a sport coat with a subtle herringbone pattern, and a white shirt stepped through.

"Ms. Warren?"

"Yes." She rose, crossed the room, and took the hand he extended. At five-seven, she considered herself on the tall side. But she had to look up several inches to meet the man's intense cobalt eyes—their hue an exact match for his tie.

She felt like she was drowning in blue.

"Detective Cole Taylor. Please come in." He ushered her through the door. "First room on your right."

Kelly eased past him, focusing on the neutral beige carpet. Better.

He followed her in silence. At the door he'd indicated, she took a quick inventory of the conference room. A large table surrounded by comfortable chairs took up most of the floor space. She claimed the nearest seat.

The detective closed the door and sat at a right angle to her. "I understand you have some new evidence to present regarding the death of your father."

"Yes." She fiddled with the catch on her purse. "I'd rather give it to Detective Carlson, since he handled the case, but I didn't want to wait two weeks."

"I'll be happy to discuss it with you." The man opened his notebook and picked up his pen. "I'm not familiar with the particulars of the case, but why don't you tell me what you have and we'll go from there?"

His tone was polite, his words professional. But there was a touch of reserve in his manner. As if he didn't appreciate her questioning the conclusions of his fellow detective. Or maybe he had a lot on his plate and didn't like wasting his time with evidence he assumed would be inconsequential to a thoroughly investigated closed case.

Too bad.

Her fingers tightened on her purse, and she lifted her chin. "Before I show you what I have, you need to know I've never believed my father committed suicide."

He studied her. "My supervisor mentioned that."

"You also need to know I'm not going to give up. Suicide went against everything my dad believed. Somebody killed him."

The words left a bitter taste on her tongue, and pressure suddenly built in her throat. Dismayed by her lack of control, she dipped her head and fumbled with the clasp on her purse. "Would you mind . . . could I have some water?"

"Sure. I'll be back in a minute."

The detective scooted his chair back and stood. A moment later, he disappeared from her peripheral vision. She heard the door shut behind her.

Kelly groped through her purse for a tissue. Blew her nose. Dabbed at her eyes. Until the past five months, she'd never been a crier. Now, tears welled up whenever she thought about the aching void her father's death had left in her life.

But tears weren't going to help her convince the police the note she'd received was anything more than an odd twist of fate. She needed to be strong, assertive, and in control if she wanted them to take her seriously instead of treating her like an emotional grieving daughter who was grasping at straws.

With one more swipe at her cheeks, Kelly tucked the tissue back in her purse. Sat up straighter. Said a silent prayer for strength.

And prepared to do battle.

Shoulder propped against the wall beside the door to the conference room, Cole checked his watch. It had taken him less than a minute to retrieve the bottle of water now sweating in his hand, but based on Kelly Warren's shattered expression when he'd left, he figured she needed an extra couple of minutes to regain her composure.

Her grace time, however, was up.

Giving the knob an extra rattle to alert her to his return, Cole pushed the door open and entered the room.

He'd half expected to find her in tears, her face a splotchy mess. Crying women, as he'd discovered in his fourteen years of police work, only looked attractive in movies. But she surprised him. A single, tiny drop of moisture clinging to the tip of one of her lush lashes and a tautness in her features that accentuated her elegant bone structure were the only evidence of tears.

He set the bottle of water on the table in front of her and retook his seat.

"Thank you." She screwed off the cap and took a long swallow, giving him a perfect view of her slender neck and the graceful curve of her jaw.

He found himself staring.

And he continued to stare as she set the bottle down and rummaged through her purse. Talk about great hair. Wavy and russet-colored, it was parted in the middle and hung well below her shoulders, held back on each side with matching jade barrettes. It looked soft and luxurious and . . . touchable.

When she lifted her chin, his lungs stalled as her emerald green eyes locked on his.

She frowned and shifted in her chair. "Is something wrong?"

Clearing his throat, Cole looked down and picked up his pen. *Get a grip, Taylor. You're dealing with a grieving daughter here. Not some hot chick who's angling to be picked up.*

"No. I was just thinking that . . . you seem familiar." *Lame, lame, lame.* He tried not to cringe.

"Did you work my father's case?"

"No."

"Then I doubt we've met." She withdrew a printed piece of paper from her purse and slid it across the table toward him. "This came with a delivery of flower bulbs this morning."

Grateful to have a reason to shift his focus, Cole picked up the piece of paper that turned out to be a packing slip for an order of two dozen Magic Carpet tulip bulbs to be delivered in late October.

"There's a message box at the top left."

At her prompt, he located the box and scanned the note.

Happy birthday, Kelly! Don't these sound exotic? We'll plant them together on your big day. I'll bring the cake! Love, Dad.

Cole tried to grasp the significance of the message. Failed.

"I'm sure receiving this was a shock, Ms. Warren, arriving so long after your father's death." He reread the message, searching for some clue he'd missed. "But many people order fall bulbs well in advance."

Her mouth tightened as he looked at her, and his gaze dropped to her lips.

Nice.

"I'm aware of that, Detective Taylor. But take a look at this." She tapped a date located near the bottom of the packing slip, redirecting his attention. "He placed this order the day before the police allege he committed suicide. In other words, less than twenty-four hours before he died, my father was planning to plant tulips with me in five months."

Okay. That was odd.

"I'll tell you what. Why don't you give me a day or two to review the case file? Then I'll get back in touch and we can discuss this."

The further flattening of her lips told him she wasn't pleased with the delay.

"Is there someone else who might be able to give this more immediate attention?"

Cole tapped his pen against the lined tablet in front of him. He was tempted to tell her none of the detectives were sitting around twiddling their thumbs. That they all had active cases that demanded immediate attention. That a few days wouldn't make any difference to her father.

But Alison was always on his case about his lack of tact. So he took a deep breath and worded his response with care.

"Ms. Warren, please understand that I'm taking this very seriously. But with Detective Carlson on vacation, I need some time to go over the facts of the case and get a handle on how the resolution was reached. Any other detective would do the same. However, if you prefer, I'd be happy to ask my sergeant to assign someone else to assist you."

She pinned him with an appraising gaze. He met it without blinking. Finally, she snapped her purse shut and stood. He rose too.

"All right. I'll wait to hear from you. Tomorrow, I hope."

"As soon as possible."

The sudden narrowing of her eyes told him his hedge hadn't gotten past her.

"Look, Detective, I realize this isn't your top priority, like it is for me. But I knew my father for thirty-three years. I talked to him every day. I saw him go through some bad times, including the death of my mother, and he was a survivor. A man of strength and faith, who turned to God—not to pills or carbon monoxide—when times were tough. I can't dispute the facts of your investigation, but I do dispute the conclusion. And I'm convinced this document"—she jabbed at the packing slip on the table—"proves there's more to this than was discovered the first time around."

He regarded her for a long moment. If John Warren had indeed been a man of strength, his daughter had inherited that attribute in spades. Her voice rang with conviction, and the resolve in her eyes was formidable.

"I have a feeling your father would be proud of you."

Cole wasn't sure where that had come from. Or why he'd spoken it. But the comment seemed to disarm her. The rigid line of her shoulders eased a tiny bit, and the angular tautness of her face softened.

"He was a good man." The soft, grief-laced words tugged at his heart. "He deserves to rest in peace. That's why I want to get to the truth. Why I want to be certain justice is served."

"That's what we want too." Cole picked up the packing slip. "If we've missed anything, I can promise you we'll do our best to make it right. Let me walk you out."

He followed her back down the hall, wishing he could give her the resolution she wanted. Verify her father hadn't chosen to take his own life. But the St. Louis County Crimes Against Persons detectives were pros. It was unlikely he'd find any mistakes. Still, the tulips were an anomaly. And if they had messed up, he wasn't going to pretend they hadn't. He'd entered this business to fight for justice, not cover up the truth.

Kelly stopped at the door to the reception area and held out her hand. "Thank you for your time."

Though her shoulders were squared and her gaze steady, a slight tremor ran through her cold fingers as he gave them a squeeze.

"I'll be in touch."

With a nod, she turned and walked toward the exit.

Cole watched her go, his gaze lingering on the russet waves

cascading down the back of a silky blouse that was tucked into the waist of her slim black slacks.

Too bad he hadn't had someone like her to take to Jake's wedding.

"Nice."

At the comment close to his ear, Cole jerked around. Mitch was checking out Kelly over his shoulder.

Annoyed, Cole shut the door to the reception area, edging his colleague back none too gently with his shoulder. "Didn't you just get engaged? To my sister?"

Mitch grinned. "Appreciating beauty isn't the same as drooling over it."

"I wasn't drooling." He hoped. "Besides, I don't mix business and pleasure."

"You could have fooled me. You were sure enjoying the view. So who is she?"

"Her father died five months ago. She's not buying our suicide verdict. It was Alan's case." Cole started down the hall.

"I remember that one. From what I heard, it was cut and dried."

Cole stopped short, and Mitch almost ran into him. "How come *I* don't remember it?"

"You were tied up with that high-profile missing person case."

"Oh yeah." He'd been immersed in it for two solid weeks—and the ending hadn't been happy.

"What did the daughter want?"

"She has some new evidence she thinks supports her position that it was murder." Cole started toward his office again. Mitch fell in beside him.

"Does it?"

"It raises a few questions. But I need to look over the case notes."

"Maybe you'll find an excuse to pay her a visit."

Cole stopped at the door to the office he shared with several other detectives and squinted at his friend. "I just told you. I don't mix business and pleasure."

"The evidence suggests otherwise—but I'll let it pass." Mitch grinned and lifted a white sack bearing the logo of a familiar fast-food chain. "I brought you a burger anyway. Consider it a peace offering."

As he handed it over, Mitch pulled his phone off his belt and checked caller ID. "No rest for the weary. Enjoy." Putting the phone to his ear, he set off down the hall.

The aroma of the burger wafting up from the bag set off a rumbling in Cole's stomach, and he headed for his desk. Funny. All of a sudden, he was hungry.

Digging into the loaded quarter pounder, he wolfed down half of it before pausing to take a drink from the almost-empty can he'd left on his desk. The soda was warm, but at least it was wet.

His hunger somewhat assuaged, Cole scooted in front of the computer and pulled up the case file for John Warren. Might as well take a look while he finished his lunch.

A quick skim gave him the basics. Warren, a retired accountant, had been found in his garage after Kelly, who was out of town, couldn't reach him and called a neighbor to check on him. Cause of death—carbon monoxide poisoning. There were no other injuries, no sign of a struggle. Toxicity tests had revealed zolpidem and an elevated blood alcohol level.

Alan's investigation had backed up those findings. An empty beer can and a small bottle containing generic Ambien tablets had been found near the body, which had been slumped against the wall of the garage, close to the tailpipe. Three more beer cans had been found in the trash in the kitchen. At his daughter's insistence, Alan had talked with a number of her father's acquaintances, including the minister at the church the two of them had attended every Sunday, and all had expressed shock and disbelief at the man's actions. He had not been under psychiatric care.

But he *had* been diagnosed recently with lung cancer and was facing surgery, followed by radiation and chemotherapy. Even his daughter had admitted he'd seemed more quiet—even a little down—in the last weeks of his life.

Cole couldn't refute Alan's conclusion. All the evidence pointed to suicide. At sixty-nine, John Warren could have decided it wasn't worth all the pain and effort to fight a cancer that was very hard to beat.

Yet he'd written an upbeat note to his daughter the day before he died, talking about plans for the future.

Kelly was right.

It didn't compute.

Still, it was possible he'd ordered the generic Ambien to have on hand in case things got really bad, and then, in a moment of despondency, decided to pack it in.

Cole tapped a finger on the shipping slip she'd left, then picked up the other half of his burger and reread the case summary as he finished off Mitch's peace offering. He had two witnesses to track down this afternoon on a hit-and-run case, and he didn't have the time to delve into the details of the Warren file now. He'd get it done, though. Later today, or tomorrow.

But based on his cursory review, he didn't expect to find any irregularities. He'd worked dozens of cases with Alan, and his colleague wasn't the kind of detective who missed things.

If all the i's were dotted and the t's crossed, however, Kelly Warren was going to be very, very disappointed.

And he didn't look forward to giving her the bad news.

2

Twenty-eight hours later, as Cole walked up the stone path to the front door of Kelly Warren's bungalow, he told himself compassion and charity had prompted this personal visit. That he wanted to soften the blow by delivering his news in person.

But that motive couldn't account for the sudden acceleration in his pulse as he pressed her doorbell. Nor could it explain his quick shave in the men's room at the office. Or his sudden urge to straighten his tie and settle his coat more evenly on his shoulders.

And no way would compassion or charity produce a surge of adrenaline at the sound of the lock being turned. Or shut down his lungs when Kelly opened the door and looked at him with those big green eyes, her hair tumbling around her shoulders.

"Detective Taylor! This is a surprise."

He saw the hope flare in her eyes—and felt like a heel.

"I thought it might be better if we talked in person. May I come in?"

"Yes, of course." She gestured toward the living room. "Have a seat."

He chose a blue wingback chair beside her fireplace. She perched on the edge of the cream-colored couch.

"Looks like I interrupted you." He gestured to the paint-spattered rag wadded in her fingers.

She glanced down, as if she'd forgotten she was holding it,

25

then tossed the cloth on the glass-topped coffee table, creating the only clutter in the immaculate room. "No. I was about to call it a day." She wiped her palms down her oversized, paint-streaked shirt and rubbed at a stubborn green stain on the back of her right hand. "Sorry. I'd have cleaned up if I'd known you were coming. I'm a commercial artist, and things can get a bit messy in the studio."

"Watercolors, right? Magazine illustrations, children's books, greeting cards . . . I'm impressed."

She tipped her head. "So am I. Can I assume you found all that information in my father's case file?"

"Yes. Detective Carlson was very thorough."

At his definitive tone—and its implication—she stiffened. "You're telling me my new piece of evidence isn't enough to reopen the case, aren't you?"

The chill in her voice didn't quite disguise the disappointment—and desperation—underneath.

Leaning forward, he rested his elbows on the arms of the chair and clasped his hands, trying for a professional but empathetic tone. "The note does raise questions, but after a careful review of the file, I found nothing to suggest any stones were left unturned. As far as I could tell, Detective Carlson followed up on every piece of information he had and discovered nothing to suggest any other conclusion."

Kelly stood and paced to the end of the room, her back to him, the rigid line of her shoulders communicating her distress.

When the silence lengthened, he tried again.

"Ms. Warren, there was definite evidence of suicide. Your father overdosed on a high-powered sleeping pill. He drank alcohol, which compounded the effect. He was found in a closed garage next to the tailpipe of a car that had keys in the ignition and an empty gas tank. There was no sign of a struggle or foul play. The Crime Scene Unit found no fingerprints or trace evidence. The neighbors saw nothing irregular. The only thing missing was a farewell letter, but less than 25 percent of people who take their life leave a final message."

"Then how do you explain the note he wrote the day before he died?"

She didn't have to turn around for him to tell she was fighting to hang on to her control. He could hear it in the quiver in her voice.

"I can't."

"Doesn't it suggest foul play to you?" She swung toward him, distress etching her features. "And why would he take sleeping pills and drink alcohol? If he wanted to kill himself, he could have just gone to the garage and turned on the car."

"Maybe the drugs and booze made it easier to take that final step."

Her eyes narrowed. "My dad was a courageous man, Detective. *If* he had decided to do something that drastic, he wouldn't have sugarcoated it. Besides, I checked with his doctor. He didn't have a prescription for Ambien. I also looked at his credit card bills to see if he'd ordered it from one of those overseas drug places that don't require a doctor's script. Nothing. So where did he get it?"

"There are domestic black market sources for drugs of every kind."

She sucked in a breath, as if he'd slapped her. "My dad wasn't into anything underhanded. If he'd wanted sleeping pills, he'd have asked his doctor." She pinned him with a fierce look. "Someone was targeting my father, Detective."

"But who would do that? And why?"

"Detective Carlson asked me the same question. I don't know. Isn't it your job to figure that out?"

"Yes, but we can only work with the clues we have. According to the case notes, you yourself said your father had no enemies."

"None that I *know* of."

"Detective Carlson interviewed all the people you suggested. They didn't offer any leads, either."

"Nor did they believe my father would have committed suicide."

"People under pressure can do uncharacteristic things, Ms. Warren." He gentled his voice. "And a lung cancer diagnosis is very tough. The mortality rate is extremely high. One of my uncles died of that disease. It wasn't pretty."

Her demeanor softened, and a flicker of sympathy warmed her eyes. "I'm sorry for your loss. And I do hear what you're saying. Even though the cancer was only stage one, we both knew he was in for a tough fight. But he *was* a fighter. He was also a man of rock-solid faith who believed in the sanctity of life and always put his trust in the Lord. Suicide wasn't an option he'd consider."

If he ever got into trouble, Cole hoped he'd be lucky enough to have a Kelly Warren in his corner. She had the tenacity of a bulldog when it came to defending someone she loved.

Cole rose, planted one fist on his hip, and raked his fingers through his hair. When he'd come here today, he'd planned to let her down easy. To suggest her father had simply hidden his despair from her. Remind her that not everyone who committed suicide posted warning signs.

But the strength of her conviction made him vacillate. "I can see I'm not convincing you."

"I knew my father, Detective Taylor." She lifted her chin, in a dig-in-her-heels gesture he was coming to recognize. "Short of finding a note in his own hand, I won't believe he took his life. Even then I'd have doubts."

"In your statement in the case file, you admitted he seemed a bit down in the last weeks of his life."

"No!" Her eyes flashed, and her nostrils flared. "I never used that word. He was a little . . . contemplative, maybe. Quieter. Who wouldn't be, after hearing a diagnosis like that? But he was not depressed."

Her vehemence was persuasive. Drawing a breath, Cole capitulated. "Okay. Let me do this. I'll talk to Detective Carlson after he returns. The two of us will review the case, maybe pull in a few more people to get some fresh thinking. Have you been through all of your father's things?"

"No. I'm getting ready to put his house on the market, but I hadn't planned to sort through everything until I officially listed it with the real estate agent." She linked her fingers and looked down at her clasped hands. "It's very hard for me to . . . to be there right now."

"I can understand that. But there's a chance you might find something helpful that only you would recognize as significant. And if you do, I promise you we'll follow up on it."

She raised her chin, and a faint glimmer of hope reignited in her eyes. "So you're not closing the door on this?"

"No. If there's been a miscarriage of justice, we're as interested in fixing it as you are."

"Okay. I'll start going through his things." She exhaled, and her taut posture eased. "Thank you."

"I'm just doing my job. And now I'll let you get back to yours."

He crossed the room toward the door, turning when he reached it. She'd followed him partway, and the late-afternoon sunlight backlit her as it slanted through the window, burnishing her russet hair and isolating her slender form in a corona of light. And she was, indeed, isolated. As he'd learned from the case file, she had no family left. Her mother had died when she was twelve, and there were no siblings.

That had to be tough. All his life, Cole had been surrounded by love. He still had his mother, and while he might complain that Alison was too independent for her own good and Jake took his big-brother role too seriously, he knew he could count on them, no matter what. That in a time of crisis, they'd both be by his side.

Kelly Warren didn't have that kind of support system.

And being strong and capable and determined didn't compensate for that lack.

For a fleeting moment, he was overcome by a powerful urge to take her hand. Link his fingers with hers and assure her she wasn't alone. That if she needed help of any kind—case-related or not—he'd provide it.

But that was crazy. As he'd told Mitch yesterday, he never mixed business and pleasure—and he didn't intend to start now.

Grasping the handle, Cole pulled the door open and stepped onto the small front porch. "I'll be in touch, Ms. Warren."

With that, he strode down the walk toward his car without looking back.

Because if he did, if he saw her solitary figure silhouetted in the doorway, he was afraid the urge to take a personal interest in this case would resurface.

And he was even more afraid that this time he wouldn't be able to resist.

At the sudden ring of her cell phone in the oppressive quiet of her father's house, Kelly dropped the file folder she'd just retrieved from his desk drawer and watched in dismay as the contents flew in all directions and wafted down to the carpet.

Muttering in disgust, she rose from her chair, hopscotched over the cascade of papers, and trotted toward the kitchen. By the time her fingers closed over her phone in the depths of her purse, it was on the third ring. She jabbed at the talk button, not bothering to check caller ID before saying hello.

"Hey, Kelly. It's Lauren. I just had a great idea. Why don't we dig our skates out of the closet and hit the rink?"

Kelly leaned a shoulder against the wall, surprised by her best friend's suggestion. Although they'd met as sixteen-year-olds in a figure skating class dominated by kids half their age, these days their get-togethers were usually over lunch or coffee. "I haven't skated in years."

"Me neither, but I'm game to give it a try. If we could pick each other up off the ice as teenagers while our junior counterparts snickered behind our backs, we can do it again. And I bet we could still do three turns and waltz jumps. Now that fall is here, I'm in the mood for winter sports."

Kelly stared out the window of her childhood home. Fall *had* arrived. In the almost two weeks since Detective Taylor had paid her a visit, the color on the three giant maples that dominated the backyard had gone from pretty to spectacular.

Her dad had loved their glorious autumn display.

The scene blurred, and Kelly turned away, blinking back tears. "I'm sure you have better things to do on a Saturday morning than risk breaking a leg at the rink. Go out with that gorgeous husband of yours. Or take the twins to the park on this sunny day. It might be your last chance before winter." Although she tried to sound upbeat, Lauren wouldn't be fooled by her too-bright tone. They knew each other too well.

"My family won't miss me for an hour or two, and Shaun needs some quality one-on-one time with the kids. I already convinced him to take them to the Magic House."

As Lauren talked, Kelly wandered back into her father's office and surveyed the papers strewn on the floor. She'd been digging into every nook and cranny of the house, searching for something—anything—that might pique the interest of the police and give them a concrete lead to follow. A reason to reopen the case.

So far, she'd come up empty.

But she wasn't yet ready to throw in the towel.

"I appreciate the offer, Lauren, but with two deadlines looming I haven't been able to put in as much time as I'd like going through my dad's stuff. I was planning to spend the morning here."

"You're there now?"

"Yes."

"You want some company? I could pick up coffee along the way."

Throat tightening, Kelly dropped into the desk chair. Lauren knew she and her father had met every Saturday for coffee—and that his death had left an aching void in that part of her week. "I stopped at the coffee shop for a takeout on my way here this morning. But thanks for being such a great friend."

"Hey, I'm just looking for an excuse to get out of the house. If I hang around, I'll have to clean bathrooms."

"Why? Use the quiet time to take a bubble bath instead."

"Ooh. Low blow. You know that's one of my favorite indulgences."

"And I bet you don't get to enjoy it very often with two five-year-olds in the house. We'll meet for coffee next Saturday. I promise."

"Hmm." A moment of silence passed. "I have to admit a warm bubble bath does sound better than a cold ice rink."

"Go for it. I'll call later in the week and set up a time for next Saturday."

"Okay, okay. You convinced me. Good luck with your search."

"Thanks. Talk to you soon."

As the line went dead, Kelly turned off her phone and leaned back in her father's chair, trying to stifle a niggle of envy. Lauren had it all. Great career as one of St. Louis's up-and-coming attorneys. Devoted husband. Happy family. A home filled with love to return to at the end of the day.

Annoyed at the flutter of jealousy, Kelly dropped to the floor and began to gather up her father's papers. Sure, she'd like all those things too, but that didn't mean she begrudged Lauren the blessings that had graced her life. Their situations were just different. After all, meeting the right man wasn't easy when you worked out of your home in a solitary occupation. Few men like Cole Taylor crossed her threshold.

Kelly froze as an image of the tall, dark-haired detective flashed across her mind—then, with a shake of her head, she got up and tapped the file against the desk to settle the papers. Talk about pathetic. She must be really hard up if she was fantasizing about strangers. Cole Taylor was in her life for one reason, and one reason only—to dig deeper into her father's death. There was no place for romance in that scenario.

Obviously, she was spending too much time alone at her easel.

As she set the file on the desk and prepared to tackle the next drawer, she was glad she'd committed to coffee next week.

An hour or two with her friend would help fill in some of the gaps in her social life.

But much as she looked forward to seeing Lauren, it didn't have quite the same appeal as a date with a handsome detective.

"Sorry I'm late." Cole circled the table at the popular West County Sunday brunch spot and leaned down to give his new sister-in-law a hug. "Welcome back from Bermuda." Straightening up, he shook Jake's hand. "How was the honeymoon?"

Jake grinned at him, wiggled his eyebrows, and tugged his bride close. Liz blushed.

"Never mind." Cole's lips quirked into a smile as he slid into the empty chair and picked up a menu. "I get the picture."

"So what have you been doing all morning?" Beside him, Alison rested an elbow on the table and propped her chin in her palm.

"Working." He hid behind the oversized menu.

She pushed it down with one finger. "You couldn't spare an hour to go to church with your family?"

Cole shot her an annoyed glance. Since he'd stopped attending services four years ago, she'd been relentless in her quest to prod him back onto the straight and narrow. She should have become an FBI interrogator instead of a Children's Division social worker. She had the dogged determination for it.

"She's right," Jake chimed in. "It wouldn't hurt you to darken the door of a church once in a while."

"Like you've been so diligent."

"I am now."

"I wonder why?" He sent a pointed look toward Liz.

"Hey—it was his choice. I only dictate people's fate from the bench," his new wife protested.

Jake reached over and twined his fingers with hers. "Judge Michaels is correct. She did get me thinking about it, but I came to the decision on my own. To use a cliché, I saw the light."

"Say . . ." Alison leaned forward, her expression speculative. "Maybe that's the answer. If we match Cole up with a nice churchgoing woman, she might have a positive influence on him."

Cole eyed the exit. Maybe he'd fake a phone call and pretend he was needed for a case.

"Yeah." Mitch joined in the fun. "How about that redhead you were ogling at work a couple of weeks ago?"

"What redhead?" Alison's head swiveled toward her fiancé.

"Let it go." Cole shot his colleague a warning look.

"No way," Alison protested, refocusing on him. "Now I'm intrigued. Who is this woman?"

"She's part of a case."

"She won't be once it's resolved." Mitch swirled the orange juice in his glass, grinning. "And you must be interested. You've brought her up a dozen times in the past two weeks."

Had he? Cole felt heat begin to creep up his neck.

Yeah, maybe.

"And I saw you googling her website the other day. Looking at watercolor paintings of woodland fairies."

Alison's mouth dropped open. "Woodland fairies!?"

Cole gritted his teeth. "I was doing research. She's a commercial artist."

"And a churchgoer. Didn't you mention she and her father always attended services together?" Mitch added.

Huffing out a breath, Cole surveyed the table. "Okay. I came for brunch, not the third degree. Alison, since you started this, I'll address my comments to you. If and when I decide to return to church, I promise you'll be the first to know. Until then, to put it as diplomatically as I can, back off."

His sister stared at him, sniffed, and went back to perusing her menu. "Fine. I was just trying to encourage you to do the right thing. From now on, you're on your own."

"Is that a promise?"

She made a face at him. "I guess that means you're not going to tell us about this woman, either."

"Nope." He took a drink of his water.

"That's okay." She tucked her arm in her fiancé's and gave Cole a smug smile. "I'll get it out of Mitch later."

Across the table, Jake stifled a chuckle behind his napkin. Liz didn't even try to hide her amusement.

Cole pinned Mitch with an intent look. The other man gave him a sheepish shrug. Meaning the tough, former Navy SEAL was putty in his intended's hands.

Good to know. From now on, he'd pick and choose his words carefully around his future brother-in-law.

They ordered, and the talk shifted to Bermuda, then to Mitch and Alison's wedding plans. Cole let the conversation flow around him, tuning out much of it, focusing on his food once his order was delivered. The topic depressed him. He'd never worried much about finding the right woman and getting married. It was just one of those things he assumed would happen eventually. Though he had to admit the women he'd been dating for the past few years didn't fit his criteria for a life partner.

As for his relationship with God—he doubted a reconciliation was in the cards.

All at once, the bite of eggs Benedict in his mouth lost its flavor, and he took a swig of orange juice to wash it down. Then he set his fork on the table and shoved his plate aside.

"What's with you?" Mitch gestured to his food. "You usually scarf down every bite of that dish."

The conversation stopped as everyone checked out his half-eaten meal. Once again, his neck warmed.

"Are you sick?" Alison frowned at him.

"No. Full."

"You sure everything's okay?" Jake narrowed his eyes.

Exasperated by the attention, Cole opened his mouth to express his annoyance.

And then he thought of Kelly Warren, who had no family left to bug her. Or care about her.

He closed his mouth.

Alison lifted an eyebrow. "Aren't you going to tell us to butt out?"

"No. I appreciate your concern."

She glanced at Jake, then back at him. "Is this for real?"

"Yeah. I know you guys have my best interest at heart."

Alison set her own fork down and gave him her full attention. "Cole Taylor, the diplomat. This is a new one. To what can we attribute your remarkable new sensitivity and tact?"

"Could it have something to do with Kelly Warren?" Mitch grinned at him.

"Who's Kelly Warren?" Alison asked.

"The redhead."

"Ah." Alison gave a sage nod. "Interesting."

It took every ounce of Cole's self-control to maintain a cool, nonchalant demeanor. "You all are jumping to too many conclusions. I've only seen the woman twice."

"Twice? She came in again?" Mitch's fork stopped halfway to his mouth.

Great. He'd walked right into that one.

Feigning indifference, he lifted one shoulder and picked up his coffee. "I delivered the bad news about my case review in person. She was on my route home."

"Very considerate." Mitch hid his grin by opening his mouth and shoving in a forkful of food.

Cole shot him a dirty look over the rim of his cup.

"I'd like to meet this woman," Alison said.

"Don't get your hopes up."

"Why not? Don't you ever want to get married?"

Cole choked on the sip of coffee he'd just taken. At least the coughing gave him a few seconds to regroup. "Alison, I know you have romance on the brain now that you're engaged, but not everyone is panting to rush down the aisle."

"You're thirty-six Cole. I'd hardly call that rushing."

"Very funny."

Liz, who'd been watching the whole exchange with amusement, finally took pity on him. "I have a suggestion. Since this is supposed to be a brunch, not a barbecue, why don't we stop grilling Cole and talk about Thanksgiving plans instead?"

As the conversation shifted yet again, Cole telegraphed a silent thank-you to his new sister-in-law. She responded with a wink.

But half an hour later, the earlier conversation about Kelly Warren—and his faith—came back to him as he maneuvered his car through a surge of traffic exiting from a church parking lot. Though he'd never admit it to his siblings, there *were* some gaps in his life. He had no significant other, and his relationship with God was toast.

Neither had bothered him a whole lot until recently. But all at once, he had a yearning for the companionship of a woman who would be more than a fun date. An intelligent woman of character and substance and courage.

A woman like Kelly Warren.

And as he merged onto the highway and accelerated into the traffic, he also felt the first stirring of a need to reconnect with his faith. A subtle longing to feel again the absolute trust and confidence in God that had once been the foundation of his life.

Too bad he had no idea how to achieve either of those goals.

3

"Cole? I got your message. What's up?"

Angling away from the copy machine, Cole took in Alan Carlson's sun-bleached blond hair and dark tan. "Wow. Did you spend every minute on the beach?"

His colleague grinned. "Not quite. But you can't go to a place like the Dominican Republic and not take advantage of all that white sand."

"I hear you. Maybe I'll get down there one of these days. I could use a break."

"It's hard to go wrong with beaches, biking, and bikinis."

"I didn't know you took your bike."

"I didn't. I rented one. Let me tell you, you haven't lived until you've pedaled up a mountain on a mule trail in the Caribbean."

Cole grinned. "No thanks. But as long as you had fun . . ."

"The whole trip was great." The man's smile faded a notch. "But it would have been better with Cindy."

"Yeah." Cole didn't know what else to say. Alan and his wife of three years had separated six months ago, surprising everyone in the department. He and Cindy had always seemed like a decent match. But the hours and risks of this business took a toll on marriages, and not all of them survived. Last he'd heard, Cindy had gone back to her hometown of Chicago. "Any chance the two of you might get back together?"

"Maybe. I'm working on it, and we're still in touch. So what can I do for you?"

Cole gathered up the papers he'd been copying while he responded. "It's nothing urgent, but once you clean out your in-box and email, I'd like to talk to you about the John Warren case."

As Cole turned toward him, the other man frowned. "The suicide? About five months ago?"

"Yeah."

"We closed that one."

"I know. But his daughter came in while you were gone. When you have a minute, I can fill you in."

"How about now?" One side of Alan's mouth hitched up. "I'm not anxious to dig into my in-box anyway."

"I hear you." Cole flashed him a sympathetic grin. "Let me make a quick detour to my desk, then we can try and find an empty conference room."

Five minutes later Cole flipped on the lights in the second room they tried, shut the door, and claimed one of the comfortable chairs. Alan sat beside him.

"So what's the story?" Alan leaned back, crossed an ankle over his knee, and linked his fingers over his stomach.

"About two weeks ago, Warren's daughter got a birthday present from her father. There was a message inside. Top left." He handed the copy of the packing slip to Alan and waited while the man read it. "Notice the order date."

Alan scanned it. Pursed his lips. "That's pretty close to the day he committed suicide."

"Very close. The day before."

The man frowned. "That's a little weird."

"His daughter thought so too. That's why she brought it in. I reviewed the case notes, and I can't argue with your conclusions. Every piece of evidence pointed to suicide. The only thing missing was a farewell note."

Alan steepled his index fingers. "I recall the daughter being very distraught. She did bring up the lack of a note, but I told her not everyone leaves one. It didn't help. She refused to accept our conclusion."

"She still isn't buying it. Her conviction, plus this message"—he tapped the copy of the packing slip—"make me wonder if we should take a second look."

The other man shrugged. "I'm not opposed to that, assuming we have something to look at. I already talked to everyone she suggested, the autopsy was conclusive, and the CSU didn't find a thing."

"I know. I went over all that with her. I suggested she comb through her father's house and see if she could find anything that might trigger some new ideas."

Alan's expression grew skeptical. "That's a little like looking for a needle in a haystack."

"True. But it was all I could come up with."

"Have you heard back from her since?"

"No. She said she'd follow up on my recommendation, but she also said it's been hard for her to go back to the house."

"I can understand that. It was just her and her father, and they were very close." A touch of desolation scored his features, highlighting a gauntness in his face that hadn't been there prior to his separation. "It's hard to lose someone you love."

"Yeah." It was a shame about him and Cindy. Alan was obviously taking the split hard. "I got that impression from Ms. Warren."

Alan cleared his throat, pulled the packing slip toward him, and examined it again. "On the surface, this doesn't make sense. But we know Warren had those pills in his possession. It's possible he wanted to have them on hand in case things got really bad, then decided they *had* gotten really bad as he thought about facing all that surgery and chemo and radiation."

"That scenario occurred to me too, but Kelly Warren isn't buying it." He lifted one shoulder. "You have to admire her persistence."

"It might be stubbornness."

Cole didn't think so. But the facts of the case, not their opinion of Kelly, were all that mattered.

He stood and picked up the sheet of paper. "You want to take one more look at the case file anyway?"

"Sure." Alan rose too. "And I'll follow up with her. Sorry you got pulled into this. I can take over from here."

Cole frowned. Alan *was* the case detective. It made sense for him to step back in. Yet he didn't want to let this one go—for reasons that had as much to do with a pair of fabulous green eyes and appealing lips as seeing that justice was done.

"Cole? Is there a problem?"

At Alan's prompt, he turned toward the door. "No. I'll put this back in the case file. I'm happy to assist if you need a hand too."

"I appreciate the offer, but I doubt it will come to that."

As they parted in the hall and Cole started back to his office, he reread the message on the packing slip. His own review of the file had unearthed no discrepancies. Alan was unlikely to find any, either.

Which meant John Warren's note would remain an unsolved puzzle.

And unless Kelly found something of interest in her father's things, the resolution of the case wasn't going to change, either.

No matter how adamantly she believed the police's conclusion was wrong.

The following Saturday, true to her word, Kelly pushed through the door of the Perfect Blend on a gust of blustery wind and wedged herself into the crowded coffee shop. Lauren waved at her from a tiny round table against the far wall, and she lifted her hand in response, then wove through the occupied tables toward her friend.

"I love this place!" Lauren rose to give her a hug, then waved her hand to encompass the colorful contemporary canvases that lined the walls. "Great artwork. How come I've never heard of it?"

Kelly slipped into her seat. "It's only been around six months. I started coming here after Dad died. It was too hard to go back to the Starbucks where we used to meet." She swallowed and summoned up a smile. She was *not* going to break down today. "Anyway, this place is now part of my regular routine. They have fabulous scones, and their cinnamon rolls are to die for."

"Perfect. I'm ready for a splurge." Lauren fished her wallet out of her purse. "My treat today in honor of this rare get-together."

"You don't have to do that."

"You're welcome."

Warmth stole over Kelly's cheeks. Her friend was forever telling her to learn to be as gracious a receiver as she was a giver, but she hadn't quite mastered that yet. "Thank you."

"Better." Lauren smiled and stood. "Let me guess. White chocolate mocha."

"Am I that predictable?"

"Consistent."

"More like boring. But thanks for putting a better spin on it." Kelly shrugged her coat off her shoulders. "Good luck fighting the crowd." She inclined her head toward the order line. "It's like this every Saturday, and weekdays aren't much better."

"Sounds like you've become a regular on days other than Saturday too."

"Yep. If I didn't go to a coffee shop two or three times a week, I'd turn into a hermit. That's one of the few downsides to working out of your house." She did another scan of the packed café. "I'm surprised you found a table."

"I almost didn't. They were all taken when I got here, but as soon as the guy at this one started to shut down his computer, I staked a claim. I don't think he appreciated me hovering over his shoulder, but I learned long ago to go after what I want.

Just ask Shaun." Lauren grinned and tapped the table. "Guard it with your life."

As Lauren maneuvered through the tables toward the line, Kelly settled back in her seat. Her friend was dressed casually today, in jeans, heeled boots, a crisp white shirt, and a leather jacket. Simple but stylish. With her chic shorter hairstyle, perfect makeup, and great figure, she was a head-turner. Even the stocky gray-haired guy behind her in line was giving her the once-over through his bottle-thick glasses.

Kelly set her elbow on the table and propped her chin in her palm. She dressed nicely when she had to, but she'd always preferred comfort over glamour. Give her a pair of well-broken-in jeans, a soft cotton shirt, comfortable flats, and a fleece jacket any day. Was it any wonder Lauren had attracted the attention of a hunky guy like Shaun while she was still single?

The line inched forward, and after Lauren paid the bill, she picked up two plates. The one she slid in front of Kelly a few moments later contained a cinnamon roll.

"I didn't order this."

"No, but you were lusting after it." Lauren deposited a plate with a blueberry scone in her own place as she took her seat. "Are you sure it's safe, though? I've witnessed one of your peanut allergy attacks, and it's not an experience I want to repeat."

Kelly leaned close to the roll and inhaled the cinnamon aroma. Bliss. "Absolutely. I had a long talk with the owner the first time I came here. He assured me they don't use any peanut products."

"Lauren!"

At the summons from the barista, her friend started to rise. But Kelly laid a hand on her arm. "At least let me pick up the drinks. What did you order for yourself?"

"A caramel hot chocolate."

Kelly grinned as she stood. "We *are* being decadent today, aren't we?"

"I can make up for the calories next week." Lauren flashed an unrepentant grin. "I'm celebrating our girls' morning out."

Smiling, Kelly wove through the tables, glad Lauren had insisted on this get-together. A couple of hours with her best friend was exactly what she needed to lift her spirits after the so-far fruitless search of her father's house.

As she joined the group clustered around the drink stand, she worked her way to the front. Four drinks were awaiting pickup, and she tried to decipher the hieroglyphics the counter clerks has scribbled on the sides of the cups. The hot chocolate was fairly easy to single out. She had less success identifying her own beverage.

Just as she was about to ask one of the baristas for help, the stooped, gray-haired guy with glasses who had been behind Lauren in line joined her at the pickup station, drink in hand, looking as confused as she felt.

"Did you order a mocha?"

At his querulous question, she turned to him. "Yes."

He gave her a sheepish grin, his mustache twitching. "I think this is yours." He hefted the cup in his hand. "I must have picked up the wrong drink. It's hard to figure out which is which. Would you like this one, or should I ask them to make you a new one?"

"I don't have a germ phobia." She smiled at him and reached for the cup. "This one is fine."

He tugged his bulky coat around him and rubbed his gloved hands together as he leaned closer to peer at the remaining cups on the stand. "There it is. An Americano." He picked up the cup. "Sorry for the confusion, miss. Have a nice day."

She watched him as he limped away, his gait suggesting an injury or a gimpy leg. It was cold out, but that guy was *really* ready for winter. Sometimes people got chilled more easily as they aged, though. She'd seen it happen with her father.

After weaving back through the crowd, she set the drinks on the table and retook her seat.

"Who was your admirer?" Lauren shot her a teasing glance as she dug into her scone.

"*You* were the one he was admiring. I was watching him

while he waited in line behind you." Kelly used the edge of her fork to cut off a generous bite of her roll. "He might be old, but those skinny jeans of yours were making him feel young again." Kelly grinned as she slid the fork into her mouth and closed her eyes. "Ah. Nirvana!"

"This is a great scone too." Lauren took a sip of her hot chocolate through the whipped cream.

Kelly grinned. "Your mustache is almost as impressive as your admirer's was."

"Very funny." Lauren picked up her napkin and wiped off the white film above her upper lip. "I never did get the hang of drinking through whipped cream—but I hate those plastic lids. So fill me in on all your news. Any exciting commissions recently?"

"I've got a contract for a dozen more greeting cards. Flower-themed. And the Department of Conservation wants me to do four seasonal covers for the magazine next year. Up-close nature scenes."

"That's cool. I assume you'll be hitting the hiking trails to get ideas and take photos, as usual?"

"Yep." Kelly smiled and sipped her mocha.

"You could look at photos in books, you know."

"And miss out on the chance to commune with nature? Hiking's half the fun of those kinds of jobs." She speared another bite of her cinnamon roll.

"For you, maybe. For me, it would be hardship duty. Give me a courtroom any day."

"That's because you're more theatrical than I am." She washed the cinnamon roll down with a long swallow of her mocha and lifted the cup. "The perfect drink for a cold day. Thanks again."

"You're welcome again. Any luck at your father's house?"

"No." She continued to sip her mocha. "I've been through his office and the kitchen drawers and cabinets. Now I'm starting on the closets. But I don't know what I might find that would produce a lead for the police to follow. Alan Carlson, the original detective on the case, called to say he reviewed everything again but didn't come up with any new insights, either. The detective I talked to while he was gone called too, and encouraged me to keep looking, but I think he was just being nice." She dug a tissue out of her pocket and swiped at her nose.

"Hey." Lauren reached over and touched her arm. "Don't get discouraged, okay? If there's anything to be found, you'll find it."

"And if there isn't?" Kelly's throat tightened, and she sniffed. "You knew my dad, Lauren. Do you honestly think he'd have considered suicide?"

Lauren caught her lower lip between her teeth and sighed. "It *is* hard to believe. But being in law, I understand the power of evidence. And the evidence in your dad's case, along with the lack of suspects or motives, puts the police in a difficult position."

A wave of nausea suddenly swept over Kelly, and her lips began to tingle. She'd assumed her sudden runny nose and the tightness in her throat were due to the emotional roller coaster she'd been on since her father's death, but all at once she suspected it was more than that.

"Kelly?" Lauren touched her arm again, her tone uncertain.

Fumbling for the shoulder purse she'd hung on the back of her chair, Kelly rose. "I need to get to the ladies' room."

She tried to take a deep breath.

Couldn't.

Please, God, no! Not an allergy attack!

As she stumbled toward the ladies' room, she groped through her purse for her auto-injector of epinephrine. Her fingers closed over it, and she pulled it out. Lost her grip. Watched in dismay as it hit the tile floor.

Before she could stoop to retrieve it, Lauren was beside her. She bent and swept it up, then propelled Kelly into the ladies' room.

"Tell me what to do." Her friend's voice was tight. Edged with panic.

46

Kelly was wheezing now. Fighting for air. She grabbed the edge of the counter as a wave of dizziness swept over her.

"Take it . . . out of the . . . carrying case. Grab it . . . around the middle . . . with the black tip . . . down. Pull off the gray . . . safety release."

After Lauren did as she was instructed, Kelly took the injector. Holding it perpendicular to her outer thigh, she swung her arm away from her body and then back against her leg. She maintained the pressure as she counted to ten. After she pulled it back, she checked to make sure the needle had fired while she massaged her thigh.

"Are you going to be okay?" Lauren hovered beside her, her face pasty.

She checked the viewing window. It was red. "I should be."

But she wasn't.

As the seconds ticked by, her wheezing grew worse. And the waves of dizziness were striking with more force instead of receding.

Something was very wrong.

The room started to fade, and she gripped the edge of the sink, gasping for breath.

The last thing she remembered was a sensation of tumbling into a dark, deep hole.

4

Cole stepped out of the ER treatment room at St. Luke's Hospital, checked his watch, and expelled a frustrated breath. Interviewing an injured witness in an armed robbery had *not* been on his agenda for Saturday. And now half the morning was shot. For no reason, as it turned out. The vagueness of the witness's description rendered it almost meaningless.

So much for his plans to join Jake for a round of one-on-one basketball.

As he started toward the exit, the wide ambulance doors swung open, and he moved aside to allow the paramedic crew to enter. Reaching for his cell phone, he cast a quick look at the stretcher as they wheeled it past. Maybe he could reschedule Jake to this afternoon, if his brother and Liz didn't have . . .

He froze as he caught a glimpse of russet-colored hair against the white sheet.

The same color hair as Kelly Warren's.

The stretcher disappeared into a treatment room, the paramedics and the nurse on their heels blocking his view of the injured woman.

He stared after them.

No way.

Kelly wasn't the only woman with hair the burnished red of autumn leaves.

Still, he eased toward the door, craning his neck for a better

48

view. He arrived just in time to watch the paramedics transfer the woman to the hospital gurney in one smooth motion. She had an oxygen mask over her face, but he could see enough to make a positive ID.

It *was* Kelly!

His heart stalled, then slammed into double time. Adrenaline propelled him into the room, where he collided with the nurse at the foot of the bed.

"Whoa, Detective." She steadied herself with a hand on his chest—and kept it there when he tried to edge around her. "I thought you were done here."

"I thought so too." He kept his gaze fixed on Kelly's face. The oxygen mask obscured much of it, but he could see that her eyes were closed.

Not good.

"What happened?"

"Are you family?"

"No. I'm . . ." What was he, exactly? The answer eluded him, and he gave up trying to figure it out. "But I know her."

A guy in a white coat shouldered into the room, aiming for Kelly.

"Sorry." The nurse increased the pressure of her hand on his chest, edging him toward the door. "We have work to do in here."

"There's a friend of hers in the waiting room who can fill you in," one of the paramedics offered as he maneuvered around Cole.

He shot the guy a grateful look. "Thanks."

With one more glance at Kelly, he exited and wove through the ER toward the waiting area. Halfway there, he realized he hadn't asked the paramedic if Kelly's friend was a man or a woman.

Stymied, he paused near the door. Huh. For whatever reason, it had never occurred to him she might have a man in her life.

And the notion didn't sit well with him.

A nurse hit the release button on the wall beside him to

admit a patient's family, and as the security door to the waiting room opened, he walked through. If her friend was a guy, and he didn't like Cole butting in, tough.

The waiting room was half full, and he did a quick sweep. Most of the occupants were clustered in groups of two or three. Two women and a man were sitting alone. The lone male appeared to be about forty. He was slouched in his chair, yawning as he paged through a newspaper.

Cole hoped that wasn't Kelly's friend. She deserved a guy who'd be pacing the halls and demanding answers, not checking out sports scores.

The solitary middle-aged woman was reading a form, glasses balanced on her nose. The other woman, a stylish blonde, was closer to Kelly's age. She was perched on the edge of her chair, legs crossed, foot jiggling while she talked on a cell phone. Her posture and demeanor spelled distress with a capital *D*.

He decided to start with her.

As he approached, she looked up. "I don't know, Shaun. We just got here and they relegated me to the waiting room. As soon as I get an update, I'll let you know. Hold on a sec, okay?" She removed the phone from her ear. "Can I help you?"

"Are you by chance here with Kelly Warren?"

"Yes."

"When you're finished with your call, I'd like to talk with you."

"Okay." She put the phone back to her ear. "Shaun, I need to go. I'll call you back in a few minutes." She removed the phone from her ear, punched the off button, and slipped the cell into her purse as she eyed his sport jacket and tie. "Are you a doctor?"

"No. My name is Cole Taylor. I'm a St. Louis County police detective."

A beat of silence passed. "Are you the one Kelly's been talking with about the note from her father?"

"Yes."

The woman held out her hand. "Lauren Casey. Kelly and I are old friends."

He took her cold fingers in his and gave them a firm squeeze. "I was in the ER interviewing a witness when she was wheeled in. Can you tell me what happened?" As he released her hand, he took the chair beside her.

"She went into anaphylactic shock. Kelly's highly allergic to peanuts. Even half a peanut can be fatal if she's not treated immediately."

The bottom fell out of his stomach. "Was she?"

"No." The woman clenched her hands on her lap. "She carries an epinephrine injector with her, but for some reason it didn't work. The coffee shop we were at called 911 right away and the paramedics got there fast, but she'd already passed out and her lips were turning b-blue." The woman's voice hitched, and her knuckles whitened. "I don't understand how this happened. She's a regular at the Perfect Blend, and she's checked out all their stuff."

The word *fatal* was still strobing across his mind. They could determine the cause of her medical crisis later. Right now, he just wanted information on her condition.

"Do you know who has authority to make decisions in an emergency, now that her father is gone?"

"Yes. Me and her minister."

"Good." He stood, took her arm, and drew her to her feet. "Because we're going to get some answers."

Her lips had stopped tingling. And she could breathe again. *Thank you, God.*

"Are you with us, Kelly?"

At the question, she opened her eyes. A middle-aged woman wearing a scrub top was fiddling with an IV beside the bed.

"Yes." Her voice sounded funny, coming through the oxygen mask.

"Welcome back. You had a close call, but the doctor says you'll be fine. Shall I let your friends come back?"

Friends? Plural? "Who's here?"

"A blonde-haired woman and a dark-haired St. Louis County police detective."

She frowned. "Why is a detective here?"

"He was in the ER when you were brought in. I think he was interviewing a witness in some case. He said he knew you and joined your friend in the waiting room."

As the woman leaned over and removed the oxygen mask from her face, Kelly puzzled over that. The only detectives she knew were Alan Carlson and Cole Taylor, and Carlson was blond. It had to be Cole. But why would he be waiting around to see her? After he'd called on Tuesday to tell her Carlson was reviewing her father's case, she hadn't expected to hear from him again.

"So are you up for visitors?"

"Yes. Thanks."

The nurse disappeared, and three minutes later Lauren appeared at the door, the man in question close on her heels.

"Oh, Kelly." Lauren crossed the room and leaned down to give her a hug. "How are you feeling?"

"Not bad. Anaphylaxis is easy to treat as long as you catch it in time."

"We almost didn't."

Kelly didn't want to think about that. Instead, she transferred her attention to Cole, who stood just inside the door, holding a cup of coffee. "Hi."

At her greeting, he moved beside the bed, across from Lauren. Twin lines creased his forehead as he scrutinized her. "You had an exciting morning."

She wrinkled her nose. "I can think of better places to get my kicks than the ER." She plucked at the blanket, trying to come up with a backdoor way to find out why he'd hung around. "I heard you were here interviewing a witness."

"Yeah. Half the department is working a double homicide, so everyone else is filling in where needed on other breaking cases."

"Are you still on duty?"

"No."

That was all he offered, leaving her in limbo about his motives for staying. Was he simply being a good Samaritan—or did he have a more personal interest in her well-being?

Lauren looked from Kelly to Cole and back again before she spoke. "So what happens next? Will they admit you?"

"I can answer that." The nurse in the scrub top came back in. "Your vitals are all back to normal, but we want to keep you for four hours from time of arrival in case there's a biphasic reaction."

"What's that?" Cole asked.

"A second wave of symptoms. It happens sometimes." Kelly turned to Lauren. "You need to go home and get ready for that twinless date with your husband. I know how much you've been looking forward to it. I'll be fine. It's just a waiting game now."

Lauren gave a dismissive flip of her hand. "We can reschedule. Besides, you'll need a ride home after you're released."

"That's what cabs are for."

"I'll be happy to give you a lift."

At Cole's offer, Kelly turned back to him. From her prone position, she had a perfect view of an endearing dimple in the middle of his chin that she'd missed in their previous encounters. Her heart skipped a beat—and her sudden breathlessness had nothing to do with peanuts.

"That's a great idea!" Lauren enthused.

Kelly stifled a groan at the speculative gleam in her friend's eyes. Lauren was shifting into matchmaking mode, and subtlety wasn't her strong suit.

Time for evasive maneuvers.

She refocused on Cole. "That's too much of an imposition. What will you do for three hours?"

"Keep you entertained?" He gave her a half-hitch smile that set off a tingle in her stomach.

"Perfect!" Lauren buttoned her jacket and squeezed Kelly's fingers. "I can see you're in very capable hands. I'll call you later tonight." Slanting a grin at Cole, she lifted her hand in a wave and disappeared out the door.

In the wake of her departure, silence descended. Cole remained by the side of the bed, and Kelly gave him an apologetic glance. "Look, you don't have to stick around. I have to believe you have better things to do on a Saturday morning than kill time waiting for me to be released. But I appreciate the offer."

He took a sip of coffee, watching her. "If you'd rather not have visitors, I'm fine with that. But if you'd like the company, I honestly don't have any other plans. Work already nixed my one-on-one basketball game with my brother."

Her heart warmed. So his reasons for staying were personal, after all. "Okay. If you're sure."

"I'm sure." He slid the hard plastic chair in the corner closer to the bed and sat. "So tell me what happened this morning. Your friend was very upset, and I didn't get a clear explanation."

"That's because there isn't one." She sighed and pushed her hair back from her face. "I have no idea what went wrong. She told you I have a peanut allergy, right?"

"Yes. Severe, apparently."

"Very. A fraction of a peanut, or eating foods cooked in or containing peanut oil, can lead to anaphylactic shock. That's what happened today. But I don't understand why. I'm very, very careful to verify the food I order at restaurants has had no contact with peanuts. I even talked to the owner of the coffee shop on my first visit. He assured me they didn't use any peanut products in their pastries, which they bake on-site, and I've had that cinnamon roll many times."

"What did you drink?"

"Same as usual. A white chocolate mocha."

Cole took another sip of coffee, his expression thoughtful. "Okay, putting aside the cause for a moment . . . your friend said you had a drug with you that didn't work?"

"Yes. I always carry an auto-injector of epinephrine. It did fire—but I also dropped it as I pulled it out of my purse."

She frowned and shook her head. "Still, I can't believe all the epinephrine would have leaked out that fast."

"Have you ever dropped it before?"

"Not that I recall."

"What happened to the injector?"

"The paramedics probably brought it in. Why?"

He lifted a shoulder. "I don't like mysteries. Maybe if you saw it, you could tell what happened."

"We have the injector." The nurse in the scrub top joined their conversation as she entered the room. "It's completely empty. When did you check it last?" She directed that comment to Kelly as she adjusted a setting on the IV.

"Six or eight weeks ago, I think. I've been a little distracted in the past few months."

"I'd like to see it," Cole said.

"Sure. I'll round it up for you."

Kelly watched the nurse exit, feeling like an idiot as she gave Cole a sheepish look. "I usually check it every week or so. It must have leaked and I never noticed."

"You've had plenty of other things to worry about."

She appreciated the empathy in his eyes. "Thanks for being nice about it. And I'm still sorry about ruining your morning."

"It's not ruined." He moved on without giving her a chance to dwell on that remark. "But even if you weren't as diligent as you should have been about monitoring the injector, that leaves us with the question of why you had the reaction in the first place."

"I guess it's possible they changed their recipe at the coffee shop. They know me there, but I didn't place the order today. Lauren did. Since I told her everything was safe, she didn't ask." A sudden yawn caught her off guard, and she sent him an apologetic smile. "Sorry."

One side of his mouth quirked up, and he stood. "You've had a tough morning. Why don't you see if you can get some sleep? I have a few calls to make anyway."

Her eyelids *were* growing heavy. And a quick nap sounded

appealing. But guilt nipped at her conscience. "I feel like I should at least keep you company."

"You can keep me company later. In the meantime, I'll be close by if you need anything." Tossing his empty cup in the trash can, he sent her one more smile before exiting.

And as her eyelids drifted closed, as she hovered in that drifting state between wakefulness and sleep, she found herself wishing his parting comment would be true for far longer than her unexpected hospital stay.

Scanning the central desk area as he exited Kelly's room, Cole spotted the nurse who'd promised to find the injector and strode toward her.

She saw him coming, and by the time he reached her she had it in hand. "Looking for this?"

"Yeah." He took it as she handed it over. It had been put back in its plastic storage tube, and he turned it end to end. Through the viewing window he could see that no liquid remained.

"My guess is a leak," the nurse offered. "A normal firing would leave a small amount of medication inside."

"Does that happen very often?"

"No. Only if the injector is damaged."

He examined it, but if there was a crack or other break, it wasn't visible to the naked eye.

She leaned closer to inspect it too. "It could be that a fine crack produced a slow leak. It might take an X-ray to pick that up."

The medical examiner's office owed him a few favors. Depending on what else he discovered, this might be the time to call one in.

"Hang on to this for me, okay? I'd like to take it with me when we leave."

"Sure thing."

As she turned to answer a summons from one of the staff doctors, Cole pulled out his cell phone and crossed to the exit, stepping outside where he could get a signal. With the help of directory assistance, he had the owner of the Perfect Blend on the line in sixty seconds.

After introducing himself as a friend of Kelly's and assuring the concerned man she would be fine, he asked whether any recipes had been altered in the past few days.

"No. And as I told the young woman when she inquired on her first visit, I never allow the use of peanuts or peanut products in my beverages or baked goods. I have a nephew with a peanut allergy, and he's had to use his injector several times after eating restaurant food he thought was safe. I know how dangerous it can be."

Cole shoved back one side of his sport jacket and propped a hand on his hip as he mulled over possible scenarios. "Have you switched ingredient suppliers recently?"

"No. We haven't changed a thing."

"Okay. Thanks for the information."

Frustrated, Cole pressed the end button and slid the phone back onto his belt. None of this was making sense.

Too wired to sit, he went back inside and prowled around until he found a small hallway not far from Kelly's room, where he could pace off some of his restless energy. This whole incident had a decidedly bad flavor. While coincidences happened, it was a stretch to think that on the one day she'd ingested peanuts, her injector had been empty.

What bothered him most, however, was that all of this had happened not long after she stirred up questions about a closed case she claimed was a homicide.

Cole wasn't a detective because he liked puzzles. He was a detective because he liked *solving* puzzles.

And as he went in search of another cup of coffee, he was already formulating more questions for Kelly.

5

The slam of a door penetrated Kelly's sleep-fogged brain, and she opened her eyes. Blinked against the bright light. Stared at the white ceiling.

Where was she?

When she spotted the IV, it all came back. The allergy attack. The clawing panic when she couldn't breathe. The ride in the ambulance.

Cole Taylor.

She turned her head to find him sitting in the chair he'd occupied earlier.

"Welcome back." He smiled and saluted her with a disposable cup.

"How long was I out?" Even as she asked the question, she twisted her wrist and peered at her watch.

"A couple of hours."

Her eyes flew open. "You waited all this time while I slept?"

"I promised I'd stay close. And I always keep my promises." He held her gaze for a moment before standing to approach the bed. "You look better."

"I feel fine. Maybe they'll spring me soon and you can get out of here." She gave the door a hopeful glance.

"I'm in no hurry." He took a sip of his coffee. "Feel up to answering a few questions while we wait?"

She looked back at him, conscious of a subtle shift in his

manner. His tone was still casual and conversational, his demeanor friendly, but she sensed he'd just slipped into his official persona. The one he used when interviewing witnesses. Or suspects. Or victims.

The one reserved for criminal investigation.

Antennas up, she nodded. "Sure."

"I'd like to hear your version of what happened at the coffee shop this morning. Can you talk me through it?"

"Okay. But may I ask why?"

He hesitated, as if debating his response. When he spoke, his words were slow and measured. "Let's just say I've been thinking about this while you slept, and I'm coming up with more questions than answers. Especially since the owner of the Perfect Blend assured me they haven't changed any ingredients. Do you have any other allergies that could have caused the crisis this morning?"

"No."

"Then the question becomes, how did peanuts get into your system? I'm hoping if you walk me through what happened from the time you arrived until you had the attack, I might spot a red flag."

Kelly frowned, getting a hint of where he was going with this—and not liking it. "Are you suggesting this wasn't some kind of freak accident? That there might have been . . . malicious intent?"

"I don't know. But I don't like the coincidence of exposure to peanuts and an empty injector all on the same day. So humor me, okay?"

A chill swept over her, and she tugged up the thin blanket that was draped over her lower body. "What do you want to know?"

"Start with your arrival, and tell me exactly what happened. Don't leave out any detail, no matter how inconsequential you think it is."

She did as he asked, relaying the events of the morning and answering his questions as she went along. When she got to the part about picking up the drinks, however, she paused and bit her lip.

He narrowed his eyes. "What's wrong?"

Kelly was glad the two of them were on the same side. This was *not* a man she'd want to meet in an interrogation room. No nuance escaped him.

"One unusual thing did happen, although it didn't strike me as odd at the time. The shop was very crowded, and when I went to get our drinks, there were several waiting to be picked up. The barista's scribbling was hard to decipher, and I couldn't find my mocha. An older man joined me, also looking confused. Turns out he'd picked up my drink by mistake. He apologized and offered to ask them to make me a new one, but I said not to bother."

The grim set of Cole's lips told her he didn't think the man had made a mistake.

"So this guy had your drink in his hands."

"Yes. But he was an older man, and I could see how he might have gotten confused. There was nothing sinister about the situation." She bunched the blanket in her fingers. "Are you thinking he put peanuts in my drink?" The whole notion was surreal.

Cole set his coffee on the cabinet, picked up the wall phone, and dialed a number after scrolling through his cell phone. "Can you think of any other explanation for what happened?"

She tried. Failed. "But why would someone do that?"

He held up a finger and asked for the manager of the coffee shop before he responded. "Do you have any enemies?"

"No."

"But you *have* started to ask questions again about your father's death. Have you told anyone you're searching his house?"

"Yes. Lauren and Dad's neighbors who stopped by while I was at his house. And my pastor."

Kelly stared at him, trying to digest his implication as he asked the manager about the trash pickup schedule. His disgusted expression told her he wasn't happy with the answer.

The instant he ended the call, she spoke. "You think someone wants me to stop asking questions badly enough to try and kill me?" The words curdled her stomach.

"I don't know, but I can't discount the timing. Unfortunately, we're not going to get an answer on your drink. The trash was picked up at noon, so short of going through a truck full of garbage, we're out of luck. And I can't muster the resources for that kind of search without more to go on."

Although she was touched he'd even consider such an extreme measure, it seemed like overkill to her. It wasn't as if she'd turned up any evidence that would convince the police to reopen the case. Nor was she likely to, given the dismal results of her search to date.

Unless . . . Maybe there was evidence buried somewhere in her father's house that only his killer knew about.

That was a chilling thought.

"Can you describe this guy?"

Cole's question drew her back to their discussion. "He had gray hair and a bushy mustache, and he wore thick glasses. I think he was on the stocky side, but I can't be sure because he was wearing a bulky coat. He was stooped, which put him at close to my eye level, and I'm five seven. And he limped."

"Any guesses on age?"

"Sixtyish, maybe, based on his gray hair and posture."

"Any distinguishing marks?"

She gave Cole an apologetic look. "I didn't pay that much attention. We only exchanged a couple of words. I'm sorry."

"It's okay. You had no reason to take inventory."

As he reached for his coffee, the nurse rejoined them. "The doctor says you're good to go. I'll unhook you from the IV and run over his instructions. Then you can get dressed and ditch this place."

Cole moved toward the door. "I'll wait outside."

As he retreated, pulling the door shut behind him, the nurse circled around the foot of the bed. "Your chauffeur?"

"Yes."

"Lucky you." The woman grinned. "With my luck, I'd end up with Barney Fife instead of a hot detective."

The nurse removed the IV, and Kelly pressed on the cotton ball covering the prick point, as instructed. She *did* feel lucky to have Cole Taylor as an escort. Yet the questions he'd planted in her mind were unnerving.

Had today's incident been an attempt on her life rather than an accident?

If so, who wanted her dead?

And most troubling of all—would he try again?

Following Kelly, Cole pulled into her driveway and set his brake. She'd insisted on picking up her car at the coffee shop, even though he'd told her he'd be happy to drive her back tonight, after she'd had a few more hours to recover. But maybe this was better. If he came back later, he'd have to cancel his dinner plans with Mitch and Alison. And his sister would be all over him, wanting details he wasn't inclined to offer.

By the time Kelly braked to a stop in her small attached garage, disengaged her seat belt, collected her purse, and turned off her engine, he was beside her door. She smiled up at him as he pulled it open.

"I'm not used to this kind of service."

You should be.

He kept that response to himself as she slid out of the car. But he couldn't imagine why an attractive, intelligent woman like Kelly was unattached.

Unless there *was* a boyfriend lurking around somewhere.

"Don't tell me your dates have bad manners." He kept his tone casual as he fished for information.

"Most guys these days seem to think women would rather fend for themselves." She slid from the car and shuffled through her key ring. "But I, for one, appreciate those kinds of courtesies. Thank you."

That didn't answer his question. He tried again, taking a more direct approach.

"You're welcome. And if you're involved in a serious relationship, I hope he doesn't let you down in that regard."

She fitted the key in the door that led from the garage to the house and turned toward him. The day had grown gray, and the garage was dim, but he detected an appealing wistfulness in her expression. "I'm not involved with anyone. But if I ever am, it will be with a man who's considerate." She fixed those green eyes on him, and her gaze didn't waver. "Like you."

Whoa!

And *he'd* been worried about being too direct.

Blindsided, Cole took a moment to regroup. He was used to flirty come-ons. For whatever reason, a lot of women seemed to find law enforcement types appealing. But Kelly's quiet sincerity put her comment in a whole different league, touching him in a way nothing—or no one—had in a long, long time.

Not since Sara.

At the memory of the gentle-spirited, dark-haired beauty, his stomach coiled into a tight, painful knot.

In the lengthening silence, soft color rose on Kelly's cheeks. She turned toward the door, her fingers fumbling with the key in the lock, clearly embarrassed by his lack of response to her candor.

Way to go, Taylor. This is earning you a lot of points.

Pushing memories of Sara aside, Cole touched her shoulder. Her hand stilled and she stiffened. "Hey. I appreciate that thought. A lot."

At his husky comment, she stole a glance at him over her shoulder, her eyes uncertain. "You didn't look like it."

He debated how much to reveal. He'd never told anyone about Sara. Not even his family. Yet he was tempted to share the story with Kelly.

But this wasn't the time. Not after all she'd been through today.

"My reaction had nothing to do with you. Your comment

just reminded me of an unpleasant episode in my past. Maybe someday I'll tell you about it." Without giving her a chance to process that pseudo-promise, he gestured toward the door. "Do you mind if I take a quick walk-through before I leave?"

She gripped the doorknob, and some of the color drained from her cheeks. "You think there's danger in my own house?"

"I didn't say that. But in light of what happened this morning, I'd prefer to err on the side of caution."

Without saying a word, she turned the key in the lock, pushed open the door, and stepped in.

He followed. Noted the absence of a keypad beside the door. Frowned. "You don't have a security system?"

"No. I've never needed one."

Everyone needed one. If people saw half the stuff he did, they'd know that.

"Okay. Give me five minutes. Anywhere you'd prefer me not to look?"

"No. But ignore any clutter you find. I didn't expect to have visitors today." She tried for a smile but couldn't pull it off.

Cole did a quick but thorough sweep of the neat-as-a-pin house. Everything was secure, but he didn't like her door locks; they were simple keyed knobs, easy to open with a bump key or pick gun. No dead bolts. No sliding bolts, except on the front door—where one was least needed. The basement windows were bottom-hinged hoppers with laughable security, and there were no stops on the main level window frames.

She needed to beef up her security, and he told her that when he rejoined her in the kitchen and found her pulling off her hiking boots.

Distress tightened her features, and she massaged the bridge of her nose. "I've always felt safe here."

He hated to be the one to put fear in her heart, but fearful people were cautious. And he'd much rather have her afraid and on alert than oblivious and vulnerable. There were too many unanswered questions that bothered him. Including the one he'd thought of as he'd followed her home from the coffee shop.

"Safety is an illusion without first-rate security. Even if today hadn't happened, I'd recommend some basic enhancements. But today did happen. And I do have one other question for you. When you took the injector out, was there any moisture inside the carrying case?"

She gave him a blank look. "I have no idea. Lauren opened it for me. Why?"

"If the medication leaked, wouldn't it have been in the case?"

Twin creases appeared on her brow. "Yes. It should have been, but I doubt Lauren will be able to verify that it was. She was really freaked."

"Would you mind asking anyway?"

"No. I'll call her this weekend."

"Okay. Meanwhile, is it okay if I hang on to the injector?"

"Sure. It's of no use to me anymore. But why do you want to keep it?"

"I never get rid of evidence while I'm in the fact-gathering stage." He softened the comment with a smile. "So what are your plans for the rest of the day?"

"I was going to do some hiking. That's the only reason I was wearing those." She indicated the boots. "I may not be as fashion conscious as Lauren, but even *I* don't wear hiking boots except for that express purpose. I don't think I'm up for that today, though."

She liked the outdoors. Nice. Most of the women he dated preferred spike heels to hiking boots.

"Where do you hike?" He leaned back against her kitchen counter and wrapped his fingers around the edge.

"Hawn State Park. Mark Twain National Forest. Weldon Spring Conservation Area." She tucked her fingers into the front pockets of her jeans. "All over."

"You aren't also a camper, by chance, are you?"

"When I can squeeze it in. Mostly, I do day hikes." She smiled, and some of the tension in her face dissipated. "I tell people it's research for my paintings, because I do a lot of nature-themed work. And I never, ever go on a hike without my camera to snap photos of ideas. But between you and me, I just like to be outdoors. Do you camp?"

"I used to, but it's been a while. Life got busier."

"I know what you mean. Plus, with winter coming, I'll get out less often now. Much as I like to hike, I'm not a cold-weather person. Once it gets below forty, I'm in for the season. Give me a warm fire over a frosty nose any day."

Now there was an appealing idea for a Friday night. A warm fire . . . Kelly beside him on the couch . . . a cup of hot chocolate in hand . . . soft jazz in the background.

Talk about a one-eighty from his typical happy hour routine.

Yet all at once the luster of the fast lane dulled. Because suddenly he wanted to be worthy of a woman like Kelly Warren.

She shifted her position, pulling him back to the present, and he realized he owed her a response. Clearing his throat, he pushed off from the counter, needing to put some distance between them. Think this thing through.

"I'm not big on cold weather, either." He motioned toward the living room. "Shall I go out the front door?"

"Sure." She picked up her boots and followed him, opening the coat closet to deposit them on the floor just inside the door. She aligned them precisely, in a spot obviously reserved for them, and when she caught him watching her, she blushed. "Okay, so I'm a neat freak. A place for everything, everything in its place and all that."

She closed the door and leaned back against it. "You know, if you're right about what happened today . . . if someone *was* trying to stop me from digging deeper . . . maybe there's something to be found after all. I might go over to my dad's later and do some more poking around."

The thought of her alone in her father's house sent a cold chill up his spine. "I saw in the case file that his house has a security system. Is it still activated?"

"Yes. I figured that was safer, since the house is vacant. I'm glad now he had one, though I never did understand why he

66

felt the need for it. The house is very modest. But he always said burglaries happen everywhere."

"They do. So keep the doors locked while you're there and reset the system when you leave, okay?" He reached into the pocket of his sport coat and withdrew a card. After flipping it over, he jotted his cell number on the back and handed it to her. "Alan's very competent, and he'll follow up on anything you find. But if you want to talk with me for any reason, use that number. I always have my cell with me. And I'd like to hear what your friend has to say about whether there was any liquid in the carrying case."

Gratitude warmed her eyes as she took the card, reminding him again how alone she was—and how tough it must be to have no family to turn to in a crisis.

"I'll check with her this weekend and give you a call. Thanks for being so thorough and professional."

"No problem."

But that was a lie. Because as Cole looked at her, he felt anything but professional. His usual on-the-job neutrality and detachment had failed him this time—prompting a request he wouldn't typically make. "Would you mind sharing your cell number with me too? In case I need to reach you quickly for some reason."

If she thought his lame request odd or unnecessary, she gave no indication. She just recited her number as he keyed it into the directory on his phone.

"Okay." He slipped the phone back onto his belt and turned the doorknob. He didn't want to leave, but there wasn't any reason to linger. At least none he could come up with. "Lock up behind me." He stepped onto the porch and pulled the door shut. A moment later, he heard the bolt slide into place.

She was as safe as she could be for now.

But as far as he was concerned, she wasn't safe enough. She needed to add a lot more security to her house.

Which gave him an excellent excuse to call her again in a few days.

Things had gone well this morning.

A slow smile twisted his lips as he dipped a cotton swab in spirit gum remover, pried up a corner of the bushy mustache, and dabbed at the dried adhesive. Leaning close to the mirror, he worked his way across the strip of bristly hair with practiced efficiency. Once the gum was dissolved, he discarded the swab in a plastic sandwich bag, peeled off the mustache, and disposed of it in the bag as well.

Straightening up, he flexed his shoulders to work out the kinks. But the discomfort was worth it. The unnatural stoop he'd assumed for the job had completely altered his usual bearing and gait.

Next, he removed the green contact lenses. Not that anyone had noticed his eye color behind the thick glasses, but details counted in an operation like this—and he was a master at details. That's why he was successful on these types of assignments.

The contacts went into the plastic bag too . . . along with the glasses.

He hadn't played a part for a while, but he'd had no trouble shifting back into that mode. And he excelled at it. He knew how to blend in, and he'd perfected the art of disguise to the point that no one would recognize him. Even his wife. Grinning, he added the bottle of temporary theatrical hair color to the bag. She'd been impressed the time he'd fooled her, just for laughs, when they were first dating.

He zipped the bag closed and set it on the vanity. A little drive in the country later today, with a brief stop on a bridge over the Meramec River, would take care of the evidence of his morning outing. Unzip the bag, shake it over the water, and the episode would be history. He'd toss the clothes in the Goodwill bin on his return trip.

But first he needed to get rid of the gray hair.

As he flipped on the shower and adjusted the water temperature, he thought back over the groundwork he'd laid last night and the steps he'd taken this morning. As far as he could see, the operation had been flawless. He hoped Kelly was dead, but even if she'd survived, her near brush with death should distract her from raising dangerous questions about her father's death.

A tiny twinge of regret pricked at his conscience as he stepped into the shower and lathered his hair, then began scrubbing out the gray. Disposing of her had been different than killing her father. John Warren had been on his last legs, anyway. What was the harm in hurrying the process along a little? Especially for such a big payoff. And the man hadn't suffered. It had been a painless, peaceful way to die.

Kelly, however, had been young. Healthy. Talented. Cutting short a life like that didn't feel right.

Soap washed into his eye, and he blinked against the sting, groping for the towel he'd draped over the shower door. He rubbed his face, doing his best to wipe out the irritant, but he couldn't get rid of it.

Kind of like his guilt about Kelly.

But what else could he have done? She'd become a threat to him—and to his plans. She'd sealed her own fate by being too persistent.

He threw the towel back over the door and resumed scrubbing his hair, trying to muffle the little voice that said he'd overreacted. That she might have backed off on her own if she didn't find anything in her father's house.

But what if she *had* found something?

That was the problem.

When you played for high stakes, you couldn't take chances. All the loose ends had to be tied up. And she'd been a loose end.

A big one.

He shut off the water, toweled himself dry, then checked out his hair in the mirror. Not one speck of gray remained. No one would ever be able to connect him to Kelly's allergy attack . . . and perhaps her death.

But you didn't have to kill her. At least, not yet.

He frowned as he stared at his reflection. It wasn't like him to second-guess. He was thorough. Professional. Dispassionate. He did his job, whatever it was, and did it well. Sometimes people died. It happened. But he'd never let it bother him before.

This time, though, he had a personal stake in the outcome. A big one. And maybe . . . okay, probably . . . panic had affected his judgment. The truth was, he could have watched and waited.

Irritated, he ran a comb through his hair. He wasn't going to belabor this. It was too late for regrets, and the operation had been clean. Once he disposed of his disguise, there would be nothing to tie him to today's incident. Worst case, even if Kelly Warren did continue to search her father's house, he would just be back to where he'd been a few days ago. If she did happen to find something that raised questions, he'd deal with it.

Things would turn out fine.

Yet as he pulled on a pair of jeans and a T-shirt, grabbed his car keys, and prepared to make a pizza run, he couldn't shake the niggling doubt that he'd made a mistake today.

One that could very well come back to haunt him.

6

Kelly reached for the phone next to her easel. Dropped her hand. Reached for it again. Hesitated.

Annoyed, she huffed out a breath. How hard was it to pick up the phone, dial Cole Taylor's number, and pass on the information she'd gotten from Lauren about the injector?

It should be a piece of cake.

And it would be—if she wasn't also thinking about offering to take him to lunch as a thank-you for his help on Saturday. She just wasn't used to asking guys out. Especially tall, dark, and handsome guys.

Rubbing her damp palms on the oversized shirt that served as a smock, she told herself she was being foolish. She owed the man for giving up a big part of his weekend for her, and a mere thank-you note didn't cut it. A meal seemed like a reasonable alternative. And it wasn't like she was inviting him out for an intimate dinner. Lunch was casual. Low-key. Nonthreatening. What was the worst that could happen? He'd say no.

But that was the scariest part of all. However, putting off the call wasn't going to change the outcome.

Summoning up her courage, she picked up the phone and tapped in his office number rather than his cell. That felt more official. Less risky.

He answered on the first ring. A clipped, no-nonsense greeting. "Taylor."

71

Her fingers tightened on the phone and she took a deep breath, striving for a pleasant, conversational tone. "Cole, it's Kelly Warren. Is this a good time?"

Though he again responded with a single word, the transformation in his voice from brusque to gracious eased the tension in her shoulders.

"Always."

Kelly shifted away from her easel and looked out the window. The day might be gray and dreary, but her heart suddenly felt lighter. "I wanted to let you know I asked Lauren your question, about whether there was any liquid in the carrying case. She wasn't 100 percent certain, but she does remember tipping the case to slide the injector out, so if there'd been any liquid inside, it would have spilled. And she doesn't recall that happening."

"Okay. That's one more piece of information to file away. How are you feeling? Any aftereffects?"

"No. Dangerous as anaphylactic shock is, recovery is quick if you catch it fast enough." She moistened her lips and plunged in. "Besides passing on the information from Lauren, I did have another reason for calling. I was wondering if you'd let me treat you to lunch one day this week as a thank-you for Saturday."

Silence.

Her stomach clenched and she closed her eyes, stifling her disappointment. At least she'd tried. "Look, I know you're busy. I totally understand if—"

"Whoa! No retracting allowed. I never turn down a free lunch. You just took me by surprise. When would you like to go?"

Her heart gave a little flutter. "Does Wednesday at twelve-thirty work for you?"

"Perfect."

His response was so quick she wondered how he'd had a chance to check his calendar. "Okay. What's your favorite kind of food? And please don't say Mexican."

"You're not a fan of refried beans?"

At his teasing tone, she smiled. "No. Nor guacamole, jalapenos, chipotle . . ."

"I get the picture." His husky chuckle came over the line, setting off a pleasant quiver in her nerve endings. "How about Italian?"

"That I can do. Do you like Maggiano's? It's about halfway between us, and their menu has safe items for me."

"Sounds great. I'll look forward to it. Thanks, Kelly."

"Same here. See you then."

As the line went dead, a smile teased her lips. Somewhere along the way they'd slipped into first names. And it felt good.

Cole's warm reception to her invitation also felt good.

Picking up her brush, Kelly considered her palette, then swirled the tip in spring green and tried to focus on the whimsical woodland scene that would soon illustrate a children's book about a gnome with the magical power to grant wishes.

But it was difficult to think about fairy tales in books when wishes were coming true in real life.

Leaning back in his chair, Cole linked his fingers behind his head, grinning like an idiot. But who cared? The woman who'd dominated his thoughts from the moment he'd caught sight of her on an ambulance stretcher in the ER had invited him to lunch.

Talk about a great way to start a Monday.

"You look happy."

At the comment, Cole swiveled in his chair to find Alan watching him from a few feet away. He didn't bother to tone down his grin. "Guilty as charged."

Alan strolled over and settled a hip on his desk. "I heard you mention Kelly. That wasn't by any chance Kelly Warren on the phone, was it?"

Unlinking his fingers, Cole rocked back in his chair. "As a matter of fact, it was."

"Why am I thinking this wasn't a business call?" One side of Alan's mouth twitched.

"Because you're a decent detective?"

"I happen to be a great detective. But even a rank amateur would notice your goofy grin. It's pretty convincing circumstantial evidence. When did you two connect, anyway?"

Some of Cole's good humor faded. "Over the weekend. She was in the ER while I was there interviewing a witness in an armed robbery. She almost died."

Twin furrows appeared on Alan's brow, and he dropped his gaze to the injector lying on the desk. "I noticed that as I was walking by. She has a peanut allergy, doesn't she?"

"Yeah. How did you know?"

"She mentioned it during the investigation of her father's death." He gestured to the injector. "Is that hers?"

"Yes, but it didn't work. Apparently the medication had leaked out."

"That happened to Cindy once, but she discovered the leak and replaced it. She was allergic to bee stings, so she carried one of these too." Alan picked up the injector and examined it. "I did see Kelly drop one of these once. It fell out of her purse when she opened it to get a tissue. Hit the floor pretty hard. I'm assuming she ate some peanuts?"

"Yes, but we can't pinpoint the source." Cole filled Alan in on what had happened, as well as his suspicions. "And here's another odd thing. She doesn't think there was any liquid in the carrying case when her friend opened it."

Alan regarded the injector. "And you're wondering why there wasn't, if the medication leaked out." He cocked his head. "I see your point. But why would anyone target her? It's not as if she's found anything that would make us reopen the case."

"Maybe someone is afraid she will. Or *knows* she will if she keeps looking."

"So are you buying into her theory now? That her father's death was a homicide, not a suicide?"

Cole picked up a pen and twirled it in his fingers. Alison was always ragging on him about his lack of tact, and this situation demanded it. He needed to come up with a diplomatic

74

response that didn't impugn the integrity of Alan's investigation. Especially since his own review of the case hadn't raised any red flags, either. "Let's just say I'm keeping an open mind. Too many little things aren't adding up. What do you think?"

The other man nodded. "I agree. But we have no solid evidence that merits reopening the case."

"I know, but we might eventually get some. Kelly's more determined than ever to go through her father's house with a fine-tooth comb."

Alan set the injector back on the desk and rose. "Well, she knows where to find us if she comes up with anything. I called her last week too, and assured her I'm more than happy to investigate any new leads she might stumble across."

Though his colleague's tone was casual, Cole didn't miss the man's slight emphasis on *I*. He was defending his turf, and Cole couldn't blame him. He was the case detective, unless or until he was reassigned. If the situation were reversed, Cole knew he'd be laying down some boundaries too—and with far less finesse.

"I told her the same thing and assured her you were excellent at your job."

That appeared to mollify his co-worker. "Thanks for the endorsement. And look at it this way. If you leave the official business to me, you can focus on a personal investigation of Ms. Warren instead." With a grin, the man exited.

Cole watched him leave, conceding the man's point. He *would* prefer to leave the official stuff to Alan. But as he slid his chair under his desk and picked up the injector, the analytical side of his brain refused to disengage.

According to Alan, Kelly had dropped the injector a few months ago. No surprise she'd forgotten that, in the midst of all her trauma. That may have been when it had begun to leak. But surely she would have noticed liquid collecting in the carrying case sometime in the past four months. And even if she hadn't, it should have been in there on Saturday. Where had it gone?

Then there was the older man who'd taken her drink at the coffee shop. Cole's instincts told him the confused customer was the key to Kelly's allergic reaction. Tough to prove, though, even if they could locate the guy.

Nevertheless, identifying him would be a first step. Perhaps he'd been caught on a security video somewhere near the coffee shop.

Cole thought about suggesting that angle to Alan, but he hated to waste the man's time on what would probably turn out to be a wild-goose chase. Why not make a few phone calls on his own? Do a little digging? If he did manage to find anything interesting, he'd pass it on to his colleague. If he didn't, the only thing lost would be his time.

Leaning forward, Cole reached for his phone.

She should be at home, painting. Her deadlines were piling up, and she was behind. But ever since her allergy attack four days ago, Kelly had felt compelled to put in extra hours searching her father's house—all the while praying that if she *did* find something important, she'd recognize its significance.

But a quick check of her watch told her she couldn't afford to spend more than a few more minutes on her quest today. Not unless she wanted to be late for her lunch with Cole.

And she definitely didn't!

Hand resting on the chest of drawers, she surveyed the bedroom her parents had shared for the sixteen years they'd been married, and which her father had occupied alone for the remaining twenty-one years of his life. By choice. A man as kind, handsome, and intelligent as her dad could have remarried, but when she'd broached the subject once, he'd told her he was happy with his memories. That he'd already been blessed with his once-in-a-lifetime love.

Kelly looked at the wedding photo of her parents that had always graced the top of the chest, wishing she could remember more about the woman her father had adored. More than that, though, she wished a congenital heart defect hadn't cut her life so short. Hypertrophic cardiomyopathy, the medical examiner had ruled. One minute she'd been playing tennis, seemingly in the peak of health. Seconds later she'd been dead.

Even now, from the distance of two decades, that whole period of Kelly's life had a surreal quality to it.

Just as the weeks surrounding her father's death did.

But dwelling on the past wasn't going to bring her parents back. Or help her find justice for her father.

Shutting off the memories, she got down on her knees to tackle the bottom drawer in the chest before leaving to meet Cole.

When it didn't budge after a firm tug on the handles, she tightened her grip, repositioned herself for better leverage, and tried again. Inch by inch, she was able to work it open despite the squeaks of protest. Obviously, this was not a drawer her dad had used very often.

A cursory inspection told her it was a junk repository. But she wasn't leaving any stone unturned.

Sifting through the jumbled contents, she found a wadded-up T-shirt emblazoned with the logo of the girls' softball team her father had coached when she was eleven; two used tennis balls that had lost most of their bounce; a transistor radio that might have antique value by now; a 1982 St. Louis Cardinals World Series cap; a forty-year-old accounting manual; and various other dog-eared tomes, pieces of worn clothing, and the detritus of someone who'd lived almost seven decades.

All of it, though, was ancient history. And unlikely to have any bearing on recent events.

Just as she was about to close the drawer, the scuffed corner of a wallet peeking out from the clutter caught her eye. A rush of memories swept over her of the beloved Sunday morning ritual of her childhood, and she tugged the wallet free, cradling the scarred leather in her hands. While her mother would finish getting ready for church, she and her father would go to the convenience store at the corner to buy a newspaper. That weekly excursion with her dad—and the glazed donut he always bought her—had been one of the highlights of her week.

But what she'd loved most was how he'd let her hold his wallet. Even before she'd understood the value of money, she'd known this wallet was important to her dad. He never left home without it. Yet he'd trusted her with it every Sunday morning.

John Warren had always known how to make people feel important—and valued.

Kelly blinked back the sudden tears that blurred her vision and stroked the worn leather, now cracked in a few places. It was stiff when she tried to bend it, like an arthritic knee, and empty when she opened it. The photos of her and her mom were gone, the plastic holders bare and cracked, and the window that had once protected her dad's driver's license had yellowed.

She bowed the compartment for bills, where her dad had always kept his singles, fives, and twenties lined up in military precision, all facing the same direction, each denomination together—the very same way she did it now. That, too, was empty.

Except . . . what was the small whitish triangle sticking out near the bottom, in the corner?

Curious, Kelly worked her finger into the space. It felt like the corner of a piece of paper. She ran her finger over the leather, detecting a vertical crack—or slit. By inserting her fingernail, she was able to create an opening large enough to ease out the small slip of paper.

Once she had it in hand, she set the wallet aside. The soiled, yellowed paper was folded in half, and she opened it carefully. Despite the grime, she could make out a sequence of digits.

It was a telephone number.

Kelly frowned and picked up the wallet again, scooting beside the window to let the light shine into the dark corner where the paper had been hidden. Although the leather was cracked in a few places from age, the slit that had given her access to the phone number seemed too precise—too deliberate—to be a random split.

It was as if her dad had created a hiding place for this slip of paper.

How odd was that?

She reread the unfamiliar local number. Was there any chance it would still be a working line? Her dad hadn't used this wallet in at least a dozen years, not since she'd upgraded him to a Gucci version with part of the payment from her first watercolor commission.

Sixty seconds later, after tapping the digits into her cell phone, she got the recording she expected. The number was no longer in service.

She checked her watch. She needed to leave *now* to meet Cole. As it was, if the streets around Galleria were deadlocked with traffic, she'd be late. Parking could be a problem too.

Switching gears, she retrieved her jacket from the kitchen, still distracted by the carefully concealed number. Puzzling as it was, what bearing could a number twelve-plus years old have on her father's death?

Yet she'd found nothing else, despite her diligent searching. And she couldn't shake the sense that this discovery was relevant.

She picked up her purse from the counter. Hesitated. What would Alan Carlson say if she told him about her find—and her intuition that it was important? Would he think she was grasping at straws and dismiss it?

Maybe.

But Cole wouldn't. Not to her face, anyway. Why not run it by him first? See what he thought before she approached Carlson?

Settled on that plan of action, Kelly detoured to her father's bedroom and put the note and the wallet in her purse. It wasn't much to go on, and she tried not to get her hopes up.

Yet as she set her father's security system and exited, she couldn't suppress a small surge of optimism that perhaps, at last, she'd stumbled upon a clue that would help her get to the bottom of her father's death.

Cole checked his watch.

Kelly was late.

Then again, he'd been early.

Too early.

But three minutes later, as he checked voice mail and returned calls to pass the time, she pushed through the front door, the blustery November wind whipping her hair around her face. She spotted him at once and waved, looking harried—and gorgeous—as she hurried toward him.

"Sorry." Cheeks flushed, she wrinkled her nose as she gave him a breathless apology. "I got tied up in traffic."

"No problem. I made calls while I waited." He slid the phone back onto his belt.

"Well, let's get a table. I'm sure you're on a tight schedule."

Nope. He'd cleared his agenda until two-thirty, in case their lunch ran long.

He hoped.

Once at the table, he helped her with her jacket, then slid into the booth across from her. "You look like you've fully recovered from the weekend's excitement."

"I have."

"And everything's been quiet?"

"Yes. No sign of the mysterious older man in the coffee shop. Are you still worried about him?"

He was. But after a few discreet calls, he'd concluded the man hadn't been caught on any security video. So he was out of luck trying to identify him.

"I think a little extra caution would be wise for a while." He kept his tone casual as he draped his napkin across his lap.

The waiter appeared, and after he ran through the day's specials, they placed their orders.

"Thank you again for the invitation." Cole settled back in the booth and smiled at her. "My typical lunch is a burger grabbed on the run. This is a treat."

"It's small repayment for monopolizing your Saturday." Before he could tell her he hadn't minded in the least, she linked her fingers on the table and gave him a serious look. "Besides, I want to pick your brain about something I found at my dad's house this morning."

His radar went up. "Okay."

"I know Detective Carlson is my official contact, and I don't want to put you in the middle, but before I go to him with this I thought I'd get your read. If you tell me I'm overreacting, I won't bother him." She unzipped her purse and withdrew a beat-up wallet and a small slip of paper, which she set on the table.

He listened as she explained how and where she'd found the items. Then he picked up the wallet and examined it. She was right. From what he could tell, the slit did appear to be deliberate—as if it had been made to create a hiding place.

"I wasn't surprised when the number was out of service." She tapped a finger on the table as she concluded her story. "And since Dad hasn't used that wallet in a dozen years or so, it may be a stretch to think this is relevant to his death. But he wasn't a secretive man. I can't imagine why he'd keep a number hidden like that."

Cole examined the smudged slip of paper. He could think of several reasons. But none of them fit the profile Kelly had painted of an upstanding Christian man. "I'll tell you what. Let me have our Communications people see if they can put a name to this number. It might end up being totally innocent, but there's a chance it could turn out to be a lead."

"Are you sure you don't mind?"

"I'm sure." He pulled out a notebook and jotted down the number. "Hang on to these until I get some more information." He slid the wallet and slip of paper back to her side of the table.

She stowed them in her purse and shot him a smile. "Okay. Enough business. This isn't supposed to be a working lunch. Why don't you tell me a little about yourself? I feel at a distinct disadvantage, since you've read so much about me in the case file."

"What would you like to know?"

Grinning, she took a piece of bread from the basket. "Tell me what you do for fun."

Socialize with women who like to have *fun.*

That was the truth of it. And with anyone else, he'd have said exactly that with the rakish grin he'd perfected. The kind of women he dated would laugh, or feign a pout, or edge in closer if the seating arrangement allowed.

But Kelly didn't fit that mold. And he could imagine her reaction if he gave his usual response. Disappointment. Disapproval. Withdrawal.

None of those were acceptable.

Because even though this lunch didn't qualify as a date, he hoped they *would* have some real dates down the road.

As a result, he did something he hadn't done with a woman in years. He spoke from the heart.

"I hang out with my family a lot. I have a brother and sister, and while we can get on each others' nerves, I love spending time with them. My mom's great too."

Her expression grew wistful, and a smile softened her lips as she rested one elbow on the table and propped her chin in her palm. "I always wished I had siblings. Tell me about yours so I can live vicariously for a little while."

He complied as they consumed rigatoni and lasagna, regaling her with tales about their growing-up years, as well as Alison's Social Services children's work and Jake's career as a deputy U.S. marshal and a member of that organization's elite Special Operations Group. She plied him with eager questions, her eyes alight with enthusiasm and interest, and as the meal wound down he realized he hadn't shared this much about his life with anyone outside the family—ever. Nor enjoyed himself so much.

"You know, if you ever get tired of being an artist, you should apply for a job as an investigative reporter. Or an interrogator. The FBI could use you." He wiped his mouth with a napkin and grinned at her.

She smiled back and buttered the last bite of her bread. "I loved hearing about your family. Talk about a high-performing bunch. How did you all end up in justice-related professions, anyway?"

"I think it's in the genes. My dad was a police officer. Just a beat cop, as he always put it. That's all he ever wanted to be. A guy on the street, helping people. He didn't care about glory or promotions or citations. He cared about justice and about keeping people safe. He was the most selfless, principled man I ever met." His voice hoarsened, and he covered the uncharacteristic display of emotion by taking a swallow of coffee and shifting the spotlight to Kelly. "How did you become an artist?"

"Unlike you, I can't claim to have followed in my father's footsteps—except when it comes to neatness." A smile tugged at her lips. "He was a numbers man. He used to kid that he couldn't draw a straight line, and there was a lot of truth to that. But he appreciated art and encouraged me to develop my talent. He always paid for extra art lessons and summer art camps and supplies . . ." Her words trailed off and her smile faded. "He was a wonderful person. Kind of like your dad."

Without stopping to think, he reached across the table and covered her fingers with his. Her eyes widened, but she didn't retract her hand.

"If I haven't said it before, I'm sorry for your loss. And I admire you for loving your dad enough to keep digging for information to prove your theory about his death."

"Some days it feels like an uphill battle." A quiver ran through her words, and the muscles in her throat contracted as she swallowed. "But when I got those bulbs, I felt like it was a message from Dad, telling me there was more to the story. It was the impetus I needed to get back in the fight, even though the case was closed."

"You're not alone. Enough has happened to make me suspicious too. Let's see what we can turn up on that number from your dad's wallet."

Their gazes locked, and a flush rose on Kelly's cheeks. Then she tugged her fingers from beneath his and picked up the credit card slip.

He missed the warmth of her hand at once.

"I didn't mean to take up this much of your afternoon." She kept her head bent as she signed the slip.

"My schedule is flexible today." He set his napkin on the table. "Ready?"

In answer, she slid out of the booth. He stayed a step behind her as they wove through the tables toward the front door, and insisted on walking her to her car after discovering she'd parked in the garage.

The blustery wind and unseasonable cold wasn't conducive to conversation as they set off at a brisk pace, and she shivered as they stopped beside her Focus in the shadowy garage. "It's much too early to be this chilly."

"I agree." He did a quick sweep of the garage as she unlocked her car. Few people were about. "No more parking garages until we get this thing sorted out, okay?"

She turned to him, her brow furrowed. "You're going to make me paranoid."

"Think of it as being prudent." He pulled the door open for her. "I'll call you about the number. And thank you again for lunch. I enjoyed it a lot."

Once more, her color rose. "Me too."

For a moment, she hesitated. As if she wanted to say more. Instead, she slid into the car.

He closed the door, stepped back, and waited for her to start the engine and pull out before returning to his own car, glad he'd reserved a full two hours for lunch.

And glad the number in his pocket gave him an excuse to call her again.

Soon.

7

A missing person's case kept him on the go for the next two days, but by Friday afternoon Cole had a chance to connect with the Communications Bureau and pass on the number Kelly had found. Identifying a line out of service for more than a decade was dicey, as they reminded him. Four or five years was usually the max, but it might be possible to track it if the phone company was still in existence.

Meanwhile, he intended to take a closer look at the medical examiner's report on John Warren. After his first meeting with Kelly, he'd focused on the summary and cause of death, skimming the details. The conclusive findings hadn't seemed to merit a detailed review.

But in light of all that had happened, he decided to follow Kelly's example and start using a fine-tooth comb with this case.

Pulling up the report on the screen, he leaned forward and read through the data. He'd sat in on enough autopsies to understand the terminology, to know that the states of rigor and livor were consistent with Alan's conclusions. But one small note in the external description did catch his eye.

John Warren had had a small round scar on the left side of his lower back.

Round.

What would cause a round scar?

A bullet?

Her father had also had a narrow three-inch scar on his left abdomen.

Were the two scars related?

Filing those questions away, Cole moved on to the results of the internal examination.

The lung cancer was noted, but nothing else jumped out at him until he came to the gastrointestinal system. There, the forensic pathologist had observed old damage to the large intestine on the left side.

Was that related to the scars?

He read the rest of the report, including the toxicology findings, which confirmed the presence of ethanol and zolpidem. That was consistent with the beer and pills found with the body and in the house.

Tapping a finger on his desk, he scrolled back to the first page. Dale Matthews had done the exam. A smart guy. Intuitive. Precise. Thorough. Cole had sat in on some of his autopsies, and he'd been impressed by the man's deductive reasoning. Matthews's off-the-cuff verbal observations never made it into the final report. A postmortem was about fact, not conjecture. But his insights were sound, and Cole was interested in his take on the scars and the damaged intestine.

Despite the small odds of reaching the man on a first try, Cole put in a call.

Much to his surprise, he caught Matthews in his office. The pathologist pulled up the autopsy as Cole gave him a topline review of the case.

"Yeah . . . I'm skimming the report as we speak. I remember this one. I don't see that many carbon monoxide deaths. What's your question?"

"You noted a round scar on the victim's back and another long one on his abdomen. And you called out some damage to his large intestine. Do you think all three could be related? Off the record."

"That would be my assumption. They're all consistent with a gunshot wound. My guess is the bullet entered the back, damaged the intestines, and was removed through the abdomen."

Matthews's conclusion confirmed his own suspicions.

Kelly's father had been shot.

"Any idea about the age of that damage?"

"The scars were old. Twenty-five, thirty years would be my guess. It's harder to tell with the intestine."

"Okay. That helps a lot. Thanks."

"Not a problem. Good luck with whatever you're working on."

As the line went dead, Cole set the phone in its cradle and leaned back in his chair. He needed to run this latest news by Kelly. If the damage was from an old war wound, she might know about it.

But he had a feeling this news was going to take her by surprise. That the injury was from a trauma her father had never shared with her.

For that reason, this wasn't a discussion he wanted to have by phone.

He pulled his cell off his belt, scrolled through his directory, and tapped auto dial. She picked up after two rings with a cheery hello.

"Hi, Kelly." He turned a pen end to end on his desktop. "If you have a few minutes, I'd like to swing by your house tonight after work."

"Sure." She sounded surprised but pleased. "Did you track down my mystery number?"

"No. The Communications people are still working on it. But I learned something else interesting today I'd like to share with you."

"Okay. I'll tell you what . . . since you're coming around dinnertime, why don't you share your news over dinner? I'm planning to grill salmon. Unless . . . it *is* Friday. You probably have other plans."

His usual Friday night routine included socializing with some of the other single detectives, but that hadn't even been on his agenda for tonight—thanks to the russet-haired beauty on the other end of the line.

"I don't have any plans. And dinner would be great. Look for me around six, if that's okay."

"Perfect. See you then."

As he dropped the phone back in the cradle, Alan spoke over his shoulder. "Sounds like you're not in the market for happy hour tonight."

Cole pivoted toward him and flashed a smile. "I got lucky early."

"You wouldn't be referring to a certain redhead we both know, would you?"

"Maybe." Cole needed to tell Alan about his discussion with Matthews. He didn't want his colleague to think he was going behind his back. Where was Alison when he needed her, to coach him through this tact business? "But it's mostly business."

The other man grinned. "Right."

"No. I'm serious." He tried to couch his explanation as diplomatically as he could. "Kelly found a phone number this weekend in a secret compartment in her father's old wallet. I'm running it through Communications. Since new information keeps appearing, I took another look at the autopsy report for Kelly's father and noticed a few things I missed on my first review. Some external scarring, and damage to the intestine. I just had an interesting conversation with Dale Matthews, whose opinion corroborated my own conclusion. We think her father was shot many years ago."

Alan's face went blank with shock. "How did I miss that?"

"Given the circumstances of his death, I doubt I'd have paid any attention to old injuries, either. Considering all the recent developments, though, I'm wondering if there's a connection."

"She never mentioned anything about her father being shot."

"I have a feeling she doesn't know."

"So that's why you're going over tonight." Understanding chased away the shock on his face. "To break the news—and see if she can shed any light on this surprising bit of history."

"More or less. Plus, she offered to feed me." Cole lifted his shoulder in a what-can-you-do gesture. "Since my mom moved to Chicago and Alison started dating Mitch, my home-cooked meals have been few and far between."

One side of Alan's mouth lifted. "I hear you. Go for it. And let me know what you find out from her. I might have to dig back in on this after all. In the meantime, enjoy your dinner."

With a wave, the other man exited into the hall.

As Cole swung back to his computer, he intended to do his best to follow Alan's advice and have a pleasant meal.

But he had a feeling his news might very well kill his hostess's appetite.

Things were not going as planned.

Kelly Warren hadn't died, and Cole Taylor was getting much too involved in the John Warren case. With four weeks to go until the last of the money was paid, his debts were piling up. The threat of garnishment on his wages was very real. But he could hold everyone off for one more month.

His main concern was *getting* the final payment. The last third had been contingent on pulling off a clean operation, the time delay built in as insurance against fallout.

The kind of fallout that was beginning to happen.

The kind that had to be contained.

He paced from one side of the sparsely furnished living room in his apartment to the other, frustration tightening the muscles in his shoulders. He'd gone clean, just like he'd promised. He was living like a pauper to conserve cash, something he'd vowed never again to do after the rattraps he'd occupied as a child because his old man had never been sober long enough to hold a decent job. He was keeping his nose clean. He didn't deserve to have things blow up at this point.

What bothered him most was that he'd brought some of this on himself, thanks to the peanut incident. Instead of distracting Kelly, it had energized her. Stiffened her resolve. Now all kinds of new developments were popping up. A mysterious phone number. An old gunshot wound. A detective who was falling for the victim's daughter and taking a personal interest in the case.

At least he was getting the latest updates from an excellent source. That was about the only bright spot in the whole picture.

Pausing by the window, he gazed out into the darkness. Night fell early this time of year. That meant the winter cold wasn't far behind. He hated winter. Once he got this thing straightened out and had the final payment in hand, he was ditching this town and going somewhere warm. Florida, maybe. Or Arizona.

And if he was lucky, he wouldn't be alone.

He clung to that hope. It was what kept him going. Sure, there'd been a few glitches, but so far none of the new information was providing any worthwhile insights. Nor did it link him to John Warren's death or his daughter's allergy attack.

And it wouldn't. He'd been careful. There was no reason for his benefactor to be displeased with his work. No reason for the final payment to be delayed.

The sudden glare of car headlights arcing across the window blinded him, and he lifted a hand to shade his eyes. Jerking back, he stumbled against the coffee table. Lost his balance. Muttered a curse as he struggled to regain his equilibrium.

As the world stabilized, he sucked in a sharp breath. In general, he was cool under pressure. But this whole situation had him on edge. He was as skittish as a neophyte blackjack player up against high rollers for the first time.

Rubbing his shin, he hobbled toward the kitchen.

He needed a beer.

"So what news did you have to tell me? We're almost finished with dinner." Kelly smiled at Cole across the small café table in her kitchen and leaned back, looking as relaxed as he'd ever seen her. Good thing, given the next topic of discussion.

Cole finished off his last bite of salmon and and set down his fork. "First, I have a question for you. Was your father ever in the military?"

"No. Why?"

"Was he ever involved in any sort of hunting accident?"

"That's two questions, and the answer is still no." Twin creases appeared on her forehead, and she picked up her water glass, holding on tight as if she were bracing herself. "What did you find?"

"A few things on your father's autopsy report I missed the first time around."

"Like what?"

"Notations about two scars and evidence of old damage to his intestine."

"How old?"

"The pathologist is guessing twenty-five to thirty years, and he said all three are consistent with a gunshot wound."

She gave him an incredulous look. "A gunshot wound? That's crazy. My father was the gentlest, kindest man I ever met. He hated guns. And if he'd been involved in some kind of violent incident years ago—a robbery, or whatever—he'd have told me. There must be some mistake."

"There's no mistake in terms of the physical evidence, but we can't prove it was a gunshot wound, either. The forensic pathologist who did the autopsy is a sharp guy, though, and I called him to discuss it. He had the same take I did."

Kelly lifted the glass to her lips and took a sip. Her hand was shaking. So was her voice when she spoke.

"This is getting weirder and weirder." She set the water down carefully. "But assuming we *are* talking about a gunshot wound, how could something that old have any bearing on what happened to my dad five months ago?"

"That's the $64,000 question." He rested his elbows on the table and steepled his fingers. "In the days and weeks leading up to your dad's death, did anything out of the ordinary happen that, in hindsight, might be significant? Did your father do anything or say anything that now seems out of character or gives you any pause?"

"No. Dad led a very quiet life. He was active at church and in the garden club, and he went on an occasional bus trip with a senior group from the community center. The only thing different he did in the last few months of his life was drive to Niagara Falls by himself on his wedding anniversary. That was where he and my mom went on their honeymoon. He was gone for about ten days. Taking a trip alone was unusual, but given the occasion, it didn't raise any red flags."

"Did you tell Alan about that, when he was investigating the case?"

"No." She shrugged. "It didn't seem relevant. Do you think it is?"

"I don't know. But any out-of-pattern behavior is worth noting. What were the dates he was gone?" He pulled a notebook out of his pocket and jotted them down as she recited them. "Did he visit anyone on that trip?"

"Not that I know of. I don't think he had friends in that area. He and Mom were born and educated in the Midwest. I suppose it's possible he knew someone along the route, but I doubt it. I think he would have mentioned it when he told me about the trip. Then again, I don't know why he never mentioned the scars or the internal injuries." She bit her lip, her eyes troubled. "I'm getting more and more confused."

So was he. Every fact they turned up left them with more questions than answers.

"Well, the trip may not . . ." At the sudden vibration of his cell phone, he shot her an apologetic look and checked caller ID. Sarge. That didn't bode well for the rest of his evening. "Sorry. I need to take this."

"Go ahead. I'll clear the table." She rose, picked up their plates, and disappeared into the kitchen.

"Taylor."

"Cole, we've got a double homicide. I'm pulling in some extra people. Let me give you the location. They'll brief you at the scene."

He jotted down the address as the man recited it. So much for his evening with Kelly.

By the time she returned with a platter of lemon bars that looked homemade, he was on his feet.

"You're not staying for dessert?" It was more statement than question, and there was a touch of disappointment in her tone.

"Duty calls. We've got a case that requires some extra manpower. It's gonna be a late night."

She sighed and started toward the foyer, platter still in hand. "I don't envy you the kind of hours you keep."

"They're not always this bad." He stopped at the door, liking her marginal security even less than he had on his last visit. "You need to get some better locks."

"It's on my list."

"Bump it to the top."

"I already made a few calls. I'm waiting for estimates. But I want to spend most of the weekend at my dad's house, anyway. With all the new developments, who knows what else I might find?"

He couldn't argue with that. "Just be careful, okay?"

"I will."

"And next time, the meal's on me."

"I'd like that." A heart-melting smile softened her lips.

His gaze got stuck on their lush fullness, and his pulse took a leap.

Man.

He did *not* want to leave.

But what he did want to do wouldn't be wise. So maybe it was better he'd been called away. It would keep him from rushing things. Making a mistake he might regret. Like crossing the line from professional to personal. Or scaring Kelly off. She struck him as a slow mover, and he needed to downshift if he wanted to stay in this race.

"I'll let you know as soon as I hear anything about the mystery number." He grabbed two lemon bars, opened the door, and stepped out into the chilly air. "Lock up."

Before she could respond, he started down the walk. And despite the frosty nip of the November wind, he felt toasty— thanks to the lingering warmth of her smile.

8

"Are you sure this is wise?" Lauren cast a nervous glance at Kelly's cinnamon roll and mocha as they claimed a table at the Perfect Blend.

Kelly shrugged off her coat, draped it over the chair, and took her seat. "Relax. I've been coming here every Saturday morning since Dad died—and a lot of days in between. The food is safe. The manager just assured us of that again. Besides, I have a brand new injector with me. Sit. Enjoy. Stop worrying."

"Easy for you to say." Lauren shot her a nervous look as she perched on the edge of her chair. "You about gave me apoplexy last Saturday. I do *not* want a repeat performance. My heart couldn't take it."

"Neither could mine." Kelly cut off a bite of cinnamon roll with the edge of her fork. "Do you really think I'd be eating this or drinking that"—she gestured toward the mocha—"if I had any concerns?"

Her expression skeptical, Lauren watched her in silence as she put the pastry in her mouth and chewed.

"Come on, Lauren, chill. I'm fine. I told you what Cole said. He thinks the older guy who picked up my drink put peanuts in it."

"That's just as freaky."

"Tell me about it." Kelly did a quick scan of the coffee shop. She knew the regulars by sight, and the older man had been a new face that day—one she hoped never to see again.

"So is our friendly detective more receptive now to your theory that your dad's death wasn't suicide?"

"Yes. Especially in light of other developments." She told Lauren about the telephone number she'd found and the new information Cole had gleaned from the autopsy report.

"Wow." Lauren took a sip of her caramel frappuccino. "When did you find out about the autopsy stuff?"

"Last night."

Her friend arched an eyebrow. "Last night, as in after working hours?"

Kelly squirmed in her seat. Lauren had always been open about her social life, even giving Kelly a play-by-play account of Shaun's courtship. She, on the other hand, had been far more reticent about her infrequent dates, none of which had amounted to anything more than a short-term relationship. Lauren claimed the reason for her dismal dating history could be summed up in two words: too picky. Kelly couldn't argue. Most of the men she'd gone out with didn't meet her high standards.

Cole was different, though. From the day she'd shown up at his office with the packing slip from the bulbs, she'd felt a connection to him. Not just the spark of attraction—although there was plenty of that—but a sense they might have much in common at a deeper level. That's why she'd ventured outside her comfort zone by inviting him to lunch and issuing that impromptu dinner invitation last night.

By no stretch of the imagination, however, could their relationship be called a romance.

Yet.

But she had hopes. Ones she hadn't shared with Lauren, afraid if she talked too much about it, she'd jinx the whole thing.

"It wasn't a hard question, Kelly. After work—yes or no?"

At Lauren's prompt, a warm flush swept across her cheeks and she tried to hedge. "Detectives put in long hours."

"So what time did he call to pass on this news?"

She was stuck. There was no dodging that question, short

of lying. And she didn't lie. "Actually, he told me in person, on his way home from work."

Lauren stopped sipping her drink. "He came to your house?"

"Yeah."

"How long did he stay?"

"Awhile. I, uh, invited him to dinner."

Lauren slowly set down her drink and pinned her with what Kelly always thought of as her district attorney look. "I see I've been out of the loop. The vibes between the two of you in the ER last week were obvious, but I had no idea things had progressed to the stage of you issuing dinner invitations. What else have I missed?"

She might as well spill everything. Lauren would get it out of her eventually, anyway. "I invited him to lunch last Wednesday to thank him for hanging around the ER and giving me a ride home."

"Let me get this straight." Lauren sat back and narrowed her eyes. "In the space of a handful of days, you've asked the man to lunch and to dinner. Plus you talked with him on the phone several times. Do I have my facts straight?"

"Yes, but all of our contact has been in relation to my dad's death. There's been nothing personal about it."

Lauren gave her a "get real" look. "Trust me. If the man wasn't interested in getting personal, he wouldn't have spent his day off in the ER, and he'd have handled any business by phone. Especially on a Friday night. Unless there was some personal interest, do you honestly think a single guy who looks like Cole Taylor would pass up a hot date to spend the evening discussing a case that could be dealt with in one quick call during working hours?"

It was hard to dispute her best friend's logic.

"No need to respond." Lauren picked up her drink and gave her a smug smile. "I can see the answer on your face. And I'm glad you're being assertive about this. That's how I got Shaun, as you recall. I asked him out first."

"These weren't dates, Lauren." Kelly pressed her fork against the crumbs of the cinnamon roll she'd shredded during their exchange.

"But you wish they had been."

She sighed. "Okay. Yeah. I do. He's a nice guy." She popped the fork in her mouth, disposing of the crumbs. "But I'd rather he focus on my dad's case than on me until we get this cleared up."

"I hear you. However, it doesn't hurt to lay the groundwork. Let the man know you're interested. You want him to want you."

Kelly thought about the banked fire that had darkened Cole's eyes to cobalt as he'd left after dinner. And the look on his face that had said he'd wanted to kiss her. Her stomach fluttered, and she gripped her cup tighter. "I think he does."

"Excellent." A satisfied smile settled over Lauren's lips.

Blocking out the charged memory of last night's parting, Kelly refocused on her friend. "Why are *you* so happy about this?"

"Because I'm your friend. I like to see you happy. And despite losing your father, despite your own health crisis last weekend, despite your frustration about the lack of proof to support your homicide theory, there's a glow about you I've never seen before. The kind a person gets when they're falling in love."

Kelly stared at her in shock. "I only met the man a month ago. People don't fall in love that fast."

"Maybe not. But you can recognize early on that someone is special—and worth getting to know better. You look the way I did a month into my relationship with Shaun."

"That doesn't mean this will go anywhere. The attraction could fade if we ever do start dating."

"It could." Lauren grinned. "But I'm betting it won't. Unless you get cold feet."

"Why would I do that?"

"Because you're a slow mover, and I suspect Cole may be used to the faster lane."

She couldn't refute her friend's assessment. Most men did want more than she was willing to give. That's why she always cut things off so quickly. She hoped Cole didn't fall into that camp. Hoped, too, that he shared her faith. That topic hadn't come up yet, but she needed to explore it before she got too carried away.

"It's better to be cautious, Lauren. And I won't violate my principles for any man."

"Caution is good. So are principles." Lauren picked up her cup. "And if Cole is the man my intuition tells me he is, he'll respect both. Shall we drink to that?"

"By all means." Kelly picked up her cup and touched it to Lauren's.

Half an hour later, after an animated conversation on a variety of topics, Lauren glanced at her watch and gathered up their cups and napkins. "Sorry to cut this short, but I promised Shaun I'd be home in time for him to meet the guys for a round of golf."

"No problem." Kelly picked up her plate and settled the strap of her purse on her shoulder. "I always appreciate it when you squeeze in time for me."

"Hey . . . you're no less important in my life than you were before Shaun and the twins. I'm just sorry I won't be here for you on Thanksgiving. I wish this wasn't our year to go to the in-laws in Columbus."

"I'll be fine." Kelly stood, not certain that was true. She and her dad had always spent the day together. Her first Thanksgiving alone would be tough.

"Maybe the good detective will reciprocate your invitations by asking you to have dinner with him that day."

Startled by the suggestion, Kelly shook her head as they walked toward the door. "He has a very close family, and I'm a stranger to them. Besides, inviting someone to a family Thanksgiving is a big deal, and we just met."

"Doesn't mean I can't pray for it." Lauren dumped their cups and napkins in the trash container.

Kelly followed, depositing her plate in the plastic bin. And as they hugged and said good-bye, she couldn't help thinking how nice it would be to spend the holiday with Cole. Even if that notion *was* ridiculously far-fetched.

Hands on hips, Kelly surveyed the two shelves in her father's bedroom closet. Like the junk drawer in his bureau, they were a mess—a mélange of items piled in haphazard fashion. For a man who'd chosen a career based on precise numerical balances, who had arranged the tools on his workbench in the garage with the meticulous care of a surgeon, who'd carefully organized and labeled every photo in the family album, the disorder of these two storage areas was an anomaly.

Then again, everyone deserved a few quirks.

But she wasn't looking forward to spending her post-church Sunday digging into the chaos.

Resigning herself to the task ahead, she positioned the stepladder half inside the closet, climbed to the second rung, and reached for an armload of stuff. As she pulled it out, a cloud of dust invaded her sinuses, and she sneezed. Five times. With each ah-choo, an item or two shook loose from the pile in her arms and fell to the carpet.

When at last her sneezing spurt subsided, she descended the ladder and lowered the collection in her arms to the floor beside the bed. Sitting back on her heels, she examined it in dismay. Tattered jerseys, a clear plastic box containing a dead flower that might have been a boutonniere, a file filled with itineraries from old trips, a tarnished silver money clip, and various loose pieces of paper and greeting cards.

Sheesh.

She'd never considered her father to be a pack rat, but she might have to revise her opinion.

Still, the junk drawer had yielded a potential treasure. Perhaps this eclectic collection would too.

Encouraged by that thought, she plunged in.

An hour later, as she pulled the last armful of stuff out of the closet, her hope had dimmed. Though she'd examined every single item, none had held any significance she could discern in relation to her father's death. Maybe the phone number was all she was destined to find. And that could very well turn out to be a dead end.

She sifted through the final armload. It was just more of the same. At first, she'd hoped some of the documents or cards in her father's hoard of treasures might yield some interesting information, but they'd meant nothing to her. A program from a theatrical production. The menu from a restaurant. A receipt from a B & B bearing the date of her parents' anniversary. Birthday cards from her mother. All sentimental keepsakes, nothing more.

A folded sheet of stationery did catch her attention, and she picked it up. A skim of the handwritten text, dated sixteen years earlier, told her it was a letter, and she went back to read it more closely.

Dear J—I've allowed extra time for this to reach you, so I hope it arrives by your birthday. I wish I could be there to deliver my best wishes in person, but of course that's impossible—and the finality of that weighs more heavily on me as time passes.

When you left so suddenly fifteen years ago, before we even had a chance to say good-bye, I knew things would never be the same again. But I didn't realize so much of my past would disappear, for only you and I know the old stories and share the old memories. Your absence has left a gaping hole that will never be filled again.

But as I think of my own loss, it is yours I regret even more. For you gave up everything. I pray the loneliness and isolation of your early years have subsided, and that life has treated you kindly. I know K is a great comfort to you, and I thank God for her presence every day. I am sure she has become the fine young woman you portray in your letters.

I want you to know that not a day passes that
I don't think of you—but I understand and accept
that you're where you need to be. Happy birthday,
J, and may the year ahead be filled with happiness
and peace for you and K. You are both always in
my thoughts and prayers.

The personal and heartfelt letter was signed with the initial *P*.
An initial that clearly represented a person who had been important in her father's life.

An initial that was connected to no person Kelly had ever heard of.

Stymied, she leaned back against the side of her father's bed, letter in hand. Why had her father never mentioned such an old and dear friend? Why could the two of them never meet again? Why had they parted so suddenly? What had her father given up? When had he been lonely and isolated? Was P a man or a woman?

Questions raced through her mind faster than she could form them, and she closed her eyes as a faint throb began to beat in her temples. Were there other disturbing items in this last pile of things from her father's cache?

Her eagerness for new information now tempered by an ominous sense of dread—of danger, almost—Kelly gingerly sorted through the remaining items. Nothing else odd jumped out at her, but she did find a faded photograph she'd never seen before, of her mother and father on their wedding day. A snapshot, rather than an official photo like the one on her dad's chest of drawers. This one showed the smiling couple lifting champagne glasses toward each other in a toast, the love in their eyes so achingly sweet it tightened her throat.

Kelly cradled the image in her hands, soaking up the unexpected glimpse into this moment of joy her parents had shared. Her mother's face, alight with happiness, was framed by the wispy tulle of her veil, while her father gazed at her with the adoration every bride hoped to see on her husband's face.

This final discovery might not solve any mysteries, but it was a wonderful memento that alone made all the hours of searching worthwhile.

As she reached up to put the photo on the bed with a few other sentimental treasures she'd set aside, handwriting on the back caught her eye. The script was unfamiliar and she flipped it over. In a flowing hand, someone had noted the date at the top. Below that was the word *newlyweds* followed by two names.

The date matched her parents' wedding anniversary.

The names didn't.

Jim and Lucille Walsh.

Right initials, wrong names. This was a photo of her parents, John and Linda Warren.

Had the photographer gone to two weddings at about the same time, perhaps, and written the wrong names on the back of this shot?

Or was this one more weird discovery to add to her growing list?

And if so, what did it mean?

Kelly hadn't a clue.

But she was beginning to feel as if she'd stepped into an episode of *The Twilight Zone*.

She picked up the mysterious letter from P and stood, a chill rippling through her. The silence in the empty house suddenly felt oppressive, and the need to hear a human voice, to share this latest discovery, drove her in search of her cell phone. She'd call Lauren—but her best friend would be equally flummoxed by the new information.

Cole's measured, calming voice was the one she wanted to hear.

Kelly dug his card out of her purse. She'd never called his cell or tried to contact him when he was off duty, but she didn't want to wait until tomorrow to pass on this news.

She took a deep breath to steady her nerves and tapped in his number, noting the tremble in her fingers. The strain of the

102

past few weeks was finally getting to her, and her stress level wasn't being helped by a growing sense of urgency that was disrupting her sleep. She was getting close to a breakthrough. She could feel it. And she had Cole to thank for prodding her to dig into the recesses of her father's house.

The phone rang three times, and just as she expected it to roll to voice mail he picked up, his tone curt, his greeting clipped.

"Taylor."

"Cole, it's Kelly. Have I caught you at a bad time?"

"Kelly. Hi." He sounded distracted, and she could hear the hum of other voices in the background. "I'm still caught up in that double homicide from Friday night. We've been at it nonstop. What can I do for you?"

The weariness in his voice told her he'd had little, if any, sleep in the past thirty-six hours. This wasn't the time to pass on her new information. It had been buried in her father's closet for years; it could wait another day or two.

"Look, why you don't give me a call when things slow down a bit? I have something I'd like to discuss, but it can keep."

"Are you sure?" In the background, she heard someone call his name, then his muffled—and annoyed—"I'll be there in a minute" response.

"Yes. Go do your job. And get some rest."

"Yeah. Like that's gonna happen anytime soon." Exhaustion hoarsened his words. "I'll call you tomorrow, okay?"

"Whenever. Don't make it hard on yourself."

"Trust me. Talking to you is no hardship. I'll be in touch." The line went dead.

Smiling, she tapped the end button and dropped the phone back into her purse. Funny. A few minutes ago, the quiet in the house had been oppressive and isolating. Now, thanks to his parting comment, she no longer felt so alone.

And although she was anxious to pass on her news and hear his thoughts, she had a feeling she was going to sleep much better tonight.

9

Stifling a yawn, Cole reached for the disposable cup on his desk and took a swig of coffee. The six hours of sleep he'd logged when he'd fallen into bed fully clothed last night didn't begin to make up for the dozen he'd lost over the weekend. The only positive news on this Monday morning was that he hadn't been made case detective for the double homicide. That honor had fallen to Alan. And since they hadn't yet come up with any decent answers, his colleague wasn't likely to get a good night's sleep for the foreseeable future.

Cole chugged some more of the lukewarm brew and tried to blink the bleariness out of his eyes. As soon as the caffeine kicked in, he'd give Kelly a call. In the meantime, he might as well plow through his emails.

Ten minutes later, in the midst of reading a mind-numbing missive on revisions to a departmental policy, Cole's cell phone began to vibrate. Grateful for the reprieve, he pulled it off his belt—only to have his pulse kick up a notch when he saw that the Communications Bureau was on the other end of the line.

The policy memo forgotten, he swiveled away from the computer screen. *Please—let this be a lead instead of a dead end.*

"Taylor."

"Detective Taylor, it's Steve in Communications. You asked us to call your cell as soon as we had any information on that number you gave us Friday. We got lucky. It's been out of service for more than ten years, and there was no single name assigned to it. But the phone company's billing records indicate it was paid for by the U.S. Marshals Service."

Cole stared at the wanted poster on the wall opposite his desk.

The U.S. Marshals Service?

Why would an accountant hide the number of a U.S. marshal in a secret compartment in his wallet?

"Is there anything else I can do for you, Detective?"

Cole blinked. Refocused. "No. That's it for now. Thanks for tracking this down."

Mulling over this new information, Cole took another swig of coffee, depressed the switch hook, and entered Kelly's number. Now that he was awake, it was time to find out why she'd called yesterday—and share this latest development.

Kelly dabbed her brush into titanium white and swirled it in the permanent rose she'd squeezed onto her palette, attempting to match the hue of the dogwood blossoms in the photo she'd taken on one of her hikes last spring, now clipped to the edge of her easel.

But despite her prodigious effort to focus on this commission for the April issue of the Department of Conservation's monthly magazine, her gaze kept straying to the curious items from her father's house, arrayed on the worktable beside her.

His worn wallet with the secret compartment, and the yellowed slip of paper with the phone number that had been inside.

A letter from P.

The wedding photo of her parents, identified with unfamiliar names.

To borrow a phrase from Lewis Carroll, the whole situation was getting curioser and curioser. And she was feeling more and more like Alice, thrust into a strange world where nothing was as it seemed.

She'd tried googling the names on the back of the wedding photo, but after scrolling through close to a hundred hits, she'd given up. What was the point of searching when she had no idea what she was looking for?

Just as she leaned forward to stroke the pink paint onto the watercolor paper, the discordant ring of her cell phone intruded on the soothing Vivaldi emanating from her CD player. Her hand jerked, and she yanked it back from the textured surface. Another half inch and she'd have painted a pink diagonal squiggle on the fresh expanse, ruining an expensive sheet of the cold-press Italian vellum she favored.

After depositing the brush in a jar of water, she wiped her hands on a rag and picked up her cell phone. Cole's number flashed on the display, triggering a lurch in her heart that was definitely *not* a delayed reaction to the startling ring of her phone.

"Hi, Cole." She swiveled away from the blank paper, toward her worktable, a smile whispering at her lips. "I hope things have calmed down since yesterday."

"Some. For me, anyway. Alan Carlson's handling the case, so I'll just be filling in where needed. Sorry I couldn't talk when you called."

"No problem. I found a couple of other things at my dad's house that raised questions, and I wanted to see what you thought."

"I have some news too. Communications couldn't put a name to the number from your dad's wallet, but they were able to find out who paid the bills. The U.S. Marshals Service."

Kelly frowned. "Why would my dad be in contact with a marshal?"

"I don't have an answer for that yet. What did you come up with?"

Still trying to process his news, she told him about the letter and the photo with the wrong names. "What do you make of that?"

Silence greeted her question—along with unsettling vibes. Her fingers tightened around the phone. "Cole?"

"Yeah. I'm here. Look, I'm toying with a theory, but I want to make a call before I jump to any conclusions."

"You mean this scenario is making sense to you?"

"Maybe. But I could be way off base. Give me a little time to do some checking. If this pans out, though, we'll have ample reason to officially reopen your dad's case."

"That's encouraging news." She picked up the wedding photo of her parents, trying to frame her next question diplomatically. "If you do, does that mean Detective Carlson will be back in charge?"

Another few seconds of silence ticked by. "In general, I'd say that would be protocol, but he's tied up with the homicide now. Let me talk to our sergeant and see how he wants to handle this. It might not hurt to have some fresh eyes on the case, and if he agrees, I plan to volunteer. Unless you'd rather have someone else."

"No." Cole was who she wanted on the case—and in her life. "At this point, you know the history better than anyone."

"Okay. Let me get back with you later today. And until we sort this out, be careful."

With a promise to do so, she set the phone back on the worktable and stared at the blank sheet of paper clipped to her easel.

The more they uncovered, the more it seemed her father had had something to hide. But what? Had he been a spy? An undercover FBI agent? A CIA operative?

The whole notion was ludicrous.

Trying to put the riddle out of her mind, she remixed the dogwood-pink hue, swirled her brush in the paint, and leaned toward the paper to stroke on a bold arc of color. Slowly a cluster of flowers emerged, each sweep of the brush easing the tension in her shoulders. The act of creation soothed her. As did the mellow Vivaldi. But not enough to subdue the hum in her nerve endings, fueled by the sense they were on the brink of an important discovery.

One that might at last establish the real cause of her father's death.

Cole didn't even put the phone down after Kelly broke the connection. The instant he had a dial tone, he punched in Jake's number, crossing his fingers that his brother hadn't been called out on a most-wanted arrest or some other mission with the Special Operations Group. He needed information on the marshals, and Jake was his best source.

When his older sibling answered on the second ring, Cole let out a relieved breath. "I need to run a theory by you and see if you can dig up some information for me."

"Good morning to you too."

At the wry amusement in Jake's voice, Cole compressed his lips. He wasn't in the mood for his brother's humor today.

"Give me a break, okay? I worked a double homicide this weekend. *All* weekend. And my Monday's starting off with more questions than answers. That's why I called. I need your input."

Cole gave him a rapid-fire download of all that had happened over the past month, beginning with Kelly's first visit to the office. He concluded with the new information.

"So I did a little math. I added up the hidden phone number that belonged to a marshal, the letter from the person who was close to Warren but a stranger to Kelly, and the wrong names on the back of the wedding photo with initials that happen to match those of Kelly's parents. I came up with WitSec."

Dead silence greeted his statement. No surprise there. The Witness Security program was an off-limits topic for marshals. Not long ago Jake had mentioned one deputy who'd gone to jail for merely paging through a WitSec folder.

"Look, I'm not asking for any inside information, Jake."

"Good. Because I don't have any. Only the guys involved in WitSec know anything about it. That's why they've never lost a witness who followed the rules. As for confirming whether Kelly's father was being protected, it wouldn't matter if I asked or you asked. We'd both get the same response—a form letter saying the marshals wouldn't confirm or deny this person's existence or their participation in the program."

Cole raked his fingers through his hair, trying to hold on to his patience. "I realize that. I'm going to check out the names on that photo myself. I'm just asking if you think my theory is plausible."

"It seems like a reasonable conclusion." Jake spoke slowly, deliberately, as if he was measuring every word. "You'll know more if you can track down those names."

That helped a whole lot.

"Okay, look . . . if Kelly's father was in the program, that means she entered the program too—as an infant. So couldn't she just go to the marshals and ask? They'd tell her if she was in the program, right?"

"Maybe. It all depends on the arrangements made at the time. *If* her family was in the program, maybe her father never wanted her to know. Maybe he wanted to leave all that sordid stuff behind. Maybe it was set up so she went off the marshals' radar at twenty-one. That might make sense, since she's clueless about it. Every situation is unique."

His brother had been indoctrinated well. A person couldn't get any more noncommittal—or use more maybes in the space of a few sentences.

Okay. Fine. He respected Jake's integrity and appreciated the safeguards built into the WitSec program. But there was one piece of information that would answer a lot of questions. One he hoped wouldn't violate any protocols.

"I do have one favor to ask, if it won't get you into trouble."

"What is it?" Jake's tone was guarded.

"I know the phone number Kelly found was billed to the U.S. Marshals Service. It goes back ten years. I'm not asking you to give me the name it was assigned to, but can you find out if it belonged to a marshal in WitSec?"

Another pause. Cole tapped his pen against the desk, doing his best to rein in his impatience. You'd think he was asking for a nuclear activation code.

"I'll see what I can do. No promises."

At least he hadn't said no.

"Thanks." Cole recited the number.

"Got it. So this Kelly . . . is she the hot redhead Mitch was talking about at brunch a couple of weeks ago?"

The sudden change of topic took him off guard. "What if she is?"

"That's what I thought. Still holding the line between work and play?"

"Yeah." Sort of.

"You realize that if her father's death wasn't suicide . . . and your theory is correct . . . this could be an extremely dangerous situation." All levity had vanished from Jake's voice.

"Yeah." Cole wasn't a WitSec expert, but he knew the basics. Only people whose lives were at grave risk entered the program. And some of the people they were hiding from had long memories—as well as a thirst for revenge.

"I'll get back to you with any information I can pass on about that number as soon as I can. Until then, be careful."

"Count on it."

As Jake severed the connection, Cole rose and headed down the hall toward the office that housed Alan's desk. One quick sweep told him the place was deserted. He had no idea where everyone else was, but he assumed Alan was either operating on fumes while he continued to chase leads or grabbing a few much-needed z's before plunging into the fray again.

"Staring at his desk isn't going to make him appear." Mitch edged past him into the room and continued toward his own desk. He sported a day's stubble of beard, and his eyes looked weary. "Last I heard, he went home to crash for a few hours."

"You need to do the same."

"My next stop. I just swung by here to take care of a couple of things." He squinted at Cole. "How come you're so chipper?"

"They cut me loose at midnight."

"Lucky you." He dropped into his chair. "If you need to talk to Alan, you'll have to call his cell."

Cole propped his fists on his hips as he debated his next move. He'd prefer to discuss the latest developments in the Warren case with Alan before taking them to his sergeant, but the man wasn't apt to be too friendly—or coherent—if Cole awakened him from a sound sleep. The only other option was to wait, and that didn't feel right, either. Someone needed to start tracking down James and Lucille Walsh. Now.

"You seem worried. What's up?" Mitch rolled his chair into his desk and shot him a curious look.

"New information on the Warren suicide. I think it merits taking a second look at the case."

"And you want to do the looking?" Mitch grinned and laced his hands behind his head. "Or is it the daughter you want to look at?"

Narrowing his eyes, Cole folded his arms across his chest. First Jake, now Mitch. The keen interest in his love life was beginning to get on his nerves. "For your information, I'm more interested in keeping her alive than looking at her. She almost died a week ago."

Mitch's expression went from amused to sober in a heart-beat. "What happened?"

He gave him a topline version of the peanut incident. "And I have new information that leads me to believe her original theory about her father's death may be accurate after all."

"You want to share it?"

"Not yet. I'm waiting for more data, and I still have some research to do." He rubbed the back of his neck. "Do you know if Paul is in?"

"Yeah. I saw him in his office as I passed by a few minutes ago. Listen . . . if you need any help with this thing, let me know."

"Thanks. In the meantime, go home and get some sleep."

"That's my plan." He yawned and rubbed his eyes. "By the way, your sister asked me to remind you to order the three pies you volunteered to bring for Thanksgiving dinner at Jake and Liz's."

Cole shot him a disgruntled look. "Tell Alison I have it under control."

Grinning, Mitch reached for his phone. "You forgot, didn't you?"

Yeah, he had. "It's been a little busy. But I'd have remembered." Sooner or later.

"Hey, don't kill the messenger." He motioned toward the door. "You better catch Paul while you can. With all that's going on, I doubt he'll stay in one place long."

"True." With a wave, Cole exited and walked down the hall toward his sergeant's office. He didn't like encroaching on Alan's turf without first discussing it with his colleague, but the potential danger to Kelly made the matter more urgent. If WitSec was involved, they could be dealing with some ruthless characters.

As he approached his supervisor's office, he spied the fifty-ish man exiting and flagged him down. "Sarge! Do you have ten minutes?"

Jacket half on, the trim sergeant turned and squinted at Cole. Paul Callahan might not work the streets anymore, but despite the salt-and-pepper in his buzz cut and the permanent shadows under his eyes, he hadn't lost one iota of his legendary acumen. The old-timers recalled how he could take one look at a person and, with astounding accuracy, assess guilt, innocence, and the gravity of a situation. He still had that knack.

Cole was glad they were on the same side.

"I'll give you five." Shrugging the jacket onto his shoulders, Paul reversed direction.

Wasting no time, Cole picked up his pace and was taking a seat opposite Paul's desk even as his boss settled into his own chair.

In less than three minutes, Cole had brought him up to speed on the situation, ending with his speculations about WitSec and a recommendation that the case be officially reopened.

"Have you discussed this with Alan?" Bristling with energy despite the lines of fatigue etched in his face, Paul pinned him with a keen look as he rested his elbows on his desk and steepled his fingers.

112

"Yes. All but today's developments. He's not at his desk."

"And he won't be, not until we get these homicides solved."

"That's what I figured. And I'm not certain we should wait on this. Besides, a fresh pair of eyes might be beneficial."

"Yours?"

Cole strove for a logical, businesslike tone. "I'd be happy to step in. I've been in touch with Ms. Warren since her first visit a month ago, and I'm up to speed on the case."

Paul tapped his index fingers together, and Cole tried not to squirm. The man had the piercing eyes of a hawk. "I agree this deserves another look. And I don't want to pull Alan off the homicides. I'll let him know what's going on. Keep both of us in the loop."

"I will." Cole let out a slow, relieved breath and rose.

"Scuttlebutt says Kelly Warren is a looker."

Startled, Cole swiveled back toward his boss. How was he supposed to respond to that?

Paul stood and rounded his desk, pausing on the threshold of his office. "Protecting a pretty woman isn't exactly hardship duty. But I have absolute confidence in your ability to maintain a professional distance while on a case." He locked gazes with Cole. "I wouldn't assign it to you if I didn't."

Then he was gone.

Rooted to the spot, Cole regarded the empty doorway. That little exchange had once again reinforced his boss's acuity. In a couple of sentences, Paul Callahan had acknowledged the appeal—and danger—of dealing with a beautiful, threatened woman. He'd also issued a warning.

And it was one Cole took to heart. If Kelly was in danger, he needed to keep his personal feelings out of the mix. They could cloud his judgment. Cause him to make mistakes.

Mistakes that could be deadly.

So until they had answers, until he knew Kelly was out of danger, he'd stick with his policy of keeping his personal and professional life separate.

Difficult as that was proving to be.

10

"Mr. Rossi? UPS just delivered this."

At his housekeeper's comment, Vincentio looked up from the desk in his study, wishing, as always, that the room was more spacious. That his whole house was more spacious. Still, it was far preferable to the tiny cell he'd called home for almost three decades. And at this stage of his life, he didn't want the scrutiny that came with ostentation.

"Bring it in, Teresa."

He squinted at the box as she set it on the corner of the polished walnut desk. His keen eyesight had fled along with his youth, but he had no trouble reading the single hand-lettered word written in bold block letters across the top of the package.

REFUSED.

Although his stomach clenched painfully, he maintained the impassive expression he'd perfected in his former life. "Thank you, Teresa."

"Would you like some tea or coffee, sir?"

"No, I'm fine for now."

With a deferential nod, she exited. A fine woman, Teresa. Honest, hardworking, dependable. A devoted wife and mother who put family first. As she should. That's why he slipped her an extra fifty now and then from the generous stash he'd secured decades ago in an offshore account. It was good to reward people who had their priorities straight. He'd done so often in the old days, when his house had been fully staffed and both his official—and unofficial—business payrolls had been burgeoning.

The days of servants and power lunches were gone now. Teresa alone kept his household running, and there was no more big-time wheeling-dealing. Been there, done that, as the young people liked to say. Now he was content with a small network of associates who could be called on to take care of what little business arose. And most of that in the past three years had been of a personal nature.

But they couldn't help him with the one thing he wanted most.

A reconciliation with his son.

Heart heavy, he leaned forward, grasped the edges of the box, and pulled it toward him. He'd hoped, by addressing the package to his new grandson, that Marco would accept the gift in the spirit it was intended: a grandfather's attempt to welcome his first grandchild into the world.

But no. His son's heart remained harder than the alabaster buried in the hills of his beloved Sicily. Every effort he'd made to reconnect, every olive branch he'd extended, had been rebuffed, until at last he'd been forced to accept the harsh truth: the breach between them would never be bridged.

Still . . . to deny him his grandson? He wouldn't have even known about the boy's birth if an old acquaintance hadn't passed on the news—three months after the fact.

The callous cruelty of that omission was like a vise around his heart.

He ran his fingers over the name on the package. Jason. That, too, was an affront. It was clear Marco—Mark now, he reminded himself with a wince—planned to deny the child not only his grandfather but also his heritage. What kind of name was Jason for a boy from a proud Sicilian family? What was wrong with Antonino? Or Stefano? Or Angelo?

But that was the problem. Marco wasn't proud of his family. He was ashamed of it.

Of his father.

All at once, a consuming fury swept over him and he vaulted to his feet. Shoving the package aside, he leaned forward and braced himself, palms flat on the desk, quivering with rage. What right did Marco have to judge him? He was a good man. A good father. He attended church every Sunday. Respected and rewarded loyalty and hard work. Provided for his family. Yes, he'd operated an enterprise the government frowned upon, as had his father and grandfather before him. And yes, he'd punished those who had betrayed him. That's how the family business worked. How it had always worked. Here, and in Sicily. You protected what was yours. Whatever it took.

But he'd modified that unforgiving code when he'd assumed control of the business. Taken a kinder, gentler approach than those who'd preceded him. Traitors were punished, yes, but innocent people associated with them were not. He'd never believed in retaliating by hurting those who were blameless.

Some had praised that stance.

Others had criticized it.

Including his father.

His hands clenched into fists as he recalled the derogatory adjectives Salvatore Rossi had applied to him on countless occasions. *Soft* had been the mildest of them. Even now, decades later, they still had the power to twist his gut.

Yet his father had been right in his prediction that mercy, benevolence, and misplaced trust would be his son's downfall. His fatal error in judgment had germinated from the seeds of kindness and compassion. Admirable qualities in the eyes of God, if not Salvatore's.

Why could Marco not see the good as well as what he perceived to be the bad in his father?

Was he the despicable character his son had renounced?

No!

Vincentio straightened up. Squared his shoulders. He would not let his son's disapproval undermine the pride he had always felt in his heritage. If Marco wanted no part of the Rossi legacy, so be it. That was his loss. But he had no right to deny *his* son the opportunity to know his nonno. The grandfather who loved him.

Compressing his lips, Vincentio opened his desk drawer and removed a box cutter. A few slashes was all it took to dispense with the tape that sealed the cardboard flaps. Then he dug into the nest of tissue and lifted out the plush teddy bear he'd selected himself at the Build-a-Bear store.

If his son wouldn't pass the gift on to the newest member of the Rossi family, he'd do it himself.

When the time was right.

Bingo.

Adrenaline surging, Cole leaned closer to the screen and scanned the article from the *Buffalo News* archives. He'd been at the computer since Paul had given him the go-ahead four hours ago to reopen the Warren case, and at first the number of hits for James Walsh had been overwhelming. Only after he recalled Kelly's comment about her father's trip to Niagara Falls had he been inspired to narrow the search to New York state.

Now he'd hit pay dirt with an article headlined "Guilty Verdict for Mob Boss."

Based on the thirty-one-year-old story, testimony from a James Walsh—an accountant for a Mafia boss's front businesses—had been instrumental in sending Vincentio Rossi to prison for twenty-eight years on racketeering and money-laundering convictions. Prior to the trial, there had been an attempt on Walsh's life, and he and his wife, Lucille—along with their infant daughter—had been placed under the protection of U.S. marshals.

It all fit. Warren's old wound. The phone number for a U.S. marshal secreted in his wallet. The names on the wedding snapshot.

Kelly's theory that her father had been murdered.

Cole tapped a finger on his desk. The fact that Warren had

died so soon after his purported trip to Niagara Falls was more than suspicious. If Rossi was still carrying a grudge against him, and if Warren had broken the primary rule of the WitSec program and made contact with someone from his past—P, perhaps?—it was possible he'd been spotted.

Proving murder would be difficult, though. The bulk of the evidence suggested suicide. Only Kelly's strong conviction and the note with the bulbs hinted that her father's death had more Machiavellian origins. If someone had killed him, he'd done an excellent job disguising the murder. And tying Vincentio Rossi to it would be even tougher.

But it couldn't hurt to have a nice long talk with the Mafia boss.

First, though, he had a lot more homework to do. And he needed to talk to both Paul and Kelly before this day ended.

As he skimmed his browser hits for more articles on the Rossi case, his cell began to vibrate. He pulled it off his belt and glanced at the display before putting the phone to his ear. "Hi, Jake."

"The answer to your question is yes. He retired ten years ago and died last year."

"I appreciate the confirmation." Cole leaned back in his chair. "I didn't know he'd retired or died, but I'd already figured out the first part." He brought his brother up to speed on what he'd discovered so far in the *Buffalo News* archives. "I've just scratched the surface, though. I need to do a lot more digging."

"It sounds like you may be on to something. If you need us for anything, let me know."

"I will. Thanks again."

Cole slid the phone back onto his belt and continued to troll for articles about the case. And there were plenty. In less than an hour, he'd compiled an impressive list of facts on the Rossi trial, begun to assemble a dossier on Vincentio, and learned some interesting background on James Walsh, thanks to a long conversation with a woman in the vital records office in Buffalo.

It was time to track down Sarge.

After punching in the man's cell number, he put the phone to his ear. Barely into the first ring, Paul barked out a greeting. Flinching, Cole yanked the phone back a few inches. "Sarge, it's Cole. I've uncovered a lot of interesting information since we talked this morning that I'd like to pass on so we can discuss next steps. Are you coming back here today?"

"I'm walking into the building as we speak. I also saw Carlson pull into the parking lot. I'll flag him down. Meet me in my office in five minutes."

A click told Cole the call was over.

He set the receiver back in its cradle, gathered up his notes, and headed for Paul's office. Hoping Alan wouldn't be too miffed he'd taken over his case . . . and found some holes.

Kelly swirled the sable tuft of her favorite #8 filbert brush into a bar of soap, then dabbed it against her palm under warm running water until the suds were white. After a final rinse, she squeezed the water out of the brush with a paper towel, reformed the hairs to their original shape, and laid the brush next to the others on the terry-cloth square beside her utility sink in the basement.

Although she'd been distracted by Cole's intimation this morning that the disparate pieces of information she'd uncovered were fitting together, she'd managed to focus long enough to complete the dogwood illustration. Tomorrow she'd get back to her woodland fairies.

As she ascended the steps to the kitchen, she heard the muffled ring of her cell phone and picked up her pace. Maybe Cole had some news to report.

By the time she dug it out of her purse, however, it had rolled to voice mail.

Before she could check her messages, though, her landline rang. She dashed across the room and snatched it out of its cradle, issuing a breathless greeting.

"Kelly? Cole. I've got some information I'd like to share in person. May I stop by on my way home from work?"

She checked her watch. "You *do* put in long hours. First you work all weekend, then you stay until seven-thirty? Did you get pulled into the homicide again?"

"No. I've been on your dad's case all day. It's officially re-opened. That's what I want to talk with you about."

Her fingers tightened on the phone. "You discovered something important."

"Very."

"You can come anytime. The sooner the better."

"Did you eat dinner yet?"

"As a matter of fact, no. I just stopped for the day too."

"Why don't I grab a pizza for us? I worked through lunch and I'm starving."

"If you worked through lunch on my dad's case, I should feed you."

"You already did that twice. It's my turn. Is pizza okay?"

"Sure. Any kind is fine. And takeout pizza is one of the few things I rarely have to worry about in terms of peanuts."

"I'll ask anyway. Look for me in less than an hour."

As Kelly hung up, she inspected her paint-stained shirt. Anxious as she was to hear Cole's news, she was glad he'd given her some warning. If she hurried, she could grab a shower and wash her hair before he got here. Not her usual routine of an evening—but then again, she didn't have many visitors as appealing as the tall detective.

Forty-five minutes later, as she brushed on a touch of mascara, her doorbell rang. Lucky she hadn't dawdled in the shower. He hadn't wasted any time getting here.

The savory aroma of pepperoni and tomato sauce greeted her when she opened the door and ushered him in. "That smells great."

"Tell me about it." He grinned, waving the box under her nose as he passed, his five-o'clock shadow clear evidence *he'd* had no opportunity to freshen up after his long day. "It took every ounce of my willpower not to pilfer a piece—or two—as I drove. Kitchen?" He hefted the box.

"Yes."

She preceded him, grabbing paper napkins and plates as she passed a cabinet. "Would you like a soda?"

"Sure."

She pulled out two Cokes and joined him at the table, dispensing the drinks, plates, and napkins.

"Thanks." He popped the tab and eased the box in her direction. "Dig in."

She took a piece, waited while he did the same, then bowed her head and said a silent blessing. She'd offered a brief prayer of thanks the other two times they'd eaten together too, and while he hadn't commented, she sensed it made him uncomfortable.

Not a positive omen for their future.

But she set aside that concern for the moment. Tonight she wanted to focus on his news. Based on the way he was wolfing down his first piece of pizza, though, he hadn't been kidding when he'd claimed to be starving. Better to give him a few minutes to take the edge off his hunger before plying him with questions.

Half a pizza and ten minutes later, after offering no more than a few words of conversation, Cole came up for air.

"Sorry." He gave her a sheepish grin as he wiped his mouth on a napkin. "I don't make a habit of devouring my food like that. Skipping lunch was a bad idea—but I had good reason."

"And I've been waiting patiently to hear it."

He surveyed her plate, and she checked it out as well. Only one bite was missing from her second piece of pizza. "Anxiously too. Sorry to keep you in suspense." He wadded up his napkin and pushed his plate aside. "Go ahead and eat while I bring you up to speed."

Her appetite had vanished, but rather than argue, she picked up her pizza and nibbled at it as she gave him an expectant look.

"Okay." He pinned her with those intent, assessing blue eyes. "On the drive over, I tried to think of a way to ease into this, but I couldn't come up with anything. So I'll give it to you straight. The picture you found of your mom and dad on their wedding day did contain the right names. Your father was a witness in a Mafia trial in New York thirty-one years ago. My assumption is that your dad, you, and your mother were given new identities and put into the Witness Security program after the trial ended."

Mafia. New identities. Witness Security program.

The words echoed in her mind but wouldn't compute.

As Kelly stared at him, the bite of pizza lodged in her throat. She groped for her can of soda. Took a swig. Swallowed.

And then, as the implications began to slam into her, she started to shake.

Her whole world, her very identity—all she'd believed about her parents—was a sham.

The aluminum crinkled beneath her fingers, and a geyser of soda spurted from the can.

On some peripheral level, she was aware that Cole rose and circled the table. He gently tugged the can from her grasp, wiped the sticky residue of soda off her fingers and the table, and pulled her to her feet.

"You can finish eating later. Let's continue this in the living room."

She didn't protest. Nor did she object when he kept a firm clasp on her fingers as he sat beside her on the couch.

"Sorry to lay all that on you at once." He gave her hand an encouraging squeeze. "Are you okay?"

She blinked and refocused on his face. Twin grooves were etched on his brow, and concern darkened his eyes.

Get a grip, Kelly. You prayed for answers. Don't cave now that you're getting them. Be grateful they're coming from a man you trust. A man who cares.

Forcing herself to take a calming breath, she nodded. "Yes. I'm just trying to . . . regroup. Are you sure about this?"

"The U.S. Marshals Service won't deny or confirm your dad's participation in WitSec, but it's a safe conclusion. I do know the number you found in your dad's wallet belonged to a WitSec marshal who has since retired and passed away."

"I thought WitSec was for criminals whose testimony put them at risk." She couldn't believe her father had been part of the Mafia—but she was finding it hard to believe *most* of what Cole was telling her.

"In general, it is. But a very small percentage of participants are people like your dad—ordinary citizens who have information the Feds need to prosecute a crime figure."

Relief coursed through her. "So my father wasn't a criminal."

"No. Not by a long shot." Cole squeezed her hand again, his gaze locked on hers. "After I uncovered the initial information, I did some digging in the case files. It appears your dad was an honorable, responsible citizen who was forced into WitSec."

She squinted at him. "What do you mean, forced?"

"An attempt was made on his life."

The pieces started to fall into place. "The old scars . . ."

"Yes. He was shot when Vincentio Rossi, the major-league Mafia boss he testified against, found out he was cooperating with the Feds. Rossi was known as a man with a long memory who always punished those who betrayed him. It was either join WitSec or face execution."

"And my mom and I—we were threatened too?"

"No. My research suggests Rossi had an unusual code. He didn't punish peripheral people or take retribution on innocent family members. You and your mom would probably have been safe, but I'm assuming she decided to give up her old life and go with your dad. If she hadn't, you and she would never have seen him again."

"Wow." Kelly caught her lower lip between her teeth as the magnitude of her parents' sacrifice began to register. "But I still don't understand how my dad got involved in all this."

"I'm still digging up background, but based on what I've found so far, your parents were from Rochester. They moved to Buffalo not long before you were born, when your dad was offered a much higher-paying accounting job in what turned out to be the umbrella organization for the front businesses operated by Rossi, whose *real* business was racketeering—mostly illegal gambling. Not growing up in Buffalo, he had no idea Rossi was third-generation Mafia. In his testimony, your dad said he uncovered some unrealistic jumps in income levels for several of the umbrella businesses—a string of coin-operated laundries, car washes, a garbage collection service. He put two and two together and came up with money laundering. Until that point, he thought the businesses were legit."

"Double wow." Kelly combed her fingers through her hair, trying to imagine her mild-mannered, straight-as-an-arrow dad in the midst of such a mess. "So he went to the FBI?"

"Eventually. But not before Rossi tried to bribe him into silence. The testimony suggests Rossi liked your dad and treated him well during the three years he worked for him, steadily moving him up in the pecking order and pay scale. When your dad questioned him about the income irregularities, Rossi assured him the funds were legit. Not long after that, your father received a sizable bonus. Plus, Rossi offered to get him a great deal on a home in a very desirable part of town. I suppose he assumed your father would be grateful for his benevolence and overlook the inconsistencies in the books."

"Instead, he went to the FBI."

"Yes. After he drove by a few of the rundown businesses Rossi claimed were generating significant income and realized there was no way he could be telling the truth. The Feds convinced him to play along while they continued to gather evidence, but Rossi found out about the investigation and put a contract out on your dad. He would have died if an off-duty street cop hadn't interrupted the hit, which took place at a convenience store your dad frequented. The police officer was wounded as well."

This all sounded more like it should be the plot of a movie than her family history. "So Rossi went to prison and we went into WitSec."

"Yes. He spent twenty-eight years behind bars for racketeering and money laundering."

"Was it my dad's testimony that convicted him?"

"It was instrumental. But three members of Rossi's organization also agreed to testify in exchange for reduced sentences."

"What happened to them?"

"They served their time. And they all died within a year of their release. Car crash. House fire. Construction accident."

The air whooshed out of Kelly's lungs. "Suicide."

His mouth settled into a grim line. "Yeah."

"None of them traceable to Rossi."

"Not yet." His eyes hardened.

"Why wouldn't those men have gone into the Witness Security program when they were released, given Rossi's reputation for vengeance?"

Cole shrugged. "Years had passed. Maybe they thought his power had diminished, since he was still in prison. Maybe they hoped he'd softened. Or they might have been confident their street savvy would keep them safe. WitSec is a last option, Kelly. Your life as you know it ends, and a lot of people would rather take a risk than make that sacrifice."

She sighed. "I'm beginning to realize that. Where is Rossi now?"

"Back in Buffalo. Keeping his nose clean, per the local cops and the FBI. I checked this afternoon."

"But he isn't. He found my dad, despite the WitSec program." She searched his face. "How could that happen?"

Cole released her hand long enough to weave his fingers with hers. "I think he broke the rules. Even though WitSec participants aren't allowed to contact friends or relatives directly or give them their new identities or location, they can funnel mail through WitSec and talk by phone on arranged calls. He only had one relative he might have kept in touch with on a regular basis. An English-professor brother, who was dying of ALS. Lou Gehrig's disease. His name was Patrick."

P. From the letter.

She'd had an uncle she'd never known.

The shocks kept coming, wave after wave.

"My guess is your dad's trip to Niagara Falls was a cover." Cole stroked his thumb over the back of her hand, the soothing motion comforting at some elemental level. "That he went back to see his brother one last time, assuming it was safe after all these years, and was spotted by someone in Rossi's organization."

Kelly closed her eyes and lifted her free hand to massage the headache beginning to pulse behind her forehead, clinging to Cole's fingers as if they were a lifeline. His solid presence was the one steady element in a life suddenly turned topsy-turvy, where nothing was as it had seemed.

"We're going to work this out. Justice *will* be done. I promise you that."

At his steely, take-no-prisoners tone, she opened her eyes. His granite-like resolve was comforting—but it was clear they were up against a canny, careful adversary.

"I want to believe that, but . . ." She frowned, trying to make sense of all she'd learned. "How did Rossi arrange my dad's death? Who did it? How did the killer make it look like suicide?"

"I don't have those answers yet."

Her mind began to race as logic kicked in, the questions forming faster than she could voice them. "You said Rossi didn't hurt innocent people. So do you still think my peanut episode was connected to my dad's death?"

Twin furrows appeared on his brow. "That piece isn't fitting. Unless he's changed his code, he wouldn't have targeted you." He reached around and rubbed the back of his neck. "But I'm not buying the coincidence theory, either."

"Is my uncle still alive?"

"No. He died while your father was in New York. He may well have gone to the funeral."

"Do you know if I have any other relatives?"

"Your mother didn't have any siblings. Your dad's brother was a widower, but he had three children. Two are in Rochester, one's in New York City. That's it, as far as I could tell."

She had cousins. Family connections. And now that her cover was blown, maybe they didn't have to be strangers once the situation with her father was resolved.

That was the one bright spot in this whole sordid situation.

"Would you like to know your original name?"

At Cole's gentle question, she blinked. Of course—her name would have been changed too. She wasn't Kelly Warren. Her heart stumbled, and she gave a jerky nod, bracing herself. "Yes."

"In WitSec, people are often encouraged to keep their first name or their initials. It's easier to cover mistakes if they start to say or write their old names. That's why your parents' real initials matched their new ones. Yours do too. You were born Kathleen Walsh. A fine Irish name." One side of his mouth quirked up as he fingered a few strands of her hair. "And the complexion and hair fit."

Distracted by his touch, she had to force herself to focus on this new piece of information. "Kathleen Walsh. That will take some getting used to."

"There's no need to change it back if you don't want to. All the records have been sealed. In the eyes of the world, you're Kelly Warren. In my eyes too."

The warmth of his smile helped chase away the disquieting chill that had settled over her. "So where do we go from here?"

"You're not going anywhere. But I'm going to Buffalo to have a long talk with Mr. Rossi. My boss approved the trip this afternoon."

She gave him a skeptical look. "I doubt he's going to admit anything."

"I'm not expecting a confession, but it's possible we'll learn something that might help us identify the man who carried out his orders. And if we find *him*, he might cave and give us the link we need back to Rossi."

"Unless Rossi takes care of him first." That seemed a more probable scenario, based on the ruthless picture Cole had painted of the Mafia boss.

"He could." Cole caught and held her gaze. "But the Buffalo police and FBI say Rossi has kept a very low profile since his release, and he's been out of circulation for a lot of years. Most of his former colleagues have died or been imprisoned for various crimes. His circle of influence has tightened considerably, and he has fewer resources at his disposal. He's also a careful planner who doesn't make rash moves. And we're not going to give him a lot of time to put into place the kind of meticulous arrangements he prefers."

She furrowed her brow. "Whoever did it, I still don't get how he convinced my father to willingly take drugs, drink alcohol, and sit behind the exhaust pipe of a car. Yet there was no sign of a struggle." The pounding behind her forehead increased. "I don't understand any of this."

"Hey." Cole squeezed her fingers. "It's my job to figure that out, and I've got a lot of resources to help me do that. You focus on staying safe. Did you schedule the installation of your new locks yet?"

"Yes. The guy's coming Friday."

He watched her in silence for a moment. "Why don't you see if you can move it up?"

"I thought you said Rossi didn't bother innocent people?"

"I said that was his pattern in the past. I'd prefer not to take chances in the present."

His quiet, intent tone told her he was worried. So was she. Dealing with speculation was one thing. Dealing with the Mafia was another.

"I'll call him tomorrow."

"Okay." With one final press of her fingers, Cole released her hand and stood. "Would you like me to put the pizza in the oven for you? You didn't have much dinner."

"No. Thanks for the thought, though. Why don't you take it home?"

"Nope. I had my share. You might be hungry later."

After all that had happened tonight? Not likely.

He started for the door and she rose to follow him. On the threshold he turned toward her.

"I'll keep you in the loop as things develop."

"I appreciate that." She folded her arms around herself. Wishing the tall detective inches away was doing the hugging. As if reading her mind, his eyes darkened and he shoved his hands into the pockets of his dress slacks. "I've always had a policy of maintaining a professional distance with the people involved in my cases, Kelly."

At his low, husky comment she hugged herself tighter and moistened her lips. "That's prudent."

"But just so you know, when this is over, I'd like to get to know you a whole lot better. If you're interested."

Her spirits rose. Maybe there was light at the end of this murky tunnel after all. "I'm interested."

Giving her a slow smile, he laid his fingertips against her cheek, his touch whisper soft. "That's the best news I could get to end this Monday."

Then he was gone, pulling the door closed behind him.

For a full sixty seconds, Kelly remained where she was, savoring his parting comments. And once more feeling as if her world had changed.

This time for the better.

11

Alan Carlson picked up the bottle of cheap scotch he'd bought on his way home, twisted off the lid, and refilled his glass. For the third time.

It had been a bear of a day.

Make that a bear of a month.

He tossed back the amber-colored liquid, then hissed out a breath as the alcohol burned a path down his throat and settled in his belly, sending out tentacles of warmth that loosened the knots of tension in his muscles.

Better.

A man deserved to relax after working almost around the clock over the weekend only to end his Monday with a kick in the gut.

After topping off the glass again, he set the bottle on the kitchen counter and wandered over to the couch. It took all of ten steps to get there in the oversized cubicle he now called home. A far cry from the three-bedroom house he and Cindy had shared.

And lost.

That's what happened when money had to go to pay gambling debts instead of a mortgage. Or utility bills. Or car payments. Or credit card debt. Every dime of it. From his paycheck. Their savings accounts. The trust fund Cindy's uncle had left her.

No wonder she'd moved out.

No wonder she hung up on him whenever he called.

Alan tipped the glass against his lips and swallowed another mouthful of the scotch. It didn't sear his throat as much this time.

Cradling the tumbler in his hands, he eased down onto the couch. He'd never been much of a drinker. A beer now and then, that was it. No hard stuff. Cindy had liked that about him. She'd also liked that he didn't smoke. Or fool around. She'd always said she'd felt blessed to find a man she could trust. One without any vices.

Until she'd found out he had one after all.

A big one.

Big enough to be a deal breaker.

His hand tightened on the glass as he recalled the day, two years into their marriage, when he'd come home from work to find her holding the latest bank statement. The one he'd hoped to intercept before she opened it. She'd met him at the door, distressed and anxious, asking what he knew about the large withdrawals from her trust fund.

He'd never been able to lie to Cindy. So he'd confessed.

Her expression of shock, of betrayal, was scorched into his memory. As vivid as if that scene had taken place a week ago instead of a year ago.

But he'd sworn to her the gambling debt was recent—and a mistake he deeply regretted. Told her truthfully that he hadn't made any wagers for the first year and a half of their marriage. And he'd argued that if he could go that long without gambling, he could stop again. Taking her in his arms, he'd promised to clean up his act. Told her he loved her too much to risk losing her or destroying their marriage.

And he'd meant every word of his impassioned pledge.

But the rigid discipline he employed on the job had failed him in his personal life. The thrill of the wager, the buzz of the high-stakes game, the euphoria of winning—of beating the odds—had been too strong to resist.

Cindy had cut him some slack for the first six months. Given him more chances than he'd deserved. But in the end, he'd lost it all. His home. His savings. His wife.

All he had left was his job.

A wave of self-loathing washed over him, and he rose. Too fast. The world tilted, and he grabbed on to the mountain bike propped against the wall, seeking support. It shifted, and he tightened his grip, holding fast to the only possession he valued. The one place these days where he could lose himself in a rush of wind and speed . . . and assuage the anxiety that kept sleep at bay. That's where he wished he was now—pumping up his favorite Weldon Spring trail.

Like that was going to happen anytime soon.

He sucked in a lungful of air, and when the horizon leveled he started toward the counter with careful, measured steps. He didn't want to have to explain a split lip from a fall against the coffee table. No one at work knew about the mess he'd made of his private life, and he intended to keep it that way. He'd come too far, taken too many chances, to fail now.

The only gambling he'd done since Cindy had walked out seven months ago had been on his vacation in the Dominican Republic. A spur-of-the-moment trip to celebrate the arrival of the second payment for the job he'd done. But that had been penny ante stuff. Not real gambling. It had been more like . . . entertainment. Yeah. That was a better way to describe it. Instead of parasailing after his cycling excursions, he'd gone to the casinos. And once he'd depleted the two grand he'd budgeted for the tables, he'd stopped. Walked away. Cold.

He should drink to that accomplishment.

His fingers refused to cooperate, however, and he fumbled the bottle, splashing more scotch onto the counter than into his glass. As it ran across the nicked Formica surface, he groped for a paper towel and wiped it up. Two seconds later, it was gone.

Just like his urge to gamble.

That was the truth of it. He had his compulsion under control now. And in time, he'd convince Cindy he'd conquered it too. The day she'd left, he'd vowed to stop. Promised that in one year, he'd have his act together, debts paid off, her trust fund restored. No matter what it took.

And it had taken a lot.

But he was almost there. His last payment was due to arrive in less than four weeks. He couldn't blow it now.

Except fate was conspiring against him.

All at once, his spirits plummeted, the numbing effect of the alcohol unable to dull the stark reality of his plight. For the past month, starting with the rotten timing of his vacation, he'd been plagued with bad luck. Had he been in town when Warren's daughter had shown up with her stupid tulip note, he'd have convinced her it was meaningless. Oozing empathy, he'd have admitted that while it was an odd coincidence, and while he understood she was having difficulty accepting the circumstances of her father's death, the simple note wasn't sufficient to warrant a new investigation in the face of such overwhelming evidence of suicide. He'd have smooth-talked her out the door, and that would have been the end of it.

But no. He'd been sitting at a blackjack table. Or cycling up a mountain. Or soaking up rays on the beach. Assuming that since five months had passed without incident, the Warren case was as dead as Kelly's father.

Man, had he misread those cards.

He wadded the liquor-soaked towel in his fist, clenching it so tightly a few drops of scotch leaked through his fingers despite his fierce grip.

Just like stray facts were oozing through the cracks in the Warren case.

To make matters worse, Taylor had gotten into the middle of it—and taken more than a professional interest in the daughter. He'd not only listened to her theory, he'd convinced her to search her father's house for more evidence.

And she'd found it.

What had been the odds of that?

Too small to make book on, that was for sure.

Bad as that was, though, the news Taylor had shared with him and Paul two hours ago had been worse.

His colleague had linked John Warren to the WitSec program. Traced him to Vincentio Rossi—a Mafia boss. Connected the dots and concluded Rossi had ordered a hit on Warren.

And now he'd persuaded Paul to let him go to New York and talk to the guy.

Muttering a curse, Alan hurled his tumbler against the tile above the counter. It shattered, sending pieces of glass exploding every direction, littering his kitchen with sharp-edged shards waiting to puncture his flesh. Slice through his skin.

A perfect analogy for the minefield that had become his life.

He grabbed the back of the kitchen chair, fighting against the raw panic clawing at his throat as the desperation of his situation slammed home.

While he'd kept his part of the bargain by taking care of Warren, it hadn't been a clean operation, as had been specified.

Meaning he'd failed a mob boss.

And the punishment wouldn't be pretty.

Raking his fingers through his hair, Alan began to pace, his feet crunching on the glass. Had he known his anonymous benefactor was associated with organized crime, that Warren had been in the crosshairs of the Mafia, he'd have said thanks, but no thanks, faster than a slot machine ate money. He wouldn't have even considered grabbing the lifeline that had now become a noose.

He tried to think coherently, but his instincts overrode rational thought, screaming at him to run. To disappear.

Yet flight would be futile. Despite the alcohol haze clouding his brain, he knew that. They'd track him down just as they'd tracked down Warren.

He had to figure out how to fix this before Taylor contacted Rossi. Try to reassure the Mafia boss a visit from St. Louis County detectives would be nothing more than a slight inconvenience, and that all the questions would disappear.

Alan had no idea how he was going to do that. But he knew one thing.

If he didn't come up with a gold-plated plan to make it happen, he was a dead man.

"Thanks a lot for hooking me up with the Mafia."

At the comment, Cole swiveled his chair toward his future brother-in-law. Mitch stood on the threshold of the office, one shoulder propped against the door frame, arms crossed, a wry quirk to his mouth. Yesterday afternoon, Paul had been noncommittal when Cole had requested that Mitch accompany him to New York. But Sarge had obviously made a decision overnight. He must have cornered Mitch the minute he arrived.

Relief eased the knot of tension in Cole's shoulders. Seeing his colleague in action after Alison had been abducted last spring had convinced him that in a dicey situation, he wanted Mitch watching his back.

And it didn't get much dicier than the mob.

"I would think the Mafia would be small potatoes compared to what you dealt with in your SEAL days."

Mitch pushed off from the door and strolled into the room. "Maybe."

The vague response didn't surprise Cole. Most of Mitch's Navy missions had been classified.

"So you want to fill me in?" Mitch settled a hip on the corner of his desk. "Paul's briefing lived up to its name. He gave me all of two sentences."

"That sounds like Sarge." Cole leaned back, linked his fingers over his stomach, and brought Mitch up to speed.

When he finished, the other man arched an eyebrow. "I'd say Kelly Warren's persistence paid off. Big time."

"And big time is what we're dealing with in Rossi."

"Yeah. So what's the plan?"

"I want to have all my ducks in a row before I set up a meeting. I'm thinking by Thursday I'll be ready to call him. How do you feel about getting on a plane next Monday?"

"Works for me. What can I do to help in the meantime?"

Cole grinned, straightened up, and rolled closer to his desk. "I'm glad you asked. Pull up a chair. This could take a while."

He needed a suicide note.

Alan opened his eyes. Blinked at the ceiling. Swallowed past the sour taste in his mouth.

Drinking half a bottle of scotch last night had scrambled his brain. And put him in a coma for . . . he peered at his watch . . . twelve hours.

But it had also led him to reconsider the idea of a suicide note. So maybe the hangover was worth it.

He sat up slowly, wincing when his stomach revolted as he eased his legs over the side of the bed. Heart pounding, he forced himself to take a deep breath. Another. Throwing up wasn't an option. He needed to focus. To hold on to the idea taking shape in his mind.

Kelly Warren had talked about the absence of a note after her father died. Had insisted that if he had decided to take his life, he'd have left her a farewell message to explain his actions, tell her one last time he loved her. And she hadn't bought Alan's response, that depressed people didn't always behave in character. Instead, she'd insisted her father hadn't been depressed.

But a note in his own hand . . . that would be difficult to ignore. Especially if the handwriting was verified by experts.

And he could make that happen, if necessary.

Alan rose, gripping the back of the straight chair beside the bed where he'd dumped his phone, badge, and Sig Sauer before crashing, swallowing past the nausea when his stomach lurched again. No more drinking for him. He'd need a clear head to pull this off fast and clean.

Coffee and dry toast high on his priority list, he padded

barefoot toward the kitchen. Lucky thing he'd thought ahead and pilfered a few things after Warren's death. The scribbled notes jammed in files, the to-do lists in the kitchen, the hand-written minutes in the man's desk from a garden club meeting. Not the kinds of things his daughter would miss, but great insurance. Just in case things went south.

Like now.

He'd even taken a few blank sheets of the man's stationery and pressed Warren's fingertips to the paper.

From the beginning he'd toyed with the idea of planting a farewell note. But involving other people in an operation increased risk. So he'd opted to forego the note—unless he ran into a glitch during the investigation.

As it turned out, no note had been needed. He'd done such a superb job staging the death that no one had questioned his conclusions.

Until the past month.

He yanked open the refrigerator, grabbed the bag of generic coffee that had replaced his preferred Starbucks brand, and slammed the door. He should have gone with the note weeks ago, when Kelly started to raise a serious stink. It would have been easier to plant it back then, before she'd searched her father's house.

Instead, he'd panicked. Given in to a knee-jerk reaction. Tried to eliminate her—or at the very least, distract her—by creating a life-threatening allergy attack. And he'd pulled it off masterfully, thanks to the disguise skills he'd perfected as an undercover detective with the Dallas PD.

But panic was always a mistake . . . on the street, and in life. One he wouldn't have made if he hadn't been desperate to erase any roadblocks to a reconciliation with Cindy.

The past couldn't be changed, though. He could only go for-ward. Guided by logic and reason this time, instead of emotion.

He fumbled with the top of the coffee bag, his fingers clumsy, his mind on the day's agenda. Once he was sober, he'd check in at the office. Then he'd stop at the bank, withdraw the pilfered papers from his safe deposit box, and contact Freddie to arrange a drop. The sixtysomething former embezzler played it straight these days—for the most part—but he was the best forger around.

And Freddie owed him for looking the other direction on a few occasions. In his eleven years as a cop, Alan had learned it didn't hurt to cultivate favors with people on the shady side of the law. They could be useful sources in investigations—if they had a personal reason to cooperate. And Freddie had plenty of those. He'd do a little job for him, no questions asked.

Once he had the note in hand, he'd figure out a plan to plant it where Kelly would find it—just as he'd considered doing in the days following the investigation if any questions arose. But he'd prefer to convince Rossi to sit tight. There was no hard evidence to tie him or the mob boss to the crime. In time, the questions would go away.

If Rossi would *give* it time.

He shook the coffee into a filter and settled it in the top of the coffeemaker, averting his face from the aroma. Usually, he liked the smell of coffee, but his stomach was still too unsettled from last night's alcohol.

Or perhaps the queasiness was due to the familiar fear vibrating along his nerve endings. The same fear he felt when luck turned against him in the middle of a high-stakes game, with the same symptoms—dry mouth, pounding pulse, fast respiration. Along with a crushing sense he was about to lose everything, but it was too late to back out.

The situations *were* similar. Except the stakes in this game were a lot higher.

And he could think of only one less-than-foolproof remedy.

A wave of uneasiness shuddered through him. Bringing in a third party was risky. As much as Freddie owed him, he could turn out to be a wild card. And assuming Rossi insisted he fix the situation rather than wait it out, Alan had no idea how, without arousing suspicions, he was going to plant a letter in a house already thoroughly searched by Kelly and the Crime Scene Unit.

It was shaping up to be a pit of a day.

Frustrated, he snatched the pot out of the coffeemaker and stomped toward the sink. But a moment later he jerked to a stop when a sudden, sharp pain stabbed the sole of his foot.

Muttering a curse, he checked out the floor. Shards of glass glinted in the morning sun streaming through the kitchen window. As he watched, blood began to ooze from beneath his foot.

He'd stepped right into the middle of the mess he'd created last night.

The juices in his stomach congealed.

A cut foot he could handle.

But like every gambler he'd ever met, he believed in omens. And this wasn't a good one.

"Want anything out of the vending machine?" Cole stretched and rose from the table in the conference room he and Mitch had commandeered. "It's way past lunchtime."

"Yeah." Mitch rubbed the back of his neck and surveyed the piles of paper in front of him. "Anything with sugar—and caffeine. Chocolate would work. I need an energy boost."

"I thought Navy SEALs ate healthier than that."

Mitch grinned. "Another myth busted." He patted his midsection. "Actually, my disciplined eating regime has gone to pot since I met Alison. She's a great cook."

"Yeah—despite her lousy coffee. But you don't look like you're overindulging."

"That's because I've increased my daily lap count. The pool has become my second home since your sister started stuffing my face."

Cole rolled his eyes. "Don't expect any sympathy from me. I subsist on bachelor fare. Trust me, I wouldn't mind having someone cook for me once in a while."

"Didn't Kelly make you dinner one night? How are *her* kitchen skills?" Mitch grinned at him.

Cole kept his expression neutral. "It was a very impromptu meal."

"Are you telling me she nuked a microwave dinner for you?"

Hardly. Those lemon bars he'd wolfed down as he'd driven away had been amazing—just like the rest of the dinner she'd prepared.

"I'll take that as a no." Mitch's grin broadened.

Cole flattened the smile teasing his lips and shot him a disgruntled look as he edged toward the door. "You sure you don't want anything more than a candy bar?"

"Nope. I'm going to Alison's tonight for that lasagna. I want to save up my calories."

Cole leaned his forehead against the door frame and groaned. "Go ahead. Rub it in."

"You're welcome to join us. She's making a whole pan. There will be plenty. And she was just saying yesterday she hasn't heard much from you lately and that the two of you need to catch up."

He knew what that meant. His sister wanted to grill him. Weighing the benefit of a home-cooked meal against a third-degree interrogation about his faith or his love life, he decided the cons outweighed the pros.

"Let's see what's going on by the end of the day." With that hedge, he made a quick exit.

His stomach rumbling a protest against the late lunch, Cole barreled down the hall, intent on getting to the vending machines as soon as possible. But as he rounded a corner he almost ran Alan over.

"Whoa! Sorry." He grinned and did a quick sidestep. "Don't tell any of the street cops or they'll cite me for a moving violation."

His attempt at humor was met with an annoyed frown. "Why is everyone always in a hurry?"

Cole's smile faded as he gave Alan an assessing sweep. The man's eyes were red-rimmed and bloodshot, and the tan he'd sported a couple of weeks ago had faded into an unhealthy gray pallor. If he didn't know better, he'd think his colleague was coming off a wild night of drinking. But even at a Friday night happy hour, Alan never indulged in more than a beer or two.

"You okay?"

"Yeah." The man wiped a hand down his face and made an obvious effort to pull himself together. "I didn't get much sleep this weekend."

"How's the homicide investigation coming?"

"It's not. The leads I've been chasing have turned into dead ends. What's happening with the Warren case?"

Cole shifted and shoved his hands in his pockets. Alan's stiff posture in the meeting with Paul yesterday had clearly communicated his displeasure about being pulled off the case.

"Nothing new. We're just fact-finding right now. I'm hoping to be ready to call Rossi by tomorrow and set up a meeting for Monday."

"It's gonna be tough to pin anything on him." He propped a shoulder against the wall, as if overcome by weariness. "There was nothing at the crime scene to tie him to the death. I suspect he's a pro at evading the law and keeping jobs like that—*if* he was behind it—at arm's length."

"He made enough mistakes to land in prison, though."

What little color remained in the man's face seeped out. "True."

"Look . . . are you sure you're okay? Maybe you picked up that flu bug that's been going around."

"Nah." He pushed off from the wall. "Just tired. Let me know what's happening on the Warren case, okay? I don't like loose ends."

"Sure. I'll keep you in the loop."

"How's the daughter holding up?"

"Okay for now. I did convince her to beef up the security at her house. Her window and door locks were pathetic."

"Yeah, I remember noticing that when I stopped there a couple of times during the investigation to talk to her. With

Rossi involved, it doesn't hurt to take extra precautions." He sighed. "Well, back to the salt mines."

"Good luck."

"Thanks. I think I'm gonna need it." Raising his hand in farewell, he continued down the hall.

Cole followed his progress for a few seconds, then continued toward the vending machines. He didn't get more than three steps before his cell began to vibrate.

Hunger kept him moving as he pulled it off his belt, but he smiled when he noted the caller.

"Hi, Kelly. I was just talking about you."

"Saying nice things, I hope."

"Always."

"Thanks." She cleared her throat, and he could picture her blushing—a trait made more endearing by its rarity in today's world. "I just wanted to let you know all the locks are in place. The installer was very thorough, so I should be well protected. I haven't quite gotten the hang of how the ones on the basement windows work, but I'll figure it out. I don't open them often, anyway."

"You want me to stop by after work and take a look? I've had plenty of experience with all kinds of window locks."

The ill-advised offer was out before he could stop it. If he wanted to keep their relationship strictly professional until her father's case was resolved, trumping up excuses to see her wasn't smart.

Her tone suggested she was as surprised as he was by the invitation. "I hate to put you out."

She was giving him a chance to retract the offer. He should take it.

Except he didn't.

"I pass close to your house anyway. It's not a problem."

"In that case, I accept—as long as you let me feed you again. I even baked some pumpkin bars in the spirit of the upcoming holiday. They were my dad's favorite."

Despite the forced brightness of her last comment, he heard

the slight catch in her voice at the end. Any lingering inclinations to recant his offer evaporated.

"That sounds great. Thank you. Look for me by six."

"I will. And Cole—thank you." Her soft expression reflected an emotion deeper than gratitude.

Or was that just wishful thinking?

He cleared his throat, reminding himself not to get carried away. Yet. "You're welcome. I'll see you soon."

As he ended the call, Cole scanned the vending machine offerings and selected a Mr. Goodbar for Mitch. The man would get his requested chocolate, but at least the peanuts would provide a little protein. He punched the button for a granola bar for himself.

Snacks in hand, he rejoined Mitch and tossed his colleague's candy bar on the table. Mitch ripped off the paper, eyeing the granola bar as Cole sat.

"Trying to make me feel guilty?"

"If the shoe fits . . ." He lifted one shoulder and bit into the chewy bar as he pulled a stack of material on Rossi's family toward him.

"I know. You're saving your calories for Alison's lasagna."

"Nope. I'm going to pass." He pulled out a sheet on Rossi's son that looked interesting.

"Better offer?"

He glanced up. The more he worked with Mitch, the more impressed he was by the man's intuitive sixth sense. Not a bad asset for a SEAL—or a detective.

"As a matter of fact, yes."

"Heading to Kelly's?"

Cole squinted at him, as annoyed as he was intrigued. "How do you do that?"

"What?"

"Read between the lines."

"Elementary, my dear Cole. Any man who skipped lunch and could still pass up Alison's lasagna has to have either a fabulous meal or a beautiful woman waiting for him. Maybe both."

"You know, we should make a great team with Rossi. Between your keen perception and my inestimable interrogation skills, we may come away with some excellent insights."

Mitch smirked and lifted what was left of his candy bar in salute. "I'll eat to that. And have fun tonight. I'll give Alison your regrets. Not that you have any."

For a moment, Cole thought about responding. Decided against it.

Because once again, Mitch's intuition was dead-on.

12

"Thank you again. This was much better than eating alone." Cole wiped his mouth on one of the Irish linen napkins Kelly reserved for special occasions and smiled as he set it on the damask tablecloth beside his plate. "And I appreciate all the nice touches." He gestured to her small dining room table, set with her best china and the Waterford crystal goblets her dad had given her for her twenty-first birthday.

At his husky tone, she dipped her head and made a pretense of brushing some crumbs into a pile on the snowy cloth. "I don't get to use my nicer things very often. Company gave me an excuse to get some mileage out of them."

True, but not the only reason. She'd originally intended to serve in the kitchen, until Lauren's advice had echoed in her mind as she'd whipped up a batch of her homemade biscuits.

It doesn't hurt to lay the groundwork. Let the man know you're interested.

And she was interested. Very. So in addition to pulling out the stops on the meal, she'd exchanged her usual jeans for a pair of black wool slacks and a forest-green V-necked angora sweater that matched her eyes.

"Well, anytime you want an excuse to break out the family silver, give me a call. I'll be glad to volunteer as a taster." Cole grinned and nodded toward her plate. "Finished?"

She checked it out. Funny. She couldn't remember eating,

but her food had disappeared sometime during the animated conversation that had started with practical matters—like locks and a case update—and evolved into a discussion of politics, hobbies, and family.

"I guess I am." She pushed back her chair and rose. "Did you save room for dessert?"

"Always. A sweet tooth is one of my weaknesses." He picked up his plate and stood. "I'll help you clean the table first."

A man who helped with kitchen chores. That definitely went into the "strengths" category. "I can't say I've spotted many faults."

"Oh, I have plenty. Just ask my sister." He chuckled and followed her into the kitchen. "She's very outspoken on the subject."

"Name one besides the sweet tooth."

"True confessions, hmm? Okay, let's see . . ." He set his plate beside the sink. "She claims I have no tact."

Kelly deposited her plate next to his and appraised him. "Maybe it's a sister thing. Family members sometimes see shortcomings no one else does."

"Nope. She's right. Not that I'd ever admit it to her face, you understand. Which brings up another one of my flaws. Stubbornness."

A smile teased her lips. "I'm guilty on that score too. But I prefer to think of it as tenacity or persistence. And that can be a positive quality." Her smile faded. "It paid off with my dad's case."

"True."

She opened the cabinet and pulled out some cups and saucers, determined not to let the lingering questions over her father's death ruin what had turned out to be a most enjoyable evening. "Coffee?"

"That would be great. I'll grab some more stuff off the table."

He disappeared into the dining room while she started the coffee, returning with the butter dish, salt and pepper shakers, and the empty bread basket.

"We made short work of these." He lifted the basket, grinning as he set it on the counter. "Or I should say, I did. You're a fabulous cook."

She shrugged off the compliment, but the warm glow in her heart remained. "Learning to cook was a matter of survival. My mom died when I was twelve, and cooking was *not* among my dad's many talents. We subsisted on macaroni and cheese and frozen dinners for weeks, until I finally dug out my mom's recipes. In the beginning we ate a lot of charred mystery meat, but my technique improved with age and practice. Are you ready for those pumpkin bars?"

"Yes. Do you take cream with your coffee?" He indicated the refrigerator.

"And sugar. The bowl's inside the cabinet on your right."

"I hope not as much as Alison. She ends up with syrup instead of coffee."

Kelly smiled at him as he withdrew the items. He might complain about his sister, but the affection in his voice when he spoke of her was unmistakable. "I use half a teaspoon. Just enough to cut the bitterness. And if that's her biggest fault, I envy her."

"Oh, she has other quirks." He set the sugar and cream on the counter. "Not only does she oversweeten coffee, she can't brew a decent cup. Tea is her thing, so when we eat at her place we always opt for instant. It's safer. She's also stubborn. Must be a family trait." He flashed her another grin. "Plus, she takes far too much interest in my personal life and my relationships—and is very vocal in her opinions."

Relationships. Plural.

Kelly turned away to remove the plastic wrap from the pumpkin bars as she wrestled with that concept. The news didn't surprise her, but hearing it put into words was a bit disconcerting. With his good looks and engaging personality, though, Cole wasn't likely to spend many Saturday evenings alone. Even Lauren had hinted as much—and suggested he might be on the fast side. Perhaps his sister agreed.

"Want to sample one while we wait for the coffee to brew?" She held out the plate, trying to come up with a diplomatic approach that would allow her to dig a little deeper into the subject.

He eyed the frosted bars. "I could be persuaded." Leaning forward, he took one.

"So are you saying your sister is nosy?" She retrieved dessert plates from the cabinet and put two pumpkin bars on each, easing into the subject.

"Yes." He swallowed the bite he'd taken before continuing. "But she also has many fine qualities. Ones I never fully recognized until she was in a serious car accident a couple of years ago and we almost lost her." His voice hoarsened, and he cleared his throat. "She's a fighter, though, and she was determined to not just survive but make a complete recovery. These days, the only visible evidence of the accident is a slight limp when she overdoes things—which she often does. Alison isn't the type to do any task halfway." He weighed the remaining half of the pumpkin bar in his hand and studied her. "She kind of reminds me of you in that regard."

The comment took her off guard, and she slid her hands into the pockets of her slacks. "Thanks. I think."

"I meant that as a compliment. In case you haven't figured it out, I admire strong, determined women."

"Even nosy ones?"

"You aren't nosy."

She crossed to the coffeemaker and fiddled with the handle of the pot. "Okay. But I am curious."

"About what?"

Turning toward him, she folded her arms over her pounding heart. "Can I be honest with you?"

"Sure." He lowered the pumpkin bar instead of popping the rest in his mouth, his expression sobering at her serious tone.

"I know you want to keep things strictly business between us until my dad's case is resolved. I understand that—and agree with it. But you also said you'd like to explore a different kind of relationship once things are settled. So I was wondering if . . . well, you said your sister is vocal in her opinions about your relationships—plural—and . . ." Kelly's cheeks began to burn. Tucking her hair behind her ear, she huffed out a breath. "I am *so* not good at this. Forget it, okay? We can talk about this later, after the investigation is finished."

Twin creases appeared on Cole's brow. "No. This is important, and it's a fair concern." He set the half-eaten pumpkin bar on the counter and faced her. "You want to know if I sleep around."

At his blunt but accurate assessment, the flame in her cheeks grew hotter. "See, I am nosy."

"I look on it more as your self-preservation instincts kicking in."

"That's a generous take." She tried for a smile, but her unsteady lips wouldn't cooperate. "The thing is, I don't operate in the fast lane, Cole. As my friend Lauren would be the first to testify, I'm a slow mover. I like you a lot already, and I think I could like you a lot more. But I don't want to get too far down that road if you're only in the market for a superficial relationship."

He looked at her for a moment, as if debating how to respond. Then he leaned back against the counter and gripped the edge. "For the past few years, my relationships with women have been superficial. But I can tell you with absolute honesty that I'm not looking for that with you." One side of his mouth hitched up. "And for what it's worth, my sister would approve of this relationship. She's been after me to find a churchgoing woman to date."

His last comment brought up a whole different issue. One that had been on Kelly's mind for a while and was just as important—if not more important—than the first one. As long as they were tackling the tough stuff, she might as well put this on the table too.

"Why does she want you to date a woman who attends church?"

His knuckles whitened and his features grew taut. "Because I walked away from God a few years ago. When I said before that Alison is vocal about my relationships, that includes my relationship with him."

A sudden hiss from the coffeemaker intruded on their quiet conversation, and Kelly jerked.

"The coffee's ready." He took a step away from the counter. "Would you excuse me a minute while you pour?"

"Sure."

He exited the room into the hall, and a few seconds later she heard a quiet click as he closed the bathroom door.

Slowly she let out her breath. Was he closing the door on their discussion too? Did he regret revealing so much personal information? Was he aggravated that she'd delved into such private subjects?

His reaction to the subject of faith also troubled her. A lot. While he'd been quick to acknowledge his dating history and told her he wanted to make a change, he'd made no such claim about his relationship with God. In fact, he'd shut down when that subject came up. Walked away.

And that kind of attitude could be a deal breaker.

Spirits plummeting, Kelly picked up the coffeepot, filled her cup, and gazed into the black depths. It was better to know Cole's feeling on the subject now, of course. Before she lost her heart completely.

As for the part he'd already claimed . . . she had a feeling that would be his forever.

Hands braced on the bathroom sink, Cole stared into the mirror. How in the world had he and Kelly gotten into such a serious discussion?

And where did he go from here?

He hadn't minded answering her questions about his social life. He'd known from day one she was a woman with rock-solid values, and meeting her had been the kick he'd needed

150

to get his act together on that score. Far more effectively than Alison's badgering or Jake's more subtle prodding, her sweet goodness had made him take a hard look at himself and convinced him he wanted to be worthy of someone like her.

No. Scratch that. Not *like* her. Her, specifically. He was becoming more and more certain of that with each day that passed.

But the faith issue—that might be a stumbling block unless they could talk it through, come to an understanding.

Except he'd never discussed that painful piece of his history with anyone.

Maybe, though, it was time. Since he'd turned his back on the Lord, lost his way spiritually, the emptiness in his soul had intensified. And Kelly, with her quiet faith and absolute trust in God, had forced him to acknowledge that lapse as well.

Could she perhaps help him rectify both his social life and his spiritual life?

With sudden decision, he opened the door, flipped off the light, and returned to the kitchen. It was deserted. He found her at the dining room table, hands wrapped around her coffee cup, her pumpkin bars untouched on the plate in front of her.

As he slid into his seat, he forced his lips into a smile. "Sorry to keep you from your dessert."

She lifted one shoulder. "I'm still full from dinner."

The subtle wariness in her eyes, the caution in her tone, told him she was afraid she'd overstepped and annoyed him the same way his sister often did. He needed to put those fears to rest.

"Me too. But these are excellent." He tapped the half-eaten pumpkin bar she'd retrieved from the counter and placed on his plate, along with the two whole ones.

"Look, Cole, I'm sorry if—"

"Don't apologize." He touched her fingers, cold despite her grip on the coffee cup. "The issues you raised are important to you—and to how you perceive the future of our relationship. That makes them important to me too. Although I'll admit I didn't expect them to be on the menu tonight."

His attempt to tease her into a smile didn't work.

"But now that you've put them on the table, let's talk about them. Starting with my recent dating history. I can't change the past, but I can shift gears and move to a slower lane in the future. And I promise you I will. Is that good enough to make you feel comfortable about moving forward with this relationship when the time comes?"

He held his breath as she searched his face. For someone like Kelly, it might not be good enough. But he hoped she could find it in her heart to forgive his past mistakes and trust his promise for the future.

She nibbled at her lower lip, her expression conflicted. "I think so. I'm still processing everything you told me, but to be honest, the faith issue is an even bigger hurdle."

"I suspected that was the case."

He slid his plate aside as his pulse began to pound. He had to be honest. A future built on secrets was a future built on sand. Yet he also knew honesty could make her shutter her heart. But he wouldn't sugarcoat the truth.

"I used to have a strong faith. Maybe the strongest of all the Taylor kids. Then, four years ago, I walked away from God. I tried to fill up the empty place in my soul with work and a very active social life and a few too many happy hours on Friday nights, but I'm beginning to realize I've been searching for consolation in all the wrong places. And I'm starting to think I need to reconnect with my faith. That nothing will fill that empty spot except a relationship with God."

She broke off a piece of pumpkin bar with the edge of her fork but didn't eat it. When she spoke, her question was cautious. Tentative. "Is there a particular reason you walked away?"

Oh yeah.

The image of Sara lying in a pool of blood, lifeless eyes staring at the ceiling as the lights of emergency vehicles strobed through the night, flashed across his mind.

When the silence between them lengthened, Kelly spoke again. "You don't have to answer that."

152

Forcing himself to block out the image burned into his memory, he refocused on the woman across from him. She was clinging to her cup, her face taut.

"I want to." Reaching over, he touched her cheek, the tender gesture meant to reassure. And it worked. She exhaled, and the tension in her features eased. "I've never told this story to anyone."

Her eyes widened slightly. Rather than wait for her to ask the question he knew she was formulating, he answered it.

"Because you need to know exactly who you're getting before we decide to take this relationship forward."

He picked up his coffee and took a slow sip, buying himself a few seconds to collect his thoughts. And for the first time in years, he turned to God, asking for the courage to at last put into words the incident that had driven him away from the faith that had always sustained him.

"Four and a half years ago, a twenty-three-year-old woman was found unconscious in an apartment complex stairwell. The neighbor who called 911 told responding officers she suspected domestic violence, and had often heard disturbances in the adjoining apartment. I went to the hospital to talk with the woman, who was suffering from a concussion and multiple abrasions. Her name was Sara."

The last word came out in a rasp. He stopped. Swallowed. He'd never spoken Sara's name to anyone. As it reverberated in Kelly's hushed dining room, the traumatic memories he'd ruthlessly suppressed morphed from past to present in a heartbeat. Clenching his hands into fists, he forced himself to keep breathing.

Kelly waited in silence until he was ready to continue.

"When I questioned her, she insisted she'd fallen down the steps. Denied she'd been abused." His words were shakier now, but he kept going. "I didn't buy it. I'd been a cop long enough to recognize the signs, and I told her that, straight up. But she didn't budge from her story. So I resorted to scare tactics. Told her situations like hers didn't get better. That her best and safest option was to walk away. She refused." He raked his fingers through his hair and focused on his black coffee. "There's not much we can do if people won't press charges or take some initiative to change their situation."

"I have a feeling you tried anyway."

At Kelly's gentle comment, he looked up. The warmth and empathy in her eyes tightened his throat.

"Yeah." He took another sip of his cooling coffee. "I discovered early on in this job that you can't save the world. Trying to do that will leave you with an ulcer or heart attack or chronic insomnia. So I'd learned to walk away from situations like Sara's and commend them to God. But there was something about her . . ."

He paused, recalling the sweep of her long dark hair against the white sheet on the hospital gurney, the velvet brown of her irises, the graceful curve of her jaw. And how her beauty had been marred by puffy red swelling and a collage of purple and black bruises.

"I don't know." He shrugged, blocking out that image. "She just seemed so scared and vulnerable. I left her my card, the name of a shelter, and a hotline number, as I always did in cases like that. But I also gave her my personal cell number and told her if she ever needed a friend, or someone to talk to, she could call me."

"And she did."

"Yes. About a month later. It was a weekend, and I was off duty. She was crying. She said her husband had gone out drinking and she needed to hear a friendly voice. So I talked to her. I'd done some homework after we met, and I knew the guy she'd married was an ex-con who'd served time for armed robbery. I also knew she was a product of the foster care system and that she'd disappeared from the official radar at the age of fifteen.

"To make a long story short, she ended up calling me periodically over the next six months. We met now and then for coffee, when her husband was passed out after a binge of drinking and it was safe. As time went by, I learned her whole story. How she grew up in a dysfunctional home and was put into the foster system, where she was abused by one of her foster fathers. That's when she ran away. She was barely eking out a living when she met her Prince Charming. Things went downhill from there."

"Why did she stay with him?"

"Fear. Like a lot of abused women, Sara was afraid if she left he'd come after her and kill her. Nor did she want to end up back on the street. So she stuck with him." His tone flattened. "But in the end, he killed her anyway."

"Oh, Cole!"

At Kelly's exclamation of dismay, he sent her an apologetic look. "Sorry. This isn't the best dinner conversation."

"I asked. I wanted to know. I'm just so sad for her."

"Me too. Because it was preventable—and because it was partly my fault." The words tasted bitter in his mouth.

Confusion clouded her eyes. "How can that be? You tried to convince her to leave."

He did his best to distance himself from the narrative. If he didn't, he wouldn't be able to finish. "I also talked with Sara about my faith. That prompted her to start attending church. She found a congregation on her own, and ended up sharing her story with the minister. Unfortunately, he convinced her that marriage vows were forever and encouraged her to try and persuade her husband to seek counseling rather than leave him. He also convinced her that prayer would keep her safe."

Cole clenched his fingers again, fighting to contain the wave of anger nipping at his self-control. "There were a few times I was tempted to go over to that church and have a heart-to-heart with the guy. Instead, I kept working on her from my end. Encouraging her to follow through on the GED program she'd started. Reminding her she had options. That she didn't have to stay with him. That there were plenty of resources available to help her until she got on her feet. That the system could keep her safe. And I did a lot of praying myself. She deserved a better life. She was smart and funny and caring . . . and despite all the bad stuff that happened to her, she never let it beat her down. She always had hope that tomorrow would be better."

He blinked to clear his vision, struggling to hold on to his composure. To finish this story—and perhaps put it to rest once and for all. "Anyway, she followed the minister's advice and stuck with her husband. Then one morning someone from her apartment building called 911 to report a guy walking around in a bloodstained shirt. I burned rubber getting there, but it was too late. She died at the scene. After a night of drinking, he'd beaten her to death."

Silence fell in the room, broken only by the faint ticking of a clock in Kelly's kitchen. Cole picked up his cup. The liquid sloshed close to the edge, and he realized his hands were shaking. He wrapped his fingers around the cup and lifted it to his lips. Took a sip. The coffee had grown cold and bitter—much like his heart had after Sara's death.

Carefully he set the cup back in its saucer and ventured a glance at Kelly. She'd lost a little color during the story, but at least it was almost over.

"I see a lot of carnage in my job." His voice came out scratchy. Worn. Weary from the pain that had darkened his soul for four long years. "But that crime scene gave me nightmares for months. On bad days, it still does. The whole experience left me angry with God and disillusioned about prayer. How could a minister, a man of God, counsel a woman to put her life in danger in the name of religion? And why did prayer fail? From the first time I met Sara, I asked God to show me what to do. To tell me how to intervene. I waited for his direction, but none ever came. So I prayed every day that he would guide Sara, and save her. But in the end, he failed her. Her minister failed her. I failed her."

Kelly leaned closer and covered his hand with hers. "I don't think that's entirely true."

At her quiet comment, he frowned. "What do you mean?"

"I agree her minister was misguided. I *don't* agree that you failed her. You tried to help. But you couldn't force her to leave her husband. All you could do was offer her reasons why she should. It was her decision to stay. As for God not answering your prayers—I think he did. Thanks to you, Sara found her way to him. And she was saved in the eternal sense. Maybe that's the role God intended you to play all along. To be the instrument of her salvation."

Cole stopped breathing as he mulled over that possibility. Had his prayers been answered after all—but in a different way than he'd hoped?

Pressure built behind his eyes, and he tried to blink it away. "That's an angle I never considered."

"Sometimes a third party can offer a more objective perspective." She wrapped her fingers around her cup. "You cared about Sara a lot, didn't you?"

"Yes." He'd started this story determined to be honest, and he intended to stay the course. "Too much. It was the only time I ever let personal feelings get in the way of my job, and it was a big mistake, professionally and personally. We never did more than talk or meet for coffee, but she *was* married—and I was falling for her. Between guilt over that and worry about her safety, my life was a train wreck. Somehow I managed to hold it together at work, but Alison cued in to my mental state and started calling me almost every day. I sidestepped all her questions, but she never stopped calling. She never knew it, but she was my lifeline."

"Kind of like you were for Sara."

"Yeah. I guess."

"What happened to her husband?"

He gritted his teeth. "He's back in prison. Where he belongs."

"And you've been in a prison too. Of a different kind."

At her soft comment, he frowned. Had he? It was true that his guilt and anger had isolated him in many ways. While that wasn't his usual concept of prison, it did fit.

"You're right. But you know what? I think I'm finally ready

to deal with that." He twined his fingers with hers and managed to summon up the hint of a smile. "Thank you for listening."

She squeezed his hand, took a deep breath, and gestured to his coffee cup. "That has to be cold. How about a refill?"

"How about a rain check? I think we could both use some time alone to digest more than our food." In truth, he'd prefer to hang around. Just being in Kelly's presence lifted his spirits. But he'd dumped a boatload of heavy stuff on her. She had to be reeling.

"You might be right. Let me wrap those up for you." She stood and picked up the plate with his pumpkin bars, her immediate acquiescence to his suggestion proof he'd read the situation correctly.

When she joined him in the foyer a couple of minutes later, he'd already opened the door. The porch light spilled in, picking out the bronze highlights in her russet-colored hair, and it took every ounce of his willpower to resist the impulse to pull her into his arms.

"I'll call you, okay?" He shoved his hands in his pockets to keep them out of trouble.

"Okay." She moistened her lips, calling his attention to their soft fullness.

His mouth went dry. "I need to leave." The words came out hoarse. And abrupt.

A flash of uncertainty ricocheted through her eyes, and she took a step back. "Okay."

She'd misread his haste. He didn't have a single regret about what had happened tonight, and she needed to know that.

Slowly, he removed one hand from his pocket and reached over to touch her lips with his index finger. She gave a soft gasp but didn't pull away. "This is why I need to leave. If I stay, I'm going to kiss you, and we're not ready for that yet." That was a lie. *He* was more than ready. "I want to be smart about this—and try to stay in the slow lane. We'll leave the kissing until after we wrap up your father's case." He managed a grin as he retracted his hand.

The longing that filled her eyes as she clung to the edge of the door set his pulse hammering. "I appreciate your restraint. And for the record . . . I hope we wrap it up really fast." She handed him the pumpkin bars.

"So do I. Now lock up." With one last touch of her cheek, he exited.

He waited until he heard the new dead bolt click into place before he continued to his car. Until all the questions about her father's death were answered, he wanted her house locked up tight.

But he was glad she was *un*locking her heart. Letting him in. And he was glad he'd reciprocated.

As he climbed into his car and took one last look at the light spilling from her windows, he couldn't help smiling. Based on what Mitch had said earlier, Alison would be calling him soon for a chat. As usual, he'd evade any personal questions.

If all went well, though, his sister would be getting an earful in the not-too-distant future.

13

The door on the side-entry garage of the suburban Buffalo ranch house opened, and from his parked position down the street Vincentio tightened his grip on the wheel of his car.

The time had come.

He watched as an older-model SUV slowed in front of the house, then pulled into the driveway and disappeared inside the garage. He'd have to reward his contact for supplying such accurate information. His son's wife—Eileen—had arrived home from her teaching job, Jason in tow from day care, within minutes of the schedule the man had passed on. And his son wouldn't be home from his job as a carpenter—Vincentio's mouth curled in distaste at the shame of a Rossi doing blue-collar labor—for at least an hour.

That gave him plenty of time to take care of his business.

After exiting the car, he retrieved the cane he rarely used, then tucked the teddy bear under his arm and walked toward the modest Lancaster house. He drove by it now and then, when loneliness overwhelmed him. On one occasion his son had been cutting the grass. Vincentio was glad he'd worn sunglasses that day, though Marco had given his car no more than a passing glance as his father had driven by, gripping the wheel with sweaty palms.

They were sweaty today too, despite the biting chill in the November air.

Vincentio Rossi with sweaty palms. He shook his head. What a difference from the old days, when he'd had nerves of steel. When he'd have laughed at the notion that a baby could produce such anxiety.

Funny how a man's priorities could change.

He paused at the bottom of the steps that led to the front door. The house was well maintained. Paint crisp, porch swept, no rotting wood. But it was small. Plain. Ordinary. And so much less than Marco could have had. A gracious two story in Amherst—or maybe Orchard Park—could have been his for the asking. Vincentio had plenty of money stashed in his offshore account, thanks to regular deposits during his working years. He'd intended most of those funds to be a legacy for his son.

But Marco wanted none of it. Dirty money, he'd called it, when Vincentio had phoned him soon after his release from prison—the one and only time they'd talked in thirty-one years.

The time Marco had said never to contact him again.

His son's rejection had been more painful than the stab wound he'd received decades ago from a disgruntled—and soon-to-be-deceased—colleague. But it hadn't come as a great surprise, given their long estrangement. So, after a few more futile attempts to connect, he'd accepted his son's decision.

A grandson, however, changed things.

A grandson deserved to know his nonno.

Hand on the railing, Vincentio climbed the six steps to the front porch, huffing too much. He should cut back on his visits to Romano's. Reduce his carbs and cholesterol. But how could he give up one of his few remaining pleasures?

Unless he had visits with a grandson to look forward to.

And maybe, God willing, he would after today.

He repositioned the teddy bear under his arm, leaned forward, and pressed the doorbell.

Ten seconds passed. Twenty. Thirty.

Was Eileen peeking through a window? Had Marco instructed the wife Vincentio had never met to ignore any contact from him?

Just when he thought his trip had been wasted, the door opened.

The young woman with strawberry blonde hair who stood on the other side was lovely. None of the photos provided by his contacts had done her justice. But it was the infant in her arms who caught—and held—his attention. Even at such a young age, his jet-black hair and dark eyes branded him a Rossi. A rush of pride warmed Vincentio's heart. Marco might try to deny his son his heritage, but he couldn't deprive him of the Rossi looks.

Suddenly Eileen eased back, and he lifted his gaze. She was staring at the teddy bear tucked under his arm, her expression wary.

"Hello, Eileen." He tried for a smile, but his stiff lips wouldn't cooperate. "I'm Marco—Mark's—father."

"I know." The words, a mere whisper, held a tremor of fear. "I've seen your picture." She eased the door a few more inches toward the closed position.

Anger bubbled up inside Vincentio. What sort of monster had Marco painted him to be, that she would be so frightened?

With supreme effort, he subdued his fury and managed to produce a smile. "I don't know what Mark has told you, Eileen, but you have nothing to fear from me. Do I look dangerous?"

He knew he didn't. He shaved in front of the bathroom mirror every day. Saw the creases in his face, the thinning gray hair, the rheumy eyes behind the thick glasses. He was just a portly old man. The grandfatherly type.

To illustrate that point, he pulled the teddy bear from under his arm. "This was in the package you and Mark sent back. I know he wants nothing to do with me, and I've learned to accept that, though the pain of it never goes away. I only ask that you let an old man have a chance to know his grandson."

He leaned on the cane, using it to full effect. "I'm seventy-four, Eileen. I have health problems. I doubt I have a lot of years left. But I'd like to spend some of them with that little guy." He nodded toward the baby in her arms and extended the teddy bear. "Won't you please at least take this small gift? And think about what I'm asking? I'll accept whatever terms you and Mark set, as long as I can spend some time with Jason."

Seconds ticked by as she appraised him. A car honked on the street behind him. A dog barked in the distance. The rumble of an airplane reverberated in the sky above. From somewhere, the smell of frying hamburgers wafted toward him, the aroma of onions mingling with the smell of baby powder.

He watched her the way he used to watch his adversaries, face placid, alert to every nuance of her demeanor. And he knew the instant she wavered. Her features softened infinitesimally. Her grip on the door loosened enough to let the blood flow back into her knuckles. Her eyes went from fearful to uncertain.

He'd won. With Eileen, anyway.

Summoning up his next smile was easy as he bent and set the teddy bear beside the door. "I'll tell you what. Why don't I leave this here and let you think about my request? I tucked my cell phone number into his pocket." He gestured toward the red jacket the teddy bear wore. "If you can find it in your heart to arrange a way for me to get to know my grandson, call anytime. Day or night."

With a polite dip of his head, he turned. Grasping the railing, he descended the steps and walked back to his car, leaning heavily on the cane. He didn't look back until he slipped behind the wheel and closed the door.

Through the tinted windows, he saw that she was still watching him. He fitted the key into the ignition. Started the car. Pulled away from the curb. But he kept one eye on the rearview mirror.

And just before he lost sight of the house, he saw Eileen bend down, pick up the teddy bear, and close the door.

Yes!

He slammed his palm against the steering wheel and grinned. No deal, no power play, no coup against his fiercest rival had ever given him such a rush of exhilaration.

Today, he'd moved a needle that had long been stuck.

Marco might not be in his corner, but he'd found an ally in Eileen—and wives had a lot of influence with their husbands. Whenever Isabella had taken him to task for some transgression, he'd always relented. Perhaps Eileen had the same power with his son.

And if she did, maybe he'd get to play nonno after all.

"Kelly, you are a lifesaver!"

"Don't be silly." She waved aside Lauren's comment. "I was happy to pick them up, and we had a blast. Didn't we, guys?"

Five-year-old Kevin looked up from her kitchen table, where the twins had been creating masterpieces for the past hour with some of her leftover watercolors.

"Yeah! We had cookies too, Mom!" He aimed his brush at a plate in the middle of the table, empty save for a few crumbs.

"Chocolate chip," Jack added without losing focus on the winged purple creature he was painting.

"I hope that was okay." Kelly wiped some drips of paint off the table. "They said they were hungry."

Lauren rolled her eyes. "They're *always* hungry. Come on, guys, wrap it up. We need to get moving."

"Oh, Mom, I'm almost done!" Kevin sent her a pleading look.

"Me too," Jack piped up.

"Okay. Five minutes. That's it." Lauren dumped her purse on the counter and sighed. "What a day."

"So what happened with the plea bargain that delayed you?"

"It threw a monkey wrench in our strategy. But hey . . . tomorrow's another day. Did they give you any trouble at day care? I called to let them know you were coming."

"Not a bit. I'm glad you thought to authorize me for pickup way back when, just in case."

"I'm glad you agreed. With Shaun out of town and my mom and dad on a cruise . . ."

"It was no problem. Honest."

"You're just being nice. I know this was a big distraction from your work."

"I was distracted anyway."

"Yeah? How come?"

Kelly motioned Lauren to follow her to the living room, and her friend fell in behind her. "Cole came for dinner last night."

"Business or pleasure?"

"Both. And I've got lots to tell you. You won't believe all that's happened in the past three days. I've tried to call a couple of times but you've been tied up."

"You have my full attention now." She perched on the arm of the couch. "Spill."

As Kelly updated her on the investigation—including the Wit-Sec and Mafia developments—Lauren's mouth dropped open.

"You've got to be kidding me."

"I had the same reaction. But it all fits. Cole is going up to Buffalo next week to talk to Rossi."

Lauren's expression grew skeptical. "A mob boss isn't going to admit anything, and all the evidence tying him to your father's death is circumstantial. Don't get your hopes up. Guys in his league know how to cover their tracks."

"If he was that adept at covering his tracks, he wouldn't have gone to prison."

Her friend conceded the point with a shrug. "Well, it can't hurt for your friend to pay him a visit." Lauren leaned closer. "I'm assuming Cole *is* a friend by now. Maybe more?"

"Not yet."

"'Not yet' as in things could progress in the future?"

"I would say that's a strong possibility."

"Now that's the kind of news I like to hear." Lauren grinned. "Tell me all."

"Let's just say I'm optimistic. But he told me a lot of things last night about his . . . social history . . . and his faith journey that I need to think through. You were right. He did drive in a faster lane."

"Past tense?"

"He says he's willing to downshift."

Lauren narrowed her eyes. "Do you think he's serious?"

"Yeah. I do."

"Good. Because I don't want you to get hurt."

"I'm not worried about that." Kelly slid her hands into the pockets of her jeans. "I trust him, Lauren."

"That's high praise coming from the woman whose middle name is caution."

"Hey, Mom, we're ready!" Kevin zoomed into the room, Jack on his heels, both clutching their works of art.

"Glad to hear it. I'm getting hungry. How does pizza sound tonight?"

"Yeah!" The twins spoke in unison.

"Okay. Get your coats and we'll hit the road."

Two minutes later, as Lauren hustled them out the door, she turned to Kelly. "I'll call you later. I'm still digesting everything you told me and I know I'll come up with a dozen more questions between here and the house. Unless you're having company again?"

"Not tonight. But Cole said he'd let me know how his phone call with Rossi went."

"In that case, you call *me* after you talk to him. I wouldn't want to tie up your phone line if he's trying to get through." She stepped onto the porch, watched the twins scramble into the minivan, then focused on Kelly again. "Because if your take on this guy is accurate, he could be a keeper."

Lauren didn't wait for a response. Raised voices in the van drew her attention, and with a flutter of fingers, she took off at a jog, yelling at the boys to cool it.

But long after her friend had negotiated a cease-fire and driven away, her parting words about Cole being a keeper lingered in Kelly's mind.

And based on everything she'd seen so far, Kelly could only agree.

◆

Mark Rossi inserted the key in his back door, pushed through into the kitchen, and smiled at the scene before him. Eileen was at the stove, stirring what smelled like a pot of homemade chili as she bounced Jason on her hip and sang along with an oldie on the radio. His gaze lingered on his son. After ten years of marriage, they'd given up any hope of conceiving. Yet two months after they'd begun exploring adoption options, Eileen had become pregnant.

It was a miracle.

In fact, his *life* was a miracle. He had a wonderful wife, a steady job, a nice home, and a son to love, despite the taint of his past.

Life didn't get much better than this.

As he pushed the door shut and turned the lock, Eileen swung toward him. "Hi. I didn't hear you come in."

He crossed the room and leaned down to kiss her, then pressed his lips to the top of Jason's head. "You were too busy singing. Very well, I might add."

She wrinkled her nose. "We both know better. I can't carry a tune in a bucket."

"You sounded fine to me."

"You're prejudiced."

"Yeah." He gave her a slow grin. "I am."

The soft blush he loved rose on her cheeks. "You want to wash up? Dinner's almost ready. I baked some bread too."

"Wow. What's the occasion?"

"Does there have to be one?" She busied herself at the stove, avoiding eye contact.

A tingle of uneasiness crept up his spine. The vibes in the room had shifted—or perhaps he was tuning in to ones that had already been there.

"What's up, Eileen?" He leaned against the counter, keeping his tone casual as he watched her. She didn't have a devious bone in her body. Yet she was hiding something. Her grip on Jason had tightened, and she was stirring the chili far more vigorously than necessary.

"Nothing much. It's no big deal." The tremor in her words belied that assurance.

Mark's apprehension edged up a notch. Eileen didn't get rattled. She was a placid, go-with-the-flow kind of woman. They'd agreed early on in their relationship not to keep secrets from each other, and even after he'd bared his soul, revealed his sordid background, she hadn't turned tail and run. She'd accepted his story as history, not current events, and told him they could create a new future together.

If his family circumstances hadn't freaked her out, he couldn't imagine what had happened today to distress her so much.

"Hey." He joined her at the stove, took the wooden spoon out of her hand, and grasped her shoulders, shifting her toward him. "Whatever happened, we'll get through it, okay?"

"Yeah." She swallowed. Moistened her lips. Inclined her head toward the corner of the kitchen. "I had a visitor today."

Mark glanced toward the rocking chair where Eileen often breastfed their son. A plush teddy bear in a red vest grinned back at him.

"Your father left it."

Her words slammed into him with the force of a punch in the solar plexus, driving the breath from his body. He jerked back. Groped for the counter beside him. Willed his lungs to reengage as he tried to process the implications of what Eileen had said.

But only two things registered.

His father had been at his house.

And Eileen had accepted a gift from him.

Anger exploded behind his eyes, white hot, quivering through every muscle. "I can't believe you talked to that monster! I told you to slam the door in his face if he ever showed up!" He hit the counter with his fist. Hard. Pain radiated up his arm. He didn't care. "What were you thinking? How could you do that, after everything I told you about him?" His volume rose with every sentence.

Eyes wide, his son stared up at him from her arms. Then he puckered his mouth and began to wail.

Eileen had paled during his tirade too, and now she bounced Jason in her arms, doing her best to soothe the frightened infant.

He'd scared his own child.

That was like a second punch in the gut.

He swiveled away and stalked to the kitchen window, glaring into the darkness. It took every ounce of his self-control to contain the rage burning inside him.

"Put Jason in his room. Settle him down. Then come back so we can talk." He barked out the terse command without turning around.

Behind him, he heard Eileen exit. Jason's cries receded as she traversed the short hall. Her soft words were indistinguishable as she tried to calm the baby, but he could tell they were laced with tears.

He hated that she was distressed.

Hated that they were both distressed.

All thanks to his father.

His blood pressure rose another notch.

Five minutes later he heard her shut the door to the nursery and reenter the kitchen. Too soon. He wasn't ready for rational discussion.

She seemed to sense that. A click told him she'd turned off the chili. The faucet came on. The microwave door opened . . . shut. Half a minute later, the smell of instant coffee permeated the room.

When the microwave pinged, he heard her remove the coffee. Stir in cream. A mug appeared in his field of vision, proffered by an unsteady hand.

A peace offering.

He let out a long, slow breath as he focused on the dark liquid. His anger was misdirected. Eileen wasn't to blame for what had happened today. He knew his father could be charming when he wanted something—and he wanted to be a

169

grandfather. Family was important to the Rossis. Eileen, with her willingness to give everyone the benefit of the doubt, would have been putty in the hands of such a master manipulator.

That was probably why his father had shown up while Mark was away.

But Vincentio Rossi wasn't going to win this battle.

He took the coffee, moved to the kitchen table, and sat. She slipped into the chair at a right angle to him, gripping her own mug with both hands, her face pale and taut.

A muscle clenched in his jaw, and he exhaled. "I'm sorry I yelled."

"I knew you'd be upset." Her eyelashes spiked with moisture, and she blinked. "I should have left the bear on the front porch where he set it instead of bringing it inside."

A tear trickled down her cheek. He leaned over to brush it away and twined his fingers with hers, gentling his voice. "Tell me what happened."

"I'd just gotten home with Jason. The doorbell rang. When I opened it, your father was standing there with that tucked under his arm." She gestured toward the teddy bear. "He's a lot older than the picture you showed me, but I recognized him."

She ran the index finger of her other hand around the lip of her mug and sighed. "He was very nice. Polite. Respectful. Gracious. And he looks like a typical grandfather. He mentioned health problems and said he really wants to be part of Jason's life for whatever time he has left. I guess I felt sorry for him."

Raising her head, she searched his eyes. "He said he'd abide by whatever conditions we set. He left his phone number inside the bear's vest and told me I could call him anytime." She combed her fingers through her hair and sighed. "I don't know . . . all those stories you told me about him . . . I couldn't relate them to the man on the doorstep. Maybe he's changed."

Fat chance.

Mark kept that thought to himself as he took a sip of coffee. Vincentio Rossi had conned Eileen. Played the sympathy card. He might be old, but he obviously hadn't lost his acting ability.

And that's all it was. An act. Sure, he wanted to see his grandson. Mark didn't doubt that. But as for him being a docile old man who'd left his life of violence and crime behind—Mark wasn't buying it. His father was third generation Mafia. The code was in his blood. While his years in prison might have convinced him to maintain a lower profile once he got out, he was who he'd always been: a murderous mob boss. A man's character didn't change.

But how to convince Eileen of that?

Mark set his mug on the table and looked at the woman whose quiet goodness and forgiving spirit had stolen his heart and helped him leave behind his ghastly past. He'd never wanted his family's sordid history to tarnish their life together. Had hoped he'd put all the stories about the ruthless Rossi dynasty to rest once and for all. But to make her see reason, he'd have to dredge up the ugliness all over again.

"Eileen, you know what my father is."

"Was."

"Is." He wasn't backing off from his position. "The man went to prison for racketeering and money laundering. Do you know what racketeering is? Gambling and bribery and drug trafficking and all kinds of other sleazy activities. There was plenty of evidence to suggest he'd arranged hits too, even if the authorities could never make any of those charges stick. He was in a dirty, violent business. He may never have pulled the trigger himself, but he murdered people."

She flinched, but he kept going, his voice cold. Bitter. "The man who came here today is a master at leading two lives. At home, he was a loving, churchgoing father. I didn't know anything about his other life until he was arrested. And at first, I didn't understand what had happened. I was only six, and my mother sheltered me from the media and stuck up for him. But the older I got and the more I read and the deeper I dug, the clearer it became that he was scum. To the core. And I don't want a man like that anywhere near our child."

Eileen reached over and rested her hand on his arm. "But

what if he isn't like that anymore? What if he really has changed? Is it right to so heartlessly cut him off?"

"In theory, no. You know I believe in forgiveness and second chances. But we're talking about Vincentio Rossi." He clenched his free hand on the table and his jaw tightened. "I don't believe he's changed. Or worse, that he thinks he's done anything wrong. Twenty-eight years in prison wouldn't diminish his pride in being part of the Rossi legacy."

The subtle downturn of her lips, the hint of disapproval in her eyes, told him she was disappointed in him—and that hurt. A lot. However, the resigned slump of her shoulders also told him she wouldn't fight him on this. For that, at least, he was grateful.

"What do you want to do with that?" She gestured again to the teddy bear.

His first inclination was to throw it out—but he deferred to her. "What do *you* want to do with it?"

"Keep it. For a while. We can always donate it to charity down the road."

He wanted to refuse. But Eileen asked little of him. He could offer this small concession—even if looking at the thing made him sick to his stomach.

"Not too far down the road."

"Okay." She gave him a tentative smile, squeezed his hand, and stood. "Do you want to eat dinner now?"

"Sure." No sense deferring the meal until his appetite returned.

Because it was gone for the night.

14

Cole ate the last bite of his nuked cannelloni and washed it down with a swig of soda. It wasn't bad for frozen food, but it couldn't hold a candle to the meal he'd shared with Kelly last night.

His pulse picked up, and all at once he was hungry again. For more than food.

Don't go there.

Gathering up his paper napkin and the disposable container that had held his dinner, Cole rose and threw them in the trash. He needed a distraction.

His planned post-dinner call to Rossi should do the trick.

If the man had daytime household help, they would be gone by now. And Cole hoped there was a better chance the former Mafia boss would be home in the evening than during the day. If he was lucky, he'd connect with Rossi himself and not an answering machine.

Cole took his notebook out of his pocket and flipped through to the phone number he'd jotted down at work. Then he sat on a stool at the counter and tapped the digits into his cell.

A man answered on the third ring.

"Hello?" The voice was tinged with . . . eagerness? Odd.

"Vincentio Rossi?"

Silence.

Cole tried again. "Mr. Rossi?"

"Who is asking?" The eagerness was gone, replaced by a distinct chill.

"This is Detective Cole Taylor with the Bureau of Crimes

Against Persons in St. Louis, Missouri. I'm investigating the death of a John Warren and I'd like to set up a meeting with you to discuss a few issues."

More silence. A basic intimidation tactic. Often effective in making the other party uncomfortable enough to start talking—and say too much. Cole had used it himself on occasion.

He waited Rossi out, watching the clock. Fifteen seconds passed before the man spoke again.

"I'll have my attorney contact you tomorrow, Detective."

A definitive click told Cole the conversation was over.

Rather than replace the phone in its holster, he tapped in Kelly's number. He'd promised her a report after he'd spoken with Rossi, so he had a legitimate excuse to call her. Strictly business, of course.

Yeah, right.

She, too, answered quickly, sounding a bit breathless.

"Did I take you away from something?" He sat back, elbows on the counter, enjoying the lilt of her voice.

"No. I'm just anxious to hear how your call went with Rossi."

"About like I expected. On the plus side, he answered the phone. The bad news is he's handing the matter over to his lawyer, who he promised would call me tomorrow. No surprise there, but lawyers always complicate things. My guess is I'll hear from the guy—and it *will* be a guy—five minutes before quitting time."

"Are you still planning to go up there next week?"

"Yes. I expect the lawyer will try to push us off, but I'm going to push right back."

His business was finished. He should hang up.

But he didn't.

Instead, he swiveled toward the counter and rested one elbow on the surface. "What are you up to tonight?"

"Nothing exciting. I'm going to work up a couple of bids for some clients. Repair a hem I ripped in one of my skirts. Charge the battery in my camera in case the weather warms up enough for me to get in one more research hike before temperatures fall for good. Although it will have to warm up a lot for me to venture out, since I'm a fair weather hiker. What about you?"

Cole surveyed what he could see of his apartment from his perch at the counter. An overflowing laundry basket stood by the door. Several newspapers were draped over the chairs and couch. Unopened mail took up half the dinette table. He couldn't remember when he'd last vacuumed.

He was tempted to ignore the mess and suggest Kelly meet him for coffee. But while a phone call might bend his no-social-contact rule, a coffee shop tryst would break it.

"I think I'm going to clean up around here and do some laundry."

A soft laugh came over the phone, tempting him yet again to cross the line from business to pleasure. "Don't tell me you have a stereotypical bachelor pad filled with dirty clothes, fungus-covered leftovers in the refrigerator, and piles of pizza boxes."

He cast a guilty glance at the refrigerator, wondering what lurked in the recesses. It had been a while since he'd checked. "No pizza boxes."

"An evasive—and telling—answer."

"No comment."

She chuckled again.

He needed to hang up before he caved. "So I'll call you as soon as we have the trip set up with Rossi."

"Thanks. If I don't hear from you tomorrow, have a great weekend."

"You too."

He waited until she disconnected, then slowly slipped the phone back on to his belt, thinking about the approaching weekend. His Friday night happy hours were history; they'd lost their allure. And the only person he wanted to date was Kelly.

It was going to be a long, empty two days.

"We have a problem." Vincentio pressed the pay phone closer to his ear and turned his back on the boisterous crowd in the noisy bar just beyond the foyer. It was hard to hear, but with the police nosing around, he didn't intend to use his cell for business anymore.

"What sort of problem?"

"I told you I wanted a clean operation in St. Louis. No questions asked."

"I was assured that had happened."

"The St. Louis County police just called. A detective wants to pay me a visit. He has questions."

"But . . . the case is closed."

"Not anymore. I want this fixed. Fast. Or there will be consequences. Pass that message on to our friend." He spat out the last word. "And find out what went wrong."

"I'm on it."

"He has until Thanksgiving." Vincentio slammed the phone back into the hook on the wall holder and held on to it for a moment, quivering with rage.

He did not need this. Especially now, after making inroads with Eileen mere hours ago. He'd been so hopeful when he'd left his son's house . . . That's why he'd snatched up the phone tonight, half expecting it to be her. Calling with good news.

Instead he'd found himself talking to a police detective.

If his son got even the faintest whiff of this new development, whatever chance he had of holding his grandson in his arms would die faster than a professional assassin took out a mark.

Vincentio pushed through the door into the night, head bent against the biting wind as sleet pricked his cheeks. Winter was coming to Buffalo early this year.

And perhaps to his life.

A loose piece of pavement caught the toe of his favorite Bruno Magli dress oxfords, and he lurched forward. Stumbled. Clutched at the car beside him. Stabilized.

Heart pounding, he took a few deep breaths. In the old days, he'd never stumbled—while walking or doing business. Yet it seemed he'd stumbled with Carlson. But paying a hit man to take out Walsh hadn't been a feasible option. A suspicious death would have been followed by an investigation that could potentially have turned up a link to him. The pseudo suicide had been perfect, and choosing an insider to carry it out had been brilliant.

According to the dossier Vincentio had read, Carlson had been the ideal candidate—drowning in gambling debts, desperate to keep his vice a secret, fearful he'd lose his job just as he'd lost his wife. All excellent incentives to do a stellar job. And having the man investigate his own handiwork had provided an extra measure of insurance.

But Carlson had been a bad choice, after all, as Vincentio's colleague had warned. He should have stuck with a pro. A man who wouldn't make mistakes. Let things slip through the cracks.

The sleet intensified, and Vincentio continued toward his Lexus, his lips pressed into a grim line as he skirted the dangerous, icy patches that had begun to form.

This time there would be no mistakes.

Or any loose ends.

A persistent, vibrating buzz close to his ear penetrated Alan Carlson's sleep-fogged brain, and he groped on his nightstand for his cell phone, eyes still closed. Bad timing for a break in the double homicide case. He hadn't gone to bed until well after midnight, thanks to his late-night drop for Freddie.

Pressing the talk button, he mumbled a greeting.

"You messed up."

His eyes flew open, and he bolted upright in bed, adrenaline surging. He didn't have to ask who was on the line. He'd been expecting this call.

But getting it in the middle of the night was not a good omen.

"I can fix it."

"How?"

"A suicide note is being prepared. I'll plant it next week, if necessary."

A few beats of silence ticked by.

177

Alan started to sweat.

"Isn't it a little late for that?"

"I can make it work."

The man's silence conveyed his skepticism.

A bead of sweat rolled down Alan's forehead. He tipped his head and rubbed it off with the sleeve of his T-shirt.

"The boss wants to know what happened."

Alan transferred the phone to his other hand and wiped his damp palm on the sheet. "The daughter got a gift from her father that he'd ordered the day before he died. The note inside convinced her he hadn't been planning suicide. I was on vacation and another detective advised her to search her father's house. She found some stuff that raised questions—including a photo with her father's real name. It didn't take long after that for my colleague to connect him to your boss."

"Bad luck."

"Yeah." All the way around. "But there's no connection between him—or me—and her father's death. You paid me in cash. I paid off my debts the same way, or with cashier's checks. I didn't make any big deposits in my bank accounts. We're clean."

"Then why are the police coming to call?"

"They're fishing."

"The boss doesn't like that sport. He prefers hardball."

A trickle of sweat seeped into the corner of Alan's mouth, leaving the acrid taste of salt on his tongue. "It's riskier trying to fix things. I guarantee the police aren't going to find any links. Patience will work to our advantage."

"The boss isn't a patient man, and he doesn't like to be hassled by law enforcement types. You want the rest of your money, you fix this. Fast. You've got one more chance to make it right. Remember that message you passed on to your mark?"

The two sentences he'd been told to relay to John Warren as the man's consciousness ebbed were burned into Alan's mind—along with the look of dull shock in Warren's eyes as he'd spoken them.

I always said I'd find you. My condolences on the death of your brother.

"Yeah. I remember."

"This doesn't get fixed before Thanksgiving, the condolences will be for you next time. I'll be in touch."

A quiet click told Alan the connection had been severed.

Just as his life would be if he didn't get the heat off Rossi.

Hands shaking, he pushed the end button. Rose on unsteady legs. Started to pace.

Freddie had promised him the letter by Monday night. The drop was already arranged, and the man would come through. No worries there.

Planting it, however, was a different story. He still hadn't come up with a plan to get it in Kelly's hands without arousing further suspicion.

He prowled around his bedroom, shivering as the cool air hit his sweat-soaked T-shirt. Maybe he'd pay a visit to Warren's house this weekend. Nose around a little. The security system wouldn't be a problem. He'd met Kelly there a couple of times during the investigation for the express purpose of watching her punch in the deactivation code, and he'd memorized it . . . just in case. She'd also given him a key to the house during the investigation, which he'd had duplicated.

Details. He was a master of details. That's why he was such a good detective. Why he'd excelled at undercover work. And he always thought ahead. Prepared for contingencies. Had an exit plan for dicey situations.

But this was the diciest situation he'd ever encountered.

He headed for the kitchen, desperate for a cup of coffee, noting the time on the hall clock as he passed. Three-fifteen. The night was half over. It probably wasn't smart to drink caffeine at this hour.

Then again, what did it matter?

Caffeine or no caffeine, there would be no more sleep this night.

At ten minutes to five on Friday, Cole's phone rang. Long distance from Buffalo, according to caller ID.

Rossi's attorney. Waiting until the last minute, as Cole had expected.

He picked up the desk phone. "Detective Taylor."

"This is Thomas Lake, Vincentio Rossi's attorney. I understand you want to speak with him regarding the death of a John Warren?"

"That's right. At his earliest convenience. We'll be happy to come to his home or meet him at a nearby precinct station."

"What do you want to discuss?"

"We have reason to believe John Warren was really James Walsh, a former employee of Mr. Rossi who was a key witness against him in the trial that sent your client to prison. We'd like to discuss the case with Mr. Rossi."

"Have you found a link between my client and your case?"

"We're in the early stage of this investigation."

Cole held his breath following that nonspecific answer. Rossi could refuse to meet with him, but that would raise suspicions. If his attorney was smart, he'd advise the man to cooperate. And Cole assumed a man like Rossi bought the best of everything—including attorneys.

That assumption was confirmed a few seconds later.

"I'm sure Mr. Rossi will be glad to assist with your investigation. How does Wednesday morning look for you?"

The day before Thanksgiving. It figured. Air travel would be a nightmare.

"That will be fine." He kept his inflection neutral.

"Let me get back to you with a specific time. I'm certain my client will prefer to meet in his residence."

That was one piece of positive news, anyway. It was amazing how much you could pick up about a person from their home-turf surroundings.

"I'll be coming with another detective. I'd appreciate the

time as soon as you have it. Let me give you my cell number so you can call me with that information this weekend."

After Lake took the number and ended the call, Cole depressed the switch hook and dialed Mitch's cell to give him a heads-up about the travel plans. After three rings, it rolled to voice mail and he left a message.

Then he started checking flight availability. As he'd expected, pickings were slim. The best he could do was a connecting red-eye into Buffalo, leaving late Tuesday night. Coming back also required a connection, but at least they'd get home by six o'clock.

He tried Kelly next, to give her the promised update, but her phone, too, rolled to voice mail. He thought about calling again later, when he might reach her in person, but ended up leaving a message. Now that the case was heating up, it would be safer to keep his distance until things were resolved.

But with each day that passed, it was getting harder and harder to follow his self-imposed rule.

"So did you forget my phone number or what?"

Bleary-eyed, Cole shifted the phone against his ear and squinted at his bedside clock. Nine o'clock. That qualified as sleeping in for him. But since he'd stayed up late watching a movie and then spent a restless night staring at the dark ceiling and thinking about Kelly, he wasn't too happy about being rudely awakened on Saturday morning by his sister.

"I've been busy." He flopped onto his back and stifled a yawn.

"Avoiding me is more like it."

He closed his eyes. He wasn't up for one of Alison's grillings. Not without a cup of coffee first.

"You're afraid I'll ask about Kelly, aren't you?"

Make that a pot.

"What do you want to know?" Maybe he could throw her off by tossing her a few nuggets.

"Seriously?"

"Yeah. Why not?"

"Mitch says you're smitten."

Cole narrowed his eyes. His so-called buddy was going to hear about *that* on Monday. "That might be pushing it."

"But you like her, right?"

"Sure. What's not to like? She's pretty, smart, fun to be with, a great cook, and she goes to church every Sunday. The whole package."

Silence.

"How come you answered that question?" Alison sounded thrown by his candor.

Good.

He grinned and stretched. "My life is an open book."

"Since when?"

"Maybe I'm turning over a new leaf." He swung his legs to the floor and padded toward the kitchen to start that coffee. "Want to know anything else?"

"Are you dating her?"

"Not yet. It wouldn't be professional."

"Meaning you plan to ask her out once the case is closed?"

"If the lady's interested."

"Do you think she is?"

"Yep."

More silence.

"What's with you today, anyway? Usually it's like pulling teeth to get you to open up."

"Are you complaining?" He pulled a can of coffee out of the refrigerator.

"No. Just trying to decide if I have my real brother on the phone, or if some alien has snatched your body."

"Cute. Anything else you want to know?"

"Not on that subject. But I did want to ask if you'd like to join Mitch and me for church tomorrow."

Cole shook some coffee into the filter, slid it into the coffee-maker, and carried the carafe over to the sink. Why not? He'd been thinking about going back, and he didn't have anything else to do this weekend.

"Sure."

In the brief silence that followed, he pictured her mouth dropping open.

"Should I attribute this change of heart to your new romantic interest?"

"Partly. She got me thinking about some things I should have addressed long ago."

This was one topic he didn't intend to expand on. And he was glad Alison had sense enough not to push her luck by pressing for details.

"Well, whatever the reason, that's great news. Want us to pick you up?"

"No. I'll meet you there. Ten o'clock service?" He filled the carafe with water.

"Yes. So what else are you going to do this weekend?"

A quick scan of the apartment reminded him he still hadn't tended to housekeeping duties. "Clean up a little around here."

"Not a bad idea. Last time I stopped by, your apartment was a sty."

"Thanks a lot. I'm hanging up now."

"Wait . . . did you order the pies for Thanksgiving?"

"I said I would, didn't I?" He'd add that to his to-do list for the weekend too.

"That means you forgot. You can't fool me with evasive answers, Cole. I lived with you for years, remember?"

"Good-bye, Alison."

Her throaty chuckle came over the line. "See you at church."

As he hung up and poured the pot of water into the coffeemaker, Cole reviewed his agenda for the next two days. Church, housecleaning, pie ordering. His weekend wouldn't be so empty after all.

But he'd much rather be spending the day with Kelly than washing socks.

15

He was in.

Standing beside the table in John Warren's kitchen, Alan flexed his latex-gloved fingers and readjusted the black balaclava that covered his head and most of his face. Gaining entry had been a breeze. But at this predawn hour on a Sunday morning, he'd prefer to be sleeping—not revisiting the scene of the crime.

That was for amateurs.

Thanks to those stupid tulip bulbs, however, he'd been forced to take unnecessary risks.

With a snort of disgust, Alan walked toward the living room, his smooth-soled shoes quiet on the oak floor. Instead of issuing threats, Rossi should be thanking him—and paying up. Despite the glitch, all the "evidence" Taylor had turned up was circumstantial. And none of it was from the crime itself. Nor would his colleague find any. The job had been well planned and perfectly executed. The wise course would be to let things rest, as he'd told his contact in the middle of Friday night. Eventually, the investigation would fizzle out and die.

Except Rossi didn't want to wait. Or deal with the police. And thanks to recent developments, the mob boss probably thought the man he'd hired to carry out his vendetta had made mistakes. Overlooked something.

But Alan hadn't done either. The job had been clean. His only slipup had been overreacting to Kelly's persistence, but there was nothing to tie the peanut incident to him or Rossi, either.

Alan paused in the living room, beside the couch where he'd sat on his two visits with John Warren. One to scope out the place and create a comfort level. The second to do the job. He'd used that technique a lot in his undercover work. It had worked on the street, and it had worked here. But only because he'd done his homework.

Like finding the right neighbor to be his unwitting accomplice.

The hint of a smile twitched at his lips. Sheila Waters had plied him with brownies and iced tea on his first visit to the neighborhood, when he'd stopped in to talk with her while investigating the robbery at a house down the street that he'd committed himself as an excuse to do some reconnaissance. She'd given him the idea of showing up with brownies at Warren's house two weeks later, when a second—nonexistent—crime had needed investigating.

Alan bent and rubbed a gloved finger over the faint stain on the walnut coffee table, a souvenir of the maneuver that had bought him the time to spike Warren's lemonade with two generous shots of Russian Standard vodka. Twenty-five bucks a bottle, but worth every penny. His research had indicated it went down sweet and smooth, without the burn on the tongue or throat produced by harsh, cheaper versions—making it the perfect liquor to add to a glass of iced tea or lemonade. Tasteless but potent—especially when mixed with a strong sleeping pill. And easy to dump into Warren's drink after Alan spilled his and the man went to get him a refill.

He traced the stain once more and stood. The whole operation had been easy. Almost too easy. Generic Ambien was plentiful on the black market, and getting Warren to ingest the innocuous-flavored sedative had been no problem. It was a simple matter of grinding up the pills, adding them to a boxed brownie mix, and playing Betty Crocker.

Alan's smile broadened. It had been a beautiful plan. He'd shown up here that evening carrying three of the laced bars—and one that was drug-free—to ask a few questions about the latest neighborhood robbery. He'd told Warren that Sheila had insisted he take a few when he'd stopped in to talk with her, and gone on to say they were making him hungry, since he'd worked through dinner. As he'd expected based on the man's previous hospitality, Warren had told him to eat a couple while they talked, and even offered him a drink. Alan had agreed— but only if Warren joined him.

It had been an easy sell.

Two brownies and two shots of vodka later, Warren had staggered as he rose to show his visitor out. Alan had helped him back to his chair and gone to the kitchen to get him a glass of water—to which he'd added a third shot of vodka.

Once Warren's dizziness had worsened, Alan hadn't had any problem convincing him he needed to go to the ER. And with his daughter out of town—a fact Warren had mentioned on his first visit, and the reason Alan had chosen this night to carry out his plan—he'd offered to drive him there. But since he'd parked at the end of the block, he'd suggested they take Warren's car to save time.

As the events of that night replayed in his mind, Alan returned to the kitchen and opened the door that led to the shadowy garage. The man's car was gone now. No surprise there. Kelly had said she was going to sell the instrument of death, as she'd called it, as soon as possible. Otherwise, the garage looked the same. It had been dark then too, as he'd helped Warren out, settled him in the passenger seat, and started the engine. On the excuse he'd forgotten his jacket in the house, he'd retreated to the kitchen—leaving both car doors open.

Fifteen minutes later, the man had been disoriented and barely conscious. He hadn't even realized what was going on when Alan helped him out of the older-model car, moved him to the rear of the vehicle, and eased him to the floor beside the tailpipe. After he'd propped him with his back against the wall, he'd squatted down to deliver Rossi's message.

Warren had stared at him, his unfocused eyes at first confused. And then, as a glimmer of understanding dawned, the color had drained from his complexion. He'd tried to push

Alan away, to stand, but in his condition, it took no more than gentle pressure against his chest to keep him in place.

Alan's smile faded. That part had been unpleasant. It had made the killing seem too real. Though it took mere minutes for the man's eyelids to drift closed and his feeble struggles to stop, it had felt like hours.

The rest had been easy. He'd slipped on a pair of latex gloves. Wiped down the few objects he'd touched during his visit. Drained three beer cans in the sink. He'd also poured out half of the beer from another can and returned to the garage to set that can, plus the unmarked bottle of pills, beside Warren—after pressing the man's fingers against them. He'd done the same maneuver with the empty beer cans before tossing them in the kitchen garbage container for the Crime Scene Unit to find.

A faint, irregular pulse had still beat against his fingers when he'd checked the man's carotid artery, so he'd gone back to the living room. Waited twenty minutes. Checked again.

There had been no discernable heartbeat.

Just as he'd done on that May night six months ago, Alan took one more scan of the dark garage where Warren had died, shut the door, and turned away. But he'd felt more confident back then. More certain he'd pulled off the perfect crime. And with Warren's daughter out of town, the odds had been in his favor no one would discover the man until at least the next day.

No one had, either. The call had come through about noon on his police radio, and he'd been on the phone with his boss immediately, volunteering to handle it since he "happened" to be in the area.

Alan returned to the living room. Funny, being a man who had sworn to uphold the law and protect the citizens, how he'd never felt any remorse about taking a life . . . but Warren had been dying anyway. All Alan had done was hurry the process along. And in doing so, he'd given himself a fresh start financially—plus a second chance with his wife. He'd finished the job with a sense of relief, not regret.

But tangling with the Mafia had turned that relief into apprehension.

Reminding himself to focus on the task at hand, Alan crossed to the hall. Light was beginning to seep around the edges of the window shades, and he didn't want to be here in broad daylight. Kelly would be going to church, as she always did on Sunday, but there was no sense lingering. He needed to find a spot to plant the letter. One that wouldn't raise suspicions, make her wonder why she—and the Crime Scene Unit—had missed it before.

Eight minutes later, after a quick sweep of the house, Alan concluded from the state of disarray in Warren's office and bedroom that Kelly had focused her search in those areas. The second bedroom appeared to be untouched, as did the basement. If Warren had left a letter, however, there was little chance he'd have put it in either of those places. Suicide notes were typically left in obvious locations. On a desk. A kitchen table. The body itself. Had a note been in any of those places, however, the crime scene tech or the investigator from the medical examiner's office would have found it.

Passing Warren's office, Alan jerked to a stop at a sudden shift in the shadow on the wall across from the doorway. Adrenaline surging, he reached for the off-duty Beretta in his concealed holster. Stopped as the shadow shifted again and he identified the source.

A wind-tossed tree limb, backlit by the rising sun.

As his pulse slowed to normal, an idea began to germinate. He reentered Warren's office, crossed to the window at a right angle to the desk, and tipped the shade. There was enough light outside now for him to confirm the presence of several large maple trees in the backyard, one close to the house. He knew about maples from the two in the yard of the house he and Cindy had shared. Thanks to their brittle wood, which made them susceptible to wind damage, he'd often made a circuit of the yard after storms, collecting downed limbs.

He squinted at the maple closest to the house. Meteorologists were predicting a major storm for this week. A first, icy blast of winter. Trees shed limbs in storms like that, and limbs broke windows—whether ripped off by Mother Nature or pulled down with a rope. Fixing this particular window would require moving the heavy wooden desk, and that might reveal all kinds of things. Stray paperclips. Coins. Post-it notes.

A single sheet of paper that a breeze had nudged off the back of the desk the night Warren died.

A breeze from the open window he'd noted on his report.

The ghost of a smile curved his lips.

It was perfect.

Or as perfect as he was likely to get in the short time frame Rossi had allotted him to complete the job.

All at once a ray of the rising sun darted through the narrow strip between the edge of the shade and the window frame. His cue to leave.

He returned to the kitchen, punched in Warren's security code next to the back door, and slipped out. While the privacy hedges rimming the yard provided excellent cover, as did the common ground in back, there was no reason to delay. He had his plan now.

But as he locked the door behind him, he hoped Rossi would give him enough time to carry it out under optimal conditions.

"Hey . . . isn't that your favorite redhead?" Mitch tilted his head toward the back of the restaurant as Cole took his seat.

"Where?" Alison craned her neck as she claimed the chair beside her brother.

"How is it your love life always takes center stage on our after-church brunch outings?" Liz picked up her napkin and draped it over her lap, grinning at her brother-in-law.

"I wish I knew." Cole shot Mitch an annoyed look. Nevertheless, he checked out the direction his colleague had indicated.

Yep. That was Kelly at a table in the far corner. She was angled away from him, but he'd recognize that hair anywhere. Besides, she was with Lauren. The man at the table, flanked by two little boys who appeared to be twins, must be her best friend's husband.

He allowed himself a few more seconds to enjoy the play of light on her russet hair, then settled back in his chair. Much as he'd wanted to see her this weekend, this wasn't the place.

Not in light of his present company.

Too bad the Taylor clan had switched a few months ago from every-other-Sunday dinner gatherings to weekly brunch.

Alison nudged him with her elbow. "Is that her?"

He picked up his menu. "Yes."

"Aren't you going to go over and say hello?"

"No."

"Why not?"

"She's with friends. I don't want to interrupt."

His sister huffed out a breath. "You're just afraid you'll have to introduce her to us."

He didn't respond.

Jake grinned and took a sip of water. "Do you blame him, Alison? Everyone at this table except you is trained to give the third degree. And you've mastered the technique on your own."

"Very funny." She made a face at her older brother and picked up her own menu, casting one more glance over Cole's shoulder toward the table on the other side of the room. "It doesn't matter, anyway. They're leaving."

Without stopping to think, Cole instinctively turned to catch one more glimpse of Kelly

And that was his downfall.

Because once their gazes connected, ignoring her—and insulating her from his inquisitive family—was no longer an option.

"Hey . . . there's your favorite detective!"

Kelly's step faltered as she and Lauren followed Shaun, a twin's hand in each of his, toward the exit of the restaurant. It was Cole, all right. But he didn't seem at all pleased to see her as he lifted a hand in greeting. His lips barely tipped up.

Disconcerted by his reaction, she returned his acknowledgment and picked up her pace.

"Kelly!" Lauren caught up and took her arm, tugging her to a stop near the foyer. "Aren't you going to say hello?"

"He's with friends." Two women and three men, to be exact. She'd taken a quick inventory of the table.

"I think he counts you in that group." Lauren looked past her with a smug twist of her lips. "Otherwise he wouldn't be coming over."

Doing her best to ignore the blip in her heart, Kelly turned toward him.

"Hi, Kelly. Lauren." He stopped a couple of feet in front of them and smiled. A real smile. Warm and welcoming . . . and it lingered on her.

That was more like it.

"Hi. What a surprise to see you here." Lauren motioned for the tall man with the twins to rejoin them and continued to chat, giving Kelly a chance to appreciate the gray tweed sport jacket that emphasized Cole's broad shoulders and the same blue tie he'd worn the day they met. The one that matched his eyes.

Too bad she hadn't chosen attire a little more flattering than a plain black skirt and simple sweater.

"We were just treating Kelly to a pre-Thanksgiving brunch, since Shaun and I are off to Columbus for the holiday. Otherwise we'd have her over for dinner, this being her first Thanksgiving alone and all."

At Lauren's emphasis on the word *alone*, Kelly tuned back in to the conversation. "I won't be alone, Lauren. You know I'm—"

"Hey! That's my candy!" Kevin yanked the wrapped mint out of Jack's hand.

"Is not!" Jack tried to grab it back.

"Whoa!" Shaun broke up the disagreement by stepping between them. "Time to leave." He smiled at Cole and extended his hand. "Nice to meet you. Lauren, we'll see you in the car."

"I'm right behind you. And you two . . ." She leaned down to the twins' level. "Behave!"

191

They dipped their heads, chastised for the moment, but Kelly was certain the dispute would erupt again once they were out of the restaurant. Jack was still eyeing the mint clutched in Kevin's hand.

Rising, Lauren shot them an apologetic look. "Sorry. One of these days they'll turn into civilized little creatures."

Cole grinned. "Don't count on it. My sister claims little boys never grow up."

"Don't tell me that!" She rolled her eyes, then leaned over to hug Kelly, dropping her voice. "Call me later, okay?"

Kelly hugged her back, whispering close to her ear. "If there's anything to report."

"There will be."

With that, Lauren released her, gave a final flutter of fingers, and took off toward the exit with her usual long-legged purposeful stride.

"So . . ." Kelly shifted out of the path of a tray-laden waiter, trying to dredge up some small talk. "Are you having a nice weekend?" As soon as the words were out, she cringed. Talk about pathetic.

But Cole's comeback wasn't. "I am now."

A rush of pleasure swept over her. That smooth response might be a standard male line, but it wasn't one that had been used on her very often.

Like never.

The only problem was, it once again left her at a loss for words.

As if sensing her discomfiture, Cole hooked a thumb over his shoulder, toward the table behind him. "Would you like to join us? Maybe have a final cup of coffee? I'm with my brother, Jake, and his wife, Liz. Mitch is the detective who'll be going with me to visit Rossi in Buffalo, and the woman with the light brown hair who's probably giving you the once-over is his fiancée—my sister, Alison."

Kelly checked out the table. Three of the four occupants were conversing, their perusal of her discreet, but Alison was displaying unabashed interest in her exchange with Cole. When she realized Kelly was looking her way, she didn't seem in the least self-conscious. Instead, she smiled and lifted her hand in a friendly gesture.

"Your sister's waving at me."

He expelled a long breath. "That figures. She's dying to meet you. Expect to be cross-examined if you join us, but I'll deflect her questions if she gets too pushy."

Kelly grinned. "I appreciate the offer. But I think I can handle her."

"Yeah?" He studied her. "Maybe. She's a lot more blunt with family members than with strangers. So do you want to join us for a few minutes?"

Meet Cole's family or spend the rest of the day alone.

No contest.

"Sure."

He took her arm, the gesture no more than politeness, but she liked his confident touch as he guided her through the maze of diners. The two men at the table stood, and Jake signaled a waiter. By the time she and Cole arrived, an extra chair had been added—between Cole and Alison, at his sister's direction.

Once the introductions were finished and Kelly and the men took their seats, Alison jumped in.

"We've heard a little about you, Kelly, but not enough. Cole can be a clam when it suits him. You're an artist, right?"

"You want to give her a chance to get her coffee before you start the inquisition?" Cole arched an eyebrow at his sister.

She shot him a disgruntled look. "This isn't an inquisition."

"Keep it that way."

Stifling a smile, Kelly turned to Alison. "Yes, I'm a watercolor artist. As for Cole being reticent, I haven't seen that. He's told me a *lot* about you." She caught Cole's grin in her peripheral vision.

Alison narrowed her eyes at her brother. "I'll bet."

"I think you're busted, Alison." Jake grinned at her across the table, draped an arm around Liz's shoulders, and spoke to

Kelly. "Our sister is the curious type—and she takes a special interest in her brothers' personal lives."

"You guys make me sound like a meddler."

"If the shoe fits . . ." Cole picked up his coffee and took a sip.

"You know . . . you three are going to give Kelly an entirely wrong impression." Jake's wife cast an amused glance at her husband and his siblings. "The truth is, despite their bickering and complaining, the Taylors are a close-knit clan."

Kelly smiled at the blonde-haired woman. "I already figured that out. And I must admit I envy all of you." She encompassed the three Taylors with a sweeping scan. "I always wished I had brothers and sisters. Or an extended family. Especially on holidays."

A bittersweet pang echoed in her heart as she thought about all the holidays it had been just her and her dad—and all the holidays to come, without him. She was glad the waiter arrived with the food orders, interrupting the conversation. She was also grateful Alison responded with a lighthearted comment once they'd been served.

"Well, I can vouch for the fact that Christmas morning in the Taylor household was a free-for-all. Thanks to two brothers who always raced to see who could rip open their presents the fastest." She spread some jam on her English muffin and took a bite.

"Maybe," Jake conceded. "But we humored *you* on Halloween long after we were too old to go trick-or-treating. Remember the year she conned us into dressing like Tweedledee and Tweedledum so she could be Alice in Wonderland?" He aimed a grimace at Cole.

"I've tried to forget it." Cole cut off a bite of his eggs Benedict and pointed his fork at Alison. "I think you still owe us for that one."

"Repaid many times over in lasagna dinners." Alison dismissed the claim with a breezy wave of her hand. "So what are your plans for Thanksgiving, Kelly?"

She managed to hold on to her smile. "Church in the morning, and later in the day I volunteered to help serve dinner at a homeless shelter."

"Wow." Alison stopped eating. "That's a really generous thing to do."

No, it wasn't. Kelly wished her motives were more altruistic, but the truth of it was she hadn't been in the mood to accept any of the invitations from members of her congregation, gracious as they were. If she did, she'd have to smile and laugh and make small talk through the whole meal. That would take far too much effort. And if she stayed home, she'd end up sitting around feeling sorry for herself.

"It's no big deal." She took a sip of her coffee and dismissed Alison's praise with a lift of her shoulders. "A lot of people do a lot more."

"All we're going to do is sit around and stuff our faces at Jake's." Alison toyed with a bite of her omelet and gave Kelly a speculative look. "What time are you serving?"

"One to four."

Her face lit up. "Perfect. Why don't you join us for dinner after you're finished? Mitch's dad is coming too, and our mom and aunt. We're not eating until five, so you could make it. We can feed one more, can't we, Liz?"

"No problem."

Too surprised to respond at once, Kelly risked a peek at Cole. He'd stopped eating, fork poised halfway to his mouth, and was staring at his sister. Obviously as taken aback by the invitation as she was.

Knowing his feelings about mixing business and pleasure, Kelly jumped in. "I appreciate the offer, but after inhaling the aroma of turkey for three hours, I think I'll just go home, put up my feet, and have a pizza."

"Pizza on Thanksgiving! Cole, convince her to come." Alison leaned across Kelly and jabbed her brother in the shoulder.

He lowered his fork to his plate without eating the bite of eggs Benedict. "You'd be welcome, Kelly."

There was warmth in his voice—but the conflict in his eyes

convinced her to hold her ground. "I appreciate that, but by four o'clock I have a feeling I'll be ready to call it a day."

He didn't push her—much to Alison's disgust, if the disgruntled frown she lobbed at her brother was any indication.

Kelly stayed another fifteen minutes. She answered some of Alison's questions, artfully deflected others. She chatted with Jake and Liz, listened to a SEAL story from Mitch. Then she drained her coffee and picked up her purse.

"I've infringed enough on your family get-together, and I have some errands to run. I hope you all have a lovely holiday."

She stood, and Cole rose too. As did the other two men. No lack of manners in this group.

"You're not infringing, Kelly. We've enjoyed meeting you." Alison smiled up at her.

"Thank you." Despite Cole's warnings, she'd found Alison down-to-earth, engaging, and fun to talk with. Much like Lauren. The kind of woman who would make a good friend. And maybe that could happen—if things progressed between her and Cole down the road.

"I'll walk you to your car."

She considered the tall detective beside her. Another display of polished manners—or something more?

"That isn't necessary. Your food will get cold."

"Yeah, but his heart will be warm." Alison smirked at her brother.

Cole's neck grew ruddy as he took Kelly's arm. "Eat your omelet, Alison."

She gave him a mock salute. "Aye, aye, sir."

After a flurry of good-byes, Cole escorted her through the maze of tables with a muttered, "Sisters."

"I like Alison. She's interested in everything."

"Including her brothers' personal lives, as Jake pointed out." Cole pushed through the outside door, into a gust of cold wind. "You'd think she'd back off a little on mine now that I'm going to church again."

Kelly stopped in the middle of the parking lot, buttoning

her wool jacket against the chill as she swung toward him. "When did that happen?"

He shrugged and shoved his hands into the pockets of his slacks. "This morning. It was time."

"So your sister's prodding paid off."

"No. If anyone can take credit for the prodigal's return, it's you. Our conversation last week gave me a different perspective on what happened with Sara."

At the staccato beep of a car horn, Cole took her arm again and guided her out of the path of traffic.

"I'm over there." She gestured toward her Focus, parked three cars down.

They completed the walk in silence as she mulled over this new development, rummaged for her keys, and hit the remote. He opened the door, and she tossed her purse onto the passenger seat, then swiveled back toward him.

He propped a shoulder against the car. "And for the record—there's nothing I'd like more than to have you join my family for Thanksgiving. But I'd rather keep things professional until we wrap up your dad's case. Assuming that happens soon, though, I'd like to celebrate the next big holiday with you."

Christmas with Cole.

Now that was something to look forward to.

"I'd like that too."

"Consider it a date." Smiling, he pushed off from the car, waited while she slid inside, and closed the door.

She pulled away, keeping his image in the rearview mirror as long as possible, and her own lips curved up. Lauren had been right.

There *was* news to report from her impromptu coffee date with Cole's family.

And it was all positive.

16

Marco hadn't called. Neither had Eileen.

And Vincentio was beginning to lose hope they would.

He drummed a finger against the steering wheel and surveyed the house he'd visited four days ago. His son was the problem. No question about that. Eileen had been touched by his plea. If it was up to her, he'd already have a date with his grandson.

But Marco was a true Rossi when it came to holding grudges. To getting even. Too bad he'd shunned the family business. He'd have made an excellent don.

With a sigh, Vincentio turned the key in the ignition. Sitting here wishing wasn't going to change his son's mind. Besides, based on the information provided by his source, Eileen got home earlier than usual from school on Monday, and he didn't want her to find him lurking in front of the house. That wouldn't help his case. Better to lay low. Give her some time to work on Marco—and hope his son's heart would soften.

In the old days, he might even have prayed for that favor. After all, attending church every Sunday had been part of the Rossi legacy. But it had been a tradition, nothing more, and he doubted God would be inclined to grant requests from unrepentant souls like him.

The corners of his lips ticked up as he shifted the car into gear. He and God were alike in that regard, both extracting a price from those who did wrong and showed no remorse. Examples of vengeance from on high were all over the Bible.

Too bad God wasn't on his side, though. He could use some divine intervention with his ill-timed police interview too. As it was, he'd have to put his fate in the hands of Thomas Lake, whom he was scheduled to see in—he checked his watch—forty-five minutes.

Vincentio eased away from the curb. It was a shame the boy's father had died six years ago. Walter had been smart. Savvy. Skilled. His son had seemed sharp enough the few times they'd talked, but the younger man didn't know his history like Walter had. Or have his father's experience.

Still, this should be a simple matter. When he'd been hired for the job, Carlson had had no idea who'd employed him, so there couldn't be any evidence to link the two of them. Nor was there any now. If Carlson had made mistakes, he was the one in the hot seat. And if he *did* get caught and tried to finger his employer, there was no proof.

But the whole thing was an aggravation.

Expelling an annoyed breath, Vincentio drove slowly past the house where his son and daughter-in-law and grandson would be celebrating Thanksgiving in three days while he sat home alone. He'd give five years of his life to be with them for the holiday, to be welcomed at their table.

Perhaps this delay was for the best, though. It would give him a chance to clear up his little problem. And if he was smart, Carlson would be working very, very hard to erase any doubt about the cause of Walsh's death.

Because this whole mess was his fault.

Vincentio's fingers tightened on the wheel. He didn't blame the detective for the tulip note. That was a freak coincidence. But he should have stuck close to his desk, just in case there were any unexpected glitches. Instead, according to the information his contact had provided, he'd missed the daughter's visit—and his opportunity to convince her the note wasn't worth investigating—because he'd taken a vacation shortly after putting the case to bed.

That had been unprofessional. And Vincentio had no respect for amateurs—especially ones whose lack of foresight and planning could destroy his hope of a relationship with his grandson.

And that would be the outcome if Marco got wind of this.

Fifty feet ahead of him, the stoplight at the intersection changed from yellow to red. Somehow he'd missed the green-to-yellow transition.

Smashing the brake pedal to the floor, he braced himself as the car skidded to a halt behind an SUV with mere inches to spare.

Heart hammering, he sucked in a deep breath. That had been close. Too close.

And he didn't like close calls. Behind the wheel—or in business.

By the time the light changed to green, his pulse had slowed. But thanks to Carlson's botched job, his nerves were still vibrating. As they would continue to do until the man got the heat off of him.

He had a powerful incentive to make that happen too. Carlson knew Vincentio Rossi didn't tolerate failure. Mistakes brought consequences, as he'd instructed his contact to tell the detective.

And they weren't pretty.

"Cole! Wait up!"

At Mitch's summon, Cole turned, his hand on the door that led to the detective unit's waiting room.

"Cutting out early?" Mitch grinned as he joined him.

"I wish. Sarge asked me to deal with a domestic violence situation before I call it a day."

"Not the best way to end a Monday."

"Tell me about it."

"I wanted to check on the flight time tomorrow. Alison and I were hoping to get together for dinner first."

"Forget it. The flight leaves at seven. We can grab a burger en route to the airport, eat there, or scrounge up a meal during our two-and-a-half-hour layover in Chicago."

"What time do we get into Buffalo?"

"Two in the morning. And our meeting with Rossi is at eight."

Mitch shot him a disgruntled look. "I bet we're on puddle jumpers too."

"I took what I could get." Cole shifted aside to let another detective exit. "Open seats less than a week before Thanksgiving are as scarce as clues in Alan's double homicide case. You want to leave your car here and drive together?"

"I guess." Mitch shoved his hands into his pockets. "Maybe Alison can meet me for lunch."

"You saw her Sunday, and you're going to be with her all day Thursday. What's the urgency?"

"It's called attraction. You know . . . like what you feel for Kelly—only stronger."

The ribbing from his colleague didn't sit well with Cole. "Speaking of my sister, I have a bone to pick with you. She says you told her I was smitten."

Mitch's ears reddened. "I don't recall using that exact term. She must have come to her own conclusions after she grilled me about the two of you."

"I thought SEALs were trained to hold up under interrogation."

One side of Mitch's mouth hitched up. "Not the kind Alison dishes out. Let's just say she has a very persuasive technique." He wiggled his eyebrows.

"Hey. We're talking about my sister here. I don't want to hear this." Cole pushed the door open and called over his shoulder. "See you tomorrow."

Mitch's chuckle followed him as he crossed the pavement toward his car, and his lips twitched. He was glad Alison had found someone like Mitch. His colleague was a lot more worthy of her than that jerk of a Legal Aid attorney she'd been serious about, who'd walked out on her after the accident that had almost taken her life. And he'd never seen his sister happier.

It would be nice to find a little of that kind of happiness himself. And maybe, after the Warren case was put to rest once and for all, he might follow in his siblings' footsteps. Because though he hadn't admitted it to Mitch, Alison's assessment of his feelings for Kelly were accurate.

He was, indeed, smitten.

"Can I offer you a beverage?" Thomas Lake gestured to a chair at the round conference table in his office.

"No, thank you." Vincentio took a seat. Not the one the attorney had indicated. He was in charge here, and Lake needed to know that. "Let's just get this over with. What do you need from me?"

The fortysomething man retrieved a leather notebook from his desk, picked up a Mont Blanc pen, and sat in the chair beside him. "I've reviewed your file, and I have one main question. Do we have anything to worry about?" He pinned him with an intimidating look designed to ferret out the truth.

It probably worked on most people.

Vincentio wasn't one of them.

No one intimidated a Rossi.

He stared back. "You tell me."

Lake held his gaze for a few seconds, then broke eye contact. Excellent. The pecking order had been established.

"Mr. Rossi, I'm sure you know that attorney-client privilege provides legal protection of confidentiality." His tone was more conciliatory now. "It will be very difficult for me to represent you properly in a discussion with the police without full disclosure."

Vincentio considered him for a moment. He didn't intend to admit anything. To anyone. "Young man, I will tell you the truth. And I will tell you what you need to know. Nothing more. If, after I do that, you feel you can't represent me, I'll find other legal counsel. Are we clear?"

The attorney gave him an assessing look. Then he opened his notebook. "Why don't you say what you have to say and we'll go from there?"

"Fine." Vincentio linked his fingers over his stomach. "James Walsh was a trusted employee of mine many years ago. Due in large part to his testimony, I spent the prime years of my life behind bars. There was no love lost between us. However, he disappeared after the trial. I assume he went into the Witness Security program. I haven't seen or heard from him since.

"Last week, a St. Louis County police detective called to tell me they were investigating the death of a John Warren. In your conversation with him, the detective said they suspect Warren was actually James Walsh. I'm assuming that name led them to me. And thanks to our connection, I'm also assuming they've concluded his death was murder rather than suicide." He leaned forward and fixed the other man with a steely gaze. "That may be true. But I can tell you with absolute certainty there is no evidence linking me to his death. None. That's what you need to know."

Vincentio sat back and re-linked his fingers. If that didn't suit Lake, he'd find someone else to represent him. Or handle the detectives himself. Why did he need an attorney anyway, when there was no way the police could pin Walsh's death on him?

"How did you know it was suicide?"

At Lake's quiet question, Vincentio frowned. "What?"

"How did you know the police thought Walsh committed suicide? I didn't mention that."

"You must have."

"No. I haven't talked with you since I discovered that piece of information." He tapped the end of his pen on the blank piece of notepaper in front of him. Watching. Assessing. Much like Vincentio used to scrutinize his associates. Looking for cracks.

"The detective must have mentioned it when I talked to him."

"Are you sure?"

No, he wasn't. He'd been thrown by the call. All he remembered clearly was that it had been brief. Perhaps *too* brief to get into details like cause of death.

Maybe he did need someone to watch his back after all. His mind might not be as sharp at seventy-four as it had been at forty-seven.

And maybe he'd underestimated Lake.

"Good catch." It was a grudging admission, but the man deserved his due.

"I'm trained to pick up discrepancies, Mr. Rossi. So are the police. A slip like that could cause major problems."

That was true. One wrong comment might not be enough to send him back to prison, but it would be more than enough to give the police license to make his life miserable.

And if that happened, any hope of spending time with his grandson would evaporate.

He pulled a handkerchief out of his pocket and dabbed at the beads of sweat forming on his forehead. "You have a point. Are you willing to represent me based on what I've told you?"

Lake set his pen down and steepled his fingers. Letting him sweat for a few moments. "Here's my deal. We can punt through this first round. If it goes beyond that, I'll need more information."

That was fair. And prudent.

"Agreed."

"All right." The man repositioned his notebook in front of him. "Now let's talk strategy."

Freddie had done a great job.

Holding the note in his latex-gloved hands to ensure only Warren's fingerprints were on the sheet—a precaution he'd instructed Freddie to take as well—Alan shifted it closer to the light beside his home computer, picked up the magnifying glass he kept in his desk, and compared the writing to the samples he'd taken from Warren's house, moving back and forth between the documents.

Amazing.

The ink pressure was consistent. There were no interrupted strokes. The size and proportion of the letters were the same, as were the slant, angles, connections, and curves. The spacing and alignment matched. There was no discernable tremor, a common flaw when forgers traced letters or words—or moved too slowly as they copied. A shaky hand in a man about to commit suicide wouldn't necessarily be a problem, but it was better not to raise red flags.

Alan sat back. He wasn't a handwriting expert, but he'd been a detective long enough to know a good forgery from a bad one.

And this was a good one.

Good enough to fool the experts at Quantico, if it got as far as the FBI lab.

He scanned the note, this time for content rather than technique. Freddie had written the message exactly as he'd dictated, and it had all the characteristics of the typical suicide note. In four brief sentences, it referenced despair, offered an apology, and contained an expression of love for Kelly.

He was set.

A yawn caught him off guard, and he glanced at his watch. Two in the morning. And tomorrow—make that today—was going to be a full day. Now that a real lead had surfaced, the double homicide investigation was heating up. But it had been safer to retrieve the letter from the drop location after midnight rather than at a more reasonable hour. Four hours of sleep wasn't much, but he'd gotten by on less in his gambling days.

And if the meteorologists' predictions were accurate, the winter storm should move in within the next twenty-four hours.

Making tonight D-day.

Did elves have blue eyes?

Kelly paused, brush poised above her palette, pondering that question. The diminutive woodland dwellers peopling the children's book she was illustrating all had green eyes so far.

But she had blue eyes on her mind.

Not that a certain detective bore the slightest resemblance to her fanciful little creatures. Still, it might be fun to try and replicate the intense cerulean/cobalt hue of those captivating irises.

As she leaned forward to dip her brush into phthalo blue, her cell began to ring. Cole, perhaps? She hadn't heard from him since their encounter two days ago at the restaurant, and there was no reason for him to call her unless there was news on the case. Not likely until after his meeting with Rossi. But she couldn't quell a surge of anticipation as she set the brush in a jar of water and reached for the phone.

A quick look at caller ID, however, deflated her hope. It was the realtor for her father's house. Reining in her disappointment, she pressed the talk button and greeted the woman.

"Kelly? Denise Woods. I'm glad I caught you. I have someone who's very interested in seeing your father's house. He's being transferred here the first of the year, and he and his wife and baby will be in town over the holiday weekend visiting his wife's parents. When he described what he wanted, I thought of your father's house. I know we haven't listed it officially yet, and a holiday week isn't ideal timing, but in this market I don't think we should pass up any opportunity. Would it be okay if I show it to him while he's here?"

The image of her father's torn-apart bedroom and office flashed across her mind—as did the layer of dust that had settled on the furniture over the past few weeks.

"I guess that would work. But I need to clean first. And I've pulled out a lot of stuff that needs to be trashed or boxed up for charity. When does he want to see it?"

"Friday."

She checked her watch. It was already after three. That only gave her what was left of today and tomorrow to get the house in shape—unless she wanted to spend some of her Thanksgiving cleaning toilets.

Not an appealing prospect.

"Okay. I can get it done."

"Great. And anything you can do to make it seem lived in will help. Fresh flowers on the table. A plate of cookies in the kitchen. That kind of thing."

"I'll take care of it."

"All right. I'll let you know what he says. Have a nice holiday."

"You too."

Kelly set the phone back on the table and gathered up the brushes that needed cleaning. So much for her plans to finish this illustration before Thanksgiving. But Denise was right; it would be foolish not to woo a potential buyer.

As she entered the kitchen, the phone rang again. Once more, her pulse took a leap. Veering off her route to the basement stairwell, she flipped on the lights, picked up the portable, and checked caller ID. Lauren.

"Hi there. I thought you were leaving at noon."

"We were supposed to, but I got delayed at work. We're finally ready to hit the road. I just wanted to call and let you know I'll be thinking of you on Thursday, and to say I'm sorry I can't have you to our house for dinner. It stinks that it's our year to travel."

"I'll be fine. I just had a call from the realtor, who has a hot prospect for Dad's house. So cleaning up the place will keep me occupied."

"That's not much of a holiday. Why don't you reconsider spending the afternoon with Cole and his family?"

Kelly wandered over to the window, eyeing the ominous, black clouds that were massing in the distance. The wind had picked up too, judging by the gyrations of the branches on her blue spruce. "Like I told you Sunday night, Cole wasn't all that enthusiastic about the idea. But Christmas sounds promising." A smile tugged at her lips.

"Hold that thought. Listen, Shaun's giving me the high sign, so I guess the kids are in the car. And he wants to try and get ahead of the storm."

"I don't blame him." She checked the threatening sky again. "It looks like we might be in for our first taste of winter. Have a safe trip and . . ." She stopped speaking as her lights flickered and went off.

"Kelly? What's wrong?"

"I just lost power. It happens all the time in storms."

"Hmm. Ours is still on. I hope it's okay at your dad's too, or you'll end up cleaning by candlelight."

"His house is on a different grid. It never loses power. That's why I stayed with him a few years ago when we had the ice storm that knocked out half the city, remember?"

"Yeah. Maybe you ought to spend the night there again. The temperature's supposed to drop, and your house could get chilly if the blower's off on your furnace."

"Not a bad idea." She heard Shaun call again in the background. "Listen, go ahead and get rolling. Happy Thanksgiving to all of you. Next week I want a full report."

"Sixteen people in a moderate-sized house, seven of them under the age of ten, for four days. And I don't even like turkey. It ought to be loads of fun."

At her friend's glum tone, Kelly grinned. "Look at it as an opportunity to bond with the in-laws."

"If we don't kill each other first."

"You'll be fine. It's only until Sunday, right?"

"Right."

"And the cousins will have a blast."

"Thanks for the pep talk. I'll call you when I get back."

As they said their good-byes and Kelly put the phone back in its stand, a gust of wind rattled the window. With the sky darkening, the house was already growing dim, and she didn't relish spending the night in absolute darkness huddled under three blankets.

Brushes still in hand, she dropped to her knees and groped

around under the sink until her fingers closed over a flashlight. Then she descended the basement stairs to take care of her brushes, propping the light on a shelf beside the utility sink as she worked. She hadn't slept at her dad's house since that crippling ice storm, but maybe it would be beneficial to return to her childhood home for one last overnight visit. To fall asleep in the place that had always been a sheltering haven from storms of every kind. The place where she'd always felt loved. Protected. Safe.

Except that had all been an illusion. In the end, someone had not only gotten in but flawlessly masked a murder as suicide. Someone on Rossi's payroll. There was no question in her mind about that. Or Cole's. Otherwise, he wouldn't be making this trip to Buffalo.

And that same someone had gone after her once too.

She stared down at the red paint staining her fingers as she cleaned the brush she'd used for the ladybug in her illustration. A shiver ran through her.

That person was still on the loose.

But Cole was on his trail, and she had absolute confidence in the handsome detective who was fast becoming an integral part of her life.

In the meantime, though, she'd use extra caution, as Cole was always reminding her to do. And her childhood home was far more secure than hers, despite the new locks she'd had installed. Whoever had targeted her father had to have gotten in when the security system was off, either a caller her dad had let in himself or an intruder who'd perhaps come in through an open window. But she'd arm it tonight and she didn't intend to open any windows or answer the door, no matter who might come calling.

Giving her fingers a final rinse, she examined them. No trace of red remained. Satisfied with her cleanup and her security plan, she gathered up the brushes and the flashlight and started back up the stairs to pack a bag for the night.

Confident that in her father's house, she'd be safe.

17

Stifling a yawn, Cole exited the jetway, stepped out of the path of the disembarking passengers at Buffalo Niagara International Airport, and twisted his wrist to check the time. Four-ten a.m. Two hours behind schedule, thanks to weather delays.

There'd be no sleep this night.

But he didn't intend to let fatigue throw him off his game. Unless they came up with some solid evidence linking Rossi to the crime, they were only going to get this one shot at the Mafia honcho.

Mitch appeared among the hoard of zombie-like travelers shuffling out of the jetway, looking disgustingly well-rested for someone who'd sat in coach for most of the night.

"You must have caught some shut-eye." Cole picked up his small carry-on and squinted at his colleague as the man joined him.

"Uh-huh. From wheels-up to wheels-down." Mitch grinned. "SEALs learn to sleep anywhere, anytime."

"Lucky you." Cole doubted he'd dozed off for more than two or three ten-minute stretches. He'd been crammed into the window seat on the cramped commuter plane, beside an overweight man who'd snored during the entire trip. "I need coffee."

"I'm with you." Mitch surveyed a shuttered Starbucks outlet two gates down. "But we'll have to get some en route. This whole place is shut down for the night."

210

"You'd think they'd have longer hours during peak travel times. At least the car rental place extended its hours for the holiday—I checked." Cole continued toward the terminal, casting a disgruntled glance at the dark coffee shop as Mitch fell in beside him. "Since sleeping on the plane wasn't an option for *some* of us, I reviewed the background material on Rossi again, looking for angles. The FBI guy I talked to in the Buffalo office doesn't think there's been any contact between him and his son since he's been released. Sounds like the son doesn't want anything to do with the Rossi dynasty. That has to rankle his old man."

"How does that help us?"

Cole checked the arrows on the overhead sign and stepped onto the escalator that led to the car rental kiosks. "It could be a trigger point. I doubt Rossi will expect us to bring up his family—but if we're not getting the answers we need, introducing his relationship with his son could throw him off balance. Cause him to make a slip."

Skepticism narrowed Mitch's eyes. "I wouldn't get my hopes up. His attorney isn't going to let him say anything incriminating."

Cole shrugged. "People can make mistakes—even if they've been well-coached. You never know when some question will hit a sensitive spot and yield a lot more information than you expect—either in words or body language." He gestured to the left as they neared the bottom of the escalator. "There's our car place. You want to drive until we get some coffee?"

"Sure. We should clean up a little too." Mitch straightened his tie and ran his hand over the dark stubble on his jaw. "I need a shave. And you need . . ." He inspected Cole. "Something. A fresh shirt, maybe. You could also use some of that stuff Alison has to disguise shadows under her eyes."

"Thanks a lot." Cole got off the escalator and set off toward the car rental counter, leaving Mitch to catch up. He knew he looked scruffy, and he'd freshen up before they saw Rossi. But as long as his mind was sharp, he really didn't care what the former mob boss thought of his appearance. He wasn't here to impress the man.

He was here to dig for answers.

And before he boarded the return flight later today, he intended to do everything in his power to get them.

Alan killed the lights on his car two blocks from John Warren's house as he drove through the silent night. Not that the precaution was necessary. The streets were deserted at three-thirty in the morning. But he hated taking unnecessary risks.

Like this whole operation.

He flexed his fingers on the wheel and frowned. Rossi should have followed his advice and let this problem die a natural death—as it would have. But he was used to calling the shots. Used to people jumping when he barked commands. Used to exacting revenge when they didn't.

And after his role in delivering that revenge to John Warren, Alan knew firsthand what it looked like.

He swallowed past the sudden, acrid taste of fear. The very fear that had driven him here tonight, despite the risk, to plant a letter he hoped would wrap up the Warren case once and for all.

The small apartment complex he'd scouted out Monday night while he'd been retrieving the note at the drop location came into sight, and he pulled into the parking lot. There had been plenty of open spots then, and there were more now. A lot of people must already have left for the holiday.

Choosing one at the far end, he angled in, then pulled a knit hat low over his forehead and tugged on a pair of gloves. He scanned the area to confirm he was alone, then exited the car and locked it manually to avoid the audible click of the automatic mechanism. He'd taped the trunk light earlier in the day, so there was no illuminating glow when he opened the lid to retrieve the backpack that contained everything he needed. The letter, encased in a protective plastic sleeve.

Night-vision goggles. A length of sturdy rope to toss over a branch on the tree. Latex gloves. A hammer to break the window.

He was set.

And if all went smoothly, he'd be home in time to grab a little more shut-eye before he had to show up at headquarters to update his boss on the double homicide investigation prior to Sarge's departure for the holiday.

Then it was just a matter of waiting for Kelly to discover the "storm" damage and find the note.

After that happened, the Warren case could be put to rest once and for all. It would be difficult to refute a suicide note in the man's own hand. The heat would be off Rossi. The man would send him his final payment, and he could start fresh with Cindy—a reformed gambler, debt-free, with a bright future waiting for him.

Thanksgiving this year would be sweet.

What was that noise?

Kelly opened her eyes and stared at the dark ceiling in her childhood bedroom. All was silent now. But hadn't she heard a beep or two? The kind made by a microwave or a smoke alarm when the batteries needed changing.

Or a security system being armed or disarmed.

A quiver of fear snaked up her spine, and she bunched the blanket in her fists.

Breathe, Kelly.

She inhaled slowly. Exhaled. Repeated the process, listening.

There were no more beeps. Nor was there any other sound, except the wind whistling around the corner of the house and the thrashing of the trees.

She wrinkled her brow. Had she dreamed the noise? Or heard a sound outside, perhaps? A garbage truck backing up, with its distinctive, piercing warning beep? She glanced at the digital clock on the nightstand. Three forty-five. No one, including trash collectors, should be out and about in the neighborhood making noise at this hour. Especially in a storm.

Or the noise might have been some sound idiosyncratic to her father's house. All houses made unique sounds at night, and it had been a while since she'd spent a . . .

A floorboard squeaked.

The breath lodged in her throat, and her fingers clenched as she tried to quell her rising panic. There was probably a very simple explanation for that noise too. Wood contracted and expanded in heat and cold. She'd set the heat lower before going to bed. Maybe it was the flooring adjusting to the change in temperature.

Or an intruder.

No. That was impossible. She'd set the alarm when she went to bed. No one knew the code except her. The realtor did have a separate access code, one Kelly had programmed just for her. But Denise wouldn't be prowling around the house in the middle of the night, nor would she have given her code to anyone. The noise had to be . . .

Another creak echoed in the quiet house.

The breath whooshed out of her lungs.

Someone *was* in the house!

Heart hammering, she eased the covers back and swung her feet to the floor. Too bad her cell phone had died this afternoon and was stuck in the charger in the kitchen, where she'd inadvertently left it when she went to bed. As for a weapon—a quick scan confirmed there was nothing more lethal in her old bedroom than a college art show trophy. At least it was handy—and heavy.

She tiptoed across the room, praying her unsteady legs would support her, and retrieved it from among the others on the shelf her father had built for her twenty years ago. Turning it upside down so the solid wood base was on top, she gripped it with both hands, inched toward the door, and peeked into the dim hall, illuminated only by a night-light.

Empty.

She waited for another noise. One that would help her pinpoint the location of the intruder.

It came ten seconds later. The muted sound of a zipper. From her father's study.

Okay. Decision time. She could try and slip past the study without being spotted, get the phone out of the charger, and dial 911. Or she could hide in a closet with her weapon and hope the intruder wouldn't search the house.

But if this person had had anything to do with her father's death, she couldn't let him get away again.

Decision made. She had to try and reach the phone.

Tightening her grip on the trophy, she crept down the hall.

Three steps later, the sudden snap of rubber echoed in the quiet house. She froze. A few seconds later, the sound was repeated.

What was that all about?

She edged to the study door and peeked around. A black-clothed figure was crouched near the desk, rummaging through a bag on the floor. A man, based on his size.

Kelly tried to keep breathing, but she could only manage shallow gasps. Knowing an intruder was in the house was one thing. Seeing him mere feet away was another. At least his back was to her, and he was intent on his task.

This was her chance to pass the door unnoticed.

With a silent prayer for courage, she crept past the door, her bare feet silent on the carpet.

Two steps past the door, however, a floorboard *under* the carpet protested.

She heard a sudden movement in the study and swung around, trophy raised.

The intruder emerged. "What the . . ."

His startled exclamation registered at some peripheral level, but all of her focus was on his face. Or what *should* have been his face. Instead, some sort of binocular-type contraption was protruding from his eyes, held in place with a piece of headgear anchored by a chin guard.

He looked like a creature from a science fiction movie.

And he was a lot bigger than he'd appeared when he'd been hunkered down in the study.

But whoever he was—*whatever* he was—he represented a serious threat.

Raising the trophy, she prepared to smash it over his head.

Unfortunately, her delay had cost her the element of surprise. As she swung the trophy down with all her strength, he sidestepped and lunged at her. She missed his head, but the walnut base did connect with his shoulder.

Muttering an oath, he grabbed her wrist in a vise-like grip with one hand and yanked the trophy out of her grasp with the other.

Adrenaline surging, she kicked at his legs and clawed at his face with her free hand, all the while trying to twist free. From his grunts, she knew a few of her blows connected. But she was no match for his muscular strength. The most effective thing she managed to do was hook her fingers into his headgear and jerk on it. He tried to elbow her, but she kept on jerking, hoping that would distract him enough to allow her to kick him in some vital place—and give her a chance to grab a lamp in the living room so she could smash something more substantial over his head.

Instead, though, her tugging loosened the headgear. The next thing she knew, the binocular-like appendage fell away—and she found herself staring into a familiar face, inches away.

"Detective Carlson?" Her words came out whispered. Incredulous.

Panic flared in his eyes, and he sucked in a sharp breath. Tightened his grip on her arm. Spat out an expletive.

Still reeling from shock, she had no time to react when he lifted his hand. But in the instant before his fist smashed into her jaw and her legs crumpled, she knew she'd found her father's killer.

And that she could very well become his next victim.

As Kelly collapsed at his feet, Alan massaged his knuckles and fought back the crushing panic paralyzing his lungs.

Kelly wasn't supposed to be here. No one was supposed to be here. Running into someone inside the house hadn't even been a risk he'd factored into the equation. He had no Plan B for this scenario.

But he had to come up with one.

Fast.

Because it wouldn't take Warren's daughter long to recover from that clip on the jaw.

Alan stepped over her prone body and paced the length of the small hall, keeping one eye on her for any sign of returning consciousness. Kelly Warren had been a problem from day one. She'd fought him every step of the way on his suicide conclusion, then reappeared with that stupid tulip note. She'd pushed, prodded, and persevered until she'd riled a mob boss—and put not only his future, but his neck, on the line.

And now that Little Miss Buttinski had pulled off his night-vision goggles and recognized him, he had a huge complication. If she hadn't done that, he could have shoved her aside and disappeared, a shadowy intruder melting into the mist. He'd have gone home and figured out some other plan to get the letter into her hands.

But that was no longer an option.

Now, she had to be silenced.

He stopped beside her, fists clenched, hate churning in his gut as he looked down. The peanut incident had already raised suspicions. A second "accident" would too. And considering Taylor's personal interest in this case, he would dig deep, searching for proof of foul play.

Alan nudged Kelly none-too-gently with his toe. She was still limp as a dishrag. Good. He needed some quiet time to work out the details of an accident that would be so plausible and so clean no one—not even Romeo Taylor—would be able to find a single hole.

And before he left this house, he'd also plant the letter. No need to break the window now, though. He'd just slide the letter behind the desk for someone to find while the house was being cleaned out following the tragic deaths of both father and daughter. When that happened, he'd point out that the window had been open the night of Warren's death and suggest the letter had blown behind the desk. Since Kelly wouldn't be around to say if she'd searched there, everyone would assume she'd missed it. And the Crime Scene Unit wouldn't have pulled furniture out from walls in the man's office when the death was obviously a suicide.

Okay. That was reasonable. It would work.

Now he had to come up with a plan to dispose of Kelly.

He started to pace again. He'd done a lot of research on her and her father over the course of the past few months, and even more on *her* after the tulip note arrived. Including surveillance. That's what had given him the information he'd needed to plan the coffee shop incident so perfectly. That, and the intel he'd gotten during their conversations after her father's death. He knew her habits, her allergies, her job . . .

Alan stopped.

Her job.

A slow smile chased away his frown as an idea began to gel. A *brilliant* idea. A perfect synergy between what he knew about her and his own expertise.

It would take planning, though, and careful timing. He needed to think this through thoroughly. Work it out step by step. The next couple of hours would be crucial, and he didn't like being rushed. But he could pull this off. He was obsessive about details. He wouldn't miss anything.

And by the time Thanksgiving morning dawned, Kelly Warren and her father would be reunited—*if* the faith that was so important to her was right, and there *was* such a thing as heaven.

A happy ending. Nice. He liked that spin.

After one more toe nudge, he headed to the linen closet at the end of the hall to gather up what he needed for phase one of his plan.

"Feeling more awake now?" Mitch grinned at Cole across the table in the all-night diner they'd stumbled upon as they left the airport.

"Not much. I need some of that high-octane stuff we have at work. Or the sludge Alison brews."

"Maybe some food would help."

"At four in the morning?"

"It's almost five."

"Eastern time. I'm still on central."

"Mind if I order a burger and some fries?"

"At four in the morning?" Cole suddenly felt queasy.

"You already said that." Mitch grinned and signaled to the waitress. "But remember—unlike you and Jake, *I* drink Alison's coffee."

"Proof you have an iron stomach."

"I won't tell her you said that."

"Thanks."

While Mitch placed his order, Cole stifled another yawn. Once the waitress departed, his partner for the day turned to him. "By the way, I ran into Alan at the copy machine yesterday. I got the feeling he wasn't happy about being left out of the loop on this."

Cole shrugged. "Sarge wanted some fresh eyes on the case. Besides, Alan's got enough on his plate with the homicide. He was probably just tired and stressed. I can relate." He took another sip of coffee, waiting for the jolt of caffeine to kick in.

"All I know is he wasn't too friendly."

"Hey . . . if he's put out, he'll get over it. In the meantime, he's got plenty of other distractions. Trust me, the last thing he's thinking about right now is the John Warren case."

Why did her jaw hurt? Could she be getting a toothache? Why was she shivering? Her favorite sleep sweats always kept her warm, even if the fleece was worn and the fabric was beginning to shed.

And why was it so hard to wake up? She couldn't even raise her eyelids.

Kelly shifted her head, and pain exploded on the side of her face, radiating up to her temple. She moaned and pried open her eyes, trying to orient herself in the darkness. This wasn't her old bedroom at her father's house. She was in his living room. On the couch. That's why the fabric against her cheek felt nubby rather than smooth. But why . . .

"So you decided to wake up."

As a shadowy figure appeared at the edge of her vision, she gasped and struggled to sit up.

That's when she realized her hands and feet were bound.

The figure moved closer. Squatted beside her.

Alan Carlson.

Her father's murderer.

"It was you." Even as she said the words, she struggled to accept them. He was a law enforcement officer. A respected detective. Cole's colleague. The man assigned to investigate her father's death.

And also the perpetrator.

No wonder he'd closed the case so quickly.

"You never had to know that, Kelly. And you wouldn't have, if you hadn't kept pushing. Now we have a little problem."

She watched his eyes. In the shadowy darkness, it was difficult to see much. But one thing was clear. The initial panic and desperation she'd glimpsed in them in the moment before he'd slugged her had hardened into cold, ruthless calculation. He'd already decided what he was going to do about their "little problem."

He was going to get rid of it.

Of her.

Terror sucked the breath from her lungs and jolted her heart into overdrive. Her skin grew clammy, and she shivered.

"Cold, Kelly?"

"No." She hated the shakiness in her voice. Hated giving this murderer the satisfaction of seeing how frightened she was. To compensate, she lifted her chin and stared him straight in the eye, her gaze unwavering.

His lips curved into a humorless smile. "You've got spunk, I'll give you that."

As he started to walk away, she jockeyed herself upright and swung her legs to the floor, trying to ignore the excruciating pain in her jaw.

At the sound, he turned. "We're not going anywhere for a while. You might as well make yourself comfortable."

Thanks to the adrenaline rush, her mind was now firing on all cylinders. She needed information. As much as possible. It would be difficult to thwart him if she didn't know his plans. And difficult even if she did, considering how incapacitated she was. But she stifled that last disheartening thought. She needed to maintain a positive attitude.

"Why did you do it?" Her voice was stronger now.

He lifted one shoulder. "I needed money to pay off some gambling debts. Your father was dying anyway. I just hurried the process along. It was a no-brainer."

At his cavalier attitude, bile rose in her throat. She swallowed past it, determined to disengage her emotions as much as possible—as Carlson had. "How did you make it look like suicide?"

A smile tugged at his lips. "I pulled that off well, didn't I?"

The touch of pride in his voice sickened her. But she did her best to mask her revulsion. "How?"

A smirk twisted his features. "It was almost too easy."

And then he told how he'd won her father's confidence under the guise of his badge. How he'd drugged him and left him to die in the garage. How he'd made sure he was assigned to the case.

As he recounted his reprehensible plan, Kelly's terror morphed to an anger as cold as Carlson's heart.

"Next to that, setting you up for anaphylactic shock with a couple of ground peanuts was a piece of cake."

She blinked, jolted by his concluding statement. "You were the old man in the coffee shop?"

A smile toyed with his lips. Genuine, this time. "I learned a lot about disguises as an undercover detective, and I'm trained to observe. To notice details. To listen. I used all those skills during the investigation after your father's death. I learned about your allergy. I learned you carried an auto-injector. I learned the security at your house was pathetic—and I'm very familiar with breaking and entering techniques. It was easy to slip in one night, take your injector out of your purse, go outside, and rap it against a rock. They're very susceptible to leakage under stress, as my wife discovered."

He'd been in her house while she slept.

She stifled the shiver threatening to ripple through her. "What if I hadn't gone for coffee that Saturday?"

He made a dismissive gesture. "There was always the next Saturday. I studied your habits, and you're very predictable. As for getting into your father's house tonight, I watched you enter the security code several times during our investigation of your father's death, and I memorized it. But I didn't expect to find you here. That was an unpleasant surprise—for both of us. Where's your car?"

"In the garage."

"You always park in the driveway."

He *had* done his homework. She hadn't been in her father's garage since the night he'd died.

"I was afraid it might get damaged by blowing limbs or hail."

"So in protecting your car, you put yourself at risk. Too bad."

He turned toward the kitchen, ending the conversation. But she hadn't learned enough about his plans yet.

"What are you going to do with me?"

He pivoted back toward her. "I think we both know the answer to that."

She swallowed. "Then why are you waiting?"

"Because this isn't the time or place. And I have things to do first."

222

He crossed the dark kitchen. She heard the basement door open. A few seconds later he came back, walked to the couch, and leaned toward her.

She shrank away, but all he did was sling her over his shoulder. When she squirmed in his arms, he tightened his grip.

"Hold still. I'm just putting you downstairs so you don't cause any problems while I'm gone."

He was leaving?

Relief coursed through her, and she quieted at once. That was an opportunity she hadn't expected. Left alone, she might be able to figure out a way to escape.

Once at the bottom of the basement stairs, he headed toward a heavy-duty shelving unit her father had had installed years ago. After lowering her to a sitting position on the floor beside it, he used a sturdy piece of metal wire from her father's workbench to secure the rope binding her hands behind her to an upright post. He jerked it tight, immobilizing her against the post. She braced, expecting the rope to cut into her wrists. But it didn't.

Confused, she checked out her ankles. Odd. He'd wrapped a thick layer of hand towels around them before tying her up.

He stood, following the direction of her gaze. "I don't want any telltale marks. When I'm finished, no one will ever know you were tied up. I'm very good at details—and planning."

The man was bragging about the meticulous arrangements he was making to kill her.

How sick was that?

He reached into his pocket and pulled out a strip of cloth. It looked like a piece of one of the rags her father had always kept in the garage.

Before she understood his intent, he knelt and whipped it taut around her head, covering her mouth.

She clamped her lips together as tightly as she could, and he gave a sharp tug. "Open up—or we'll do this the hard way."

When she didn't respond, he kneed her in the rib cage. Hard.

She gasped.

He pulled the strip of cloth between her teeth, so tight it stretched the corners of her mouth back. The cotton clung to her tongue, sucking out all the moisture.

She gagged.

A muscle flexed in his jaw. "You brought this all on yourself, you know. You should have let the dead rest in peace." He rose, crossed to the stairs, and started up. A few seconds later, she heard the basement door shut, then the creak of floorboards overhead. The security system began to beep. A faint shudder in the house told her the back door had been closed.

She was alone.

Her body sagged, and she began to shake. Violently.

When at last the trembling subsided, she tugged on her wrists. They didn't give. Nor was the heavy-duty shelving going to budge. It had taken two burly men to set it up. She wasn't going to be able to free herself, and there was no chance she'd be able to overpower Carlson. He was big and he was strong.

That left her just one weapon.

Her brain.

She'd have to outwit him.

And she'd have to do it as soon as he returned. He'd made it clear he didn't intend to take her life here. But once they left, all bets were off.

Kelly took a deep, shuddering breath and forced herself to shift into analytical mode. Psyched herself up for a battle of wits. Carlson had bragged about his attention to detail. To planning.

Well, he was about to meet his match.

18

"Nice place." Mitch surveyed Rossi's house as Cole pulled behind a late-model BMW parked at the curb.

"Not by his previous standards." Cole scanned the tidy brick two-story colonial as he shifted into park. "Before he went to prison, he lived in a sixty-five hundred square foot mansion that sold not long ago for close to two mil. I checked." He set the brake and scoped out the quiet neighborhood of upper middle class homes. "This is quite a comedown."

"Maybe prison changed his priorities."

"Or maybe he just wants to keep a low profile."

"If he does, he can't be looking forward to our visit."

"He isn't. When I called, he passed me off to his attorney faster than Alison can throw a zinger."

Mitch grinned. "That fast, huh?"

"Yeah." Cole turned off the engine. "So are we clear on the plan?"

"You're taking the lead, I'm jumping in as needed—or if I see an opportunity to press an issue. Like we tag-teamed that felony assault case a few months back."

"Let's hope the technique works as well today."

Mitch gestured to the BMW. "Wanna bet that's the lawyer's car?"

"I don't bet on the obvious." Cole opened his door, circled around the back of the midsize rental, and met Mitch at the end of the brick walk that curved toward the front door. "Ever dealt with a former big-league crime boss?"

"Nope." Mitch matched him pace for pace as they walked toward the door. "But a bad guy is a bad guy. And most of them don't change."

Cole stepped up onto the small, white-columned porch and pressed the bell. "That's why we're here."

At the discreet knock on the door of his study, a nerve in Vincentio's hand spasmed, and he linked his fingers on his desk to disguise the tremble. "Yes?"

Teresa cracked the door. "The gentlemen have arrived, Mr. Rossi."

He glanced at Lake, who sat in a wingback chair across from him, placed a bit behind the two less-comfortable visitor chairs facing the desk. The attorney's location allowed him to be part of the conversation if he wanted to step in, but it was far enough back to facilitate discreet nonverbal communication with his client. The detectives would see through that strategy at once—but there wasn't a thing they could do about it. This was his house. His furniture. His world. That's why he'd had them come here.

On his turf, he was in control.

"Show them in, Teresa."

The housekeeper exited. Half a minute later, when he heard her open the front door, Vincentio's pulse accelerated. So different from the glory days. Nothing had fazed him then. But he was still a Rossi, with roots planted deep in the Sicilian soil. Part of a powerful family that had been feared, envied, admired, and respected. He might have lost that legacy of power thirty-one years ago because he'd trusted the wrong man. Because he'd been soft, as his father had always said. But there would be no mistakes today.

He took a deep breath. Straightened his shoulders. Lifted his chin.

This was a game he did not intend to lose.

When the two detectives came in, Lake rose. Vincentio didn't. If they noticed his lack of hospitality, however, they gave no indication.

One of the men stepped forward. "Mr. Rossi?"

"Yes." He recognized the voice from their phone conversation.

"Detective Cole Taylor, St. Louis County PD." He withdrew a business card and laid it on the desk. As if he suspected his host wouldn't take it if he held it out.

The man had sound intuitive skills. The kind Vincentio had once found valuable and still respected.

Taylor gestured to his companion. "Detective Mitch Morgan."

The man's sidekick gave a perfunctory nod.

"Thomas Lake, my attorney." Vincentio indicated the fourth man in the room.

Once greetings were exchanged and Lake shook hands with the two visitors—displaying the courtesy his client had neglected—Vincentio gestured toward the chairs across from the desk. "Let's get started, gentlemen. I'm sure you both have better places to be the day before Thanksgiving."

Morgan took a seat, leaned back, and crossed an ankle over a knee. Taylor opened a notebook, settled it on his lap, and pulled out a pen.

"Mr. Rossi, as I told Mr. Lake on the phone, we have reason to believe a John Warren who died in St. Louis in May was, in fact, the James Walsh who once worked for you—and whose testimony helped secure your conviction for racketeering and money laundering. Mr. Warren's death was originally ruled a suicide, but we've reopened the case. Could you tell me where you were on the evening of Thursday, May 20?"

An odd question. This detective was smart enough to know he wouldn't have carried out a hit himself. But he played along.

"Here in Buffalo. I haven't left the city since I was released from prison."

"Have you seen James Walsh since your release?"

"No."

"Even when he came back to New York in April to visit his dying brother and attend his funeral?"

"Like I said . . . I don't leave the city. And the last I heard, his brother lived in Rochester."

"But you knew his brother had died."

He shrugged. "It came to my attention."

"Doesn't it seem an odd coincidence that a month after James Walsh surfaced for the first time in thirty-one years, he wound up dead?"

"*Supposedly* surfaced. I don't believe you have a definitive link between John Warren and James Walsh." Vincentio lifted one shoulder. "Even if you did, stranger things have happened."

"Did you know he had lung cancer?"

He stared at the detective, trying to mask his shock. James Walsh had been afflicted with the same disease that had taken his beloved Isabella?

How ironic.

And given the poor survival rate for that iteration of the disease, the man might have died on his own in a few months. Suffered a lot in the interim too, as had Isabella. If he'd known, he could have waited for nature to carry out the death sentence.

But then he wouldn't have had the satisfaction of exacting revenge.

"A difficult way to die." He kept his inflection noncommittal. "At least he was spared that ordeal."

"Have you ever done any business in St. Louis, Mr. Rossi?"

The sudden shift in topic didn't surprise him. He knew how cops operated. They liked to keep people off balance.

He lifted the corners of his mouth in a smile that held no humor. "My business days are ancient history, and a seventy-four-year-old memory isn't reliable. Details of things that happened three decades ago aren't always clear."

"I was thinking of more recent business."

"Such as?" A chill crept into his voice.

"You tell me. It's difficult to believe a man who once led a mob dynasty would give up his old life completely."

Vincentio considered the comment, keeping an eye on Lake in his peripheral vision. The detective was getting more direct now. But they'd agreed the attorney wouldn't intervene unless the questioning took on an accusatory tone.

A point he suspected they were fast approaching.

"I went to prison for almost three decades, Detective. Things change. Power shifts. Life goes on. The world I came back to was very different than the world I left. In many ways."

His gaze strayed to the family picture on the credenza, taken a year before his incarceration. Isabella, with her long black hair, had looked beautiful that day. And grinning five-year-old Marco had been so proud of his first suit. Those had been the happiest days of his life, though he'd only recognized that in hindsight.

"Your family?"

At the query from Taylor, he turned his attention back to the detective. "Yes."

"I understand your wife is deceased."

"Yes."

"But your son lives here."

"Yes." His chest tightened with familiar regret.

"From what I've been able to gather, you two aren't close."

He leveled a cold stare at the dark-haired detective. "My family situation has no bearing on the case you're investigating."

"We often find links in the oddest places."

"My son knows nothing about your case. Or my business."

"So you do still carry out some business."

"Gentlemen . . ." Lake glanced at Vincentio. "As I'm sure you realize, that's a common figure of speech. Let's focus on the case you came to discuss. Beyond a possible connection that's thirty-one years old, perhaps you could tell us why you think my client might have any knowledge about Mr. Warren's death."

Lake was forcing their hand. A smart strategy. Vincentio

picked up the cappuccino Teresa had delivered to him just before the detectives arrived, balanced the cup and saucer in his hand as he sat back in his chair, and took a sip.

"I'll be happy to." Taylor responded to Lake but kept his focus on Vincentio. "Kelly Warren, John Warren's daughter, received a gift of tulip bulbs from her father a month ago. The gift had been ordered the day before he died, and the enclosure note talked about planting them together in the fall. Ms. Warren believes this proves her father had no plans to commit suicide, and she asked us to take another look at the case. Not long after she began to go through her father's things, searching for other clues, she suffered a near-fatal episode of anaphylactic shock. She's allergic to peanuts, and we have reason to believe that incident was not an accident. That someone wanted her dead too."

The liquid sloshed in Vincentio's cup, and he tightened his grip. Carlson had tried to kill Walsh's daughter?

That hadn't been part of the game plan.

"If the intent was to keep her from digging deeper, it had the opposite effect." Taylor eyed the spilled cappuccino in the saucer. "In her search, Ms. Warren discovered a letter we believe was written to Mr. Warren by his brother, as well as a photo of her parents on their wedding day—with their original names on the back. She also found the phone number of a U.S. marshal in her father's old wallet. All of that led us to make the connection to you, Mr. Rossi. After there was an attempt on his life before your trial, Walsh and his family disappeared. We assume they went into the U.S. Marshals Witness Security program."

"You're making a lot of assumptions, gentlemen." Lake sat back, forcing the detectives to turn away from the desk to keep him in sight. A ploy that gave Vincentio a chance to regroup. He scooted his saucer back onto the desk and wiped both his lips and his damp palms on the napkin Teresa had left. "But should any of them turn out to have credence, why would you think my client was involved in this death after all these years?"

"The other three members of his organization who testified at the trial all died within a year of their release from prison."

Vincentio was impressed. The detective had done his homework. "Those were accidents."

Taylor shifted back toward him. "You knew they'd died?"

His neck grew warm. "I have friends who kept me informed of significant events while I was in prison."

"Three accidents . . . a suicide . . . then someone tries to kill Warren's daughter when she starts making waves. And the only common denominator is you. A little too coincidental, don't you think?" Taylor's expression hardened.

"Since you've obviously done some research on me, you should know I never held family members accountable for mistakes made by my associates. I hold no grudge against Walsh's daughter."

"But you did against Walsh."

"There was no love lost between us. That was common knowledge."

"So what happened to Kelly Warren?"

"I have no idea."

"That must mean your hired gun slipped up."

Lake rose abruptly. "Gentlemen, this interview is over. If and when you have something more substantial to offer than innuendo, speculation, and circumstantial evidence, let us know. I'll show you out."

Without waiting for a response, Lake crossed the room, stopped at the door, and waited.

Taylor looked at Morgan, and the two men rose.

"Thank you for your time, Mr. Rossi." Taylor didn't offer his hand.

Vincentio gave a stiff nod.

He watched them exit. Listened for the sound of the front door opening, closing. Leaned back in his chair as Lake reentered. The man's expression was inscrutable as he retook his seat.

"Well?" Vincentio prodded.

"They don't have a thing that will stand up in court. Or even enough to get it that far. Yet. The circumstantial evidence, however, is formidable." He rested his elbows on the arms of his chair and steepled his fingers. "*Did* you know about the attempt on the daughter's life?"

"No."

"I didn't think so. But whoever did that made a mistake." He rose and picked up his briefcase. "I won't ask any further questions at this point. Let's wait and see if our friends come up with anything more concrete. If they don't, I doubt we'll hear from them again. If they do, we'll talk."

"They won't find a thing that will link any of this to me."

"Let's hope you're right. I'll let myself out."

Lake exited, and once again Vincentio heard the front door open and close. A few moments later, Teresa appeared on the threshold. "May I get you anything, sir? A refill on your cappuccino?"

He looked at the cup on his desk. The liquid that had sloshed out had stained the side of the cup and pooled in the saucer. What remained in the cup had grown cold.

Like a dead body lying in a pool of blood.

Funny. For all the violence in his world, he'd never witnessed a hit. His dirty work had been delegated to others, allowing him to keep his hands clean while rivals or disloyal men died.

But he'd never ordered a hit on a woman. The very thought sickened him.

A coil of rage snaked through his stomach. Carlson had blown this job. Leaving for an ill-timed vacation had been bad enough, but targeting a woman was—

"Mr. Rossi?"

At Teresa's prompt, he blinked. Stifled his anger as best he could. Nodded. "Yes. Another cappuccino would be nice."

With a dip of her head, she entered the room, picked up the cup and saucer, and disappeared.

Left alone once more, Vincentio pushed himself to his feet. The simple move taxed him, and he rested both palms on the desk, trying to shake off a weariness fueled by worry and a pulsing anger that had started with the call from the police and ratcheted up in the past fifteen minutes after he'd learned about the murder attempt on Walsh's daughter.

He couldn't do anything to contain the worry, though it wasn't prompted by the investigation into Walsh's death. The police would find no evidence linking him to that. The worry that kept him awake at night had far more to do with whether this glitch could somehow affect his chances of getting to know his grandson.

As for the anger—that would be assuaged. Carlson would pay for his mistakes.

That was one outcome Vincentio *could* control.

"So what's your take?" As Cole guided the car toward the nearest fast-food restaurant, he spared Mitch a quick look.

"He's guilty as sin. But we're never going to be able to prove it unless we track down the go-between—or go-betweens— who set up the job. There's a strong chance the perpetrator doesn't even know who hired him. Or didn't at the time. So I don't think we'll find any incriminating evidence there."

"Yeah." Cole drummed his fingers on the wheel. "I think he was telling the truth when he said he didn't know about the attempt on Kelly's life."

"I do too."

"But he didn't like my questions about his son. They seemed to unsettle him. I wonder why, if they've been estranged for years?"

"Interesting question."

Cole braked behind an SUV as he approached a red light. "You want to pay the son a visit? We have a couple of hours to kill before we have to head back to the airport."

"It couldn't hurt."

"I need some food first, though." He motioned out the window. "I see some golden arches up ahead."

"I wouldn't mind a breakfast sandwich and some more coffee. We can plan our strategy while we eat. In the meantime, I think I'll call Alison."

Cole rolled his eyes. "I'll be glad when you guys get married. Maybe some of the infatuation will wear off."

"Not a chance, buddy." Mitch grinned at him as he pulled out his phone. "You're just jealous. But look on the bright side. Kelly will be waiting in the wings once this is over."

As Mitch shifted away and tapped in Alison's number, Cole swung into the parking lot and joined the line at the drive-up window to wait his turn. Just as he'd been waiting his turn to find the right woman. His experience with Sara had been a detour on that journey, but now he was back on track. Thanks to Kelly.

And if his instincts were correct, one day in the not-too-distant future a beautiful redhead would be coming *out* of the wings to play a starring role in his life. Just as Mitch had predicted.

Giving him a huge incentive to wrap this case up as quickly as possible.

The cramps in her arms had long passed the mere painful stage. Her mouth felt as parched as the Arizona desert she and her mom and dad had visited once on a family vacation. And she had to go to the bathroom. Urgently.

Those were the only reasons Kelly was glad to hear the sudden beeping of her father's security system, announcing Carlson's return. She had no idea how much time had passed since he'd left, but faint glimmers of sun had been peeking through the shutters on the basement windows for what seemed like hours. The storm must have moved on.

A few minutes ticked by. Then the basement door opened, admitting a shaft of light into the dingy cellar. Feet appeared, followed by legs, a torso, and a head.

For a fleeting instant, Kelly thought she'd been rescued. The geeky-looking guy with the sideburns, glasses, and salt-

and-pepper hair wore a beige shirt, blue jeans, and a white hard hat like the ones the phone company service people used.

But when he approached and dropped down on one knee in front of her, she saw the latex gloves. It was Carlson. In another disguise.

She tried to say "bathroom," but the word came out garbled.

She made another attempt.

He must have picked up her desperation. Reaching behind her, he loosened the gag and tugged it out of her mouth.

"Bathroom." The words didn't sound a whole lot clearer, with her dehydrated tongue sticking to the roof of her mouth and her puffy jaw, but he got the idea.

He pulled out a pocketknife, flipped it open, and cut through the rope around her ankles and wrists. After closing the knife, he stood and pulled a pistol from a concealed holster on his belt.

Kelly froze.

"Get up."

She tried to follow his instruction, never taking her gaze off the pistol. But her legs and arms were numb, and it was a struggle to rise. Once she made it to her feet, she clung to the edge of the shelving.

"Move." He gestured toward the steps.

She hobbled toward them, praying she wouldn't fall, trying to get a handle on his mood. When he'd left, he'd been confident, cool, in control. Now he seemed on edge.

Perhaps the magnitude—and risk—of whatever he was planning to do with her was finally hitting home.

Maybe that would work to her advantage.

She half walked, half crawled up the steps. After she reached the top, she hurried as quickly as she could toward the hall bathroom. But he grabbed her arm and jerked her back as she rushed inside.

"Not so fast."

Carlson edged past her, the gun inches away from her face. "Stand against the wall. Over there." He gestured a few feet down the hall.

She complied.

He did a rapid survey of the bathroom and motioned her in. "You have three minutes."

Sidling past him, she started to shut the door, but he stuck his foot inside the frame. "Forget it. I don't want to have to break down a locked door to get you out."

She eyed the toilet. It wasn't visible from the crack in the door. Besides, there was no time to argue.

When she finished, she braced herself on the sink. A quick check in the mirror confirmed her jaw had turned purple. But at the moment, her parched mouth was a bigger concern. She twisted the tap and leaned down, slurping thirstily.

"Time's up." He pushed the door open. The edge of it hit her in the hip, but she kept drinking until he pulled her away from the sink and shut off the water.

Taking hold of her arm, he propelled her back to the kitchen. Back toward the basement door.

Now was the time to put the plan she'd developed into action.

"Wait." She pulled back.

"What's wrong?" He frowned at her over his shoulder.

She glanced at the clock on the wall beside the stove. Eleven-thirty. She went with the lunch plan instead of the coffee plan. "A friend of mine is supposed to swing by and pick me up for lunch at one. She has a key, and if I don't answer, she'll come in. I—I don't want to put her in danger."

The furrows on his brow deepened. "What friend?"

"Lauren. The woman I had coffee with the day you spiked my drink with peanuts."

As Carlson studied her, she prayed he'd buy her story . . . and take steps to protect his own hide.

Without speaking, he suddenly changed direction. After dragging her into the living room, he indicated her purse on the couch. "Get out your cell. And while you're at it, give me the keys to your house."

"Why?"

He shoved her toward the sofa. "Just do it."

Her fingers closed over the phone and she dug deeper for the keys. When she withdrew them, he held out his hand.

"Toss them to me."

She complied.

"Now call your friend—and put it on speaker so I can listen in."

Uh-oh.

If Lauren answered, she was sunk. Her friend would immediately question Kelly's weird message. Better to call her home number instead of her cell. Lauren would check it by the end of the day; her type A personality compelled her to keep on top of things.

Trouble was, that was hours away.

And Kelly didn't know if she had that much time.

"Tell your friend you took a hike to do some research, and you've been delayed."

The man had done some serious surveillance if he knew about her hiking. That creeped her out even more. But he'd missed one very important detail.

She never hiked in cold weather.

Lauren knew that.

So did Cole.

Thank you, God!

As she started to enter the number, he took her arm. Pressed the cold barrel of the pistol against her neck. "Make it sound convincing."

Finger shaking, she continued to tap in the digits. The answering machine kicked in, and her pulse accelerated as she listened to the greeting. This might be her one shot, and she didn't want to blow it. She'd already planned to raise as many red flags as she could, and Carlson had given her another one. All she could do was pray Lauren got suspicious enough to call the police.

At the sound of the tone, she tightened her grip on the phone. "Hi, Lauren. I'm going to have to cancel lunch. I decided to take one of my research hikes this morning, and I got delayed. Maybe we can catch up at Hacienda for some Mexican food next week. In the meantime, don't overindulge on turkey tomorrow, no matter how tasty it is." He pressed the gun harder against her neck. "Gotta run. If you want to try for coffee Friday instead of lunch next week, give me a call." She pushed the end button.

"Okay." Carlson backed away and waved the gun toward the basement door. "Downstairs."

"Are you leaving again?"

"Shut up and move."

She followed his instruction slowly, her mind racing. She had no idea when Lauren would get her message, and right now, her hands and legs were free. There might not be many more opportunities like this. Was there any chance she could knock Carlson over somehow? Make him drop the gun? Grab it herself? He'd said he didn't want to leave any marks on her body that would indicate foul play. So he wouldn't shoot her. Or strangle her. Or smother her.

But there was no question in her mind that he was planning to kill her. Most likely in a violent way, since the bruise on her jaw didn't seem to concern him. And she couldn't count on Lauren getting her message in time.

As she approached the top of the stairs, an idea came to her. Maybe she could turn suddenly halfway down and lunge at his legs. He might topple forward. Drop the gun. She could dodge him, scramble up the stairs, and lock the door. She didn't doubt he could kick it down, but she'd have a head start. If she ran outside screaming at the top of her lungs, *someone* would hear her. Sheila Waters, next door. Or a passing car. Or another neighbor. It was her best shot.

She started to descend. Three steps down, she looked over her shoulder. He was just two steps behind her.

This was her chance.

Whirling around, she ducked and lunged for his legs.

She heard his muttered oath. Even better, she heard his gun hit the concrete floor of the basement below. When she felt

238

him totter and grab for the railing, she slipped past him and scrambled to the top. Once in the kitchen, she turned to slam the door and slide the lock in place.

But he'd recovered faster than she'd expected. As she pushed the door closed, it slammed back against her, sending her sprawling on the floor.

He was on her before she could catch her breath, sitting on her legs, pinning her wrists to the floor, his face inches from hers. The fury in his eyes sent a cold chill straight to her core.

"That wasn't very smart."

Chest heaving, she licked her dehydrated lips and watched him. Wondering if he'd change his mind about where to kill her. If this would be where she died after all, just as her father had.

For what felt like an eternity he stared at her, a pulse beating in his temple. But at last he rose, grabbed her arm, and yanked her to her feet. "Let's try this again."

He didn't let go of her as they descended, or when he bent to retrieve his gun. Once he had it in his hand, he shoved her away and pointed it at her. "Lay on the floor. Face down. Put your arms straight out."

Shaking, she lowered herself to the concrete and did as he instructed.

She heard him moving about, and then her legs were pulled together and she could feel him wrapping the towels around them again. This time, though, whatever he secured them with wasn't a rope. It was even tighter.

"Roll onto your back and sit up."

She did so, checking out her ankles. They were bound with a plastic restraint.

The kind cops like him carried.

"Put your hands behind your back."

He disappeared behind her, and in less than thirty seconds her wrists were once again secured. Grasping her arms from behind, he dragged her back to the shelving post and trussed her tightly to it with the wire he'd used before.

She watched him pick up the dreaded strip of cloth, and

her stomach clenched. "Please . . . no one can hear me down here and—"

"Unless you want another knee in the ribs, open up."

Pressure built behind her eyes. This wasn't a battle she was going to win. She opened her mouth.

He tugged the cloth tight, and once more it sucked the moisture out of her mouth. She gagged again.

This time he took no notice. After giving her bonds one final check, he rose and crossed to the steps, his earlier cockiness replaced by deadly intent.

The familiar beeping of the alarm sounded, followed by the opening and closing of the back door.

Once again she was alone.

But he'd be back. And the next time he left, she knew she'd be with him.

As a tear trailed down her cheek, she let out a shuddering breath—and sent a silent prayer heavenward.

Please, Lord, let Lauren get my message and pass it on to Cole. Because that's my last hope.

19

"You think he'll show?"

At Mitch's question, Cole looked toward the entrance of the small, deserted park Marco Rossi—or Mark, as the man had corrected him during their brief phone conversation two hours ago—had specified as a meeting place.

"Yeah. Although he didn't sound happy about it." Cole burrowed his hands into the pockets of his slacks, wishing he'd brought his trench coat. St. Louis was chilly; this was full-fledged winter. But he hadn't expected to be spending any time outdoors.

"It would have been easier for him if we stopped by his job site or met him at a nearby café."

"I got the distinct impression he didn't want to have to explain to anyone who we were or why we wanted to talk with him."

"If he's that obsessed about disassociating himself from his father, Rossi may be telling the truth. His son might not know anything about his life or his business."

"We're here. We have the time. It's worth a try." Cole tipped his head toward the entrance of the park. "Here he is. Right on schedule."

Cole watched the tall, raven-haired man with dark eyes stride toward them. His work boots, jeans, flannel shirt, and thermal vest were a world removed from the suit and tie his father had worn this morning, but there was no disguising the distinctive Rossi features.

When he drew close, Cole stepped forward. "Mr. Rossi?"

"Yes. Detective Taylor, I assume." He held out his hand, and Cole took it, then introduced Mitch. Mark shook hands with him too. "Thank you for keeping your identity confidential when you spoke with my boss."

"We didn't want to put you in an awkward position. Our research indicated you and your father are estranged."

Mark snorted. "That's a polite way of putting it. If I never see the man again it will be too soon. He's scum." He practically spat out the last word.

Cole exchanged a look with Mitch.

"Sorry if that sounds harsh." Mark shoved his hands into the pockets of his vest, not sounding in the least sorry. "But it's the truth. That's why I keep my distance. We may share a name, but I want people to know that's *all* we share." He glanced around the empty park. "Sorry if this was inconvenient, but I wanted a place where there wasn't any chance I'd run into someone I know. I did eat up a lot of my lunch hour getting here, though. So how can I help you? You said you were conducting an investigation that involved my father?"

Cole gave him a quick recap of the case. As he spoke, Mark's lips thinned and compressed.

"Near the end of the meeting, I mentioned you," Cole concluded. "Your father said you knew nothing about his business or his life."

"That's true. Nor do I want to." The man's eyes hardened. "But if you're asking me whether I think your case fits his MO, the answer is yes. I did a lot of research on him in my younger years, and even though he was never convicted of murder, I have no doubt he arranged multiple hits. That was how the Rossi empire operated. If you were disloyal, you died. From what I learned, however, my father took great pains to cover his tracks. My guess is it will be very, very difficult to tie him to this crime."

Not what he wanted to hear. Stifling a sigh, Cole withdrew a business card from his pocket and handed it to Mark. "If by chance you have contact with him or learn anything relevant to our case, I'd appreciate a call."

The man took the card. Read it. Pocketed it. "Oddly enough, he did make contact. Last week."

Cole's antennas went up. "Why?"

"When he got out of prison, he tried to connect with me. I blew him off, and he let it rest. But now I have a son, and the Rossis were always big on family. He sent a gift in the mail, but we refused the package. So last week he showed up at my door with a teddy bear. Gave a sob story to my wife about how he's getting old and wants to spend time with his grandson. She fell for it. I didn't." His jaw tensed. "On one hand he wants to be a loving grandfather, and on the other he's still setting up hits. How sick is that?"

Very. But Cole treated the question as rhetorical and let it pass. "You wouldn't happen to know the names of any of his colleagues, would you?"

"Sorry. I wish I could help you." Mark narrowed his eyes. "But I'll tell you what. I don't appreciate being dragged into his sordid affairs. So I think I'll pay him a visit tonight to pass that message on. I can do a little digging while I'm there, if you want me to."

Cole grabbed at the unexpected offer. "We'll take any help we can get."

"Consider it done. He's gotten away with too many murders—and ruined too many lives. Mine included, for a long time. For him, being a Rossi is a status symbol. For me, it's a stigma. I thank God every day I found a woman who was willing to marry me despite my family history. If her parents weren't in poor health, we'd leave this town behind in a heartbeat." He checked his watch. "I need to get back to work. If I ferret out any information that seems helpful, I'll call you tonight."

"I appreciate that." Cole extended his hand, and the other man took it in a firm grip. After shaking hands with Mitch too, he turned and trekked back toward the entrance, leaving them alone in the silent park.

"That was interesting." Mitch watched the man walk away.

"Yeah. He is one angry dude."

"I might be too, if I had Rossi for a father."

"At least he's willing to help. And I'm glad we contacted him. He wouldn't be going to see his father tonight if we hadn't."

"That doesn't mean Rossi will tell him anything."

"A mob boss who wants to see his grandson badly enough to tote around a teddy bear might open up a little if he thinks it will help his cause."

"I'm not getting my hopes up. In the meantime"—Mitch looked at his watch—"we have a plane to catch . . . which I guarantee is overbooked. And we're already cutting it close. I don't know about you, but I do *not* want to spend Thanksgiving in Buffalo."

"Me, neither." He started toward the exit, and Mitch fell in beside him.

"So did you pick up the pies yet?"

Cole shot him an annoyed look. "I'm getting them tonight, okay? The bakery's open late. Don't you ever think about anything but food?"

"Sure." He grinned. "Alison's also on my short list of things to think about. Right alongside pumpkin pie."

"I think I'll tell her you said that." Cole's lips twitched as they passed through the iron gate at the entrance to the small neighborhood park and walked toward their car.

"If you do, I'll share your Superman story with Kelly."

Cole stopped abruptly and faced Mitch. "Alison told you about that?"

"Let's see, how does it go?" Mitch tipped his head. "When you were ten, you decided your Superman cape gave you the power to fly from the garage roof to the deck. That bit of youthful exuberance and stupidity landed you in the emergency room. Eight stitches later, you were grounded for a month. Did I get it right?"

Warmth rose on Cole's neck. "Alison is in big trouble. That's a family secret."

"I'll be family soon."

"Don't remind me."

Mitch chuckled. "How about this? I won't tell your story to Kelly if you don't tell Alison I put her in the same category as pumpkin pie."

"Is that a bribe?"

"Think of it as a trade."

"Deal."

"Okay. Now let's get on that plane and go home."

Mitch struck out for the car again, and Cole followed, fishing the key out of his pocket. The trip had been a long shot, and so far it had been a bust. But maybe Mark's confrontation with his father tonight would produce some usable information.

As he slid into the driver's seat, Cole readjusted his priorities for the evening. He'd get the pies—but the first thing he planned to do when the wheels touched down in St. Louis was check his voice mail.

And hope Mark Rossi had left a message with some helpful news.

"Shaun. Shaun!" Lauren raised her voice, trying to catch her husband's attention. But half a dozen of the under-ten cousins were in the midst of a raucous foosball tournament in her in-law's basement family room, while the fathers cheered from the sidelines.

She finally caught his attention after she resorted to flapping her arms.

"What's up?" He kept one eye on the game as he joined her.

"Your sister dropped your mom's bowl of homemade cranberry sauce and I volunteered to go to the grocery store and get some of the canned stuff."

He rolled his eyes. "That sounds like Caitlin. She's always been a klutz. And my mouth's been watering for my mom's cranberry sauce for two years." A shriek came from behind him, and he cringed. "Want some company?"

"The din getting to you too?" She grinned.

"Remind me never to complain again about the noise at our house when the twins get rowdy."

"I'll keep that in mind." She took his arm. "We're outta here. The decibel level is worse than a rock concert."

"Joe!" Shaun called out to his brother-in-law. "Caitlin dropped Mom's cranberry sauce. We're going out to get some canned stuff. Watch the boys, okay?"

"Sure. Sorry about the cranberry sauce." He gave them a sheepish smile.

"I grew up with her. I'm used to it." With a wave, Shaun turned toward the stairs.

Three minutes later, after retrieving their coats, they stepped out into the cold—and quiet.

Lauren closed her eyes, took a deep breath of the frosty air, and smiled. "Peace."

"Hey." He took her hand, and she looked at him. "Thanks for being a good sport. I know this is a lot of family together-ness for an only child."

She squeezed his fingers and tugged him toward the car. "No problem. As long as it's only every two years."

Unfortunately, their reprieve was shorter than she'd hoped. The store was less than a mile away, and in fifteen minutes they were once more in the car, mission accomplished.

"Are you ready to go back?" Shaun stuck the key in the ignition but didn't start the engine.

"No. But we don't have any excuse to delay. Do we?" She gave him a hopeful look.

"I haven't checked my voice mail today. Have you?"

"No." She picked up her purse from the floor and began to rummage for her phone. "It won't buy us much time, but I'll take whatever I can get."

"Me too." He pulled his phone off his belt and grinned at her. "Don't rush."

"Trust me, I won't. I'll even check the home machine."

"Sounds like a plan."

Angling away, she started with her work number, scribbling notes as she listened and returning a couple of calls that could have waited until after the holiday, just to eat up a few more minutes. Shaun seemed to be doing the same thing. His muted discussion about the pros and cons of different stone for a house he was designing was definitely not urgent.

Once she finished with work-related calls, she dialed into their home service. Only three messages. Too bad.

The first was a reminder about a dental appointment next week. The second was from the library, letting her know a book she'd reserved was waiting. The third, left three hours ago, was from Kelly.

And it was weird.

In the background, she heard Shaun close his phone and slip it back onto his belt. Shifting toward him, she frowned. "There's a strange message on our home machine from Kelly."

"What do you mean, strange?"

"Listen."

She put the phone on speaker and replayed the message.

Shaun's brow wrinkled. "What's with the lunch bit? I thought she knew we were leaving last night?"

"She did. She also knows we won't be back until Sunday, so why did she mention getting together Friday? And at Hacienda, of all places. She hates Mexican food."

"The turkey comment is also odd. She knows you don't like it."

"It's all odd. Including the hiking thing. Unless St. Louis has warmed up a whole lot since yesterday, she wouldn't have ventured out. She only hikes in nice weather. Besides, she told me she was going to focus on cleaning her dad's house so the realtor could show it Friday."

The creases on Shaun's forehead deepened. "Let's listen again."

Lauren keyed in the code, and the message replayed.

"She sounds out of breath," Shaun noted. "Like she's in a hurry."

"Or scared." A chill rippled through Lauren.

"Why don't you try calling her?"

She was already punching in Kelly's cell number as he spoke. After three rings, it rolled to voice mail. "Kelly, it's Lauren. I got your message. Call me ASAP, okay?" She pushed the end button. "I'm going to try her home number too."

When it rolled to voice mail as well, she left the same message. "It's strange she's not answering either phone."

"Didn't you tell me she might stay at her dad's last night because her power was out?"

"Yes."

"Try his number."

"It's been disconnected." Lauren tightened her grip on the phone. "I'm getting really bad vibes, Shaun."

"This does sound fishy." He exhaled and tapped his finger against the steering wheel. "You could call that detective who's been working on her father's case. Ask him to look into this."

"He's in Buffalo. Kelly told me he wasn't getting back until tonight."

"Could you get a message to him?"

"Maybe."

Using her most official-sounding attorney voice, Lauren gave her name and law office affiliation to the woman who answered the phone in the Bureau of Crime Against Persons, stressing her urgent need to talk with Cole despite the fact that he was out of town.

"I'll try to reach him, but he may be on a plane. Is there anyone else who might be able to assist you while you're waiting to hear from him?" the woman offered.

Lauren considered that. She had no idea how long it would take Cole to return her call, and she needed to talk with *someone*. Fast. Maybe the detective who'd originally handled Kelly's father's case would be helpful.

"I still want to talk with Detective Taylor. But if Detective Carlson is available, I could speak with him in the interim."

"He isn't in the office either, but I should be able to reach him. You'll hear from someone shortly."

As Lauren thanked her and ended the call, Shaun started the car and backed out of the parking spot.

"She's in trouble. I can feel it." Lauren bit her lip and checked her watch. "I'll give it ten minutes. If I don't hear from Carlson or Cole by then, I'm calling 911."

At the vibration of his cell, Alan stopped riffling through the hall closet in Kelly's house and yanked the phone off his belt. The office. He had to take it.

Pressing the talk button, he put it to his ear. "Carlson."

"Detective Carlson, this is Jennifer in Communications. We received a call a few minutes ago from a woman with an urgent need to speak with Detective Taylor. Since he isn't available, she asked that you call her. Her name is Lauren Casey. I can give you her number whenever you're ready."

Alan's stomach knotted. Why would Lauren call—unless Kelly had managed to imbed a distress signal in her message? But he'd listened to the whole thing. Nothing had sounded amiss.

"Detective Carlson?"

"Hold on a second." Dropping the hiking boots he'd pulled out of the closet, he strode toward the kitchen and reached for the pen and notepad Kelly kept on the counter. "Ready."

The woman recited the number. "I left a message on Detective Taylor's cell with this contact information too."

He stifled the expletive that sprang to his lips. Breathed in through his nose. "Okay. I'll get in touch with her right away."

Alan gave the end button a vicious stab. Kelly Warren had been nothing but trouble from the beginning. The sooner he got rid of her, the better.

But first he needed to do some damage control. He'd call

Lauren. Find out what had triggered her concern. Reassure her. Then he'd call Taylor, leave him a message that he had things under control. Fortunately, the man was out of town. But lover boy would be sticking his nose into this the instant he got off the plane. Lucky he'd run into Mitch Morgan at the copy machine yesterday and quizzed him about today's trip or he wouldn't know their flight was landing about six.

Twisting his wrist, he checked his watch. Three-forty. That gave him almost two and a half hours to take care of the new problem.

He could make this work.

But he didn't like the quiver in his finger as he punched in Lauren's cell number. He couldn't afford to let his nerves get the upper hand. He needed to remain focused. Attuned to details. That had always been the secret of his success.

Lauren answered on the first ring.

"Ms. Casey, this is Detective Carlson. How can I help you?" Despite the churning in his stomach, his greeting came out steady. Calm. Composed.

"Thank you for calling me back so fast. I received a voice mail from Kelly Warren that concerns me. She talked about canceling a lunch date for today, but I'm in Columbus, Ohio, for Thanksgiving—and she knew that. I think she was trying to let me know she's in trouble."

Okay. This might not be as bad as he'd thought. The tension in his shoulders eased. He could talk around a little communication problem.

"Maybe she just got her lunch dates mixed up, Ms. Casey." He used his most conciliatory tone. The one designed to calm distressed victims and witnesses. "I'm sure she's been under a lot of stress, given everything that's been happening with her father's case."

"No. Kelly's more organized than that. And I talked to her last night about our trip. Besides, she also mentioned meeting at a Mexican restaurant. That's totally out of character. She hates Mexican food."

His fingers tightened on the phone as a ripple of anger snaked through him. Her conversation had seemed so innocent. Yet she'd duped him.

He wouldn't underestimate her again.

At the moment, though, he needed to deal with her friend. "Do *you* like Mexican food, Ms. Casey?"

"Me?" Her tone was puzzled. "Yes. Why?"

"Isn't it possible she was trying to be accommodating, since she was canceling a lunch date?"

"But I told you—we didn't have a lunch date! And she knew that." Impatience—and annoyance—sharpened her words.

"I'll tell you what, Ms. Casey. I'm not far from Ms. Warren's house." He stared at a magnet on Kelly's refrigerator, trying to look at the bright side. If someone did happen to spot activity at her house, he now had a legitimate reason for being here. "I'll swing by. See if anything looks suspicious."

"She may have spent last night at her father's house. She lost power at hers."

"I'll check that out too. Communications told me you also called Detective Taylor, so I'll touch base with him as well. We'll let you know if we find anything suspicious. And if you hear from Ms. Warren, please call me." He recited his cell number. "Until we have more information, try not to worry. This may turn out to be an innocent misunderstanding."

Silence greeted his comment.

"Ms. Casey?"

"Yes. I'm here." Her voice had chilled.

He tried again to placate her, using the most gracious tone he could muster. He didn't want her contacting the office again to complain he'd been unresponsive. "You did the right thing calling with your concern. And please contact me directly if you have any other thoughts about what might have been behind her message. Day or night. That's why we're here."

"All right. Thank you." Her words held a hint of warmth now.

Good. He didn't have time to mollycoddle her.

"We'll be in touch." He pressed the end button.

As he slid the phone back on his belt, the magnet on Kelly's refrigerator caught his eye again. Some mumbo jumbo from the Bible, judging by the cross at the top. He leaned closer to read it.

Those whose steps are guided by the Lord, whose way God approves, may stumble, but they will never fall, for the Lord holds their hand.

Alan sneered at the final phrase and turned away.

Not this time, Kelly.

Not this time.

20

"I knew that delay in Buffalo was going to be a problem. This connection is going to be tight." Mitch checked his watch and fell into step beside Cole as they exited the jetway at O'Hare.

"Yeah, but I'd rather have mechanical problems on the ground than in the air."

"And I'd rather get home for Thanksgiving. Come on." Mitch picked up his pace as he wove through the crowd of passengers.

Cole did too. He didn't want to miss the holiday, either. Or the surprise visit he planned to make to Kelly's house before tomorrow ended, bearing a piece of pumpkin pie.

If he got home in time to pick up the dessert he'd promised to bring.

Six minutes later, the tension in Cole's shoulders eased as they approached their gate with five minutes to spare. But it ratcheted up again when they got closer.

"This doesn't look promising." Mitch frowned at the crowded waiting area. "Everyone should be on board by now."

"I'll find out what's happening." Cole made a beeline for the desk. One of the uniformed airline employees glanced up as he approached. "We just got in on the delayed Buffalo flight. What's the problem here?"

The woman gave him a frazzled look. "The plane arrived late. They've finished servicing it, so we'll begin boarding momentarily. The pilot expects to pick up some time during the flight to St. Louis."

"Thanks."

He wove back through the crowd and passed on the news.

"Better than I expected." Mitch set his bag beside him and pulled his phone off his belt. "I think I'll check messages and make a couple of calls."

"I bet Alison's on your call list again."

"Eat your heart out, buddy." Mitch turned away.

Chuckling, Cole pulled his own phone out of its holster. Two messages since they'd left Buffalo. Not bad. He tapped in his code, still smiling as the mechanical voice announced the day and time. Three-thirty-four.

"Detective Taylor, this is Jennifer in Communications. We had a call from a Lauren Casey who said she needed to speak with you about an urgent matter. When I told her you were unavailable, she asked me to pass the message on to Detective Carlson. But she wanted you to respond too. Here's the number."

As the woman recited it, Cole fumbled in his pocket for a pen and notebook, his good humor evaporating. If Lauren was trying to reach both him and Alan, the message had to be about Kelly. That was the only common denominator.

And "urgent" sounded ominous.

Once he found his pen, he hit replay and jotted down the number as the woman recited it for the second time. Then he moved to the next message, left ten minutes later. Hoping to hear Kelly's voice.

No such luck. It was Carlson.

"Cole, it's Alan. I just spoke with Lauren Casey, Kelly Warren's friend. She said Kelly left her an odd message earlier today, and she hasn't been able to reach her. I told her I'd swing by Kelly's house and check things out. It's probably nothing, but with all that's been happening I figure it's better to be safe. I'm also going to run by her father's house. Lauren says she may have spent the night there because the power was out at her house. I understand she also left a message for you with Communications, so I wanted you to know I was on it. I'll call you if I find anything worth reporting."

Mitch elbowed him. "They're boarding."

He punched in the speed-dial code he'd programmed into his phone for Kelly's cell. "I need to make a call."

"What's up?"

He gave Mitch a rapid-fire update as the phone rang. "Alan said he'd check things out, but that was almost an hour ago. I'm assuming he doesn't have any news or he would have left another message."

Kelly's phone kicked over to the answering service, and he depressed the end button without bothering to leave a message. "Kelly's still not answering. I'm going to try Lauren."

"You want me to check in with Alan?"

"Yeah. Thanks."

Lauren answered her phone on the first ring.

"It's Cole, Lauren. I just got your message. Tell me what's going on."

As she recounted the odd call Kelly had made five hours ago, his stomach tightened. The message was filled with red flags, from the nonexistent lunch date and turkey reference to the Mexican food suggestion.

"And I forgot to tell this to Detective Carlson, but the whole hiking thing doesn't make sense." A slight quiver ran through Lauren's words. "Kelly *never* hikes when it's cold. She wouldn't venture out in the kind of weather that was being predicted for St. Louis."

"Cole." Mitch nudged him. "Final boarding call."

Bending, he picked up his small bag and followed his colleague toward the jetway. "Hang on one second, Lauren." He pressed the mute button. "Did you reach Carlson?"

"No. It rolled to voice mail."

Cole handed the agent his boarding pass, pocketed it after she finished, and started down the jetway as he resumed his conversation with Lauren. "I'm getting on the plane to St.

Louis as we speak. Alan's an experienced guy, and it sounds like he's doing the same thing I'd be doing if I were there. I'll call him and you the minute we touch down."

"When are you landing?"

"We're boarding a little late . . . my guess is around six-fifteen."

"Sir . . ." The flight attendant stopped him as he stepped from the jetway onto the plane. "I need you to turn off your cell phone and take your seat as quickly as possible. We're ready to depart."

He acknowledged her comment with a nod. "Lauren, I have to hang up. We're taking off. Sit tight. I'll be back in touch as soon as I can."

As they inched down the aisle, Cole filled Mitch in on his phone call, pausing when he came to his row.

Mitch stopped, twin furrows etching his brow. "Maybe Alan will have some news by the time we land. If not, we'll figure it out."

"Yeah."

The flight attendant gestured to his seat, and he slid in and buckled up.

Knowing this was going to be the longest hour of his life.

He was back.

The beeping of her father's security system pierced the silence, triggering a burst of adrenaline that sent a tingle to Kelly's nerve endings.

Heart pounding, she peered at the shadowy stairwell. The weak light that had wedged through the shutters in the basement had waned, then disappeared, so she assumed night had fallen. Meaning Carlson had been gone four or five hours. Plenty of time for Lauren to have received her message and acted on it—assuming she'd checked her voice mail.

Kelly prayed she had.

She could hear Carlson moving around upstairs. After a

few minutes, the basement door opened and he came down the steps. In the darkness, she couldn't make out his features, but the stiffness in his posture radiated an almost palpable tension.

In silence, he dropped to one knee and freed her from the shelving unit, leaving her wrists bound. Then he cut through the plastic restraint on her ankles and hauled her to her feet.

After being immobile for hours, her legs refused to cooperate as he tugged her toward the stairs. She stumbled, but he kept moving, half dragging her across the basement. At the bottom of the stairs, he shoved her ahead of him.

"Go up."

She tried, but her shaky legs refused to support her. After two steps, she stumbled, and without her hands to cushion her fall, she went down hard. Her shoulder connected with the edge of a riser, and she slid back down to land in a heap at Carlson's feet.

Muttering a curse, he snagged her left arm and started up. She bounced along behind him, doing her best to get her footing and avoid bumping against the edge of each riser, but her knees, shins, and left hip took a beating.

When they reached the top, he continued toward the hall, dumping her at the entrance to the bathroom. He dropped to his knee behind her, and she felt a tug on her wrists. Suddenly the pressure was gone. Her arms were free.

"Put on the clothes in the bathroom. Don't take off the gag. You have five minutes." He pulled her to her feet, shoved her inside, and flipped on the shower light, which was muted behind the smoky glass. Keeping one foot inside the frame, he closed the door.

Kelly gripped the edge of the vanity and stared into the mirror. Her jaw had gone a deeper shade of purple, her hip and shins were throbbing—and Carlson no longer seemed to care about inflicting injuries.

The end of his little game must be getting close.

Fighting back a fresh wave of panic, she scanned the clothes he'd left for her. Jeans. Wool socks. Flannel shirt. Gloves. Hat. Ski jacket. Hiking boots.

Why did he want her dressed in outdoor gear?

She tried to focus. To analyze. When she'd called Lauren earlier, Carlson had told her to say she'd gone hiking. At the time, she'd thought that was a spur-of-the-moment excuse, a piece of information from his surveillance that had unexpectedly come in handy. But maybe not. Maybe all along he'd planned to take her somewhere in the woods, kill her, and leave her, making the whole thing look like a hiking accident.

Just as he'd made the anaphylactic shock look like an accident.

Except Lauren wouldn't buy it. Her friend knew she *never* hiked in cold weather. Cole wouldn't accept it, either, no matter how well Carlson pulled off the crime. He'd keep digging for proof it wasn't an accident. Searching for the perpetrator.

But Carlson was masterful at covering his tracks. No one suspected he'd killed her father, nor did anyone connect him to her near-fatal allergic reaction. And she was certain he'd be meticulous this time. Cole and Lauren might know her death was a homicide, but without proof, Carlson could walk away free.

That possibility made her sick to her stomach.

"You have three minutes."

At Carlson's cold comment, she went into action. If she balked, she had no doubt he'd dress her himself—and none too gently.

She used the facilities, then donned the attire he'd laid out as fast as she could. But tying the laces on the hiking boots was a problem. Her fingers were still too numb from the pressure on her wrists, and they were shaking.

All at once he pushed the door open, and she jerked. He had his gun in his hand now, and he surveyed her as she sat on the toilet seat, fumbling with the laces. "Hurry up."

In the light, she could see his eyes. And at the roiling rage in their depths, her heart stumbled.

"I found out about your little plan, by the way."

She froze, and the breath whooshed out of her lungs.

"Your friend called me for help."

Oh, God, please! No! She'd never even considered the possibility Lauren would call Carlson if she couldn't reach Cole.

"Yeah. Me. How about that?" A mirthless smile twisted one corner of his mouth. "She was concerned about your message. She told me there was no lunch date, and that you hate Mexican food. That was very clever, Kelly. But it's not going to make any difference. This game is over. Go in the kitchen." He backed away and motioned her out the door.

She rose, holding on to the vanity for support, and slowly walked down the hall, her thoughts in a frenzy. Without Cole or the police on her trail, she was doomed. She had to try to do *something* else to save herself.

As if reading her mind, he spoke from behind her as they entered the kitchen. "Just so we don't have a repeat of that earlier episode on the stairs, we're going to do what we did before. Lie on the floor and stretch your arms out to the sides."

This was where she had to take her stand. Once he tied her up again, she'd be helpless. And he wouldn't shoot her, not with all the care he'd taken to avoid leaving suspicious marks on her body. The gun was to intimidate, nothing more. That was to her advantage.

She took a surreptitious glance around the kitchen. The coffeepot was within arm's reach. If she grabbed it, swung around, and threw it at him, it might distract him long enough to give her a chance to lunge at his legs. Knock him off balance. He might drop the gun, and—

All at once, he hooked his foot around her ankle and jerked it back.

Thrown off balance, she pitched forward and crashed to the floor.

He was on top of her in an instant, pressing the heel of his hand against the back of her neck, smashing her cheek to the floor with such force her eyes began to water.

"We're done playing games, Kelly."

Though moisture blurred her vision, she saw him reposition the gun in his hand, lift his arm, and swing it down. The butt of the pistol connected with her temple.

Stars exploded behind her eyes.

Bright, white light filled her field of vision.

And then it went out.

The microwave pinged, and Vincentio rose from the solitary place Teresa had set for him at the table before she'd gone home to prepare for the Thanksgiving celebration she would enjoy tomorrow with her extended family.

The kind of celebration he wished was on *his* agenda.

Instead, he'd be eating his turkey dinner alone. Even Romano's was closed.

Although the meal Teresa had left for him smelled appetizing, he wasn't in the least hungry. His day had started badly, with the visit from the detectives, and he'd been feeling out of sorts all afternoon. Maybe he was catching a flu bug.

Or maybe he was just sick at heart.

Vincentio peeled back the plastic wrap from the veal scallopini and set it on the table. A glass of wine might help.

He crossed to the well-stocked rack on the far wall and perused the bottles. A special vintage tonight, perhaps. To lift his spirits.

As he debated his selection, then reached for a bottle of Chianti Rufina Riserva, his hand jerked at the sudden chime of the doorbell.

Shifting toward the foyer, he frowned. Who would show up at a man's house unannounced the night before Thanksgiving?

Without removing the wine, he crossed the kitchen and approached the front door. He didn't have many enemies these days, but caution had been ingrained in him since birth—especially in suspicious circumstances. And the timing of this visit was suspect.

The light was off in the foyer, and he didn't flip it on. Instead, he moved to the door and put his eye to the peephole that offered a wide-angle view of his well-illuminated porch. The face of his visitor was distorted, but he had no trouble identifying him.

It was Marco!

Maybe he wouldn't be spending Thanksgiving alone after all!

Hope burgeoning, he pulled back the two slide locks, twisted the key in the deadbolt, and smiled as he swung the door open.

Marco, the teddy bear gripped in his fingers, didn't smile back. "We need to talk."

Clinging to hope, Vincentio gestured his son into his house. "The living room is on your right."

In silence, Marco entered and walked to the center of the foyer, where he turned to him, his stance wide-legged and defiant. As if he was preparing to do battle. "This will work fine. I'm not staying long."

Vincentio closed the door, the heaviness in his chest squeezing the air from his lungs. He needed to sit, but that would leave Marco towering over him. Not the kind of position one took with an adversary.

And much to his regret, it was clear his son fell into that category. There had been no softening of his heart.

"Suit yourself." Vincentio walked over to the inlaid wood credenza against the wall. The one he and Isabella had bought on their trip to Venice when she'd already been carrying their only child. Laying his hand on top of it, he steadied himself and straightened his shoulders.

"First of all, I don't want your gifts." Marco's eyes smoldered as he flung the teddy bear onto a carved settee against the far wall. "Second, I don't want you to show up at my door again. Ever. And third, I do not appreciate being contacted by police investigating your latest hit."

The floor shifted beneath his feet. The detectives had gone to see Marco? "What are you saying?"

His son shot him a venomous look. "Two St. Louis County detectives called me at work today."

"Did you talk to them?"

"Yes. I met them on my lunch hour. It sounds like you're up to your old tricks, Dad." His bitter tone turned the last word into a pejorative term.

Anger began to churn in Vincentio's stomach. "What did they tell you?"

"Everything." He planted his fists on his hips and glared at him. "You arranged the deaths of all those people who testified against you. Including James Walsh, an innocent bystander who tried to do the right thing. Even after thirty-plus years, you still sought revenge. I don't know what beats in your chest, but it's not a heart." Revulsion curled his lips. "How do you live with yourself?"

Vincentio clenched the hand hanging at his side. "You don't know anything. I spent twenty-eight years in prison thanks to that man."

"No." Marco closed the distance between them, stopping inches away, fury darkening his eyes until they were black. "You spent twenty-eight years in prison because you're a criminal. That's where you deserved to be. Where you still *should* be, considering all the people who died because of you."

"I never killed anyone." His words came out tight. Choked.

"Ordering a hit is the same as pulling the trigger. Maybe worse. Pointing a gun at someone takes guts. Paying someone to do your dirty work is cowardly."

White-hot anger erupted inside him, and Vincentio lashed out, striking his son hard across the cheek. Marco's head snapped sideways, but he didn't flinch. He just stared at him, his expression cold as the ice already clinging to the ground on this holiday eve.

"That's the Rossi way, isn't it, Dad. Punishing those who stand up to you. Even when they're right. Violence solves so many problems." Sarcasm sharpened the edges of his words, which cut deeply as a knife.

Vincentio's fingers began to tingle, and he stuck his hand in his pocket. In all the years before he'd gone to prison, he'd never once struck his son. How had he sunk this low?

Because Alan Carlson bungled the job he'd been well paid to do.

That was the truth of it. Walsh's death would be history if the man hadn't gotten cocky and gone on vacation. The investigation wouldn't have been reopened, police detectives wouldn't have visited his home, and the door to a reunion that had cracked following his visit to his daughter-in-law might be swinging open instead of slamming shut.

Rage once more coursed through him—but he stifled it as best he could. He had to make one last effort to reach his son.

"I didn't kill anyone, Marco."

His son's gaze strafed him. "Can you look me in the eye and tell me you had nothing to do with James Walsh's death?"

He stared back. "If I said yes, would you believe me?"

"No."

"You believe those cops instead."

"They don't break the law. They uphold it. *That's* an honorable calling."

"You don't know a thing about honor." He ground out the words. "I can't believe you're a Rossi."

"I wish I wasn't."

Any other time, that insult would have been intolerable. But for the sake of his grandson, he fought down his anger. He could deal with his bruised pride later.

"Did it ever occur to you I might have changed during my years in prison?"

"No." His son's response was immediate. "And everything I heard today proves that."

"I can see the police turned you against me, just when I was hoping we could make a fresh start."

"A fresh start was never a possibility. And for the record, they didn't turn me against you. You did that yourself. Long ago." Disgust mottled his features. "So who did you get to do it, Dad? Some slimeball in St. Louis looking for a fast buck?"

The question took Vincentio off guard. Why did his son care how the deed had been accomplished? Unless . . .

Another surge of anger rippled through him, and he tightened his grip on the edge of the credenza. "The cops asked you to come here tonight, didn't they?"

"No. This was my idea. I wanted to make sure you got my message."

"But they asked you to question me."

"No. I offered to."

Vincentio sucked in a sharp breath, as if he'd been punched in the stomach. "You'd work against your own father?"

"If he's a criminal. So now you have another traitor in your midst. Are you going to order a hit on me too?"

"Get out." Vincentio could barely choke out the words.

"My pleasure." Marco strode across the room, opened the door, and looked back. "Don't ever contact me again. And may God have mercy on your soul."

He closed the door behind him with a sharp click.

For a full thirty seconds, Vincentio remained where he was. Then his legs grew weak and he began to tremble. Holding on to the credenza, he lurched along the length of it and sank onto the antique chair at the far end.

His son was lost to him.

And he would never be part of his grandson's life.

A suffocating anguish settled over him, along with the searing pain of loss, absolute and final. He bent forward, wrapped his arms around himself, and rocked until slowly the ache eased enough to allow his brain to engage.

Two things were clear.

There would be no family holiday gatherings in his future. Ever.

And Alan Carlson was going to pay.

21

The instant the flight attendant gave the all-clear for electronic devices, Cole powered up his cell phone. There was one message—from Mark Rossi. He checked that first.

"Detective Taylor, I spoke with my father. He didn't admit anything, and I didn't have any luck when I tried to dig for information. But after talking with him, I'm more convinced than ever he was behind James Walsh's death. I'm sorry I couldn't get anything more for you."

Dead end. Cole wasn't surprised, but he'd hoped for more.

He punched in Kelly's number. After three rings, it rolled to voice mail. Next, he tried Alan. The man answered on the second ring.

"It's Cole. I got your message, and I talked to Lauren Casey. What do you have?"

"Nothing. I drove by both houses and even looked in the garage windows. Her car's not in either place, and she's still not answering her cell."

"I know. I just tried." The seat belt sign went off and Cole stood to pull his small carry-on from the overhead compartment.

"I'm en route to a rendezvous with a nervous tipster in the homicide case, then I'm out of here for the holiday. You want me to do anything else before I fall off the radar?"

"No. I'll pick it up from here. Thanks."

Cole inched down the aisle, stepping aside in the jetway to wait for Mitch. When his colleague emerged, he started forward again, noting that Mitch, too, had ditched his tie sometime during the flight. "I just talked to Alan. He didn't come up with anything. Kelly's still not answering. I'll call Lauren as soon as we get onto the concourse."

Once inside, he set his bag down and tapped in her number. Again, she answered on the first ring. "Any news?"

"No. Alan didn't see anything out of the ordinary at Kelly's place or at her father's house, and her car isn't at either location." He massaged the stiff muscles in the back of his neck. "I'd like to get inside her house and take a look around, but search warrants take time."

"I can give you permission. I know where Kelly keeps an extra key, and I have her power of attorney for emergencies. I think this qualifies."

"It does for me. I'll worry about the red tape later." He stooped to pick up his bag and motioned with his head for Mitch to follow as he started toward the main terminal. "Where's the key?"

"Under a statue of St. Francis in the backyard. The statue's in the middle of the garden with the stones around the edge, and the key's wrapped in a tiny ziplock bag. She told me she put the new one there after she had all the locks changed a few weeks ago. Cole . . . do you think we need to get more people involved in this?"

"Yeah. I'm going to have a BOLO alert issued on her car as soon as we hang up. Worst case, we can consider a GPS trace on her cell."

"Forget it. Her cell is ancient. Five, six years old at least, and a bare-bones model."

Great.

"Okay. We'll pursue other avenues."

"Will you keep me informed?"

"I'll call as soon as I know anything. Talk to you later." He tapped the end button.

"You going to Kelly's house?" Mitch dropped back to allow a young mother juggling an infant and a diaper bag to edge past him in the opposite direction.

"Yeah. I'm also going to swing by her dad's place. Carlson said Kelly might have spent the night there because her power was out. I can run you by the office first, though, so you can pick up your car."

"Would you like some company?"

Cole looked over at him. "We've been on the go for twenty-four hours. You've got to be beat."

Mitch lifted one shoulder. "You stuck with me a few months ago when Alison was in trouble."

"She's my sister."

"And you're about to become my brother-in-law. This is what families do."

Cole's throat tightened, and he focused on the keypad in front of him. "Thanks. Now I'm going to get that BOLO alert in the works. And cross my fingers we find something in Kelly's house that will give us a clue to where she is."

A sudden jolt, followed by an explosion of pain in her head, nudged Kelly back to consciousness. When she opened her eyes, however, everything was pitch black. But she could feel a vibration. There was a hum too. Like a car engine.

She was in the trunk of a car.

Battling the haze muddling her brain, she tried to brace herself against the bumps. Yet she kept sliding. Like she was lying on a slippery surface. And what was that scratchy feeling around her neck?

She had no idea how much time passed before they reached their destination, but all at once she stopped sliding. The engine vibration ceased. She heard the soft click of a car door opening. Another soft click as it closed. A key was fitted in the trunk lock. She tensed as the lid rose.

The trunk light didn't come on, and the sky was black.

No moon or stars added even the barest hint of illumination, meaning the clouds had returned. But while the face above her was in shadows, the soft voice was clear. Too clear. And it sent shivers down her spine.

"We're almost done, Kelly."

Leaning down, Carlson slid his arms under her knees and shoulders. Then he lifted her out of the trunk and propped her beside the car. *Her* car, she realized, before the world tilted and her knees buckled. He grabbed her with one hand as she started to slide, holding her in place as he loosened the scratchy thing around her neck with his other hand.

Although her vision was blurry, she now understood why she'd been sliding around so much. She was encased in an oversized plastic garbage bag from toes to neck.

And she'd watched enough police shows to know why.

Carlson didn't want to leave any trace evidence in her trunk that would suggest she'd made this trip under duress rather than driving herself.

He pushed the bag down her body. When he got to her feet, he cut the plastic restraint and removed the hand towels that had protected her ankles. "Step out."

Once she complied, he stuffed the bag, towels, and restraints into the backpack he'd placed on the lid of the trunk. Then he removed her knit cap and pulled off the shower cap that had encased her hair underneath. That, too, went into the backpack before he tugged the knit version back over her head and tucked her hair inside it. He grazed her bruised temple with his knuckles, sending a shaft of pain shooting through her skull, and she moaned again.

He ignored her.

As he locked her car, tucked the keys in the pocket of her jacket, and hefted his backpack into place, she peered at her surroundings, blinking as she tried to focus. They were in a far corner of a gravel lot, surrounded by woods. The kind of spot she often parked near trailheads.

So her theory had been correct. He was going to stage a hiking accident.

A frigid gust of wind whipped past, and she shivered as Carlson took her arm and propelled her toward the dark woods.

And as he set off down the trail, dragging her along beside him, she knew that short of a miracle, this would be her last hike.

"I have another assignment for you." Vincentio pressed the phone against his ear with his right hand and splayed the fingers of his left hand on his desk.

"I'm always happy to be of service."

Yes, he was. For a price. But Vincentio was willing to pay handsomely for this particular service. Especially from a trusted colleague, a man of sound judgment whose advice he'd overridden when he'd selected Carlson for the Walsh job. A man who had demonstrated his loyalty and reliability many times over.

"First, I want you to check with our friend in St. Louis to confirm he's followed through on his plan to correct the problem. Assuming he has, his usefulness is finished. He's caused me great trouble and has taken actions I do not approve of. There are consequences for that. Am I clear?"

"Very."

"Good. I want this done fast, and I want it done clean. No questions. No links. And I want it done within the next twenty-four hours. I'll pay fifty percent over the usual price. Can you handle this?"

"The timing will be a challenge . . . but I know someone in the area who I believe can pull this off. A professional. I'll contact him at once."

Vincentio didn't miss the slight emphasis on the word *professional*, a dig at *his* choice of an amateur for the Walsh job. He let it pass. "Excellent. I'll arrange payment as soon as this call is finished. It will be in your hands tomorrow. Let me know when the job is completed."

"Of course." The line went dead.

Authorizing the payment took only one phone call. Then Vincentio set aside the throwaway, nontraceable cell phone he'd picked up last weekend for emergency use and leaned back, elbows on the arms of the chair he'd ordered three years ago from a family-owned leather shop in Agrigento.

Marco had claimed he was a killer. But for him, doling out punishment was simply taking care of business. Protecting the family honor. Lives were lost, yes, but not without reason. The killing in his world wasn't meaningless, like the senseless violence that was all over the news these days.

Still . . . this would be his last hit. He'd settled all his scores. He had no more enemies.

Except his son.

His throat constricted, and he picked up the glass of wine he'd poured after Marco's visit. Took a sip. It went down smooth, warming him. He put it to his lips again. He and Isabella had always sat together with a glass of wine at night, after Marco went to bed. It had been his favorite part of the day. Loving. Intimate. Filled with quiet laughter and gentle touches. Far preferable to drinking wine alone.

But that was his lot in life now, thanks to the bungling ineptitude that had sent detectives to his son's doorstep—and quashed his hope of a relationship with his grandson.

His fingers tightened on the stem and he lifted his glass in mock salute to the man who'd ruined everything.

"Good riddance, Carlson."

And then he drank to the man's demise.

Cole fitted the key in Kelly's lock and turned the knob. "Let's take a quick walk-through first and see if anything jumps out at us."

Without waiting for Mitch to respond, Cole flipped a light—at least the power was working now—and moved to the kitchen. It was neat as a pin, as usual. No dishes in the sink, no clutter on the counter, the flour, sugar, and tea containers aligned. It looked the same as it had on his previous visits.

"Does someone actually live here?" Mitch scanned the pristine space.

"She's very neat."

"No kidding." He gave the place another once-over. "At least it should be easy to tell if anything is out of order. You want me to check the basement while you do a sweep up here?"

"Yeah." He gestured to the right. "That's the door."

While Mitch focused on the lower level, Cole checked out the bedrooms. Both appeared undisturbed, as did the closet in each. Nothing was amiss in the bathroom, either. He switched on the light in Kelly's office. An easel was positioned to catch the light from the large window during daylight hours, and despite his worry, the charming half-finished illustration of an elf using a mushroom as a table tugged at his lips. As in the other rooms, everything in her work space was neatly organized. Brushes were arranged by size and shape, tubes of paint were sorted by color in a plastic tub, stacks of different types of paper shared shelf space with her camera, palettes were . . .

His gaze swung back to the camera. She'd told him not long after they'd met that she never went hiking without her camera. Yet here it was. Further evidence that hiking hadn't been on her agenda today.

He exited into the hall and moved to the living room. It, too, looked as it had on his last visit. No furniture was out of place, and there was no clutter. The glass-topped coffee table held only the small bronze casting of a man holding a child by the hand that he'd noticed on previous visits.

Nothing in the tiny entry raised any red flags, either. Hoping Mitch had had better luck, he started back to the kitchen. As he passed the coat closet, he opened the door, gave it a cursory perusal, and began to close it again.

Then he froze.

The spot where she kept her hiking boots was empty.

"Find something interesting?" Mitch joined him in the small space.

"Yeah." He pointed to the bare spot. "Her hiking boots are gone, but her camera isn't."

Mitch squinted at him. "And that's significant because . . . ?"

"She always keeps her hiking boots here. Since they're missing, that would suggest she did go out to the country. But she told me she never goes on hikes without her camera. She uses it to take pictures of ideas for illustrations. Besides, she never hikes in cold weather."

The other man shrugged. "Maybe she just decided to wear the boots today."

"No. She only wears them for hiking. She was very specific about that too."

"Did you check her other closets?"

"This is where she keeps them, Mitch. Everything in its place, as she once told me." He gestured around the living room behind him. "Have you ever seen a better-kept house?"

"You have a point."

"So if she doesn't hike in cold weather or without her camera, why is she wearing her hiking boots?"

Twin furrows appeared on Mitch's brow. "Okay. Let's back up a little and think this through. You're still convinced someone deliberately spiked her drink with peanuts at the coffee shop, right?"

"Right. But Rossi seemed taken aback by that news. Like it wasn't part of his original plan. That might suggest that whoever killed Kelly's father was getting nervous about her digging into his belongings and acted on his own."

"Because he didn't want his boss to find out the suicide ruling was being questioned."

"That's what I'm thinking. Rossi isn't known for his tolerance of mistakes."

Mitch propped a shoulder against the wall and shoved his hands in his pockets. "That might explain why the killer went after Kelly originally, but why would he target her again? Now

272

that we've established a connection between Kelly's father and Rossi, another incident with her would only put more suspicion on our friend in Buffalo. That would be the last thing the perp would want to do."

"Yeah." Cole sighed. "That's where I get stuck. It doesn't make sense."

A few beats of silence passed, and then Mitch's expression grew speculative. "Okay. Think about Rossi's attitude when you called, and again during our visit. He was *not* happy. He was probably putting pressure on our man to get the heat off of him. How would our guy do that?"

Cole shrugged. "The only way we would drop the investigation at this point is if we had definitive proof of suicide."

"Like a letter, or some other convincing piece of evidence."

"Yeah, but there wasn't anything. The CSU technician or Kelly would have found it."

"Unless our guy happened to know something we don't that would make a later discovery credible."

Cole furrowed his brow. "Like what?"

"I don't know. But he's no dummy. He'd have gotten away with this whole thing except for the tulip fluke. And he got into the house once; what's to say he couldn't get in again to look the place over, try to get some ideas? And with the pressure on from Rossi, he'd want to do that fast."

As Mitch's implication sank in, the bottom dropped out of Cole's stomach. "Maybe while Kelly happened to be there."

"That would explain her odd message and why she's dropped off the radar."

Cole started to pace, his mind racing. "It's a stretch . . . but possible. Okay. Let's go with it for a minute. If he did run into Kelly at the house, he'd have to get rid of her. But he wouldn't want it to look like murder. He was already doing damage control at Rossi's bidding, so he wouldn't want to raise any suspicions beyond those generated by mere coincidence."

"Right." Mitch scrubbed a hand down his face. "But to pull off John Warren's murder so cleanly, he had to have done a lot of research—and a lot of surveillance. Some of that was probably directed at Kelly. That means he's familiar with her patterns—which would explain how he knew about the peanut allergy and her hiking trips."

"And he could use a hiking accident to try and cover up her murder." Cole's tone was grim. "Trouble is, he missed a couple of key facts—the camera and her aversion to cold." He pulled his phone off his belt. "We need to have Communications make sure the BOLO alert is picked up by outlying municipalities, as well as the Department of Conservation and the park rangers in the St. Louis area. If we're right, and he wants this to look like a hiking accident, he'll have to leave her car in a visible place so it doesn't seem suspicious. I also need to call Lauren and see if she knows whether Kelly has an extra key for her father's house." He started to dig through his pocket for her number.

Mitch touched his arm. "You know we're making a lot of leaps here."

Like he needed to be reminded.

A muscle in his jaw ticked. "You have any other ideas? At least the pieces fit."

A moment of silence passed. Then Mitch dropped his hand. "We could track her cell."

"It's too old to be GPS enabled."

Mitch's lips compressed into a flat line. "Okay. I'll take care of the alert while you call Lauren." He reached toward his belt as he stepped into the hall.

Cole pulled out Lauren's number and tapped it in again.

She didn't bother with a greeting. "Is there news?"

"Not yet. I'm in Kelly's house now. Her hiking boots are missing, but her camera's still here."

"That's weird."

"I know. I want to check out her father's house. Do you know if she has an extra key around here? And do you by chance have the security code?"

"No. But the realtor has both. That's why Kelly was over

there today. With a potential buyer planning to look at the house on Friday, she wanted to do some cleaning. I can't remember the realtor's name, but check the drawer next to the dishwasher. That's where Kelly keeps business cards. I bet hers is in there."

Cole was already halfway to the kitchen. Once there, he located the drawer, pulled it open—and found Denise Woods's card on top of the stack. "Got it."

"Kelly's in serious trouble, isn't she?" A tremor ran through Lauren's words.

"If she is, we're going to do our best to get her out of it. I'll be in touch when we know more. Keep your phone with you, okay?"

"Absolutely. And since I have power of attorney, I give you permission to search wherever and whatever you deem necessary. We don't have time for warrants."

"I'm with you. Besides, I think we're into exigent circumstances at this point, anyway. I'll be in touch."

As he secured his phone on his belt, Mitch rejoined him. "They're recommunicating the BOLO alert and targeting the conservation agents and park rangers. I also filled Brett in on the situation. He said to keep him informed and let him know if we need anything."

Cole would rather be dealing with his own sergeant on this, but the holiday-duty officer was a sharp guy too. "Okay. You want to handle the driving to Warren's house while I try to track down the real estate agent?"

"Sure."

As they exited the house and Cole tossed Mitch his car keys, he paused under the porch light to tap in Denise Woods's number.

And prayed John Warren's house would yield some clues that would lead them to Kelly.

Halfway to his destination along the Weldon Spring trail, Alan's cell began to vibrate against his hip.

Talk about lousy timing.

He hesitated and glanced at Kelly. She stumbled to a stop beside him and listed to the right. He tightened his grip. She'd been weaving like a drunken sailor, slowing him down a lot more than he'd expected. On his bike, he could cover the first mile or so of this relatively level, well-maintained trail in minutes. Walking, he'd expected it to take fifteen, max. The slow progress was making him edgy enough. He didn't need phone calls.

Letting Kelly sink to the leaf-covered ground, he yanked the phone off his belt. The number for the incoming call was blocked. Bad sign. It could be Rossi's man.

If so, that was not a call he could ignore.

"Yes?" He spoke softly, scoping out the darkness through his night-vision goggles for any sign of unwanted company among the leaf-shorn trees.

"The boss wants to know if you've completed the plan you outlined to us about a certain piece of correspondence."

"It's done. It should be discovered in the next few days."

"Then your final payment will be delivered shortly. I'll call with the drop location."

"How shortly? I was just getting ready to leave for the weekend."

There was a slight pause. "Where are you going?"

"Kansas City. But I can change my plans."

Another pause. "No. We'll work it out. I'll be in touch."

The line went dead.

Alan slid the phone back into its holder. At least Rossi was making the final payment promptly, now that he'd kept up his end of the bargain. And once he had the money in hand, he could put this whole unpleasant episode behind him. Focus on convincing Cindy to reconsider their divorce.

Pulling Kelly upright, he started forward again. But despite the tremors coursing through her, she continued to resist, dragging her feet.

Annoyed, he swung toward her, repositioned the backpack

to hang off one shoulder, then bent and hefted her to his other shoulder. He ignored the guttural sounds of pain coming from behind the gag. He needed to finish this job. As soon as possible.

Once more he resumed his trek. Fortunately, the trail was in reasonable condition. He should pick up some time now.

And if all went well, in less than fifteen minutes Kelly Warren would be history.

22

"Here he comes." Mitch gestured over the steering wheel to a police car speeding down John Warren's street. "That was a smart idea to have a street officer pick up the security code and key from the realtor."

"I figured it would be faster than having her meet us here." He opened the glove compartment and pulled out four latex gloves, tossing two to Mitch. "Let's go."

Two minutes later, after unlocking the door and deactivating the security system, Cole flicked on the lights in John Warren's kitchen.

Mitch scanned the room. "Not quite as pristine as his daughter's, but close."

"I see Kelly's touch here." Cole gestured to a bouquet of fresh flowers on the table beside a plastic-wrapped plate of cookies. Swallowing past the sudden lump in his throat, he refocused on the task at hand. "You want to divide up like we did at her place?"

"Works for me."

As Mitch disappeared through the door in the corner of the kitchen, Cole tackled the first floor. Nothing seemed out of the ordinary in the modest living and dining room. The smell of lemon-scented cleaning solution wafted from the bathroom as he walked down the hall, and he poked his head in. One single long strand of russet-colored hair was draped across the white porcelain in the sink. More evidence Kelly had been here.

He continued down the hall, checking out all the rooms. When he reached the one at the far end, he flipped the light switch.

Three things struck him at once.

This had been Kelly's childhood bedroom. A shelf of awards and trophies, all bearing her name, graced one wall. But there was a gap—perhaps the spot usually occupied by the large trophy now balanced on one edge of her dresser? If so, why had it been removed?

The second thing he noticed was the unmade bed. Not Kelly's style.

And finally, her overnight bag stood beside the dresser, a green sweat suit stuffed—not neatly folded—inside the open top.

Someone other than Kelly had been in this room. Had touched her things.

The knot in his stomach tightened.

Cole returned to the hall and checked the last room. Her father's study. He paused on the threshold and eyed the carpet. It was clear Kelly had vacuumed it during her visit. Symmetrical tracks were visible in the plush pile, but there was also a traffic pattern. There had been some foot activity in the center of the room, and there were indications someone had walked to the desk.

"Cole!"

At Mitch's summons, he retreated to the kitchen and crossed to the basement door. Mitch was standing at the bottom of the steps.

"You might want to come down. I've got a red flag."

"I found several up here too." He joined Mitch in the basement and followed him to a shelving unit.

"What caught my eye was that green fuzz on the ground. When I bent down, I saw that hair." Mitch indicated a spot on the floor where another long strand the same hue as Kelly's lay atop the green fuzz. "And while I was down there, I noticed this." He dropped to his haunches and indicated the support beam of the shelving.

Cole got down to his level and scrutinized the spot. The heavy-duty steel unit looked as if it had been in place for many years. The color had darkened a bit, but in the spot Mitch indicated there appeared to be a narrow rub mark that had slightly brightened the finish.

He checked out the green fuzz again. "That's the same color as the sweat suit stuffed into the overnight bag in her bedroom." He relayed his other observations as well. "I don't like how this is adding up."

"Neither do I."

A faint chime sounded, and Cole canted his head. "Is that the doorbell?"

"I think so."

He rose and crossed to the stairs, taking them two at a time, Mitch on his heels. Once in the foyer, he checked the peephole.

"It's an older woman. A neighbor, maybe?"

"I'm not taking any chances." Mitch pulled out his Sig Sauer and took a position in the hallway.

Cole didn't argue.

After releasing the locks, he opened the door halfway. "May I help you?"

"Yes, young man, you may." The short, wiry, gray-haired woman adjusted her glasses and stared at him. "I'm Sheila Waters from next door, and I'm very concerned about what's been happening at this house. When I saw that police officer pull up"—she gestured over her shoulder toward the patrol car—"I decided to march over here and find out what's going on. I've been worrying ever since I saw that man drive a car out of the garage. There's not supposed to *be* a car in that garage. Kelly sold her father's car months ago."

Cole's fingers clenched around the edge of the door. "What man?"

"I have no idea. Just like I don't have any idea who *you* are."

"Detective Cole Taylor, ma'am." He pulled out his credentials and flipped them open.

"Another detective?" She leaned forward to examine the badge, straightened, and huffed out a breath. "What is this neighborhood coming to?"

"Ma'am, if you saw someone take Kelly's car, we need to talk."

"It wasn't Kelly's car. She always parks in the driveway."

"We think it *was* Kelly's car, ma'am." No wonder the perp had been surprised by her presence, if she always parked in the driveway. He turned to Mitch. "Get the CSU unit over here."

"I'm already on it."

The woman peered around him into the shadowy hall. "Is that Detective Carlson back there?"

"No, ma'am. You know Detective Carlson?"

"Of course. He was asking questions about a robbery in this neighborhood just two weeks before poor John died. And he came back to investigate the so-called suicide. But as I told him at the time, I knew John Warren for twenty years, and that man would never have taken his own life." She peered at him. "If that *was* Kelly's car, why was that man driving it? Where's Kelly?"

"That's what we're tying to determine, ma'am." A cold gust rocked the older woman, and he motioned her in. "Let's get out of the wind. Mitch, you want to tell that officer to hang around?"

"Yeah." He slipped through the door, phone pressed to his ear.

"Ms. Waters, what time did the man pull out of the garage?"

"I don't know exactly, but it was during the first commercial break in the six o'clock news. I got up to close the blinds in the front window, and I saw the garage door open. He didn't have the headlights on, which seemed strange. There was enough illumination from the streetlight for me to see he had glasses on, like the guy I spotted earlier around the back of the house."

"What guy?" Mitch slipped back inside as Cole asked the question.

"I think he was a phone company repairman. He had on a white hard hat and he wore glasses too. Had a little gray in his hair, from what I could see below the hat." The woman cocked her head and squinted at him. "You know, it was the oddest thing about that man. I saw him from the back at first, and his build made me think of Detective Carlson. I so enjoyed meeting your colleague. We had a nice chat over some brownies during the robbery investigation. Such a nice man. Handsome too."

Cole frowned and shot Mitch a quick glance as he responded to Sheila. "He did come by today to check on the house after we became concerned about Ms. Warren, but that would have been sometime after four."

"No. This was before noon. And I only caught a glimpse of him before he disappeared around the back of the house. I assumed there was some damage to the phone lines in the neighborhood from last night's storm."

"Did you notice anything else today out of the ordinary?"

"No. Not until that police car pulled up. Is Kelly in trouble?"

"That's what we're trying to find out, ma'am."

"Well, you keep trying. I watched that little girl grow up from the time she was thirteen. I don't want to see anything happen to her too."

"We'll do our best to make sure she's safe. Thank you for stopping by." Cole eased her toward the door and pulled it open.

"If you need me for anything else, you just come right over."

"We'll keep that in mind."

As he closed the door behind John Warren's neighbor, Cole turned to Mitch. "What do you make of that?"

"We have a solid departure time now."

"I'm talking about Carlson."

"She was obviously taken with him."

"No." Impatience nipped at his voice as he started to pace. "I mean the fact that she thought he looked similar to the phone guy."

282

"Coincidence?"

"What if it's more than that?"

Mitch frowned. "Like what?"

"Like what if Carlson's involved in this?"

A beat of silence passed. "That's a real stretch. As far as I know, Carlson has a clean record. And he's a solid detective. I've worked a few cases with him."

"I have too."

"And she said this guy wasn't him once she saw his face. He had glasses and gray in his hair."

"Did you know Carlson was an undercover detective with the Dallas PD before he joined County?"

Mitch blinked. "No."

"He doesn't talk much about it. But after he and Cindy split, we made the Friday-night happy hour rounds together for a while, and he told me a few things about it. I got the impression he had a real knack for the work."

"You think we should talk to him?"

Cole pulled his phone off his belt. "Yeah. And while I get him on the line, why don't you check and see if the phone company had anyone in this area today?"

"Okay." He motioned toward Cole's phone. "That could be an awkward call."

"I know." He tapped in the man's number. "But I'd rather be embarrassed than take a chance on Kelly's life."

Who was calling him now?

Alan stopped, shifted Kelly on his shoulder, and dug out his cell.

Cole.

Weighing the phone in his hand, he debated whether to answer. He'd already told the man he had a clandestine meeting with an informant in the double homicide and was leaving for the holidays. He'd hoped that would deter him from calling him again.

The phone continued to vibrate. What would he gain by answering?

Nothing.

Decision made, he slipped the phone back into its holder and set off again. He wanted no more delays with this task. Once he was finished, he'd retrace his steps to the trailhead, jog the three miles to the fast-food restaurant near the I-64 entrance ramp, and get a cab back to his car. Then he'd head for his sister's in Kansas City. She'd be surprised to see him, since they rarely talked and he'd ignored the message she'd left on his voice mail, inviting him for the holiday. But she wouldn't turn him away if he showed up for dinner tomorrow. And he'd told Taylor he was going out of town for the holiday.

The phone stopped vibrating. Finally.

Maybe now he would be left in peace.

"No answer." Cole tapped the end button. "I wonder if Cindy's heard from him?"

"I thought they were separated."

"They are. But he told me they were still in touch, and that he was working on a reconciliation. That might be where he's going for the holiday."

"I guess it's worth a call." Mitch pulled out his phone too. "I'm going to check in with Alison. Let her know what's going on."

Cole glanced at his watch and grimaced. "I missed the pie pickup."

"I think she'll understand."

Yeah. She would. But he'd make it up to her somehow after this nightmare was over.

Two minutes later, Communications had located Cindy's number in Carlson's personnel records—along with the number for a sister he hadn't known existed. Another call to make if the one with Cindy didn't pan out.

He tapped in Cindy's number, and she picked up just as he thought the call would roll to voice mail.

She listened to his explanation, then responded in a cautious tone. "I'm not sure why you think he'd be coming here for Thanksgiving."

Cole's neck grew warm. Bad call on this one. "I got the impression you two were in touch and there might be a reconciliation in the works."

"Did he tell you that?"

"Not in those exact words, but it was implied."

An annoyed sigh came over the line. "The man is truly delusional. Our divorce became final this week—giving me much to be thankful for this holiday."

Cole furrowed his brow. "I'm sorry if I misinterpreted what he said. It sounded as if you were talking about getting back together."

"He was the one talking about it. He even showed up a few times and hung around outside my apartment. I had to threaten to have a restraining order issued to get him to stop bothering me. The man had more problems than I thought."

Cole's frown deepened. "Look, I don't want to pry into your personal business, but we're in the midst of a situation that could be life-threatening. And we're starting to think Alan may be involved. Are the problems you mentioned the kind we might need to know about as part of this investigation?"

A few moments of silence ticked by. "I don't know. But I hate to make his life harder than it already is, even if I'm grateful he's out of mine."

"I understand that." Cole motioned Mitch over as the other man wrapped up his call. "And if the information you give us isn't relevant, it won't go any further. Mitch Morgan, another County detective, is here with me. It's just the two of us. Can I put you on speaker while we talk?"

"I guess so."

"Hold one second." He pressed mute. "The divorce became final this week. She had to threaten to issue a restraining order to keep Carlson from bugging her. She said he had other problems too." He released mute and pressed the speaker button, holding the phone in front of him. "So what other problems are we talking about, Cindy?"

"Mostly gambling. He says he's stopped now, but he's told me that before."

Cole exchanged a look with Mitch. "How serious is the gambling?"

"Very. We lost our house and all the money in our savings account. He went through the trust fund my uncle left me too. That was the last straw. When I walked out, he was not only broke, he owed some major bucks at several casinos. He kept trying to convince me he'd reformed and that he was taking other security jobs on the side to pay off his debts and replenish my trust fund. He sent me a bank statement a few weeks ago showing a healthy balance, so I guess he was telling the truth about that. But I'm not willing to take another chance his reform is permanent."

As Cole watched, Mitch's lips settled into a grim line.

That was his reaction too.

"Cindy, this has been very helpful. Let me give you my number in case you hear from Alan. But if you do, please don't tell him we called."

"Okay. Good luck with your case."

"Thanks." Cole hung up and slid the phone back onto his belt. "I'm liking this less and less."

"Me too."

"Motive, undercover experience, opportunity. It's all there."

"Getting himself made case detective would also be a brilliant move."

"Yeah." Cole exhaled and jammed his fingers through his hair. "It was the perfect setup for a perfect crime."

"If we're right, it's not perfect anymore."

"It might have been, if Kelly hadn't thrown him a curveball by catching him in the act of whatever he was doing at her father's house. But he's a methodical planner, and he didn't have the opportunity to plan this one. That's why he's made a few mistakes."

"None that tell us where he took Kelly."

Like he needed to be reminded of that. Gritting his teeth, Cole fought back a surge of panic. "If our theory is on target, though, her car is sitting somewhere as we speak, waiting to be discovered. And we *will* discover it."

Mitch didn't respond. He didn't have to. Cole could read his thoughts in his eyes.

Yes, they'd find the car.

But would they find it in time?

Finally.

They were here.

Alan got down on one knee and let Kelly slide to the ground. Placing his palms on his thighs, he sucked in lungfuls of cold air. He was in great shape, but carrying a hundred-and-twenty-pounds half a mile had taxed even his stamina.

He remained on his knees for a full minute, breathing hard and waiting for his pulse to slow. It finally did. But not as much as he'd expected.

Because now he'd arrived at the moment of truth.

He had to kill Kelly.

There wasn't any option, of course. And he'd killed before. He could do this. Still . . . it was different. With her father, he'd let the carbon monoxide do the killing. And the first time with Kelly, the peanuts had been the instrument of death. It hadn't been as if he'd put a gun to their heads or stuck a knife in their backs or wrapped his hands around their throats and squeezed.

Slowly he rose and walked toward a small plateau that jutted out from the path, where a cliff-top bench offered hikers a respite—and a great view—on sunny days. At the edge of the limestone bluff, he paused to look over. It had to be forty-plus feet to the bottom, and sixty feet beyond the base the Missouri River flowed by, dark and quiet. He'd chosen well. This was not a high-traffic spot—especially on the eve of a holiday and with more stormy weather in the forecast.

Odd, how he and Kelly had often spent time in this same area. She'd mentioned her hiking trips to Weldon Spring once, while he was "investigating" her father's death. Little had he known that information would one day prove useful.

Shifting around, he looked at her still form. She'd gone limp during the last stretch as she'd bounced on his shoulder. That was a plus. If she was unconscious, he could pretend she was already dead.

He did a quick sweep of the ground. Rocks were plentiful here, as he knew from his more pleasant excursions, and with the night-vision goggles, it took only a few seconds to spot one that would do the job. Seconds later, he hefted it in his hands, testing the weight. Yeah. It was plenty heavy for his purposes.

After setting the rock next to Kelly's crumpled form, he bent to cut the restraint off her hands as she lay on her side. When a sudden gust of wind rustled the few dried leaves that remained on the trees, his pulse accelerated and he did another scan of the area.

All was clear.

Willing his nerves to settle down, he stuffed the restraints and the hand towels that had protected her wrists into his backpack. Picked up the rock. Stood.

This was it.

The putrid smell of decaying leaves invaded his nostrils, and all at once he felt sick to his stomach. But not just from the odor. His life was like those leaves—slowly disintegrating. To win back his wife, he'd become a man she could never love. He'd killed once, and he was getting ready to kill again. He was no better than the criminals he'd chased for his entire career.

But Cindy never had to know that. No one did. And he had no choice now. There was no turning back. Kelly could identify him. If she lived, his life was over.

Inside the latex gloves, his palms grew clammy as his fingers tightened on the rock. He positioned himself over her head. Inhaled. Lifted the rock.

All at once, she stirred.

His grip on the rock tightened.

She rolled onto her back, opened her eyes, and stared up at him.

The roiling in his stomach intensified. He couldn't smash her face. And he couldn't ignore the plea in her eyes.

He'd thought he could do this . . . but he wasn't a killer. Not this kind of killer.

Arms shaking, Alan lowered the rock and forced himself to think. She had to die. Just as her father had. But he had to find a less direct method.

He walked to the edge of the cliff again. The odds of surviving a fall from this height were miniscule, at best, even without prior injury. Plus, an ice storm was predicted. Between injuries and exposure to freezing weather, she wouldn't last the night. And the odds were very small anyone would notice her car before then. Nor would hikers be on this trail for the next couple of days, if by chance she managed to call for help.

Maybe he didn't have to kill her before he threw her over the edge. Maybe all he had to do was make certain she stayed where she fell and let nature take care of the rest.

Okay. He could handle that.

He moved back beside her. She was trying to stand, but a slight shove sent her toppling again. Positioning himself beside her legs, he planted one foot on her ankle to hold it in position, lifted the rock and slammed it into her knee.

He heard the crunch of bone. She jerked, and her guttural moan of pain as she writhed beneath his foot clawed at his insides. But he could have smashed the rock into her skull instead. She was lucky he had no stomach for direct killing.

After tossing the rock back where he'd found it, he untied the gag, pulled it from her mouth, and stuffed it in a plastic bag that he tucked into his backpack. She was moaning, low in her throat, and when he picked her up again, her leg dangled uselessly. She was conscious, but her eyes were glazed with pain.

The weakness in his legs surprised him as he walked to the edge of the cliff and lowered her to her feet, holding her up so she wouldn't crumple. He pulled off her hat. Tossed it into the chasm. Yanked off one glove. Threw it over as well. Unzipped her jacket halfway. Took a deep breath.

This was it.

Heart pounding, he swallowed, looked toward the river, and shoved her over the edge.

He didn't watch as she fell, but he could hear her crashing through some brush attached to the ragged, ledged face of the cliff.

At last all was silent.

He looked over the edge. It took him a moment to locate her, more to the right than he'd expected, lying on her side. Her leg was twisted. Her jacket had come unzipped and flapped open, exposing her even more to the elements.

And she wasn't moving.

Swallowing past the bad taste in his mouth, Alan returned to his backpack and lifted it. Using the edge of the sport shoe he'd soon discard, he smoothed out the thick carpet of leaves. The ground was hard and dry, so even in exposed areas, there would be no footprints. That, at least, had worked in his favor. And he'd pulled socks over his shoes in the gravel parking lot, so there would be no sign of a third party there, either.

With the night-vision goggles still in place, he did one final survey of the area. It appeared undisturbed. As if no one had passed this way today.

Hefting the backpack to his shoulder, he started back down the trail.

It was done.

23

Deputy Trent Adams stifled a yawn and took a swig of luke-warm coffee from the insulated mug that was standard equipment on his late-night patrols. Not that eight o'clock qualified as late-night, but it felt like it. He and Angie had been on the go all day preparing to host their first Thanksgiving dinner as a married couple. She was freaking, and he was beat. What he needed tonight was a quiet, uneventful shift.

A sudden ping on his roof refocused his attention, and he set the coffee back in the cup holder. It seemed the meteorologists had been right for once. Too bad. Things could get messy if many people decided to venture onto Highway 94 in the middle of a sleet storm.

His headlights picked out the sign for the entrance to the next trailhead parking lot, and he slowed. Normally, he'd drive by. Weldon Spring was Department of Conservation territory. But his boss had made a big deal out of a BOLO alert in a missing-person case, and his instructions were to check every nook and cranny in his patrol area.

Swinging onto the gravel surface, he aimed for the back of the lot. Once he did a quick circuit, he'd mosey over to the fast-foot outlet near I-64 and replenish his coffee. After his hectic day, he'd need a steady infusion of caffeine to . . .

His headlights arced across a car in the far corner and he slowed, frowning. On a night like this, the lot should be empty.

He backed up, turned the wheel the other direction, and pulled up behind the car. It was an older model Focus. Dark blue.

Like the car in the BOLO alert.

Tamping down the flutter of excitement in his stomach, he squinted at the number on the license plate. Then he angled in his seat and pulled up the alert on his computer screen.

The plate matched.

Adrenaline surging, he reached for his radio.

So much for his quiet night.

"There were no telephone crews in this area today." Mitch slid his phone back on his belt as he rejoined Cole beside the CSU van parked in front of John Warren's house.

A frigid breeze blew past, and Cole felt a sting on his cheek. Just what they needed. Sleet. This was as bad as Buffalo weather. Once again he regretted leaving home without his coat last night.

"I'm not surprised." He shoved his hands into the pockets of his slacks and glanced at the house. Lights shown from behind the shades in every room. "Let's hope Hank finds something."

"He will, if there's anything to find. Hank's the best crime scene investigator I've ever worked with."

"Yeah, but temperamental. And cranky."

"You're just mad because he threw us out."

"We weren't contaminating any evidence."

"We had better things to do, anyway."

Cole shot him a disgruntled look. "Unless you had more luck than I did, canvassing the neighborhood was a bust. So was my call to Carlson's sister. She hasn't heard from him in months, and she's not expecting him for Thanksgiving."

"Maybe the officers interviewing Kelly's neighbors will turn up some usable information."

"I checked. Nothing there, either."

Cole knew he could have let the street officers do all of the door-to-door questioning here in her father's neighborhood too, but he hated feeling useless. Without any leads to follow, suspects or witnesses to interrogate, or evidence to analyze, there wasn't much he and Mitch could do except grunt work. They needed a break, or a new piece of information to follow up on.

"Look, we're spinning our wheels here." His fingers closed over the keys in his pocket and he pulled them out. "Why don't I run you by the office so you can pick up your car? I want to get on the computer and see what I can dig up on Alan."

"You know, we could be totally off base on that idea."

"Maybe. But it all fits. And he's still not answering his phone. If he's not headed for Chicago or K.C., then where . . ." His phone began to vibrate, and he pulled it off his belt, checking caller ID. "It's dispatch." He tapped the talk button. "Taylor."

"Detective Taylor, we have confirmation from the St. Charles County Sheriff Department that the car we issued the BOLO alert on earlier has been found in their territory."

His heart stuttered as he tightened his grip on the phone. "Is there . . ." His voice rasped, and he cleared his throat. "Is it empty?"

"Yes."

"Hang on." Depressing the mute button, he tried to breathe as he tossed the keys to Mitch. "They have Kelly's car. I'll meet you at mine in two minutes." Without waiting for a reply, he took off at a sprint for John Warren's front door and resumed his conversation with dispatch. "What's the location?"

He listened as she gave him the information, taking the steps to the porch in one leap. "Okay. Hold again." He opened the front door and sped across the foyer toward the hall. He found Hank in John Warren's office. "I need some stuff from the back bedroom. Now. The pillowcase and clothing items from the overnight bag."

"I'm not done in there yet."

"Give me what you can. Enough for the K-9 unit."

As the man rose, grumbling under his breath, Cole turned

away and took the phone off mute. "Okay. Patch me through to Brett Layton."

While he waited for the call to connect, he returned to the small foyer and began to pace.

"Layton here."

"Sarge, it's Cole Taylor. Mitch Morgan is with me and we're about to head out to the Weldon Spring trailhead where Kelly Warren's car has been found. I want to run a theory by you and talk about ordering a thermal scan and getting a K-9 unit out there ASAP."

Hank reappeared, the requested items in a plastic bag. Cole took it from him and exited the house, sprinting toward the running car where Mitch waited, giving the unit supervisor a full download.

And praying whoever had taken Kelly hadn't yet had a chance to carry out his lethal plan.

As the sleet intensified, coating the roadways and ground with an icy glaze, Alan cursed. The three miles from the trailhead to the fast-food outlet where he often got a cold drink after biking had been a lot slower going than he'd expected. Especially since he'd tried to stay away from the two-lane highway and hug the woods. He'd finally had to leave his cover as he approached the I-64 overpass, but at least the roads were deserted except for an occasional lone car creeping along. He'd slipped and slid across the bridge, then picked up his pace.

At last the outlet was in sight.

Detouring into the deserted parking lot of a small office building, he checked for security cameras. All clear, as he expected. Modest operations didn't often spring for elaborate security.

In the back, he found the requisite dumpster. After pulling the plastic garbage bag out of his backpack, he tossed in the towels, restraints, shower cap, and the socks that had covered his sport shoes in the trailhead parking lot. Then he wadded the bag into a small bundle and pushed against the ice-encased lid with one hand.

It didn't give.

Annoyed, Alan set the bag on the ground, tugged his leather gloves higher on his wrists, and pushed with both hands. The ice seal broke. Excellent. He picked up the bag, lifted the lid, and tossed it inside. He'd dispose of the latex gloves at the fast-food outlet.

The sleet was coming down harder now, and he ducked under an overhang on the office building as he pulled out his cell to order a cab. It could take a while to get one on a night like this, but he was in no hurry. His job was finished. All he had to do was drive to his sister's in K.C.—but he wasn't going that far tonight. An hour out of town, at most, in this weather. He'd finish the trip tomorrow.

As he suspected, the cab company made no promises about a pickup time. So he didn't rush to get to the restaurant. And once there, he spent a few minutes in the restroom, cleaning up, checking that his disguise was still intact, and disposing of the gloves.

Much to his surprise, the cab pulled up ten minutes later as he was sipping a cup of coffee at one of the tables by the window. He downed the last few mouthfuls and exited into the storm, head bent against the relentless pounding of the sleet.

"Picked a bad night to be out, buddy." The driver looked over his shoulder as Alan slid into the cab.

"A bad night for car trouble too."

"That what happened?"

"Yeah." He'd worked out his story on the miserable jog up Highway 94. "I met a friend from out of town for a quick cup of coffee, and when I went out to my car afterward it wouldn't start. My wife's up to her neck in pies or I'd have called her."

"I hear you. I wouldn't tell this to the wife, but I volunteered to work this shift. Too many relatives under one roof at our house. And too much noise." He checked a clipboard beside him. "You're going to Chesterfield?"

"That's right. Valley View Apartments." The friend who'd lived there had moved a few months ago, so even if he ran into anyone, he wouldn't be recognized.

"Okay. Sit back and relax. I'll get you there, but no promises how long it will take with this weather."

Alan buckled his seat belt, already thinking ahead to part B of the plan. Once he got to Chesterfield, he'd call another cab from a different company. He'd instruct that one to leave him a couple of blocks from where he'd parked his car, near John Warren's house. He'd walk to his car, point it toward Kansas City—and start thinking about how he was going to celebrate his final payoff from Rossi.

Things were going exactly as he'd planned.

"There's the entrance to the parking lot." Cole leaned forward in the passenger seat and peered through the sleet. They were having trouble keeping the windshield clear even with the defroster running full blast. If Kelly was out in this, he hoped she was dressed warmly.

He refused to consider the possibility that her attire might not matter.

Mitch swung in, tires crunching on the icy gravel as he drove toward the far corner, where two St. Charles County squad cars and a Department of Conservation vehicle were parked.

Cole's phone began to vibrate, and Brett's number flashed on the screen.

The supervisor wasted no time on preliminaries. "We have a no-go on the thermal imaging. The weather's too dicey for the helicopter. A St. Charles K-9 unit is en route to the trailhead, with an ETA of five minutes. One of our own K-9 units is on its way too. A CSU van has also been dispatched. We had a patrol officer do a drive-by at Carlson's house, but there was no activity. And unless we have more to go on with him than supposition, that's about as much as I want to do at this point. What's your location?"

"We just pulled in to the trailhead parking lot. We're going to need paramedics standing by."

"A team in St. Charles is already on alert and prepared to move. Keep me in the loop."

As Brett ended the call, Cole looked at Mitch. "He's not buying Carlson's involvement."

"I can't blame him. It's a stretch. And we don't have any hard evidence."

"Yet."

Mitch didn't respond as he pulled to a stop behind one of the police cruisers. Before the brake was set, Cole was out the door and jogging toward Kelly's car. A young deputy came forward as he approached.

Cole pulled out his credentials and flashed them at the man without stopping. "St. Louis County PD." He didn't pause until he was a dozen feet from the car. "You checked the trunk, right?"

"Yes. Those were the orders from my captain. My slim jim worked, so I was able to pop it from the inside. But I wore gloves."

"Good." At the sound of crunching gravel, Cole shifted toward the entrance.

"That's one of our K-9 units." The deputy waved the Suburban over.

Cole started back to his car to retrieve Kelly's things, but Mitch met him halfway, plastic bag in hand.

He took it from him. "This better work. The helicopter's grounded."

A burly man, balaclava pulled over his head and wearing combat boots, cargo pants, and a thermal jacket, emerged from the Suburban. Cole moved forward and introduced himself.

"Rick Stephens." The man returned his handshake, then shook hands with Mitch. "You guys aren't exactly dressed for this weather." The man gave them a once-over as he opened the back door of his vehicle.

"We just flew in from Buffalo. A hike in the woods wasn't part of our game plan."

Rick reached inside, pulled out an insulated black wind-breaker, and tossed it to Cole. "This will help." He leaned in further and retrieved some rubber boots and a ski mask. "So will these. You won't be making any fashion statements, but they'll keep you warm."

"Thanks."

"Trent!" The man leaned around Cole. "See what kind of cold-weather gear you can scrounge up for our friend here." He motioned to Mitch.

The deputy acknowledged the instruction with a wave.

"Okay." He snapped a leash on the energetic German shep-herd pacing around the back of the car. "Bo is an excellent tracking dog. If the victim's here, he'll find her. Tell me what you know."

Cole gave him a rapid-fire briefing as he slid his arms into the windbreaker, replaced his shoes with the boots, and pulled on the ski mask. Mitch did the same with the gear the young deputy rounded up for him, ditching his dress shoes as well for a pair of mud-caked work boots that Rick dug out of the back of the Suburban. The deputy had also come up with gloves for both of them, and Cole gratefully slid his fingers into the fleecy warmth. Better.

"So the last sighting of the car was about six-fifteen in Kirk-wood." Rick checked his watch as he retrieved night-vision bin-oculars and a small backpack from his vehicle. He slipped the pack over his shoulders and handed the binoculars to Mitch. "These may come in handy."

"I'm estimating it took him forty-five minutes to get here," Cole said.

"That would be about right. Which puts their arrival at two and a half hours ago." Rick squinted in the direction of the trailhead and wrapped his hand around the leash as Bo sniffed the ground at his feet. "If the victim was mobile, they could have covered a fair distance in that amount of time. This trail is over five miles long. If she wasn't mobile, we might not have far to go. But with the weather worsening, we'd better get moving. That the scent we're after?" He gestured to the bag in Cole's hand.

"Yes." Cole handed it over.

The man opened the bag and poked through it, extracting the pillowcase. "Let's start with this." Setting the bag with the remaining items on the backseat of the Suburban, he walked over to Kelly's car, then let Bo take a whiff of the fabric.

The dog found the scent in seconds, near Kelly's trunk, and tugged on the leash, urging Rick toward the trailhead. Cole pulled out his Sig Sauer and followed. Mitch fell in behind him.

"One of you come with us too. And bring a radio and flashlight." Cole issued the instruction over his shoulder to the deputies as he started down the path.

The ice crunched under his feet as he picked his way down the trail, the only other sounds the panting of the dog straining on the leash and the rattle of wind-tossed branches. The sky, black as death in the absence of moon and stars, offered no hint of illumination to guide them. A flashlight would help, but if the perpetrator was still in the area, artificial light would alert him to their presence.

And make it easier for him to pick them off.

Cole tightened his grip on his pistol. He hoped there would be no violence this night.

But with Kelly's life hanging in the balance, he'd have no qualms about using his weapon.

"We made a lot better time than I expected. I guess the sleet scared all the amateurs off the road." The cabbie pulled into the apartment complex parking lot.

Alan tugged his wallet from the pocket of his slacks. "It's the second building. You can stop by the white Taurus."

As the cab slowed, he checked the meter and pulled out some bills, calculating the tip. A little more than normal because of the weather and the holiday, but not enough to make him a memorable passenger. He handed the money over the seat when the car came to a stop. "Thanks for getting me here so fast."

The man took the fare and grinned at him. "I wouldn't want your wife to be any madder at you than she is now."

Alan had already mentally moved on to the next phase of the operation, and he had to remind himself of the story he'd concocted. "I appreciate that. Have a nice holiday."

"You too."

He slid out of the car and started toward one of the units, using the ice as an excuse to walk slowly. By the time he got to the sidewalk, the cab's taillights were disappearing out the exit.

When he was certain the car was gone, he melted into the shadows, hugging the wall as he skirted the building. No lights shone from the windows in the corner unit, and he took shelter under a small overhang on the patio in the back.

As he pulled out his cell to call the second cab, the device began to vibrate against his fingers. His hand jerked at the unexpected motion, and he fumbled the phone, almost dropping it onto the icy concrete.

Biting back a curse, he tightened his grip and checked caller ID.

The number was blocked.

Could Rossi's man be calling him back already to arrange a drop? He'd said the payment would be made soon, but Alan had assumed they'd wait until after the holiday. It could be someone else on the line . . . but he didn't want to risk missing the drop call. He wanted his final payment.

He tapped the talk button and put the phone to his ear. "Carlson."

"Your payment is ready. And we're accommodating your travel plans. The drop will be between two and six tomorrow morning at the Shelford Motel at the I-70 Warrenton exit. Take a room at the far end. Leave a note on the door that says 'Knock for pizza delivery.'"

A click told him the call was over.

Alan frowned. The Shelford Motel? It sounded like the kind

of place cockroaches called home. The kind of place he'd spent far too much time in as a kid. Why pick a dump like that?

On the other hand, what did it matter, as long as he got his money? Once he had it in hand, he could stay at the Ritz anytime he chose. With Cindy, if fate was kind.

A spray of sleet lashed against his face, and he shifted away from the wind, punching in the number for the second cab company. With luck, he'd be in his car and on the road in less than an hour. And Warrenton wasn't far. Even in this weather, he should be able to make it in ninety minutes, tops. Giving him plenty of time to catch a little shut-eye before all his money problems were solved.

Once and for all.

24

Her face was tingling. No, *stinging*.

Fighting her way back to consciousness, Kelly tried to lift her hand. Pain shot through her wrist, and she gasped. That, in turn, produced a searing pain in her rib cage. As did every breath she took.

She went still. Or as still as she could manage, given the shivers convulsing her—which produced yet more pain that radiated to every nerve ending in her body.

Through her haze of agony, one thing was clear.

She hurt too much to be dead.

That meant Carlson hadn't succeeded.

Yet.

Gritting her teeth, she tried to shift slightly to see the leg he'd smashed with the rock. But even that small movement sent a wave of blackness crashing over her. *No!* She had to stay conscious. Had to keep thinking. Had to believe that if God hadn't taken her yet, he had further plans for her here.

She opened her eyes and forced herself to refocus. She remembered falling.

But into what?

The stinging on her face intensified as another shiver rippled through.

What was that steady pinging hum against the dead leaves near her ear?

Sleet. It had to be sleet.

A wave of panic clawed at her throat. She was in an ice storm in the middle of nowhere, and she was too hurt to move.

Her shaking worsened, intensifying the waves of pain.

Think, Kelly! Don't let Carlson win!

Choking back a sob, she tried to focus on a plan of action. But first she needed to figure out what parts of her body were functional—and how she could use them to save herself.

She wiggled her fingers. The right hand was working, but the left hurt too much to use. She eased her right hand away from her body. No problem. That meant her wrists weren't bound anymore. She couldn't move her smashed right leg, but the left one seemed okay. And her ankle restraints were gone too. She rolled her tongue around in her mouth. No gag.

Did her voice still work?

She tried to speak. Nothing came out but a croak. She wet her chapped lips with her tongue and tried again. Better. The sound was audible. She could call for help.

But who would hear her?

It had been too dark, and she'd been too woozy, to notice much about her surroundings when Carlson had hauled her out of the trunk of the car. The area had seemed remote, though. Not the kind of place people ventured in bad weather—or on a holiday. That must be what he was counting on. Besides, he'd probably expected her to die in the fall . . . a poor hiker who'd ventured too close to the edge of an icy precipice and plunged to her death.

But she wasn't dead, and she didn't intend to be. Someone would come along eventually. She just had to hang on until daylight. The odds of being discovered would be far better then. She'd save her voice until first light too. No sense wearing it out in the dark, when there was little chance anyone would be close enough to hear it.

In the meantime, she needed to stay as warm as possible. She still had her thermal jacket on, but judging by the cold seeping into her stomach from the frozen ground, it had come unzipped. Closing that gap was imperative if she wanted to conserve warmth. She had to find some cover too.

Kelly peered into the dark. There was a pine tree a few yards away, silhouetted against the dark sky. Its sheltering branches would protect her from the sleet if she could drag herself over there.

Her left wrist and right leg weren't going to be of any help, and the pain in her ribs burned with every breath, undermining her resolve.

But she didn't want to die. Didn't want Carlson to win. Didn't want that scumbag to go unpunished for what he'd done to her father.

She wanted justice.

Praying for fortitude and courage, Kelly blocked out the pain as best she could and worked her elbow under her. Then, fighting back tears, she leveraged herself up an inch or two. Bending her left knee, she dug in her toe and pushed. She managed to slide a couple of inches toward her destination—but the toll in pain was immense.

Tears flooded her eyes.

She couldn't do this.

Yes, you can.

The voice was clear. Just as it had been when she'd almost caved under the trauma of her father's death.

I am with you always.

The beautiful, comforting words from Matthew—her mainstay in those days of inconsolable grief—echoed in her mind. As did the quote from Psalms that had hung on her refrigerator since her father's funeral.

The Lord *was* with her. He *was* holding her hand.

And with his help, she would survive.

Leveraging herself up on her elbow again, she dug in her toe, pushed, and continued to drag herself toward shelter.

"Uh-oh."

At Rick's ominous pronouncement, Cole's pulse skyrocketed.

After fifteen minutes on the trail, Bo had veered off the path toward a bench. He was now sniffing in circles.

"What's wrong?" Cole started toward the dog. Bo sat, ears perked, in passive alert position.

"Not so fast." Rick grabbed his arm. "Bo." He tugged on the leash. "Back, boy."

The dog responded, trotting back to sit at Rick's feet, panting clouds of breath into the cold air.

"What's going on?" Cole could feel the tension emanating from the man.

"The victim's scent stops here." Rick's tone was grim. "And we're on the edge of a forty, forty-five-foot cliff."

The bottom dropped out of Cole's stomach as he peered into the darkness. "How do you know?"

"I've hiked this trail plenty of times in nice weather."

Cole swallowed and held out his hand to Mitch. "Give me the night vision binoculars."

In silence, Mitch moved beside him and handed them over. Cole was glad he couldn't see the other man's face.

Pressing the binoculars to his eyes, he eased closer to the edge of the bluff. Steeled himself. Sent a silent plea heavenward. Then he looked down.

The sleet continued to fall steadily, though it wasn't as heavy now. Visibility had improved. But not enough. Between the sleet, the green night-vision tinge he'd always found disconcerting, and the film of moisture blurring his vision, Cole couldn't make out any details in the landscape below.

"I don't see anything."

"Let me try. I'm used to using these." Rick joined them.

Cole relinquished the binoculars and took a step back.

The other man moved closer to the edge than Cole considered wise, positioned the binoculars in front of his eyes, then looked straight down and began a slow sweep of the terrain.

Heart pounding, Cole waited for the words he knew were coming. Kelly was down there. K-9 dogs were well-trained. If her scent ended at the edge of the cliff, she'd gone over. And it fit with the hiking-accident theory he and Mitch had constructed—made all the more plausible by the ice storm that had slickened the sloping ground. Move a little too close to the edge, lose your footing . . . it was all over.

People didn't survive forty-plus-foot falls.

"I've got her."

Cole closed his eyes. Felt Mitch edge closer to him. Tried to keep breathing.

"Where?" His question came out hoarse as he stepped toward the K-9 handler.

Rick pointed to the right. "A few feet this side of the tall pine tree." He lowered the binoculars and held them out.

Bracing himself, Cole fitted them to his eyes and swept the area Rick had indicated.

He saw her at once this time. A crumpled, still form among the denuded underbrush that had already succumbed to the harshness of winter.

A wave of nausea swept over him, and his vision blurred. He eased the binoculars back slightly. Blinked. Reseated them and focused on Kelly.

When they caught Carlson, he was going to kill the man with his bare hands.

Kelly wouldn't approve of his thirst for revenge. Nor would God. But that was how he felt. The man had now taken not one, but two innocent lives, and if it was the last thing he ever did, Cole intended to—

He froze.

Had Kelly's arm shifted?

Or was he just seeing what he wanted to see?

He kept his gaze riveted on her slender form. And then, as he watched, her leg moved up in tiny increments.

"She's alive!" He ripped the binoculars from his eyes, thrust them at Rick, and whipped toward the deputy. "Radio for the paramedics. We need them here *now*!" Cupping his hands around his mouth, he shouted toward the base of the cliff. "Kelly! It's Cole! Hang on! We're coming down! Don't try to move!"

"Cole." Mitch put his hand on his shoulder. "It's more than forty feet down."

"I know that! But she moved! Rick, take a look. Watch her right hand and left leg."

The man already had the binoculars trained on Kelly. "Yeah. I see it. She *is* moving. Man, that's amazing. No one survives a fall like that."

"The paramedics are on their way," the deputy informed them. "They'll go in at the Katy Trail access point about a mile down 94. It'll take them a little time to cover that distance on foot, though."

"What's their ETA to Kelly?"

"Twenty, twenty-five minutes. Maybe more, in this weather."

"Not fast enough." He swung toward Rick. "Is there a trail down from here?"

"Yes, but it's not safe in good weather, let alone in this crud."

"Where is it?"

The man gestured behind him. "About three hundred yards through the woods."

"I'm going down. Show me."

"I'll go with you."

At Mitch's comment, Cole turned to him. He couldn't make out his features in the dark, but his colleague's tone was firm.

"That's not necessary. There's no reason for both of us to take a risk."

"Yeah, there is. Alison would kill me if I let you break your neck."

Cole thought about arguing. Decided against it. He wouldn't mind having the company of a Navy SEAL—or a friend—on this journey.

"Trent, let me have your flashlight." Rick reached for it and passed Bo's leash to the deputy. "Hang on tight. He'll want to follow. I'll be back for him as soon as I show them the trail access."

Rick set off through the woods at a fast clip, and Cole picked up his pace, more upbeat than he'd been minutes ago, yet trying not to be overly optimistic. Rick was right. Kelly might have beaten the odds by surviving the plunge, but no one fell that distance without sustaining serious injuries.

Possibly fatal injuries.

And as Cole plowed through the ice-encrusted brush behind their guide, he prayed Kelly's weren't in the latter category.

Vincentio rummaged through his medicine cabinet, scowling at the contents. Where were the antacids? He always kept a bottle on hand. And he needed a few tonight. Must be the veal scallopini, although he'd never had any problem with that dish in the past. He'd have to ask Teresa if she'd altered the recipe, added some spice that hadn't agreed with him.

Frowning, he leaned on the vanity and tried to remember where he'd put them. Downstairs, perhaps? Yes. That was it. He'd left them in the kitchen last week, after another bout of indigestion. But was it worth a trip down the steps and back up again at—he checked his watch—nearly eleven o'clock? Just thinking about all that exertion fatigued him. On the other hand, he doubted he'd sleep unless he neutralized his stomach acid.

Resigned, he pushed himself upright and exited into the hall, his steps labored as he traversed the dim passageway in the quiet, empty—lonely—house. A house that would never ring with the laughter of his family or the clink of wineglasses raised in happy toasts. A house where he would never get to play the part of a benevolent nonno. His grandson would never even know of his existence until he was old enough to ask Marco, and then his son would vilify him, making Jason despise him as much as Marco did.

That wasn't the kind of legacy a man wanted to leave.

But Vincentio was nothing if not a realist. And that was how his life had played out. It was what it was.

Tightening his grip on the railing, he took the steps one at a time. Isabella had always preferred two-story houses. That was why he'd bought this one when he'd been released from prison, knowing it was the kind of house she'd have chosen. But the stairs were getting more and more difficult to navigate. Maybe it was time to move.

At the bottom, he stopped to catch his breath. A necessity he despised but accepted. People got old. And no amount of money could return the youth that had been stolen from him during his years in prison.

Money could solve some problems, however. Fix some injustices. It was doing so at this very moment. But that was smaller consolation than he'd expected on the eve of a holiday meant to be shared with loved ones.

He flipped on the light in the kitchen. Spotting the jar of antacids on the far side of the room, he started toward it—until the sudden ring of his cell phone shattered the tomb-like silence.

Pulse pounding, he jolted to a stop. Then he shook his head. A Rossi, spooked by a ringing phone. How sad was that?

He crossed to the counter and pulled the phone out of the charger. The ID was blocked, but he knew who it was. His colleague had wasted no time. "Yes?"

"I have confirmation the document was delivered. Final arrangements have also been made to handle the other matter. It will be disposed of by dawn."

"Excellent." Vincentio picked up the bottle of antacid tablets. "I'll be in touch should I have further need of your services in the future."

"Always happy to oblige." The man hung up.

Vincentio settled the phone back in its charger, shook out four tablets, and popped them in his mouth. He chewed them as he retraced his steps across the kitchen and turned out the light, anxious now to go to bed. Perhaps, with the Walsh matter finally resolved, he would sleep better than he had for the past few nights.

At the base of the stairway, he grasped the railing and hauled himself up to the first step. The second. The third. Pausing, he drew in a deep breath. Coming down had been much easier.

He looked up at the remaining nine steps. Maybe he should get one of those stair-lift contraptions so he could ride up and down while he debated whether to sell the house. Too bad he didn't have one now. But wishing wasn't going to get him to the top.

Sighing, he began his ascent, taking one step at a time.

Five steps from the top, Vincentio suddenly felt as if a sumo wrestler had belly flopped onto his chest.

The crushing weight sucked the air from his lungs and he clutched at his throat. His legs gave out, and he sank to the steps. He tried to remain upright. Tried to hold on to the spindles in the railing. But there was no strength in his hands. He felt himself sliding down . . . down . . . down.

So this was how the Rossi legacy—and his life—were going to end. The heart his son claimed he didn't have was going to betray him.

And as the world around him faded, he welcomed the darkness.

Cole dropped the last three feet from the serpentine bluff-side trail to level ground. His ankle twisted when he landed on a rock, and he winced. He'd made it all the way down the treacherous descent in ill-fitting boots and *now* he messes up his ankle? But at least they were at the bottom. And the sleet had stopped.

Ignoring the ache in his shin, he pulled the flashlight out of the backpack Rick had given him and set a course straight for Kelly, pushing through the leafless saplings and dense brush in his path, Mitch on his heels.

They didn't talk on their trek.

Instead, Cole used the time to pray. Hard.

When at last he spotted the deputy's flashlight at the top of the bluff where Bo had delivered the bad news, he felt as if they'd been walking for an eternity.

He also had a better perspective on the height of the cliff—

and the length of Kelly's fall. How could she possibly have survived?

But she had. He'd think about the *how* later.

He aimed the flashlight at the base of the tall pine tree and swung it back in Kelly's direction.

The instant the beam of light caught her, Cole began pushing through the brush that separated them. She didn't seem to have moved since he'd spotted her from above, fifteen minutes ago, and her absolute stillness set off a tremor in his hands. She looked limp. And lifeless.

When he reached her, he handed the flashlight to Mitch. "Hold this, okay?"

"Yeah."

Mitch circled around behind her and dropped to one knee as Cole did the same on her other side. His colleague positioned the light on her upper body, giving Cole his first clear, close-up view at the woman he'd hoped was destined to play a major role in his life.

If he'd eaten any dinner, he'd have lost it.

She lay half on her side, half on her stomach, her hair tangled around her head, ice pellets clinging to the russet strands. Her eyes were closed, and her death-like pallor emphasized the angry purple discoloration on her jaw and temple, as well as the long, bloody scratch that ran from her forehead to the bottom of her cheek.

"Check her respiration and pulse."

At Mitch's quiet comment, Cole leaned closer and put his unsteady fingers against her neck. Nothing. He probed harder.

Finally he felt a faint, irregular flutter against his fingertips. *Thank you, God!* "I've got a pulse."

He checked her chest, watching for a rise and fall. Again, nothing. If there was movement, it was too small to see. He leaned down, putting his cheek beside her mouth and nose. He felt no breath, but a slight, pulsing warmth told him she was breathing. Barely.

"I've got respiration."

"Okay. Let's take a look farther down." Mitch swung the light over the rest of her body. No skin was visible beneath her jeans and hiking boots, but a bulge around her right knee had tightened the jeans, and the leg had an odd twist.

"I see it." Mitch spoke as Cole pointed out the injury. "But I'm more worried about stuff we can't see. Fractured skull, punctured lungs, ruptured spleen, broken ribs." He swung the light back to her face. "Hold on to this while I see what's in Rick's medical kit."

Cole took the flashlight as Mitch opened the backpack, trying not to think of worst-case scenarios as he leaned down. "Kelly? Can you hear me?"

No response.

She'd been conscious fifteen minutes ago, though. That had to be a positive sign.

Didn't it?

"Let's put this over her." Mitch handed him one end of a mylar blanket. "It will help preserve body heat and protect her from the wind."

Cole took the blanket and stretched it over Kelly, gently tucking it under her. "How much do you know about first aid?"

"I learned some basic stuff in SEAL training for field emergencies, but not enough to help much in this situation. My recommendation is to keep her as quiet and warm as we can until the experts get here. They shouldn't be that far behind us." Mitch gestured to her torso. "Did you notice her jacket?"

In truth, nothing much had registered in Cole's consciousness except Kelly's visible abrasions and her unnerving vital signs. "No."

"There's a hole in the front. Like the jacket got snagged on a limb from one of the scrubby trees growing on the face of the bluff as she fell. That branch could have gone through *her*. But it seems to have pierced the jacket instead. That would have broken her fall. Crashing through all that scrubby stuff would have slowed her down too. That's the only explanation I can come up with for how she survived." He looked down at her again. "It's about the closest thing I've ever seen to a miracle."

Cole touched Kelly's cheek. He could buy a miracle. He'd been praying hard enough for one.

And he wasn't about to stop praying until he knew she had not only survived the fall, but that she would survive *beyond* the fall.

25

"They're here."

At Mitch's terse comment, Cole shifted his attention from Kelly to the dark woods behind him. A light bobbed among the bare trees in the distance, identifying the location of the rescue team. "It's about time."

Mitch checked his watch. "We've only been here fifteen minutes."

It felt like forever.

Cole dropped his gaze to Kelly again, keeping his hand cupped over her cheek and the top of her nose. Warming such a small area of exposed skin wouldn't help much, but it was better than doing nothing. With the high probability of spinal and neck trauma, moving her to check for injuries had been out of the question.

The sound of crashing brush grew louder, and Mitch stood to aim the flashlight in the direction of the new arrivals. "Over here!"

"Hang on, Kelly." Cole braced himself with a hand on the ground, dead foliage crunching under his fingers as he leaned close to whisper in her ear. "Help is here. You're going to be okay."

His encouraging words produced no response from her, but *he* believed them.

He had to.

"Sir, please move aside."

The authoritative command came from behind him, and with one more stroke of Kelly's cold cheek, Cole stood and stepped away.

The paramedic was already assessing Kelly as he drew close. "You two . . ." He gestured to the uniformed firefighters behind him. "Give us some light."

One of the firefighters positioned himself at Kelly's feet, the other at her head. The two beams in tandem from the powerful electric torches created a circle of illumination almost as bright as sunlight. Highlighting every visible injury in excruciating detail.

Cole groped for the trunk of the bare tree beside him and held on.

The lead paramedic—Adam, according to his name tag—dropped to his knees beside her and pulled back the mylar blanket. Then he reached for her bare right hand and pressed his fingers against her wrist, assessing her breathing at the same time. "Airway's open, but let's get a mask on her. High flow O-2." He repositioned his fingers on the carotid artery in her neck.

The switch from wrist to neck meant he was having difficulty getting a pulse.

Cole's own pulse kicked up a notch.

"BP's low. She'll need a large-bore IV, normal saline. Let's cut that pant leg and splint the knee first. Same with the left wrist. Then we'll get her on a board and in a collar." He flicked a small penlight in each eye, examined the bump on her forehead, and carefully ran his fingers over her scalp. "No evidence of a depressed skull fracture."

Leaving the other paramedic to deal with her wrist, he shifted down to her knee. As he split the leg of her jeans, revealing a mass of swollen bruising where her kneecap should have been, Cole closed his eyes. Sucked in a lungful of air. Tightened his grip on the tree.

"Did you notice the broken brush?"

It took a moment for Mitch's quiet question to register. When it did, Cole opened his eyes. His colleague gestured to the fringes of the light. For about six feet, a narrow section of the ice-encrusted brush was broken and trampled. As if something had been dragged across it.

Or some*one* had dragged herself across it.

Mitch nodded to the pine tree a few feet behind him. "My guess is she was trying to get to some shelter." He shook his head. "Amazing."

No kidding.

Cole looked back at Kelly. The paramedics were using elastic wrap to secure the fiberglass splints encasing her leg and wrist.

When they finished, Adam reached for the backboard and glanced at Cole and Mitch. "You two take over the lights for a minute while we immobilize her."

Sleet started to spit again as Cole took the torch from one of the firefighters, glad to have something useful to do. The paramedics situated a backboard beside Kelly, and the two firefighters took up positions on her other side.

"On the count of three. One . . . two . . . three."

They log-rolled her onto the backboard and strapped her in place.

"Get the cervical collar on." Adam shot one of the fire-fighters a glance. "Check with medevac. If they're not still grounded, get a helicopter out here stat."

As he spoke, the other paramedic fitted the collar on Kelly. Then he pulled an oxygen mask over her nose and mouth while Adam prepared to start the IV.

The sleet intensified as the minutes ticked by, only the spatter of ice crystals against the dead leaves breaking the silence.

Finally Adam straightened up. "All right. Let's get her out of this weather. Bring the basket over."

One of the firefighters retrieved the plastic litter, and, working together, the four men lifted the backboard into it. Once she was secure, the paramedics tucked another thermal blanket around her.

"Okay." Adam grasped a handhold on the basket, and the other three took up positions around it. "On three. Nice and smooth. One . . . two . . . three."

As Cole watched, they lifted in unison—a well-oiled team that had been through this exercise many times. At least Kelly was in skilled hands.

"We'll move forward on three. Steady as possible." He gestured toward Cole and Mitch. "Keep the light focused on our path. Okay. One . . . two . . . three."

Cole aimed the beam on their path as they began their trek through the dark woods, but at every slight jolt of the basket on the rough terrain, he cringed—and wondered what additional damage Kelly might suffer from even this highly professional rescue effort.

It was the longest walk he'd ever taken.

When they emerged from the woods, both patrol cars, the conservation vehicle, and the K-9 unit vehicle were parked beside the ambulance and a fire truck. One of the deputies joined them. "The helicopter's still grounded."

"Okay." Adam continued toward the ambulance without slowing. "Let's hook her up to a cardiac monitor and some warm saline and get her out of here. We need a Level 1 trauma center. Alert Mercy we're on the way."

"I'm assuming you're going in the ambulance." Mitch's comment was a statement, not a question.

"Yeah." Cole watched them load Kelly as he stripped off the borrowed cold-weather clothing and passed the items back to Rick Stephens with a quick thank-you.

"I'll get one of the deputies to give me a ride back to your car and meet you at the hospital."

"Why don't you take it home?" His fingers fumbled the laces as he tried to tie his shoes. "I can get it tomorrow."

Mitch pulled the keys out of his pocket. "You're not getting rid of me yet. And if I follow you, your car will be at the hospital when you need it." He gestured toward the ambulance. "Go."

He didn't waste time arguing. But as he climbed aboard, he called out to Mitch. "Thanks."

The other man lifted his hand in acknowledgment, then turned away and walked over to the young deputy.

As the paramedic closed the ambulance door and the vehicle began to roll, Cole didn't relish the thought of hours in the ER. Pacing. Worrying. Praying.

On the other hand, he hoped he wouldn't need his car anytime soon.

Was that Cole's voice again? Or was she only imagining it?

Kelly tried to pry her eyes open. No luck. So she concentrated on listening instead. The wail of a siren dominated, but in the background she could hear the rumble of male voices—none of them distinguishable.

Until one asked a question. "What's her BP now?"

It *was* Cole!

Fighting a mind-numbing lethargy and the radiating pain that had turned her whole body into one big, throbbing ache, she tried again to lift her eyelids. But all she could manage was a flicker. And every breath sent another wave of pain crashing over her.

Last she'd checked, though, her voice had worked—and talking didn't require much effort.

"Cole?" The muffled word vibrated in front of her face, as if her mouth was covered. She tried again. Louder. "Cole?"

The murmur of masculine conversation stopped. She heard a shuffling sound. Felt a gentle touch on her forehead.

"Kelly?"

Was that Cole? It sounded sort of like his voice, but it was tighter than usual. And hoarse. And raspy.

Once more willing her eyelids to lift, Kelly tried again. This time she managed to raise them.

Cole's face, inches from her own, wasn't quite in focus. But it was clear enough for her to distinguish the lines etched at the edges of his eyes and the corners of his mouth, as well as the twin vertical crevices imbedded in his forehead.

"Welcome back." His mouth twitched, as if he wanted to smile but his lips wouldn't cooperate.

"Where . . ." She couldn't muster the energy to formulate the rest of her question.

"You're in an ambulance. Kelly . . . who did this to you?"

Talking sapped her energy more than she'd expected, but his urgent tone told her she had to answer his question now . . . in case she didn't make it. "Carlson. Dad . . . too."

A muscle clenched in Cole's jaw and his expression hardened. "That's what we figured."

"Stay?" She wanted to reach for his hand, but it hurt too much to move.

As if sensing her intent, he found hers instead and linked their fingers. "Count on it."

"I need to get back in there." The terse comment came from above her head.

Cole gave her fingers a gentle squeeze. "The paramedics have to do their job, but I'll be right here. Close enough to touch. Okay?"

"'Kay."

He relinquished his grip, and she missed the warmth of his hand at once. But as she began to drift back into pain-free oblivion, a sense of peace settled over her. No matter what happened now, she'd accomplished the goal she'd set the day her dad's note arrived in the mail with the tulips. She'd identified his killer. Even if she wasn't able to see this through to the end, Cole would make sure justice was done on her father's behalf. He was that kind of man.

And because he was that kind of man, she hoped she'd be around not only for the conclusion of her father's case—but for the beginning of a romance with one very special detective.

As the ambulance backed toward the doors that led directly into the ER treatment area, Cole angled away from Adam to continue his phone conversation with Lauren. "We just arrived at Mercy. I'll call you with the email address and fax number in a few minutes, since you have health-care power of attorney."

"Okay. I'll authorize them to give you info too." He heard her exhale. "What about Carlson?"

"The BOLO alert's been issued. We'll get him."

"I still can't believe he did all this. He was supposed to *protect* people, not kill them." Her words were laced with incredulity—and revulsion.

"Yeah." Cops like Carlson made Cole sick to his stomach. They were the rare exception, but they gave all of law enforcement a black eye.

"What's your own assessment of Kelly's condition?"

He refocused as the paramedics prepared to open the back doors of the ambulance, picturing the horrendous bruises on her ribs that Adam had found after he'd cut away her clothes en route. But on the plus side, there'd been no evidence of a punctured lung.

"I don't know. She was conscious for a couple of minutes during the ride here, and I saw her move. But she fell more than forty feet. And she's really beat up." His voice choked. "Look, I need to go. Are you sure you want me to call again when we get an assessment? It could be the middle of the night."

"I don't care how late it is."

"Okay. I'll be back in touch."

By the time he scrambled out of the ambulance, the paramedics were wheeling Kelly through the double doors. The instant they stepped inside, two nurses converged on them, with a white-coated physician not far behind. Cole followed as they rolled her toward a treatment room, but it was too crowded inside the small space so he hovered at the door.

"Are you a relative?" A black-haired nurse paused on her way into the room.

He did *not* want to be booted, courtesy of HIPAA rules. Pulling out his badge, he flashed it at her. "St. Louis County detective."

"Okay. You might want to hang out in the waiting room. It's a lot more comfortable."

Cole eyed the hard plastic chair in the corner of the treatment room. Not appealing, even if there *was* space for him, and he did need to talk to Mitch. But he couldn't leave Kelly yet.

"In a few minutes."

"Whatever." The nurse slipped back into the room.

Twenty minutes later, after watching the medical team start another IV, trundle in a portable X-ray machine, and take blood, he was growing antsy. And listening to them toss around terms like neurogenic shock, comminuted fracture, subdural hematoma, and spinal cord trauma wasn't helping.

Shoving his shaky hands into his pocket, he snagged the same black-haired nurse as she exited. "Shouldn't you be taking her for a CT scan or MRI or something?"

She gave him a "you're bothering me" stare.

He stared right back at her.

Huffing out a sigh, she leaned toward him, not in the least intimidated by his height advantage. "We aren't moving her an inch until we know she's stable enough to be moved. In case you haven't noticed, we've been busy examining her for less obvious injuries, looking for blood in her urine, monitoring her vital signs, doing a neuro check, and drawing blood so we can evaluate gases, CBC, and CMP. Any other questions?"

The heat rose on his neck. He didn't know what most of that meant, but it all sounded important. "No."

"Take my advice. Find a comfortable spot in the waiting room. It's going to be a long night, and she won't be coherent for a while, even when she does regain consciousness." The nurse sidestepped him.

Cole took another look into the room. He could only glimpse a portion of Kelly's masked face, but it was clear she was still out. The nurse was right. He wasn't doing any good here.

Mustering what little remained of his energy, he rounded up the ER fax number and email address for Lauren. After calling her to pass on the information, he finally plodded toward the waiting area.

When he entered the quiet room, empty on this holiday eve except for two men seated halfway down a row of chairs, Mitch rose.

So did Jake.

Cole blinked at his older brother. "What are you doing here?"

"I made a few calls on the drive in," Mitch said.

Jake closed the distance between them and clasped his shoulder. "How is she?"

The comforting contact from his big brother about did him in. "It's too soon to tell. She . . ." He stopped. Cleared his throat. "She did regain consciousness briefly in the ambulance, but she's out again now. They said it could be hours before we know much."

"Typical ER." Jake scowled. "I hate these places."

"Look . . . you both don't need to hang around." Cole aimed his next comment at Mitch. "You've been up for over forty-eight hours. Go home."

"I am." He handed Cole the keys to his car. "As soon as Alison gets here to pick me up."

"She's here."

They all turned as she hurried in. Without slowing her advance, she went straight to Cole and pulled him into a fierce hug. "You okay?"

He buried his face in her hair and somehow managed to choke out a single-word response. "Yeah."

She held on to him, as if sensing he needed a moment to recover, and he clung to her, this woman who'd known her own share of trauma. As had Jake.

When at last she pulled back, she kept a grip on his arms and studied him. "How is she?"

"I don't know yet."

322

She released him and reached for Mitch's hand. "Call the minute you have news."

"It could be hours."

"I don't care."

He nodded. Tried for a smile. Failed. "Sorry about the pies, by the way."

Alison's lips quirked. "You'll have a chance to redeem yourself. We postponed Thanksgiving until a week from Sunday." She looked up at Mitch and scrutinized his face. "You need sleep. Come on." She tugged on his hand but aimed her parting remark at Cole. "I'll be back tomorrow."

"Thanks. All of you." Cole included Mitch in his sweeping gaze. "You guys are the best."

"Remember that the next time you think I'm too bossy." Alison tossed that comment over her shoulder as she led Mitch toward the exit.

As the door whooshed shut behind them, Jake gestured to a sofa halfway down the wall. "Not the most comfortable spot for sleeping, but better than that tepee we used to set up in the backyard in our mountain man days. No mosquitoes, either. Why don't you stretch out?"

"I wouldn't be able to sleep."

"You might want to try. If you don't get a few z's, you'll be a zombie in another six or eight hours, when Kelly might really need you. And I'll be here the whole time. Checking for news every fifteen minutes. Watching your back. Just like in the old days."

Moisture clouded Cole's vision—a rare phenomenon that had been happening with alarming frequency in the past few hours. He could attribute it to stress and fatigue and worry. And that was partly true. But he also knew it was prompted by love and gratitude and relief. All his life, whenever his big brother had been in charge, everything had turned out okay. Maybe he should take Jake's advice and put the worry in his hands—and God's—while he tried to get a second wind.

"Okay. I'll give it a shot."

He slipped out of his sport jacket and wadded it up to form a pillow. Jake tossed him his thermal jacket as well, and he folded that on top. Then he stretched out, took a deep breath, and closed his eyes.

Far more quickly than he'd expected, his body began to shut down. And as he drifted toward sleep, his last conscious thought was a prayer.

Please, God, let there be good news when I wake up.

26

At the soft knock on the motel room door, Alan came instantly awake. Reaching for the Beretta on the nightstand, he swung his feet to the floor and checked his watch. Two-thirty.

Rossi's man was punctual.

He rose and padded silently to the door in his stocking feet. The gun was overkill, but who knew what kind of derelicts were wandering around at this hour in a dive like this?

Pausing beside the window that faced the parking lot, he looked through a broken slat in the blinds. His car was the lone vehicle at this end of the dark lot. No surprise there. If this hadn't been a command performance, he'd have followed the lead of most other potential customers and risked the icy road rather than stay in a dump like this. When he'd driven down to the last unit after checking in, he'd seen only two other cars, both parked near the office.

He eased sideways and scoped out the door. The dim light above the entrance had been on earlier—one of the few that had been working—but it must have burned out since. As best he could tell, though, there was no one standing on the other side. Whoever had made the drop had melted into the shadows.

After one more scan of the parking lot, Alan flipped the lock, slid back the bolt, and eased the dented aluminum door open.

The note he'd left about the pizza delivery was gone.

But no delivery had been made.

Frowning, he surveyed the covered walkway to his right, which led back to the office. It was deserted.

Where was his money?

He looked again at his car. Squinted. Was that a small bundle tucked partway under the passenger door, out of sight of the office or any other guests? Yes.

Alan blew out a breath, annoyed. Why hadn't the guy left the package by his door? Now he'd have to venture out onto the ice-covered pavement.

Resigned, he shut the door, grabbed his jogging shoes, and pulled them on. At least he was still wearing the jeans and sweatshirt he'd put on after tossing his hiking clothes in a convenient dumpster as he'd left St. Louis.

Half a minute later, he returned to the door and opened it again, the Beretta back in his hand. He stepped out, edged to the left, and checked around the side of the building.

Empty.

Where was the person who'd delivered the package?

Alan did one more sweep of the lot. Surely he'd hang around long enough to make certain it was retrieved, given the amount of money involved. Had he taken an adjoining room? Was he watching from behind one of the dirty windows?

But what did it matter, as long as the drop had been made?

Walking gingerly, he crossed the slick sidewalk outside his room and moved beside his car. A small, black, soft-sided briefcase was wedged behind the front tire. Alan dropped to one knee, reached for it, and tugged.

If it hadn't been for the sudden crackle of ice giving way under weight, he'd never have known he had company.

Whirling around, he saw the dark figure looming over him an instant before the gun was kicked out of his hand.

Alan lunged for it—but the slick surface betrayed him. He sprawled on the ice and knocked the gun with his own hand, sending it skittering across the frozen pavement. Out of reach.

He attempted to grab for it, but a vise clamped over his ankle and yanked him back toward the car. Adrenaline surging, he twisted around—just in time for a fist to connect with his jaw, snapping his head back. Dazed, he caught the glitter of a steel blade a mere second before it was thrust into his chest from under his rib cage. Toward his heart.

"I have a message for you." The voice came from afar. "Paid in full."

Alan slumped to the pavement. He hardly felt the second thrust. Or the third.

All he knew was that he'd finished his life the same way he'd finished his gambling career.

As a loser.

"Cole."

As Jake's quiet summons penetrated his sleep-fogged brain, Cole fought his way back to consciousness. Feeling as if he'd been drugged, he swung his legs to the floor and tried to focus on his watch. Three-forty-five. He'd been out for three hours.

A disposable cup of coffee appeared in front of his face, and he reached for it gratefully, cradling it with both hands as he took a long gulp. Then he looked up at his brother.

Before he could form the question, Jake answered it. "She's still with us. The doctor's here with an update."

He turned his head. As a sandy-haired man in a white coat walked toward them, he started to stand.

The man waved him back down. "Don't get up. We've all had a long night."

Jake sat beside him, and the doctor pulled a chair in front of them.

Bracing himself, Cole tightened his grip on the flexible cup, sending a surge of coffee dangerously close to the edge. "Is she going to be okay?"

"I think so."

It wasn't the definitive answer he'd hoped for. Then again, the news could have been a lot worse.

"Let me give you the positives first." The doctor rubbed his eyes, rested his elbows on the arms of the chair, and clasped his hands in front of him. "We expected to find spinal, neck, and/or head injuries, but the skull is intact. So are the spine and neck. There's no bleeding in the brain, no fluid or blood in the abdomen, and her kidneys appear to be okay." He shook his head. "All I can say is, she is one lucky young woman. She has serious injuries, but to be honest, based on what the paramedics told me, she shouldn't be alive."

Cole's hands began to tremble, and he carefully set the cup on the small end table beside him. "Define serious injuries."

"Besides two fractured ribs, she has a broken kneecap that will require surgery. We're going to wait on that, though, until the swelling goes down. She also has a severe concussion, a sprained wrist, minor frostbite on her nose and the fingers of her right hand, and major bruising. To use an old cliché, she looks like she's been run over by a truck. And I'm sure she feels that way too."

"What's the prognosis?"

"None of her injuries are life-threatening, unless she develops complications."

"Such as?"

"Pneumonia. Hematoma from the bruising. New symptoms that appear in the next twenty-four hours suggesting latent damage. Barring any of that, the biggest issue is the kneecap. It's broken in three places and will have to be put back together with screws and pins. She'll require physical therapy, but even with that, there may be some permanent loss of motion, including the ability to fully straighten or bend the knee. The orthopedic surgeon will give you more details."

"Is she back in the treatment room?"

"Yes. And she's waking up, but she's very groggy and disoriented. Partly from the concussion, partly because she's hurting. We're limited in how much pain medication we can give her, because narcotics interfere with the ability to breathe, and restricted breathing can lead to pneumonia. Do you want to come back?"

"Yes." Cole grabbed his coffee, rose, and turned to Jake. "Would you call Alison? And Kelly's best friend, Lauren, if I give you the number?"

"Sure."

Cole dug Lauren's number out of his pocket and handed it over. "You don't have to stay, Jake."

His big brother took the slip of paper and pulled out his phone. "You're stuck with me. Deal with it."

Cole tried to say thanks, but the word got stuck in his throat. So he just nodded and started to follow the doctor—until Jake's question stopped him.

"What's wrong with your leg?"

Only then did he realize he was limping. "I twisted my ankle in the woods."

"Get it checked out."

"It's fine."

"Cole . . ." Jake's warning tone was accompanied by the big-brother look Cole remembered from their childhood. The one that said Jake would sit on him if he didn't fall in line.

"Okay. Fine. Later." With that, he resumed his trek to the treatment room.

His aching ankle probably did need attention, but he stopped feeling the pain when he got to the threshold of Kelly's room and took in the purple discolorations on her jaw and temple, the angry scratch running down the side of her face, the IV drips in her arms, her elastic-bandaged wrist, and the outline of her elevated leg beneath a sheet.

And that was just the damage he could see.

Taking a steadying breath, he rounded her bed and stopped beside her.

Unfortunately, she looked even worse up close. Under the harsh lights, her pallor beneath the oxygen mask was more pronounced than it had been in the woods. And her eyes were closed.

"I thought she was conscious." He directed the comment to the nurse standing beside the IV but kept his gaze fixed on Kelly.

As he spoke, her eyelids flickered. "Cole?"

Her voice was a mere whisper, but it was the sweetest sound he'd ever heard. "Yeah." He leaned closer. "I'm here."

She blinked. Wrinkled her brow. Blinked again. "Everything's fuzzy." The words came out slurred.

"That's okay. Things will clear up later."

"Caw revin cosh."

Cole leaned closer and took her undamaged hand. "What, sweetheart?"

"Caw revin cosh."

"She's been saying that ever since she started coming around." The nurse adjusted the drip.

"Soo kishin." She squeezed his fingers.

Soup kitchen. That's what she was trying to communicate. And *revin cosh* must be the name of the minister in charge. His throat tightened. Despite her injuries, she was worried about her commitment to serve Thanksgiving dinner to the homeless.

As Mitch had said earlier, amazing.

"Don't worry about that, Kelly. Just rest."

"Call. 'Kay?" She peered at him, obviously trying to focus, and tightened her grasp.

"Okay. I'll take care of it."

She relaxed her grip, but her features contorted. "Hurt."

"I know." His stomach clenched, and he smoothed the hair back from her forehead. The soft strands were dry now, the ice crystals long gone. He wished he could make her pain melt away too. Bear the hurt for her. Fix all the broken parts. But that was beyond his ability.

He could stay by her, though. Hold her hand. Comfort her. And he would—for as long as she needed him. Just as soon as he enlisted Jake to call Lauren again and see if she knew how to track down the minister at the soup kitchen. Got his foot looked at, as he'd promised. Checked in with the office to see if there were any results from the BOLO alert they'd issued on Carlson.

And said a prayer of gratitude for the blessings he'd received on this aptly named Thanksgiving Day.

Someone was holding her right hand—about the only spot on her body that didn't hurt.

Kelly opened her eyes. The room was bright, but not from artificial illumination. She eased her head to the right, moving as little as possible. Sunlight was filtering through the blinds on a large window, so sometime during the night she'd been transferred to a regular room.

But what she noticed most of all was Cole, sitting close beside her bed, one foot propped on a pillow on a straight chair.

"Hi." With a smile and a gentle squeeze of her hand, he eased his foot down and stood.

She studied his face. Purple smudges formed half circles beneath his lower lashes, and his five o'clock shadow had turned into a bad-boy stubble. Creases were etched into his forehead, at the corners of his eyes, and beside his mouth, and his clothes looked as if they'd spent a week crammed into a too-small overnight case.

"You need sleep."

He lifted one shoulder. "I caught a couple of hours last night."

"You need more. Go home."

"Sound advice."

At the vaguely familiar voice, Kelly shifted her attention to the foot of the bed. When she found Jake Taylor occupying the other chair in the room, she sent Cole a silent question.

"He kept me company last night."

"What time is it?"

"Eight-thirty."

Kelly looked back at Jake. "Make him go home."

His lips quirked into a grin. "I'll tell you what. I'll step into the hall and you do your best to convince him." He crossed the room and exited, pulling the door shut behind him.

"I promised I'd stay, and I never break my promises." Cole stroked his thumb over the back of her hand.

She already knew that.

"I'm releasing you from *that* promise. You're dead on your feet. Just tell me three things. Did you get Carlson, what's wrong with your foot, and what's my prognosis?"

He gave her a skeptical once-over. "Are you certain you're ready to deal with all that?"

"I'm a lot stronger than I look."

"I'm finding that out." He smiled, and some of the tension in his features eased. "Nothing on Carlson yet, but we have a BOLO alert out on him. It's only a matter of time. My foot had a close encounter with a tree root last night. It's just bruised. You, however, are a different story."

She listened as he gave her a recap of her injuries, trying to take it all in. The knee was a problem, but other than that, it sounded as if time would cure everything. Phenomenal, considering how far she'd fallen.

"They want to hold off on the surgery for a few days to let the swelling in your knee go down. I think you're stuck here until then. But after that, you should . . ." Cole pulled the phone off his belt and checked caller ID. "I need to take this, okay?"

"Sure."

Kelly couldn't pick up much from the monosyllabic conversation on his end, which consisted mostly of "where?" "when?" and "I agree." But given his grim tone and the granite set of his jaw, the conversation concerned recent events.

He didn't linger on the call. After he finished, he slipped the phone back onto his belt and shifted toward her, his features hard. "That was Mitch. A maid discovered Carlson's body beside his car at a motel about an hour outside of St. Louis. He'd been stabbed multiple times. His wallet was gone, so it appears to have been a robbery."

Stunned by the news, she almost missed Cole's emphasis on the word *appears*. "You don't think it was a robbery."

"No. I think Rossi took care of him. He had to be furious that we managed to connect him to your father, all because

Carlson wasn't there to run interference with you when you came to the office with the tulip note—a piece of information I guarantee he ferreted out. And during our conversation with him on Wednesday, it was evident he had no idea there'd been an attempt on your life. Twisted as his ethics were, he never sanctioned punishing innocent people. That would have been a black mark against Carlson too."

Kelly released a long, slow breath, trying to block out the burning pain in her ribs. "My guess is it will be as difficult to connect Rossi to Carlson's death as it is to connect him to my father's."

"I agree. CSU technicians are at the site, but I doubt they'll turn up anything. Most of the hired guns employed by people like Rossi are pros. Carlson was the exception—and he paid the price."

"He was a pro in other ways, though." She told him how he'd damaged her auto-injector, disguised himself at the coffee shop to spike her drink with peanuts, and conned her father into ingesting alcohol and drugs.

A muscle in Cole's jaw twitched as she finished. "How did you find all that out?"

"He told me. I guess he figured he didn't have anything to lose, given his plans for me. He seemed proud of how he'd pulled it all off." She fought back a wave of nausea. "When I asked him why he did it, he said he needed the money."

"Yeah, he did. We found out he was a compulsive gambler with a lot of losses to pay off. He may have been delusional too. In other words, he was a mess."

"I can think of a less polite term to describe him." She didn't even try to disguise her anger or bitterness.

Cole took her hand. "I'm with you. But let's talk about something happier, okay?" He touched her cheek, his fingers warm and gentle, and when he continued, his voice took on a husky, intimate tone. "You remember a few days ago, how I said I'd like to spend the next holiday with you, assuming we wrapped up your dad's case?"

The tenderness in his eyes helped her switch gears. "Yes. I'm already looking forward to Christmas."

"No need to wait that long. We deferred Thanksgiving until a week from Sunday. I'd be honored if you'd join my family for the celebration."

Happiness welled up inside her, softening the anger in her heart and alleviating her pain better than any drug a doctor could prescribe. "If I can get there, it's a date."

"We'll get you there—if you're out of the hospital. I have two strong men I can round up to help me if necessary." He leaned closer still, until his breath was a whisper of warmth against her cheek. "However, I think we should begin the celebration sooner." His lips aimed for hers. "And I know just how we—"

A discreet knock sounded on the door, and he jerked back as Jake stuck his head in the room. "Any luck convincing him to go home?"

"I'm working on it."

"Good." Jake eyed the two of them, grinned, and retreated.

"His timing stinks." Cole shot a disgruntled look at the closed door.

She squeezed his hand. "I know right where we left off."

He turned back to her, and the ardent light in his eyes made her feel like it was Christmas and Thanksgiving and her birthday all rolled up into one. "Me too."

Bending down once again, he wasted no more time on words. Instead, he claimed her lips in a kiss that was gentle, tender, careful—and far too short. Lifting her uninjured hand, she wrapped it around his neck and tugged him back for more.

He didn't resist.

At last, with obvious reluctance, he eased back. "Just so you know, I can do a lot better than that. And I'll prove it as soon as you're back on your feet."

"That's a great incentive to get well fast." The words came out breathless—and not because of her broken ribs.

Smiling, he brushed the tip of his index finger across her lips and straightened up. "You sure you'll be okay by yourself if I run home long enough to shower and grab a couple hours of sleep?"

"As long as I know you're coming back."

"Count on it. Sooner rather than later." Smiling, he backed toward the door, winked, and slipped out.

For a long moment, Kelly looked after him, a smile lingering on her lips.

Turning away at last, she discovered that a sunbeam had shimmied through a slat in the blinds to cast a luminescent rainbow on the white sheet. Struck by the symbolism, she touched the arc of vibrant, radiant color. For just as the storm outside had passed, so, too, had the tragedy in her life given way to a bright, new future.

The road ahead wouldn't be easy. She knew that. Her physical injuries would take months to heal, and the emotional trauma might always be with her. But she was alive. And no matter what tomorrow held, she felt certain Cole would be by her side.

Life and love. Two great gifts.

It was, indeed, a day for thanksgiving.

Epilogue

4 ½ MONTHS LATER

Cole slid the suit jacket off the hanger in the backseat of his car, slipped his arms through the sleeves, and adjusted his tie. It was a little warm for formal attire, but at least the kids had a nice day for their Easter egg hunts.

A memory from a long-ago Easter surfaced, and a smile tugged at his lips as he strolled toward Kelly's front door. Alison had barreled straight for a cache of eggs, oblivious to everything in her path—including a mud trap that had sucked her shoes off. He and Jake had ribbed her for weeks.

Still grinning, Cole pressed Kelly's bell. Maybe he'd tell that story after church, when they all gathered for brunch at her house. And share the "shoeless wonder" nickname he and Jake had coined.

Then again, maybe not. She might decide not to feed him.

Thirty seconds ticked by, and he leaned on the bell again. He *was* ten minutes early. It was possible Kelly was finishing her hair or makeup, but since she was as punctual as she was tidy, it was more likely she'd been ready and waiting for half an hour. She was probably in her beloved garden. Which would be perfect, because he'd planned to coax her there, anyway.

After retracing his route, Cole followed the stepping-stones that led to the backyard. As he rounded the side of the house, his speculation was confirmed. She was down on one knee near the statue of St. Francis—a position that only hours of grueling physical therapy and her singular commitment had made possible—the fingers of one hand splayed on the ground for balance, the full skirt of her floral-print dress resting on the grass where it had drifted around her as she peered at the ground.

He paused, enjoying the view, until the trill of a cardinal drew her attention. Kelly lifted her head, giving Cole a brief moment to admire her flawless profile before she caught sight of him.

A radiant smile brought a glow to her face, and she started to rise. Too fast.

As she teetered, he closed the distance between them in a few long strides and took her arm.

"Thanks." She brushed off her hands, her smile morphing into a frustrated frown. "But I should be able to do that by now without any help."

"Hey." He stroked away the furrows on her brow, hating Carlson anew for all the extra pain he'd put her through by slamming that rock into her knee. "You're getting there. The doctor said you've made remarkable progress."

"It's too slow."

"Maybe you're too impatient."

She made a face, then lifted one shoulder in concession. "That's possible."

"Probable." When she affected a pout at his correction, he chuckled. "Happy Easter."

Her pout dissolved into a smile. "Thank you. The same to you. And guess what? I found a present better than Easter eggs." She gestured to the ground.

He looked down at the first tulip of the season, a double-petaled, two-toned beauty. "One of the ones your dad sent?"

"Uh-huh. Isn't it beautiful?"

The catch in her voice tugged at his heart, and he pulled her close. Tucking her cheek against his chest, he cradled the back of her head with his hand and rested his chin on her soft hair. "Yeah, it is. Just like the woman who planted it."

"You're prejudiced."

"Guilty as charged. But don't you want the man who's in love with you to think you're the most beautiful woman in the world?"

She pulled back to look up at him, surprise flickering in her eyes. In the months they'd been dating, he'd never been that direct about his feelings, though he'd dropped plenty of hints and innuendos. In light of the trauma that had brought them together and all the medical issues she'd faced, it had seemed more prudent to let their relationship develop at a slower pace.

But he was tired of moving slow. He might have chided *her* for being impatient, but he was just as guilty when it came to getting started on their future together.

Taking her hand, he motioned toward a wooden bench beside a rosebush that was sprouting its first new shoots of the season. "Let's sit for a minute and enjoy the garden, okay?"

She gave him a curious glance, then checked her watch. "Do we have time?"

"I'll get you there before the organ strikes the first note of the opening hymn. Trust me."

She locked gazes with him. "I do."

The quiet conviction in her tone helped quell the flutter of nerves in his stomach as he led her to the bench.

"By the way, I had a nice chat with one of my cousins in Rochester last night." Kelly sat, brushing her silky skirt aside to make room for him. "She invited me to visit this summer so I can meet all three of them."

He joined her, forcing himself to switch gears—temporarily. "I'm glad you connected with them. There's no reason not to build that relationship now, since the vendetta died with Rossi."

The cardinal warbled again, and she lifted her face to the sky, watching as the scarlet bird took flight. When she continued, her voice was more subdued. "I think about how he died sometimes. Lying there for four days before his housekeeper found him. Wouldn't it be sad to have no one who cared enough to call and check on you, especially on a holiday?"

"Only if you'd done nothing to deserve that kind of treatment. Rossi's own choices brought him to that end."

"That's true." Her gaze shifted to her father's tulips.

Cole moved closer and draped one arm on the back of the bench behind her, his fingers skimming her shoulder. Time to get this conversation back on track. They'd wasted enough breath on a man who'd gotten what he'd deserved. "So now that you've reconnected with your cousins, have you given any more thought to reclaiming your original name?"

"Not much." She tilted her head as she studied the tulips, her expression pensive. "I've been Kelly Warren my whole life. I'm glad I know the truth about my background, but I don't see any reason to change my name."

"I think you should."

She swiveled toward him, clearly taken aback. "Really?"

"Yes." Pulse accelerating, he reached into the inside pocket of his jacket and pulled out a small velvet box. "But I think you should change it to mine."

As she stared at the box, he flipped it open to reveal a one-carat solitaire on a gold band, every facet sparkling in the brilliant morning sun.

Her hand flew to her throat. "Wow."

He waited—but that was all she said.

The air whooshed out of his lungs, and he swallowed. "Wow is good. But I was hoping to hear a yes."

A tiny smile twitched at the corners of her lips as she switched her focus from the ring to him. "And I was hoping to hear a question."

She was going to make him go the whole nine yards.

Okay, he could do that. Even if Alison claimed his verbal skills were pathetic.

He removed the ring from the box with fingers that weren't quite steady and took her hand.

"I'm not too good at saying the right things at the right time. Plus, I tend to be too blunt—and not all that diplomatic. So I'm sorry if this isn't flowery enough, but here goes."

Clearing his throat, he tightened his grip on her finger. "Even though I've been in love with you for months, I thought we both needed time to regroup after everything that happened. But I'm tired of waiting. I want to share the rest of my life with you—sooner rather than later. You're everything I could ever want in a woman, and I promise to love you with all my heart as long as I live. So . . . will you marry me?"

The tiny lift of her lips suddenly swelled into a megawatt smile. And even before she gave him her answer in words, he saw it in the rush of tenderness that softened her eyes and in the love shining in their depths.

"I think I'm about to change my name after all."

"Is that a yes?"

She put her arms around his neck and leaned close. "You're the detective. What do you think?"

Smiling, he tugged her left arm free, slid the ring on the third finger, then pulled her to her feet and into his arms—where she belonged. For always.

"I think this deserves further investigation."

She grinned and snuggled closer. "I'll cooperate in any way I can."

"I'm counting on that. Because this case will take a lot of up-close-and-personal research."

And without wasting any more words, he got down to business.

Acknowledgments

Because my suspense books are research intensive, I spend hours on the Net digging for information. But despite that huge investment of time, the final touch of authenticity always comes from the information and advice I receive directly from the experts who do the jobs I depict, day in and day out. Only they can answer the questions specific to the scenarios in my book.

I am blessed to have many such people who graciously and generously give me their time and expertise whenever I need help. For this book I offer special thanks to:

Lieutenant Tom Larkin, Commander of the St. Louis County Police Department's Bureau of Crimes Against Persons, who went above and beyond in answering my questions and reviewing the final text. It is only because of his input that I was able to portray my fictional detectives with such a high degree of real-world accuracy.

U.S. Marshal Don Slazinik, who validated the tight security and incredible secrecy surrounding the Witness Security program and who answered what few questions he could. No wonder the U.S. Marshals have never lost a protected person who followed the WitSec rules!

Fellow author and nurse Patricia Davids, who reviewed and fine-tuned the medical sections of the book.

And Marc Ulses, Assistant Chief/Fire Marshal of the Frontenac Fire Department, who answered my many questions about the paramedic/rescue scene at the end of the book and reviewed the final copy.

As always, my thanks also to the incredible team at Revell—editorial, marketing, sales, cover design, promotion. I feel blessed to work with such masters of the business.

And finally, all my love to my wonderful husband, Tom, and my fabulous parents, James and Dorothy Hannon, who have supported and encouraged me every step of the way on my writing journey.

Irene Hannon is a bestselling, award-winning author who took the publishing world by storm at the tender age of ten with a sparkling piece of fiction that received national attention.

Okay . . . maybe that's a slight exaggeration. But she *was* one of the honorees in a complete-the-story contest conducted by a national children's magazine. And she likes to think of that as her "official" fiction-writing debut!

Since then, she has written more than thirty-five contemporary romance and romantic suspense novels. Irene has twice won the RITA award—the "Oscar" of romantic fiction—from Romance Writers of America and is a five-time finalist. Her books have also been honored with a Carol award, a HOLT medallion, a Daphne du Maurier award, and two Reviewers' Choice awards from *RT Book Reviews* magazine. In 2011, *Booklist* named *Deadly Pursuit* one of the Top 10 Inspirational Fiction titles of the year.

Irene, who holds a BA in psychology and an MA in journalism, juggled two careers for many years until she gave up her executive corporate communications position with a Fortune 500 company to write full time. She is happy to say she has no regrets. As she points out, leaving behind the rush-hour commute, corporate politics, and a relentless BlackBerry that never slept was no sacrifice.

A trained vocalist, Irene has sung the leading role in numerous community theater productions and is also a soloist at her church.

When not otherwise occupied, she loves to cook, garden, and take long walks. She and her husband also enjoy traveling, Saturday mornings at their favorite coffee shop, and spending time with family. They make their home in Missouri.

To learn more about Irene and her books, visit www.irene hannon.com

What a lousy night to get lost.

Moira Harrison peered through the April rain slashing across her windshield. Even at full speed, the wipers were no match for the torrential onslaught. The faint line bisecting the narrow strip of pavement—the only thing keeping her on the road and out of the ditch filled with churning runoff immediately to her right—faded in and out with alarming frequency.

Tightening her grip on the wheel with one hand, she cranked up the defroster with the other. Fogged-up windows were the last thing she needed. As it was, the high-intensity xenon headlights of her trusty Camry were barely denting the dense darkness of the woods-rimmed rural Missouri road. Nor were they penetrating the shrouding downpour.

So much for the premium she'd paid to upgrade from standard halogen.

She spared a quick look left and right. No light from house or farm broke the desolate blackness. Nor were there any road signs to indicate her location. Maybe St. Louis–area natives would be better able to wend their way back to civilization than a newcomer like her. But she doubted it. Dark, winding rural roads were confusing. Period. Especially in the rain.

With a sigh, Moira refocused on the road. If she'd known Highway 94 was prone to flooding and subject to sudden closure, she'd never have lingered for dinner in Augusta after she finished her interview and risked subjecting herself to this poorly marked detour.

Instead, she'd have headed straight back to the rented condo she now called home and spent her Friday evening safe and warm, cuddled up with a mug of soothing peppermint tea, organizing her notes. She might even have started on a first draft of the feature article. It wouldn't hurt to impress her new boss with an early turn-in.

A bolt of lightning sliced through the sky, and she cringed as a bone-jarring boom of thunder rolled through the car.

That had been close.

Too close.

She had to get away from all these trees.

Increasing her pressure on the gas pedal, she kept her attention fixed on the road as she groped on the passenger seat for her purse. Maybe her distance glasses were crammed into a corner and she'd missed them the first time she'd checked.

Five seconds later, hopes dashed, she gave up the search. The glasses must still be in the purse she'd taken to the movie theater last weekend. That was about the only time she ever used them—except behind the wheel on rainy nights.

It figured.

The zipper on her purse snagged as she tried to close it, and Moira snuck a quick glance at the passenger seat. Too dark to see. She'd have to deal with it later.

Releasing the purse, she lifted her gaze—and sucked in a sharp breath.

Front and center, caught in the beam of her headlights, was a frantically waving person.

Directly in the path of the car.

Less than fifty feet away.

Lungs locking, Moira squeezed the wheel and jammed the brake to the floor.

Screeching in protest, the car fishtailed as it slid toward the figure with no noticeable reduction in speed.

Stop! Please stop!

Moira screamed the silent plea in her head as she yanked the wheel hard to the left.

Instead of changing direction, however, the car began to skid sideways on the slick pavement.

But in the instant before the beams of the headlights swung

348

away from the road—and away from the figure standing in her path—one image seared itself across her brain.

Glazed, terror-filled eyes.

Then the person was gone, vanished in the darkness, as the vehicle spun out of control.

Moira braced herself.

And prayed.

But when she felt a solid thump against the side of the car, she knew her prayers hadn't been answered.

She'd hit the terrified person who'd been trying to flag her down.

The bottom fell out of her stomach as the car continued to careen across the road. Onto the shoulder. Into the woods. One bone-jarring bounce after another.

It didn't stop until the side smashed into a tree, slamming her temple against the window of the door to the accompaniment of crumpling metal.

Then everything went silent.

For a full half a minute, Moira remained motionless, hands locked on the wheel, every muscle taut, heart pounding. Her head pounded in rhythm to the beat of rain against the metal roof, and she drew a shuddering breath. Blinked. The car had stopped spinning, but the world around her hadn't.

She closed her eyes. Continued to breathe. In. Out. In. Out. When she at last risked another peek, the scene had steadied.

Better.

Peeling her fingers off the wheel, she took a quick inventory. Her arms and legs moved, and nothing except her head hurt. As far as she could tell, she hadn't sustained any serious injuries.

But she knew the person she'd hit hadn't been as lucky—a person who might very well be lying in the middle of the road right now.

In the path of an oncoming car.

Her pulse stuttered, and she fought against a crescendo of panic as she tried to kick-start her brain. To think through the fuzziness.

Okay. First priority—call 911. After that, she'd see what she could do to help the person she'd hit while she waited for the pros to arrive.

Plan in place, she groped for her purse. But the seat beside her was empty. Hadn't it been there moments before?

With a Herculean effort, she coerced the left side of her brain to engage.

The floor.

Her purse must have fallen to the floor while the car was spinning.

Hands shaking, she fumbled with the clasp on her seatbelt. It took three jabs at the button before it released. Once free of the constraint, she leaned sideways and reached toward the floor—just as the car door creaked open behind her.

With a gasp, she jerked upright. A black-shrouded figure stood in the shadows, out of range of her dome light.

Her heart began to hammer again as a cold mist seeped into the car.

"I saw the accident. Are you all right, miss?"

The voice was deep. Male. And the only clue to his gender. The monk-like hood of his slicker kept most of his features in shadows.

But she didn't care who he was. Help had arrived.

Thank you, God!

"Yes. I . . . I think so. I banged my head against the window, and I'm a little dizzy. But . . . I hit someone on the road. I need to call 911. And I need to help the other person."

The man leaned a bit closer, and she glimpsed the outline of a square jaw. "You've got a nasty bump on your temple. Moving around isn't a good idea until the paramedics check you out. I'll help the person you hit." He tipped his head and looked across her. "Is that blood on the passenger seat?"

As Moira shifted sideways to look, she felt a jab in her thigh. "Ow!"

"Watch the glass. Lean a little to the right." The man restrained her with one hand on her upper arm as she complied. "Hold on a second while I brush off the seat."

He was silent for a moment, and she shivered as the wind shifted and the rain began to pummel her through the open door, soaking through her sweater.

"Okay. I think I got most of it."

He released her, and she collapsed back against the seat. As he retracted his hand, she caught a quick glimpse of his gold Claddagh wedding ring. The same kind her dad wore.

Somehow that comforted her.

"Stay put." He melted back into the shadows, beyond the range of the dome light. "I'll call 911 and check on the other person. Give me a few minutes."

With that, he closed the door.

Alone again in the dark car, Moira tried to keep him in sight. But within seconds he disappeared into the rain.

As the minutes ticked by and the full impact of what had happened began to register, her shivering intensified and her stomach churned.

She could have been killed.

And she may have killed or seriously injured someone else.

Wrapping her arms around herself, Moira closed her eyes as a wave of dizziness swept over her.

At least help had arrived.

With that thought to sustain her, she let the darkness close in.